A Road of Stones

A ROAD OF STONES

a novel

WARNE PALMER

Book I: The Low Field 20 Trilogy

ISBN: 069241021X
ISBN 13: 9780692410219
Library of Congress Control Number: 2015904580
Warne Palmer, Warren, OH

For My Parents

1

COLTON CALDWELL AND his best friend, Travis Law, bounced along the unpaved country road that led deep into the forgotten corner of Low Field County. His uncle often described the area as Godforsaken swampland. Travis's late model Ford pickup truck left a plume of purple exhaust and dust in its wake as he sped down the center of the lane in an attempt to avoid the ruts and holes washed out by another year of weather. It was a high-speed game of chicken in an attempt to not crack an axel or break a steering rod. Only once every three or four years, the county road department would make a feeble attempt to re-grade the seldom-used thoroughfare because it was exceedingly low on the priority list from the hundreds of miles of county roads that required annual maintenance. The area contained mostly unusable land with only a few farmhouses tucked into the woods at the highest points of the topography. The left front wheel caught the edge of a pot hole bouncing the boys a foot off the bench seat. Colton's head hit the door frame and he swallowed a healthy portion of his chew.

"Slow down Travis," he choked.

"Damn, I know. I tried to miss it but was as big as a dumb hot tub."

"Well what's the hurry anyway? Let's just relax and watch for groundhogs," Colton suggested.

"I'm getting thirsty for that beer you brought."

"I'd like some of that too but I'd also like to shoot some varmints while we're out here."

"My uncle's place is just a few more miles," said Travis somberly. "Sorry Colt. Is your head still bothering you as much?"

"One thing I can count on every day is at least one massive headache."

"Sorry dude."

"That's okay Travis. Thank god I earned those GI benefits now so I can maybe get things straightened out."

Colton turned up the radio. Country station Froggy 105 met their joint taste and had a strong enough transmission signal to be received throughout the county, even in this remote and desolate edge of pastoral civilization.

"Turn that up; that's my cousin Randy Travis."

Colton just shook his head. It was one of Travis's oldest jokes.

"Travis, that joke quit being funny when we graduated from the fourth grade," Colton said. "Besides, this song is so old our parents probably listened to it when they were young."

"That's why it's called a classic gold record," said Travis. "In fact, I'm pretty sure this one went platinum."

"Sometimes I think you're stuck in the past," Colton said.

"Ah, you're just jealous. When my cousin dies and leaves me a fortune I'm going to show up at your house with a brand new Ford truck, and the bed's going to be filled with a big heaping load of *I told you so*. Now, please be quiet so I can enjoy RT," said Travis lowering his jaw trying to match the deep baritone pitch of the vocals while singing.

"You're a total idiot, my friend."

Travis held up the middle finger of his right hand to Colton. Colton grabbed at it but Travis pulled it away too quickly. Colton smiled and sat back in the seat and looked out the side window. The sleeve of his flannel shirt fluttered in the wind's draft. It felt good to riding again with Travis in his pickup. He wore a comfortable pair of distressed jeans and cowboy boots that he had owned for years. He took off his faded red ball cap from high school and set it on the seat between them. With his left hand he reached down and picked up the handgun case from between his legs.

"What kind of gun did you buy?" Travis asked.

"This my friend is a M9 Beretta—it's the standard Marine issue semi-automatic, double-action handgun that became my new best friend in boot camp. It's a lethal, kickass weapon that we use to kill bad guys all over the world, and I just want to see if it can blow the head off of a groundhog from fifty meters."

"Well, keep your eyes peeled; there are plenty of hogs in this swamp."

The two friends, nineteen and twenty respectively, rode along slowly enjoying the music and the October sun which cast a metallic glow on the yellowing spires of wild grasses that waved mystically back and forth in the breeze. Suddenly, Colt held up his left hand in a position suggesting Travis slow the truck. He pointed to a ground-hog listlessly foraging on a root or clump of grass fifty yards ahead. Colton closed his hand slowly forming a fist as a signal for Travis to stop the truck. He eased it off the road into the grassy berm. Colton quietly slipped a clip into the gun and, with a soldier's stealth, opened the door and moved to a position near a fencepost where he extended his arms and rested his hands and weapon on the top of the weathered tree branch poised to fire.

He waited patiently. It seemed like minutes went by and Travis wondered why he didn't just start blasting the unsuspecting creature, but Colton held his position patiently like a sniper training his sight on the groundhog and waiting for the slightest advantage in his shot. Finally, the creature lifted its head, instinctively sensing something foreign in his environment, and Colton squeezed the trigger with motionless precision. The blast echoed through the trees startling Travis with its ferocity. Animal matter and fur from the ground-hog exploded into the air and the creature fell limply to the side;

its disfigured carcass rolled briefly before settling in a final flaccid position.

Travis walked around the bed of the truck, laughed and said simply, "Sweet."

Colton moved with dead seriousness toward the fallen adversary, his gun pointed down at the dead creature as he was taught in basic training a few months earlier.

"Damn, the Marines taught you some skills," Travis proclaimed.

"We did this every day Travis. It's a necessary skill to possess if you are going to survive in a warzone. My brothers and I had to be aware of everything around us and always have each other's back."

"Okay then," said Travis sardonically, "but I don't think the dimwit of a groundhog had a fair chance since young Rambo was back in Low Field stalking him."

"All the better for him; it's a good way to go," avowed Colton.

"Well that deserves a beer," said Travis as he ripped open the box of beer from the truck bed and tossed a can to Colton. He pulled back the tab on his can and held it up to his friend. "Welcome home, Colt!"

"Thanks Bud."

2

TRAVIS'S UNCLE HAD constructed a make-shift pier that stretched a short way into the pond on his property. A rowboat dock was his original idea but over time the water end of the structure was expanded to accommodate friends and relatives who simply wanted to sit and fish or sunbathe. The midday sun cast a shimmering twinkle upon the small ripples of water. Clouds gently redistributed the beams of light in a mesmerizing procession. The early fall leaves colored the edges of the water a fiery hue of ginger. Travis fished, occasionally hooking a bluegill or croppy then releasing them back into the pond with a sullen toss. Colton tenderly handled his gun back and forth while they reminisced about high school, got caught up on the current status of old friends and shared their respective plans for the future. The beer and snacks progressively disappeared as the lunch hour approached.

Bored, Colton would occasionally stand and fire the gun at a passing bird or a turtle's head that would peak fractionally above the surface of the water. Travis added some sport to the random target practice by having Colton turn his back away from the end of the pier until an empty beer can had been tossed into the pond behind him. The ex-Marine private first class crouched in an athletic, alert standing position and, upon Travis's exhort of "Go," would quickly turn, locate the floating object and squeeze one shot after another until the bullet's impact caused the can to pop from the water, summersaulting uncontrollably through the air. When they became bored again,

Travis suggested they ride the ATVs around the property. The two muddy vehicles were stored in his uncle's barn under a pair of sea-blue tarps. The six beers they had each consumed removed common sense and caution from the ride and they both got thrown from the vehicles several times, although neither was injured. Muddy around their pant legs and boots, they put things away and got back into Travis's pickup to head back to town.

"Man, I'm hungry," stated Colton.

"Me too; where to do you want to go?" asked Travis.

"How about *The Roundup*?" Colton suggested. "It's on the way."

"Yeah, that sounds good."

As they pulled into the dusty, gravel lot some lunch hour patrons were filing back to their vehicles mindlessly sliding toothpicks between their teeth, fishing keys from their pockets and continuing conversations about work and life. A brawny, tan man in a yellowish cowboy hat and work jeans recognized the boys and pointed at them.

"Hey boys, what are you two up to this fine day?" the man asked rhetorically. "Colt, I didn't know you was back home; last I heard you were at basic training in Georgia. You must be finished."

"Hey Mr. Thomas. Yeah, just got home," Colton replied.

"Well, how did it go?"

"Actually, I got hurt and they said I couldn't be in combat, so I chose the honorable discharge rather than sit at some desk for four years. I mean, I didn't want to leave, but ah, my head got banged-up pretty good so now I'm home," explained Colton.

"I'm sorry to hear that. Uncle Sam missed out on one hell of a soldier."

"Thank you, sir," said Colton.

"Well, it's good to see you and you tell your momma and daddy I said *hey*," said Mr. Thomas.

"Will do, sir. Good to see you as well and please tell Molly and Amy hello for me," said Colton.

"Me too," added Travis as he waved with a slight lift of his arm, tapping the air with his index finger.

They walked inside the dim restaurant and sat in a wooden booth stained in dark walnut. The walls were also covered with wood planks stained the same deep-coffee shade of brown. Framed posters of NASCAR drivers and race cars hung high around the perimeter of the room along with pennants, jerseys and an array of other sports-related memorabilia and random farm antiques. On one wall hung dozens of Ohio license plates nailed up in symmetrical rows, many of them decades old. A pool table with worn, faded felt took up one corner of the room and a dart board hung on the wall near the hallway that led to the restrooms.

"That was a nice touch by you to say hello to both of his daughter," posed Travis. "The poor guy is probably wondering if you slept with one of them in high school."

"Actually, if we are counting, I slept with both of them," stated Colton. "I'm kidding. Only Molly. Not really; but you can't tell me you didn't undress her with your eyes a few times in school."

"Oh, god yes; she was hot as a firecracker," admitted Travis. "You know Colt, I feel for you. Being the star quarterback who was worshipped by all the girls in Low Field had to be quite a burden."

"Yeah, if I wasn't so stupid in love with Kelsey back in the day, I could have fathered a slew of Caldwell babies in this piss-hole of a town," proclaimed Colton.

"Well the welfare system thanks you for your abstinence, young man...well done!" mocked Travis.

An attractive waitress with burgundy hair pulled back in a braided pony tail under a ball cap approached the table. She wore a loose denim shirt covering a spandex t-shirt and form-fitting crimson pants tucked into a pair of high boots. Her fresh complexion and easy smile rounded out her look—cute.

"Oh my god, Colt," she shrieked. She bent over and hugged him, kissing his cheek. "I can't believe you're here. I heard you were in Iraq."

"Hey, Tammy; I didn't know you worked here."

"Yeah, since last summer. Are you on leave?" she asked.

"Nope, back home for now. I banged up my head again and they sent me packing," Colton replied with a blush. He hadn't seen her since high school graduation.

"That's too bad, but hey, I'm glad your home with all your body parts," she said with a wink. "Hey, Travis. How are you doing?"

"Hey, Tammy. I'm fine, thank you for asking."

"Colt, why don't you come over Friday night and we'll make a fire out back and get caught up?" she inquired. "You too Travis; I'll call Kristen and see if she can come over too."

"That sounds great Tammy," Colton shook his head in affirmation.

"Great; about 7:00? Now, what can I get you boys to eat?" Tammy asked with a sense of excitement.

They ordered and sat back proud of their prominence throughout the area.

"Damn, she looks better than ever, don't she?" Travis asked rhetorically.

"Yeah I didn't see that blossom coming when we were in school," Colton agreed.

"Well it's nice to see we still got it," said Travis.

"We still got it or she's hard up; that was pretty quick," Colton admitted.

"I'll choose that we still got it," affirmed Travis.

They drank several draft beers and snacked on shelled peanuts as they waited for their food. They threw darts even though neither of them knew the nuances of the game. Travis talked nonsense about girls and high school, but all Colton could think about was Kelsey. She was his first true love in high school. The way he felt about her was special and unique—she was on his mind all the time. He knew he would never feel the same way about any other girl, now or in the future. Lunch was filling, and Tammy charged them for a few less drafts than they ordered. They paid at the bar and said goodbye to the people working.

"See you Friday, Tam," Colton promised as they swung open the door blasting their eyes with a flash of sunshine that danced off the sandy parking lot. Travis lifted his arms back and stretched his chest and shoulders. He patted his stomach and smiled. Gusts from a brisk fall wind buffeted the area occasionally lifting puffs of dust from the lot. To the west, heavy grey clouds were thickening. The air had cooled. They both pointed to the horizon and nodded. Colton got in the passenger side of the cab and rolled his head back and forth in circles stretching his neck muscles.

"That was good."

"Double good," said Colton referring to the food and Friday night's date.

"That's the easiest date I've ever made. I have really missed the benefits of hanging out with you," Travis said shaking his head.

"You're a good sidekick, T," conceded Colton. "Well, at least you don't scare off the girls."

"Oh, that's nice. You have a way of making me feel all warm and fuzzy inside, you big dummy."

"I just speak the truth like my mama taught me," declared Colton.

"Well I'm sure your mama and Pastor Mike are both real proud of you; and your path to heaven is paved with the blessings of all the virgins in Low Field."

"Like I said before," Colton responded, "you're an idiot Travis, but I do love you and truth be told, I missed hanging out with you too, even though you're an idiot."

"Proud of it," declared Travis.

The ride back toward town was quiet as both Travis and Colton got somber from the effect of too much beer and food. Country songs played from the radio and occasionally one or both of the boys sang along. As they got closer to Low Field, Colton asked Travis for a favor.

"Hey, Travis, would you mind dropping me off at the high school? I can get a ride home with Clay."

"Sure. I wanted to stop by Pruitt's anyway; my oil light came on a few days ago and I need to have Wade check it out."

They approached the school. A dozen or so buses were parked adjacent to the building and the School Zone lights were flashing in pulsating rhythm.

"Where do you want dropped off?" Travis asked.

"Just pull into the student lot and we'll look for Clay's jeep," answered Colton.

"Sure. I want to get out of here before the gates of hell open," joked Travis.

"Can't blame you for that," Colton agreed.

Travis stopped the truck behind Clay's older model vehicle. Colton shook Travis's hand and picked up his gun case.

"Great day Travis, thanks," Colton said. "Give me a call or text about Friday, okay?"

"Yep; as soon as I get home I'm going straight to the shower. Come Friday, I want to resemble a god in every way, or at least look better than usual."

"You do that," said Colton.

"Hey, you want me to take your gun for you and drop it off later?" asked Travis.

"No thanks; I'll just toss it in the back of Clay's jeep."

"Okay Colt; later," Travis said as he shifted into gear and pulled away.

Colton opened the back passenger door of his brother's jeep and set the gun case on the floor. He started walking toward the school. What he really hoped for was that he'd run into Kelsey at dismissal. He wasn't sure if she knew that he was home.

3

WHEN COLTON ENLISTED after graduation, they agreed it was best for both Kelsey and him to break-up and feel free to see other people. He looked at it as a way ultimately to galvanize their relationship. Colton conjectured that she would miss him so much that in time she would come to agree with his position that they should get married after she graduated this year from Low Field High School. Early in the summer when he first left town, they still talked on the phone and sent text messages to one another on a regular basis, but with the succeeding weeks, their contact became more infrequent. Finally, after a few months, she quit responding to his texts all together. He received one cursive, final text in August that broke off the communication once and for all.

Colt quit texting me we agreed to take a break and we need to do that was all she wrote in the last text message he received one hot, humid evening while in Georgia.

Wow, he thought. I guess she really wants some time apart. But he remained confident she would come back to him. In his heart he knew she loved him as much as he loved her. They had been inseparable for three years and that kind of deep sharing of everyday life experiences with a person you love doesn't just get wiped away in a few weeks. In Colton's vision, they would have kids, live a great life in Low Field and grow old together. He'd give her some space and time, and he'd enjoy himself as well. He might as well take a little time to experience life on the wild side, especially if he was going to marry Kelsey next summer. It was all good.

Colton turned and went back to Clay's jeep. He thought better of leaving the handgun unattended in Clay's jeep. Instead, he took the gun out and tucked it into the waist of his jeans and slid the empty case deep under the front seat of the car. He pulled out the front of his t-shirt and flannel shirt, making sure both were hanging low enough to conceal the bulge near his belt buckle. Now it was time to look for his girl. As he walked through the lot toward the school, he saw two of his old football teammates from the past.

"Hey Captain," one of them said loudly as he walked toward Colton and shook hands with him with raised fists, both wrapping their fingers around their thumbs as if they were about to arm wrestle. Then they bumped chests and with their free hand lightly slapped the other boy's back .

"Hey Josh," Colton replied. He turned to the other and repeated the greeting, "Bobby, how have you been?"

"Good Colt. You look good; not an ounce of body fat on you after basic training," said Bobby.

"Have either one of you guys seen Kelsey? I was going to surprise her," Colton explained.

"Not yet; she'll be out in a few minutes," said Josh. He looked at Bobby and then both dropped their eyes to the ground and got quiet.

"What? What's up with you two?" asked Colton. "Come on, I looked into your eyes in every huddle the last two years. I can read you two like a book. What?" Colton implored.

Finally, Josh's eyes met Colton directly and he said, "Kelsey always gets a ride from the dude in that shitty white pickup over there." He pointed across the lot.

"Who is that?" asked Colton.

"Daron; you know, that black kid with the two last names who moved out here a few years ago," Bobby said. "Remember, he played football for about a week and then quit." He paused for a moment and then asked, "Colt, have you seen or talked to Kelsey recently?"

"Not really," Colton replied with a look of concern. "Why, what's wrong with her?"

Josh slapped Bobby across his chest with the back of his hand.

"Tell me; what's going on," demanded Colton with concern in his voice. Neither Josh nor Bobby volunteered a response. Finally, Colton insisted they tell him what they were thinking. "Come on; say what's on your mind."

"Word is Kelsey might be pregnant," Bobby answered.

"What! Who's saying that? How do you know?" Colton asked in quick succession and disbelief.

"She's in my second period class and every day she asks to go to the clinic to see the nurse. The girls in the class keep saying she's having morning sickness," explained Bobby.

Josh stepped forward and in an attempt to end the conversation stated, "It's probably nothing more than a dumb rumor Colt; don't even think about it." He grabbed Bobby's coat sleeve and pulled him in the direction of the school. "We better get going Colt; good to see you man."

Colton shook his hanging head and squeezed his forehead. The sides of his head started to throb. He pinched his eyelids together a few times and shook his head. He couldn't get any more words out; he held up his hand to say goodbye and started walking across the lot toward Daron's truck. Just then the dismissal bell rang loudly on the side of the building and almost instantaneously students burst through the doors of the school.

4

Low Field, Ohio was located thirty-five miles west of Akron in a rural expanse of the state. Specifically, it showed on a map as a small dot at the intersection of state routes 933 and 17. The town consisted of a few cheaply built, dilapidated buildings that spread a few hundred yards in all four directions away from the unadorned crossroads. The business structures were mostly abandoned. The makeshift library, a gas station, several churches and the high school made up the rest of the forlorn town. The region was just beyond the rings of suburbia that flourished during the late 20th century then stopped fifteen miles short of the township border. Roadside storm culverts were filled with a mix of wild sunburst daylilies, spread from years of human inattentiveness, and litter, sucked from the beds of pickup trucks that sped through the town ignoring the posted speed limit. A short distance to the west of the solitary traffic light was the high school, a proud old building from a different era. It stood as a reflection of the conservative nature and forlorn economy of the community—good enough.

Kelsey Boyd, an attractive senior with chestnut hair beyond her shoulders and a finalist for queen in next week's homecoming festivities, was waiting in the main office for the secretary to finish a phone call so she could pick up her friend Erin's homework assignments and books. Her clothing was form-fitting on her slender, athletic body, but she wore layers which contributed to a more respectable appearance. The make-up she wore was light and her good complexion gave her face a glowing, natural appearance, even at the end of the school day. She was getting impatient and thought about leaving but Erin had already missed three days with an illness. Kelsey felt obligated to wait and pick up Erin's books today so she could take them to her friend's house on the way home. It couldn't wait another day. Kelsey's escort for the game and current boyfriend, Daron Roberts-Scott, was waiting in the student parking lot to give her a ride. She pulled out her phone thinking she'd better send him a text so he didn't leave without her.

B right there getting Erin's books she texted.

A few seconds later the vibration of her phone acknowledged his reply, *Ok*

The secretary waved Kelsey over to her desk with a hand motion. The phone was pressed to her ear but she whispered a silent question, "Erin's books?" Kelsey nodded an affirmation and Mrs. Cunningham pointed to the small stack on the corner of the counter. She covered the speaker portion of the phone and said, "I sent the homework request to all of her teachers but only three sent down assignments. We got her books so at least she can get started on some of it."

"Thanks Mrs. Cunningham. You're the best!" said Kelsey.

"No problem honey. Thank you."

As soon as she stepped into the hallway, one of her friends, Amanda, was running toward her and calling to her, "Kelsey, there you are, come on; Colt's out in the parking lot arguing with Daron. I think they're going to fight."

"What? Oh crap! Let's go," said Kelsey and both girls took off running toward the exit doors. Their gait was more like a fast shuffle made awkward as they struggled through the hallway thrown off balance by the heaving bundles of books, backpacks and purses they were toting.

Kelsey couldn't see past the buses when she got to the door. The student body continued to empty the school—the younger students filling the buses while the older pupils walked to their cars. Both lots were full of stilted traffic. As they made it around the corner of the last bus, they could see Daron's white S10 in the middle of a lane with students surrounding it like a whirlpool. When they got closer to the scene, it was apparent why the crowd had gathered.

Colton and Daron confronted each other at the driver's side of the truck. Colton was gesturing like a bird trying to fly with upside down wings. It was the same arm movement he used in the glory of years past to incite the football crowds on Friday nights. Both of the boys were fit, muscular and stood over six feet tall. Daron, exerting restraint and good sense, stepped away from Colton and got back into the driver's seat of the vehicle. Colton pushed up against the door blocking it inadvertently with his body, trapping Daron inside in a vulnerable position while he continued to rant uncontrollably.

Kelsey pushed through the crowd and yelled, "Colt, what do you think you're doing? Leave him alone. Why are you even here?" She was confused by his sudden appearance back in Low Field let alone at the school. She got in the passenger side of the truck, dropped her backpack and Erin's books on the floorboard and slammed the door shut.

"Back up, Colt. Let's go Daron," she insisted, leaning toward the window. The truck's engine backfired with a loud boom when Daron started it, drawing even more on-lookers to the altercation.

"Kelsey, what are you doing with this guy?" Colton asked loudly. "Are you pregnant?"

"What? Don't be ridiculous; who told you that anyway?" Kelsey insisted with a look of bewilderment on her face.

"Word gets around."

"Mind your own business Colt," she demanded. "Quit putting on a show and let us go."

Colton stopped his verbal assault for a moment. Daron re-entered the argument and angrily retorted, "Colt, get a life man. She's not your girl anymore. You aren't even in school anymore; time to move on, man."

Colton leaned in the driver's side window and said, "Kelsey, I won't let you turn into trailer trash with one of these kind."

"Screw you Colt," Daron fired back with increasing adrenaline and rage as he pushed Colton's head back out of the cab.

"Your kind move out here from some ghetto and try to take over. Dirty people. You're not going to ruin Kelsey. I'm not gonna let you, you black trash," screamed Colton.

"You got no right to say that shit, Colt. I outa kick your ass, right here, right now," Daron yelled.

"Stop it; stop, both of you," Kelsey screamed and pleaded, holding tightly to Daron's arm.

"Well, bring it on mister tough guy," Colton taunted sarcastically.

Colton backed up a step from the door and lifted his shirts exposing a handgun tucked in his belt. He pulled the gun from the waist of his pants and waved it in the air. His face was twisted and cartoonish. The crowd of students pulled back. The buses were now leaving the lot from the front of the school; there was movement, confusion and the noise of diesel engines. Bus fumes coughed from the buses and clouded the air. The deputy was standing in the road stopping traffic wearing a hideous neon yellow vest and waving the buses out. One of the girls shrieked "GUN" and pandemonium ensued.

Colton's younger brother of two years, Clayton, had been serving an afterschool detention in the library when one of his friends notified him with a text message of the argument in the parking lot. He hastily gathered his belongings and stuffed them carelessly into his back pack. The teacher monitoring the punishment voiced an obligatory warning.

"Mr. Caldwell, if you leave, your detention doubles," he stated unequivocally.

"I know, Mr. Kurtz; I'm sorry, I've got to go," Clayton stated as he rushed from the room and ran down the hallway.

Back in the parking lot some students instinctively started running away from the circle of people or ducking behind cars, while others stood in stunned disbelief of the action taking place in front of them. Daron opened his door quickly and forcefully, thumping Colton in the midsection and knocking him to the asphalt. His head made a sickening thud like a rotten melon when it snapped back against the pavement. Daron tried several times to get the truck in gear. The sudden squeal of tires and roaring engine parted the students who moved in an action of involuntary self-preservation. The vehicle backfired loudly again mixed with the sound of screeching tires; a cloud of smoke filled the air. From the ground, Colton reacted without thought. He pulled the gun, leaned up and aimed at the bed of the bolting truck.

Clayton rushed to the mayhem just in time to witness his brother grasp below his right hand with his left in the standard firing grip and extend his arms.

"No, Colt!" he screamed, although his words were indistinguishable from the other sounds of panic in the area. Students crouched and leaned away from the line of fire.

One, two, three rapid bangs echoed amongst the screams; bursting flashes ricocheted off the truck as in a movie. Daron pulled the truck to the left in a hard turn across the stopped traffic, swerved recklessly back to the right and sped down the road. Colton fell back to the blacktop unconscious, his right arm extended, and the gun lay softly in his hand. The history of concussions that had kept him out of football games the last two seasons ending his dream to play in college and to be a Green Beret had put him down once more.

People were shouting at the deputy. His inelegant dash was complicated by his age, the stiff bulletproof vest he always wore, and his simultaneous attempt to draw his pistol as he ran toward the scene. Students were crouched down beside cars, and most covered their faces instinctively in self-defense. Deputy Perry approached the scene, surveying the area trying to quickly determine the point of danger.

One of the students pointed at the shooter and followed the deputy sensing the risk was abated. Colton Caldwell laid on the ground, still as a mannequin, blood forming a pool beneath his head. Clayton ran to his brother. The officer turned his attention to a circle of students calling him from another part of the lot. His worse fears were realized—two more students down and bleeding.

The deputy issued a forceful command, "Call 911! Anyone with a phone, call now!"

Clayton leaned over Colton staring at his unconscious face. He tapped his cheek as he had seen a thousand times on television.

"Colt; Colt, you okay?" he asked softly.

A few seconds later, Colton's head rolled to the side and his eyes blinked slowly.

5

WITHIN MINUTES THE high school principal, nurse and a handful of teachers ran to the area asking the students they passed for an explanation of what had happened. Mrs. Andrews, the school nurse, had grown-up in Low Field. Her daughter attended the high school. The nurse ran to a female student writhing on the pavement and applied pressure to the girl's midsection, just below her ribs. It wasn't her daughter, thank god, but she knew the wounded girl very well. Abby was twisting in anguish; pools of tears were welling around her eyes and the strain on her young face showed that she was both scared and in deep pain. Her teeth were clenched tightly yet her moans of agony were audible to everyone who stood and stared, unable to avert their eyes or shift into action.

"You're going to be okay. Abby, you're going to be okay; just try to relax. Take a deep breath. Help is on the way," the nurse calmly reassured her as she compressed the wound with a towel one of the students had given her.

The principal and some students were on their knees beside the second gunshot victim. He rolled rhythmically from side to side grasping the upper portion of his left leg just below the hip. He grimaced, opening and closing his eyes, and groaned deeply between breaths.

"Oh, god, it hurts. Damn; man, Mr. Daniels, why me?" the boy lamented. The principal rolled then slipped his jacket under the boy's head.

"It's okay Will. Try to stay calm," counseled the principal.

A science teacher pushed his way close to the scrum and quickly assessed that a tourniquet was needed. He took a scarf from a nearby student and snugged the knot securely above the wound. Others brought blankets from their cars and helped to cover the two students with gunshot wounds. The faint sound of sirens started to fill the air, and adults ran to the area abandoning cars in the street; others running from the porches of the run-down homes that faced the school. Several students sat on the pavement with scrapes from being knocked down in the melee. Many stood holding their cell phones in front of them capturing the scene with their cameras. Others made phone calls and some sent text messages to parents and friends, quickly spreading the news of the school shooting throughout the community.

Deputy Perry took the gun from Colton's hand, removed the clip and carefully slipped the weapon into his coat pocket. He told Clay to stay with his brother.

"Make him stay down and hold this on his head to see if you can stop the bleeding," the officer instructed pulling his hankie from his pants pocket and handing it to Clayton.

Following his training with reflexive proficiency, the Sheriff Deputy took out his cell phone and made two calls to report the incident—the first was to the township police and the second was to the Superintendent of Schools.

Superintendent Jim Collins was in his office with a board member discussing the pros and cons of placing a new levy on the ballot for a special election before the May primary when his secretary knocked hastily and opened the door.

"I'm sorry to interrupt but there's been a shooting at the high school; they need you there right away," she said without delay or unnecessary courtesy.

"Oh shit," the superintendent said quietly.

"Excuse me John," he replied to the office guest.

"Sure, go," said the man sensing the urgency of the moment.

The superintendent grabbed his coat, bolted from the room and out of the building, searching his pocket for keys as he jogged to his car.

Collins thought daily about this darkest possibility. His blood pressure simultaneously raced and pulsed as his stomach knotted. His teeth were clenched as he drove furiously down the road toward the chaos. *Not on my watch* had always been his mantra, although in his heart he knew that all of the best planning and due diligence in the world needed to be cloaked with good luck to prevent a tragedy. His thoughts swirled in confusion; uncharacteristically, he flashed his head lights and passed several cars on his way to the high school. He wished he knew more about the events he was racing toward, but ultimately it didn't matter. He would be there in a moment. His life and career would never be the same. He knew this disaster would occupy many of the coming hours, days, weeks, and months.

Jim parked and ran to the scene. His chest was pounding and his breathing was labored. At this point he hoped for the best case scenario such a situation could offer—no deaths.

6

DARON AND KELSEY's hearts were speeding faster than his truck as they crossed out of town on Main Street in the direction of her house. Their hands were literally shaking from adrenaline and the emotional trauma of what they had both just encountered. He pulled the truck into the wide gravel parking lot that fronted a small manufacturing plant. He put his face in his hands, exhaling and inhaling deep breaths. His torso rose and fell in unison with his breathing.

Finally, he looked up and asked Kelsey, "Are you okay?"

She was still shaking—her face was flushed with a stern look of anger while tears dripped over her pronounced cheekbones.

"I can't believe that. Did he really shoot at us? I just can't believe it," she said incredulously.

"Me neither, but I think he definitely shot at us," Daron echoed. "What should we do now?"

Sirens were audible throughout the community. A police car presumably responding to the incident raced past them in the opposite direction. Gradually they both regained their composure. Their breathing quieted to a state of normalcy.

"Maybe we should go back to the school," Kelsey said searching in her purse for her pulsating phone.

"Okay. Or we could drive ourselves to the police station?" proposed Daron.

"I don't know, let's just sit here a minute. My phone is blowing up with messages. Maybe I should call my mom?" she wondered aloud.

Her phone rang and *Stephanie Boyd* showed on the screen. "Never mind, it's my mom. Hi mom. No I'm fine. Mom, Colton was being a jerk and then he flashed a gun at us so we just got out of there. But we think he shot at us. He did? Oh my god," she said before turning to Daron to explain. "My mom said he shot two students."

"Oh shit, what a dumb ass," Daron replied with a sick realization of the immense problem. "What in the world was he thinking? I wonder if he was high or something; he did seem messed up, didn't he?"

As Kelsey continued to recount her actions of the past ten minutes and Daron contemplated their options, two police cruisers pulled into the lot aggressively braking in the gravel and pinning them from moving—one car in front of the truck and the other behind it. The officers swung open the car doors, pulled their weapons and aimed them at the two young people. Kelsey and Daron instinctively raised their hands to demonstrate to the officers their willingness to cooperate.

"Out of the car, now!" screamed the young office from in front of the truck.

Daron and Kelsey slowly opened their respective doors and slowly got of the truck continuing to show their hands the best they could.

"Sir, we didn't do anything," offered Daron.

Kelsey told her mom what was happening.

"Stay on the phone, Kelsey," her mom insisted.

"Shut up and put your hands on the hood," demanded the policeman from the front who kept his gun pointed with deadly seriousness at Daron. The officer from behind aggressively pulled each of Daron's arms behind his back and handcuffed him.

"Give me the phone," he said roughly.

"It's my mom and I'm going to keep the phone right here so she can hear what you're doing," Kelsey responded holding the phone toward the officer.

He wrestled the cell phone away from Kelsey.

"Ma'am, this is Patrolman Hurst. Your daughter has to come with us to the police station in Low Field. There was a school shooting and she is a suspect. We have to take these kids back to the police department in town to sort things out. You can meet us there anytime," he stated and hung up the call. He slipped the phone into the side pocket of his jacket.

Then he repeated the act handcuffing Kelsey with a pair of handcuffs handed to him by the other officer.

Daron quietly pleaded, "Sir, I'm just saying, we are the victims here; we didn't do anything except flee from a psycho who was threatening us with a gun. And we stopped here and waited as soon as we got a safe distance from the school."

"There'll be plenty of time for explaining everything," said the officer as he finally returned his weapon to its holster. He pinched the small communication device on his appellate and announced that the suspects in the white pickup were in custody. Daron and Kelsey were separated into the rear seats of the two police cars. They looked at each other through the side windows, both shaking their heads in disbelief. Now both fully realized the severity of the school altercation. Their lives had been turned upside down in an instant, and Colton was to blame.

7

A HALF HOUR LATER, the piercing pitch of sirens had receded save for the approaching ambulances that had to travel to the scene from neighboring communities. The countless emergency lights on the assortment of response vehicles, however, continued to pulsate with regularity, signaling the scene of a momentous problem. After running too hard to the scene, Jim Collins knelt beside Abby for several minutes surveying the scene and waiting for his breathing to become normal again. He, like so many others, launched himself into helping the injured and wounded. People wanted to talk to him but he remained diligent with the purpose of providing aid to the victims. He figured there would be plenty of time later to piece together the sequence of events. He knew much of his time in the coming days, week and months would be consumed by this event anyway, so there was no reason to neglect the priorities of the moment in order to start administrating the issue.

He folded his jacket and placed it gently under Abby's head. He held her bloody hand and maintained eye contact with the frightened girl. The superintendent didn't know every student by name but he knew Abby. The district had made a practice of purchasing one piece of student art each year and hanging it proudly in the Board of Education offices as a tribute to the district's outstanding art teachers and the talented students who flourished to the program. Each student artist was awarded a scholarship as payment for the chosen work when they graduated. Abby Olson already had two works selected to be showcased as district winners and she was likely to become the first three-time *Low Field Student Artist of the Year* in this, her senior year.

Collins had two young children himself from a late marriage and he couldn't help but transpose his daughter's image on Abby's face as he gazed with profound sorrow at her pained expression. A school shooting was the unthinkable act and it had occurred during his tenure. He was filled with an overwhelming feeling of despair and emptiness.

"The first ambulance needs to take Abby," he stated quietly to the nurse who was providing primary care to the student.

"Absolutely," she agreed.

"What's taking them so long to get here?" he rhetorically asked himself shaking his head.

Local law enforcement personnel quickly secured the crime scene the best they could unwinding neon yellow caution tape around the expansive area and moving bystanders behind the makeshift barrier. Considering the number of people who had actually been involved and the additional responders, official and unofficial, who had descended on the public parking lot, it was a logistical puzzle they solved in short time. They cleared paths and parking spots for the ambulances and directed them to the students in the order of highest priority.

In total, five ambulances took students away for treatment. A police officer and the middle school principal rode with a groggy and bleeding Colton, his wrists handcuffed together in the back of a vehicle. Nurse Andrews assisted two paramedics in stabilizing Abby for her ride to the closest hospital emergency room in Akron. Without hesitation, the nurse climbed into the back of the vehicle and sat on a small stool near Abby maintaining sensory contact with her hand. The ricocheted bullet that pierced her abdominal area rendered her injuries the most critical. The high school principal, Mr. Daniels, accompanied Will to the area urgent care before he was also sent to Akron General, and two other students were taken to the local urgent care facility as a precaution—one with a twisted knee and the other with minor scrapes and bruises—both sustained while evading Daron's fleeing truck.

Media and parents continued to flood the school property repeatedly asking the same questions and getting the same sketchy answers from the superintendent and the deputy. During the late afternoon and evening hours, the local police took statements from many shaken students in several classrooms just inside the side entrance of the school. Anyone who was a first-hand witness to the event was asked to go to this restricted area and write down an account of what they had seen and heard before leaving the premises. When the police released the students, most of them looked for a way to escape the scene quickly, happy to be unhurt in the fracas and grateful to be safely united with friends and family. The media pursued each of them loudly asking questions. A few of the students stopped and made somewhat incoherent, long-winded statements but most continued their exodus from the turmoil as quickly as possible within the secure arms of their parents.

Superintendent Collins knew from past experience that in these kinds of tumultuous and chaotic situations, the less he said the better, especially when he really didn't know all of the facts. Each of the board members, as well as his wife, had called his cell phone wanting clarification and updates from the rumors they had heard through their mobile devices. For an hour or more, he spoke to them, local government officials and neighboring school superintendents, repeating what he knew almost a dozen times. Finally, it was time to face the gathering of media who kept pressing him for a statement, desperate to file a report regarding the breaking story and securing the lead spot on the upcoming six o'clock news broadcast. The early fall sunset was spreading darkness upon the parking lot and the camera lights literally blinded him when he tried to make eye contact with the camera lenses. He hastily scribbled a short list of notes and stepped forward toward the cornucopia of microphones and portable audio recorders.

"My name is James Collins and I am the Superintendent of the Low Field Local Schools. On behalf of the Board of Education, our staff and faculty members, our parents and all of our community, we are both shocked and saddened by the events at our high school this afternoon. At this time we know that a weapon was discharged during school dismissal wounding several of our students. They have been taken to a nearby hospital and an urgent care facility for medical treatment, and their families are now with them. We will update all of our parents later this evening with additional information through our emergency telephone notification system. I would like to thank the first responders for their timely actions in assisting the wounded students. We ask that everyone please keep our students in your thoughts and prayers tonight. Thank you."

There was a burst of questions from the members of the media that stunned the superintendent momentarily.

"Mr. Collins, Michael Witlow, WJAK Akron News Network; what can you tell us about the shooter's identity? We've heard he's a decorated ex-Navy Seal; can you confirm that sir?" barked one reporter.

Jim responded with a quizzical expression, "Right now, the facts are sketchy, at least the information that I have is preliminary, but it does appear that the problem was a dispute between several students, and one of them is a former student who is not an ex-Navy Seal. The Low Field Police Department and our administrators will work collaboratively on the investigation of this unfortunate incident in that it is both a police issue and a school issue."

He paused and then added, "It is important for me to explain that this confrontation does *not* appear to be some sort of a random mass shooting or act of terrorism, but, we will be working through the evening with the local authorities gathering information and trying to

determine exactly what happened, and we will have additional statements later this evening or we will issue a Press Release in the morning. Again, at this time we ask for your patience while we continue
the investigation. Please excuse me."

8

K ELSEY AND DARON were separated in the two interview rooms of the Low Field Police Department. The township had recently constructed the multi-purpose facility primarily as place to hold the monthly Trustee meetings and to conduct other community business. It also served as an upgraded location for the law enforcement unit, but it functioned more as a clean, updated office and work space for the three full time officers and four part time employees rather than a secure facility or jail in which to manage people in a crisis. The simple two-by-four stud and drywall construction, as well as the beige vinyl siding that was used to finish the exterior, gave the building's appearance one of an inexpensive spec-home from the road. A small illuminated sign out front proudly heralded the structure as the Township Administrative Building. The long-overdue facility was built on one edge of a wide parcel that was counterbalanced at the opposite end by a relatively new structure used by the Volunteer Fire Department. The political functions and vital services of the community were now unified on one site including a place for the police department to handle its business in the north wing of the administration building.

Stephanie Boyd stood at the small counter and window that separated the dispatch operator from the lobby and waiting room. She impatiently asked the heavy-set, grim woman for updates on the status of her daughter. Her demands to see Kelsey only served to harden the employee's stern resolve to make her wait even longer. At the top of the hour, another brawny person, this one a male officer, replaced the dispatch operator. She informed the man of the location of the various people in the interview rooms, grabbed her purse from beneath the desk and left the building, not hiding her annoyance with Kelsey's mom. Mrs. Boyd decided to remain standing near the counter to send the signs of impatience and disgust with her body language. She stood and repeatedly sent text messages to Kelsey's phone that went unanswered.

A hallway led toward the back of the building. In the first interview room to the right Daron was seated on one side of a plain folding table opposite Officer Hurst. A legal pad and pencil were in front of Hurst. One wall of the room had a large glass panel that Daron conjectured from his experience of watching countless television crime dramas with his mother was a two-way window. An artificial tree with a braided trunk planted in a basket pot sat alone in one corner of the room. He recounted his altercation with Colton in its entirety over and over again to the officer—finding that explaining the details of the episode lasted three times as long as the actual quarrel. Patrolman Hurst asked many seemingly superfluous questions in an attempt to verify Daron's truthfulness in his retelling of the facts and confirm the accuracy of his memory of the row. Once the patrolman was satisfied with the consistency of the story, he told Daron to write a full account of the events along with a list of witnesses who could verify his version of the argument.

Kelsey was having a similar experience in the neighboring room with an older man whom she recognized as the Chief of Police. She could actually hear the muffled sound of Daron's voice coming through the walls and ceiling but could not perceive his statements with clarity. It didn't matter because she was sure their stories would match. As far as she was concerned, Daron and she had not done anything wrong; in fact, they had escaped from the tense situation as a way to protect themselves and others. The words her mom and grandmother had often quoted to her and her younger brother growing up were a simple guide for life: *It's always the right time to tell the truth and do the right thing.* She was following that advice now.

9

QUICK WORD OF the shooting spread through the community through social media and cell phones like a powerful wave from a strangely fused news and gossip tsunami. As soon as the affected parents could free themselves from work, they headed to the various sites to locate and support their children. Colton's father, Roy Caldwell, drove a semi-truck and trailer back and forth to Saint Louis most weeks. He was an independent contractor for a small trucking company that covered overflow shipping of retail packages for the major carriers and sometimes the U. S. Postal Service. When his wife called to inform him about the incident, he yelled and swore loudly and she could hear him banging the steering wheel or dashboard of the cab. She knew Colton's actions would incite his violent temper so she chose to bear the news to him now while he was still on the road and not later after he had arrived at home.

Roy decided to stop at the Police Department with his rig as he was passing through town rather than go back out later. He knew the Chief of Police, Harlan Hadley, very well. They were only a few years apart in age and had grown up together in Low Field. As kids, they played many sports together culminating as teammates on the high school varsity football and baseball squads. Roy was determined to get to the bottom of this nonsense immediately. Colton wouldn't have done anything as foolish as fire a weapon at a group of kids, and he was sure he could take care of everything with swift, aggressive action starting directly at the top of the power structure in Low Field. He'd stop by and talk with Harlan.

As he approached the outskirts of town, he could see the flashing lights of the emergency vehicles. He slowed the semi and eased it off the road onto an extended gravel berm that served as a local fruit and vegetable stand on weekends. He turned on his flashing lights and took another pill. Getting down the steps of the truck was noticeably more arduous to him because of advancing arthritis and even walking a few hundred yards down the road to the new township building was a demanding proposition for his stiff joints and muscles.

He held the door of the police department for an attractive woman who arrived at nearly the same time. She had a concerned look on her face.

"Ma'am," he said as he tipped his soiled cap.

"Thank you," she simply replied. The woman stepped to the window and identified herself to the dispatch officer who was also serving as the receptionist.

"I'm Brenda Roberts. I believe my son Daron is here," she said.

"Sure; have a seat Mrs. Roberts. Your son is in the interview room I think with Chief Hadley."

"May I go and be with him?" she asked.

"No ma'am; he's eighteen now and the Chief is conducting the interview," replied the overweight officer.

"I'd like to go into the interview," Daron's mom insisted. "Can you please go ask the Chief if I can join them?"

"Okay sure; just calm down and have a seat. I'll be right back."

Roy Caldwell had been standing behind Mrs. Roberts listening intently to their exchange. As the officer awkwardly pushed himself up and out of the desk chair, Roy stepped forward and said, "Hey Carl, since you're going back there could you ask Harlan if I can speak to him for a moment?"

Kelsey's mom moved forward and greeted Daron's mom who hadn't seen her standing near the far end of the room.

"Brenda," she called looking up from her phone. "Hi. I asked to go back with Kelsey too. I've been sending her messages not to talk to anyone but I think they've taken her phone. I'm very irritated with them."

The two women stood facing each other shaken and talking softly. They were trying to understand the events of the afternoon and explained to one another what they had heard from third party reports. Stephanie Boyd gestured toward the man and whispered to Daron's mom that the man was Colton's father.

"We need to get back there with our kids," Mrs. Roberts said.

The three parents of Colton, Kelsey and Daron stood awkwardly within a close proximity of each other. Roy approached them as they waited for a response from the interrogation area.

"Excuse me, Stephanie, how have you been?" he asked with obligatory politeness.

"Fine, Roy. What the hell is wrong with Colt that he would shoot a gun at our children and into a crowd of students?" she blurted out with exasperated rage.

"Now, we don't know the facts yet, do we?" Roy tried to suggest. "I heard the black kid hit my son first with his truck, in fact, he might have, sort of run him over from what I heard."

"What?" shrieked Mrs. Roberts. "First of all, the *black kid* is my son and his name is Daron. And *Daron* from what I heard from several eye witnesses did nothing to your son."

"Don't be so sure about that, Daron's mom," he said sarcastically raising his deep voice.

"Well, I know he didn't run your son over unless he had no other way to get away from a crazed man with a gun who was threatening him," she said loudly.

Stephanie stepped toward Mr. Caldwell and said, "Roy, Colton is the one in big trouble here because he instigated this entire mess.

You better get a good lawyer and hope all of those children he shot are okay."

"Don't you worry about my son," Roy said glaring at Kelsey's mother and pointing his finger at her. "He's the best thing that ever happened to your daughter and you ought to be sticking up for him right now."

"What?" she said incredulously. "Are you crazy? Colt's always thought he was above everyone else in this town, but not now. He's in big trouble, in fact, huge trouble, and I certainly won't stick up for him or allow Kelsey to ever see him again after this debacle."

The ruckus the three adults were making in the reception area could be heard from the back and both the Chief and dispatch office both quickly reappeared to intervene between them.

"Ladies; Roy," said the Chief commanding their attention. "Listen please; we've all got a lot on our minds right now, but please, I need you all to be calm. Your kids need you to be calm. Roy, come on into my office and wait for me. Ladies, why don't we go into the back here and you can join your children."

The Chief grabbed Roy's arm and started to pull the bigger man toward the officer.

"Carl, take Roy back to my office," he said. As Roy was being led away, he looked back at the women with a sardonic expression on his face and said,

"My boy didn't do anything that we can't fix; you better keep your kids away from us. We Caldwells have been in this community for three generations. This is our town. You understand me? This is *our* town," he bellowed as his face flushed red with anger.

"Okay Roy; that's enough," demanded the Chief. "Carl, get him out of here."

10

SCHOOL WAS CANCELLED the next day. The administrators, police and the technology coordinator spent much of the night combing through the surveillance video and the statements from students. Many of these eye-witness accounts of the incident were written with such poor handwriting that it rendered them largely unreadable and caused the adults to repeatedly comment about the need to teach penmanship. They were trying desperately to amass a complete and accurate interpretation of exactly what had happened the day before. The elementary school principal, Mrs. Andrews and a Low Field police officer visited the hospital rooms of the injured to check on them and obtain additional written statements.

Later that evening, law enforcement officers drove to the homes of Colton, Daron and Kelsey and tried to gather additional background information from parents, siblings, other relatives and neighbors about the trio. The authorities were anxious to piece together the full back story to the incident so they could be confident they had the correct answers to everyone's questions. Most of the people were either not home or too upset and confused to speak to the officers that evening. Instead the officers left business cards and asked everyone with more information to come into the high school library at eight o'clock the next morning in order to be interviewed by the police and give statements regarding the three young people who were involved in the shooting.

The time frame for the entire event was approximately ten minutes in length—roughly 2:55-3:05 PM on Thursday, October 13th.

How could so much in the lives of people, the reputation of a school district and the collective soul of a community change in such a short amount of time? The team of officials wrote a composite statement that would suffice as the historic Press Release of the event. Because of the throng of curious media personnel and vehicles ensconced in the parking lot since the previous evening, the decision was made to hold a brief press conference at 1:00 PM on Friday to read the statement and answer a few follow-up questions. Since the shooting suspect was an adult and no longer a student, it was decided that the Chief of Police would be the most appropriate spokesperson for the group.

A great flurry of activity ensued after the high school principal was sent outside to inform the media that the press conference would be delayed slightly but would take place in about fifteen minutes. The weary group of people exited the main doors of the high school and the Chief stepped forward to a wobbly podium that a custodian had carried out from the cafeteria.

"Good afternoon. I'm Harlan Hadley, Low Field Township Chief of Police. Since the events of yesterday afternoon, the Low Field Police Department and the Low Field Local Schools have been conducting a joint investigation into the shooting that occurred here in the parking lot of our high school during dismissal. In all, four students were injured and required emergency medical treatment; two remain hospitalized in Akron with gunshot wounds—one is in guarded condition and the second is listed in serious but stable condition. The names of these students, all of whom are minors, are being withheld at the present time. The gunman has been identified as Colton Caldwell, 19, of Low Field Township. He too received medical treatment last evening and now is in the custody of Low Field County Sheriff's Department. The investigation is considered ongoing at this point. Now I'd be happy to answer any questions," the Chief concluded.

"Is there any indication that the shooting was a premeditated or planned attack by the gunman?"

"No, it appears that the incident was more of a domestic dispute between Mr. Caldwell and one other male student."

"What about the girl?"

"It appears the argument occurred because of a changing relationship the female student had with the two males."

"Chief, there is a theory that has been floating around today that the shooter, ah, Mr. Caldwell, had been recently discharged from the Marines and that this shooting might have been intended as retaliation on the government for his release from the Marine Corps. Do you have any indication that the event was a deliberate, calculated revenge mass shooting?"

"No, as I just said we consider this incident to have been a domestic dispute."

"Sir, Ohio law contains strict provisions regarding the possession of fire arms within school zones, but I have not been able to locate any of the required public postings related to that statute on the doors or on signage on the school property. In light of that, what charges do you anticipate will be filed against the defendant?"

"I am reticent to discuss the specific filing of charges that the Prosecutor's Office could deem appropriate in this case," he said pausing. "Certainly reckless endangerment and discharging a weapon in a public place are two offenses that I might recommend for their consideration."

"Chief Harlan, the shooter's father was interviewed last night and stated that his son suffered multiple concussions during his career as a star football player at Low Field High School and he also informed the media that his son had a traumatic brain injury during basic training. It is his belief that his son's actions were a direct result of these injuries not being properly diagnosed or treated by the school district or the Marine Corps. Do you have any thoughts regarding his statements?"

"No," the Chief simply stated with a shake of his head. "One final question."

"What about the driver of the pickup truck? Any charges being considered as they relate to his actions?"

"Yes; that young man is still a minor but we are taking a look at his statements and those of eye witnesses and the surveillance video to determine his culpability in the incident. We are also studying his actions as an operator of a motor vehicle in light of the situation. As I said earlier, the investigation is on-going."

One of the deputies stepped forward and handed the chief a scrap of paper. He nodded and from his side jacket pocket pulled out the paper from which he had read the initial statement. He held up his fingers in counting succession as he announced the three items from the paper.

"Sorry, a few announcements—First of all, there will be members of the clergy and counselors available Saturday afternoon in the high school library for any students or parents who would like to meet with them. Secondly, a prayer service for the injured students will be held at 1:00 Sunday afternoon in the school cafeteria and there will be a community meeting immediately afterwards to discuss school safety and some new procedures that will be implemented when the students and staff return to school next week. And thirdly, Superintendent Collins asked me to announce that the schools will re-open on Monday. Thank you."

11

THE LOW FIELD Diner was a small restaurant about a half mile south of town on the corner of state route 17 and Alden Avenue. The red brick building was originally an insurance agency but was converted into a restaurant twenty years ago by a hardworking immigrant couple who somehow found their way to Low Field. Over the years, *The Diner*, as it was referred to by the people who lived locally, became the epicenter of the town for the exchange of community news, opinions and grass-roots gossip. The shooting at the high school had the place abuzz on Friday morning. Tables of patrons offered their views of the situation to one another throughout the open room of the restaurant. Several groups slid tables together and became larger groups and a few people who started in booths unstacked chairs from a grouping tucked in a corner and joined the bigger table by wedging chairs between other guests who shifted sideways to make room. Even the row of folks along the eight stools at the counter leaned forward or backwards to look past each other and share opinions down the line as they ate the breakfast meals and drank coffee.

One grey-haired older man in a worn flannel jacket rubbed his unshaven chin and spoke in a deliberate pace as he looked around the table. His sleeves were rolled up just short of his elbows revealing a tattoo of an anchor slightly twisted from years of sun and thinning skin.

"I reckon Roy's boy was just going to take care of his problem as he saw fit. That's the way his old man worked—if somebody did you wrong, you took care of the situation yourself," he stated.

"He let that other boy know that he wasn't going to allow him to mess with his girl, that's for certain," another man joined in by saying.

"What kind of girl is she to move on to another guy as soon as Colt went off to war?" asked a woman in the group.

"That's a low-life two-timer, if I ever heard of one," laughed a different man. "They're a dime a dozen and Colt probably should have just walked away from that girl."

"Yeah it just shows that he ain't right no more," said a man as he set down his coffee cup. "His brain is all scrambled from football. We never had a decent offensive line any of the four years he played quarterback, and on top of that, he played middle linebacker the first three years. That boy got his bell rung too often."

"For sure," another man agreed.

"I heard he got messed up during basic training, too, which didn't help."

"What happened?" asked another man.

"They said a drill sergeant was disciplining Colt for picking on some Chinese kid is his battalion and he picked him up and dropped him on his head," said a man chewing a piece of toast.

"Really?" said another is disbelief.

"That's what I heard," the man said swallowing. "I guess he couldn't shake a headache and they put him in a hospital. A few days later he collapsed and they discovered he has some kind of aneurism in his brain or neck. Roy told me he got discharged right after that."

"Poor kid."

"Yep and only home a few days and finds out his girl is out messing around behind his back. Can't blame him for losing his cool," a man said shaking his head back and forth.

"I'd have done the same thing," said the grey-haired man wanting to rejoin the conversation.

A man with a toothpick said with a wry smile, "The craziest thing though is I would have figured he was a better shot; all he hit was the tailgate of the truck."

"But he was on his back trying to shoot," offered a man.

"Yeah, but like most men, he probably does pretty good work on his back," laughed the woman.

"Well, he sure spent lots of time on his back playing football in this hard-luck town; we all know that," confirmed a man with a smile.

A few members of the media came in for breakfast or a coffee and saw the opportunity to film and capture some of the locals' reactions to the shooting. A few people stepped outside onto the porch to make statements on camera for television networks but most were unwilling to comment publically about the occurrence. An older couple was sitting in a pair of sun-bleached rocking chairs having coffee and agreed to a brief interview.

"All I can say is I had a feeling something bad like this was going to happen around here. People in this town are backward and stupid," commented the man without hesitation.

The woman was nodding her head in affirmation when the cameraman turned the large camera resting on his shoulder in her direction. She held her purse on her lap with both hands.

"He's right unfortunately. When we first moved out here after the war, this was a nice little town. There used to be a good connection between people who lived out here, but ever since they started merging the townships together to save the schools, things have turned rotten," she said with surprising insight.

"Why did that start to happen?" asked the newswoman.

"There weren't enough kids no more. The graduating classes were so small at all these little high schools that the state started combining the districts together," the man offered. "My wife here used to work in the cafeteria at the elementary school before they closed it. They said it would lower everyone's taxes but that was a load of bull."

"Now the buses run for hours every morning and afternoon wasting money because the kids come from all over creation and the two schools are miles apart. These kids don't have anything in common no more. It's like they're a bunch of strangers forced to go to school together; it don't make sense," she said with conviction looking straight into the camera lens.

"I hate to say it but the children are bad and the schools are bad too," the man offered finally. "That's why we ain't surprised this happened in Low Field."

Inside *The Diner* conversations circled round and round in ebbing highs and lows as new patrons took the place of coffee-weary others. Those who were leaving tossed money on the table, grabbed their jackets and returned their caps to their heads as they headed out. Each one was issued a reminder as they left the table.

"Don't forget the meeting Sunday afternoon. That should be a good show."

12

KELSEY'S MOM, STEPHANIE Boyd and Wyatt Simmons, her stepfather stood in their kitchen arguing. Simmons general disposition was one of a man who was living a life of disappointment. The years of unappreciated toiling miles away in heavy construction to pay for two families had become a monotonous drudgery for the intelligent man. He postponed college enrollment following high school in order to save money. The plan was to work for two or three years and stockpile enough funds that his educational endeavors would not be compromised by part-time employment. Once he started school, he wanted to have sufficient savings so that he could finish what he started without interruption and without taking loans. If he needed to borrow money and go into debt to pay for graduate school, that was okay, but not for his bachelor's degree. The two or three years seamlessly turned into five and his quick mind and good work ethic landed him a foreman position with greater financial reward. After he met his first wife, Sherri, they bought a nice house on an expensive property and started to have children; his focus changed and his dreams evaporated. When he turned thirty, he accepted the fact that he would never attend college.

Several years later the constant pressures of work and parenthood led he and Sherri to divorce. He consoled himself with work and beer. Six months later he had committed himself to be a better father to his kids and regain purpose in his life. Stephanie worked in the offices at the construction company, and within a few months of their first date, they were married and he adopted her two kids, Kelsey and Brian, from her first marriage. Initially Wyatt was the perfect step-dad, but as the novelty of the situation subsided and the children grew older, their relationship evolved from congeniality to complacency and finally bitterness.

The paper-thin walls that separated the kitchen from Kelsey's bedroom did little to stop the sounds of the ensuing argument of the adults. Since she got home from the Police Department Thursday evening, she closed the door to her bedroom and remained in her sanctuary almost exclusively for the next twenty-four hours. Her mom's and Wyatt's marriage was increasingly strained and Kelsey's involvement in the shooting only served to heighten the situation. She could hear Wyatt's powerful voice from the kitchen.

"It all started last summer when they broke up and she started hanging around with those kids in that recycling club. You'd think they would be good kids but they're not. They just use it as an excuse to be away from home and hang out together and none of the parents suspect anything because it sounds like a good cause. They probably just use the money to buy drugs smoke dope together," Wyatt conjectured.

"Don't be ridiculous. Anyway, the more I think about it, Colton was no good for her. He was just filling Kelsey's head with moving away with him and living in base housing while he was off at war. No plans for her other than being his wife and having his kids. Why, so she could become a nineteen year old Marine widow?" her mom reasoned.

"That boy Daron is no better," countered Wyatt.

"We hardly know him, but to me he seems nice enough. I'm just worried about her being more than just friends with him. Young people today are just foolish when it comes to interracial dating—even though his skin is not that dark. People in this community pass judgment. It's not right but it happens."

"People are saying this whole thing is her fault," Wyatt said.

"That's nonsense. Where did you hear that?"

"The gas station. They said the boys were arguing over her being pregnant."

"What?" Stephanie threw the dishcloth on the counter. "My daughter is not pregnant, and Colton is a bully and a stalker as far as I'm concerned. This whole predicament is his doing, not Kelsey's," her mom said.

"You need to forbid her to see him or any other boy for the rest of the year," Wyatt insisted.

"She's in the homecoming court with Daron next Friday and they have a dance on Saturday. Kelsey's been waiting for this year's homecoming for three years and I'm not going to change her plans one bit," her mom stated with resolve.

"You think she should stand in that stadium in front of a crowd of people after what just happened?" Wyatt asked.

"Homecoming is important to her."

"She should have thought about that yesterday, if it was so important to her. All she thinks about is boys; she's boy crazy, if you ask me," Wyatt said.

"No she's not and I didn't ask you. Dating is normal. It's good for her but it's not the most important thing—not what I want her to be focused on," admitted Stephanie.

"She's needs to get a trade, so she can make a living and take care of herself. She turns eighteen next month," Wyatt said.

"I don't know what to do," lamented Stephanie. "I want her to go to college and have a future."

"You need to take her out of that school. It's a poison. Look at that neighbor girl—straight A's; got a scholarship to college and now she's pregnant and home with her parents."

"She made some bad decisions," Stephanie admitted. "She's not the first and she won't be the last—we have no room to pass judgment. I just want Kelsey to get through this year and go away to college."

"Hell, the die was cast. No kids from this place make anything of themselves. They just stay here, have kids and the circle goes round and round. Stephanie, you need to take her out of that school before it's too late. You hear me? You need to take her out of that school tomorrow!" screamed Wyatt.

Their argument upset Kelsey as much as her mother and Kelsey's head was spinning. She was exhausted from responding to text messages and email for hours. Tears streaked her face as she emailed Erin again. How could anyone think it was her fault? She didn't have anything to do with it really. Erin agreed, at least that's what she said.

Kelsey hated Wyatt. She wished her mom had never met him, let alone married him. It was all a financial arrangement. She knew her mom sacrificed her own happiness to give her and her brother a chance for a better life. When they were little, Wyatt was nice to them all, almost too nice. As she got older, his behavior and attitude toward her became awkward and disconcerting. As the opportunities for overtime hours dried-up and money got tighter, his drinking increased and dominated his time at home. He became more like a stranger to her rather than a stepfather. She wouldn't let him touch her anymore, not even a hug. Over the years it became obvious that he resented her and her brother. Wyatt projected a feeling that they really weren't his kids, and he resented them even more. He frequently made comments about how much of his money was being spent on them and his own two boys, and that none of them appreciated the sacrifices he made at work for their benefit. She couldn't wait to graduate and leave—for good. The phone rang and she heard her mother answer it.

"Hello."

Stephanie listened then whispered to Wyatt, "Homecoming is postponed."

As the phone call continued and a scowl formed on her face— her skin started to flush and her expression turned to one of disgust.

Her body language became tense and rigid. She started to repeat the principal's statements out loud for Wyatt's benefit.

"Why is she not allowed to participate in Homecoming? What? Wait a minute, Mr. Daniels. You're saying Kelsey's suspended for ten days and you're recommending she be expelled from school because of the shooting. Why? She didn't do anything. She was just there like the rest of the kids. Colt did wrong, not Kelsey. This isn't fair. Everyone says you make terrible decisions. Yes, I will call the superintendent and a whole lot of other people too," she said with anger as she slammed the phone into the receiver.

13

ABBY AND WILL were wheeled into areas close to each other in the Akron hospital emergency room. Their clothes were cut from their bodies and stuffed into large, clear plastic bags. Will's wallet, keys and watch were placed in an envelope and Abby's purse was placed in a second plastic bag which also got placed into her clothing bag. The emergency room doctor performed an initial assessment of both students and decided on two different courses of action for their respective conditions. The bullet had passed through the outer portion of the large muscles on Will's left thigh. The femur was fine but there was a need to examine the soft tissue around the wound to prevent the threat of infection and determine if there was any damage to nerves, ligaments or tendons. The doctor performed a brief surgical procedure in the room Will had been brought to by the paramedics. He cleaned and stitched the wound shut and then had Will admitted to a room on the second floor of the hospital. Typically, Will's family doctor would now assume control of and monitor his subsequent treatment, care and convalescence.

The emergency room doctor stabilized Abby and told her parents that because of the seriousness of her wound it would be best for a specialized surgeon to properly evaluate her condition following several tests he would order. The surgeon would use the results to make a diagnosis and discuss his recommendations with them the next morning. In all likelihood she required a rather complex and delicate operation. She was moved to an intensive care unit room and sedated.

Her parents had sat by her side for hours and hours. The gurney she lay on was rolled in and out of the room several times as technical machines became available to perform tests on her abdomen. In her room Abby slept peacefully; her mom held her motionless hand. It was the hand of an artist, a serious artist. Abby had won ribbons for her art at the county fair almost every year that she entered. She always loved to draw and paint, but now that she was a mature and more sophisticated in her view of the world, her art had soared to new levels of importance. Her portfolio had been reviewed by several colleges for scholarship consideration and she had offers from the prestigious art departments at both Carnegie Mellon and Kent State University. One of her works from last year, *Winter Solstice*, won a national award from The Guggenheim Museum of Art in a competition for high school students. Seeing her work displayed in New York last summer fueled her passion to create almost to the level of an addiction.

The bullet that entered her abdomen had perforated her large intestine and nicked her spinal column just below the waist. After two days, she had not regained feeling in her legs. A team of doctors already performed two different surgeries within the first 48 hours and their prognosis grew bleaker each hour the numbness lingered. The medical staff and her parents were now forced to wait and hope for a minor miracle. There were several serious issues, most notably severe nerve damage to her spine. It would take months of healing and rehabilitation before they would know if she would ever walk again. The split seconds of Colton's gunfire had become a life altering moment for Abby and her parents.

Will was luckier. The shot that hit his leg entered and exited the hamstring muscle midway between his hip and his knee. It was deeper than a flesh wound, but, in time, the doctors said that they expected him to make a full recovery. However, playing in next week's district golf tournament was out.

For most people, the news would have been disappointing but not the end of the world. But for Will the news was devastating. Just two days prior to the shooting, he had won the individual medalist honors at the sectional golf tournament by eight shots. The district tournament meant everything to him. All summer, he tirelessly worked at his game. He traveled to three neighboring states playing tournaments and attempting to qualify for national competitions. In July, he finished fifth at an AJGA tournament in Indiana and won an OJGA event outside of Cleveland in a playoff.

But now his plans for the future depended on his success in the Ohio High School Athletic Association District Golf Tournament, and hopefully, the state tournament. His surge up the junior rankings had come only this summer, just prior to his senior year, so he was only on a few recruiters' lists for his class; however, most of the college coaches who still had a spot or two open on their team rosters would be in Columbus evaluating the most talented golfers in the state, and he needed to be there to display his talents. His goals at the beginning of the season were to become the first golfer in Low Field High School history to compete at the state tournament and to secure a scholarship to play golf in college. Missing next week's district tournament was simply not an option.

14

KEITH BYLER'S NEIGHBOR was in his yard raking leaves when the teachers' union president pulled into his driveway. The rows of Cape Cods were painted different shades of ugly and there was a modest lack of character among the houses. The October sky was changing into its typical winter pattern—a gunmetal grey quilt that covered the area for months. On rare days it would be pulled back to expose radiant sunshine that would soak the area for a few hours and turn the empty looks on the residents' faces to smiles.

Bill Henry was a retired cop from The New Lake Township PD. He looked like an older professional football player. His jet-black dyed hair caused a visual disconnect between the hair on his head and the aging lines on his face. One of the things Bill did since he left the force was teach a concealed carry weapon class at the nearby Fish and Game Club. During his career he had seen more than his share of assaults and murders and believed violence was best counterbalanced by having more people prepared for the unexpected, the unthinkable. As a result, he was a strong proponent of the state law that gave trained citizens the right to carry a sidearm for personal protection. A layer of compassion existed deep below the calloused, hardened layer of his personality. However, a career of seeing graphic human disputes and grief linked with his own life experiences had transformed his everyday demeanor into one that was habitually direct and authoritative.

"Sorry to hear about the shooting Keith," he said to his neighbor. "How are those two kids doing?"

"Okay, by and large, but the word is the girl might be paralyzed. It's too early to say for sure, but she's got a tough road ahead of her," said Keith. Then he asked, "Bill, if some of the teachers took your class, could we carry weapons to protect ourselves and others at school."

"Well, the law prohibits concealed carry in school zones. There are a few provisions that allow the gun to be in the car, but I suppose it would take the Board of Education's approval for a teacher to be armed in the school," answered Bill.

Keith volunteered his position, "There are a lot of us who feel that we can't just sit back any longer, unprepared, hoping that the next crazy doesn't come and shoot up our school. We want to protect our students, plain and simple, and this seems like the best way to do that."

"I understand, Keith. That's why these laws were put in place. So people could protect themselves in life and death situations. At least until law enforcement personnel can get there," Bill responded.

"I think it would help our case with the Board and the superintendent if we already were certified for concealed carry, don't you?" Keith asked.

"Definitely. We could do a special class out at the club whenever you want—in one or two weekends, we could do the course and meet the required hours for shooting and gun safety. Then, the teachers could get their background checks. It takes a couple sessions to complete everything, but there are guns out there for the people to use and in forty-five days we'd have your folks ready," Bill offered.

"That would be great. Most of them have no experience with guns; I mean they're teachers," Keith laughed. "I've got an old pistol I inherited from my dad, but most of these people don't own a gun. So, they'd need some advice on what to buy. It would really help if you could help us with that too."

"Sure, that's not a problem. A friend of mine is a gun dealer from Akron and I'm guessing he'd let me bring some samples out to the club for your people to try," Bill responded. "There's some really good weaponry available that women and men can handle pretty easily and will give them peace of mind." He paused for a minute and then added, "It's too bad the world's come to this, but the nuts have no qualms about doing anything they want to for money, attention or for some sick legacy. So we all have to be ready for them."

"Thanks Bill. I'll talk it over with the teachers and let you know," Keith said as he shook his neighbor's hand and walked toward his house.

"No problem my friend, no problem at all," concluded Bill.

He returned to his chore of raking the multitude of dead leaves in his yard into neat mounded piles. Before he bagged them for recycling or cremation, the raked leaves resembled freshly dug grave mounds the size of children.

15

UNBEKNOWNST TO THE people of Low Field, there were, in fact, two meetings scheduled for Sunday—one public and one private. The first was the publically announced community meeting to be held in the afternoon at the high school. The second was a special meeting of the Low Field Teachers' Association for later that evening. Attendance at the union meeting was strictly for members only. A private room in the back of the VFW Hall with a separate rear entrance was reserved with short notice. The manager was a friend of Keith's and made it easy for the teachers to conduct clandestine gatherings here. The hall was located near the opposite end of the school district's boundaries, miles from the high school, and the teachers were asked not to discuss the meeting announcement with anyone, even family members or friends.

The 1:00 prayer service was conducted by Pastor Mike of the Community Fellowship Church next to the high school. He was a highly-educated young man who had married a woman from a nearby community who wanted to return home and live near her parents when the couple started a family. He taped a simple note on the double doors of the school asking people to join together next door in the church to pray for the students of Low Field, especially, Will and Abby, whose enlarged senior photos hung in front of him on the pulpit. His comments, as always, were judicious and perceptive, and although the service lasted less than twenty minutes, his use of power point technology added significant interest and enjoyment to the experience for those who attended. The pastor's perspective emphasized an unselfish caring for one another and the significance of God's grace during difficult times. He concluded the service with a brief, artful use of moving religious music and ceremony that stirred even the most callous members of the gathering.

Pastor Mike had a strong connection to young people and the weekly attendance at the once fledgling church had swelled in the months since his arrival because of his vibrant personality and the efforts he made to relate his messages to them. As a concluding act, he asked everyone to stand and pray with him while raising their arms and holding the Low Field student symbol of support, the simple formation of the letter *"L"* made by extending one's index finger and thumb in the shape of that letter while closing the other three fingers in a fist. People swallowed hard and wiped tears from their faces when he finished the prayer and they all said in chorus, "Amen."

Although the meeting at the high school was specifically conducted to share information with students and parents, the overflow crowd also included local media affiliates and throngs of school supporters and detractors from the community. Some of the representatives from town were genuinely concerned citizens with a strong civic conscience while others were simply the kind of people who slowed down to witness the misfortune caused by auto accidents—spectators who took pleasure from any type of controversy or malaise in town, especially when it involved the schools. All of the seats were taken so the late arrivals stood lining the walls, in some places two and three people deep.

A weary panel of officials comprised of Chief Hadley, Mr. Collins, Deputy Perry and Mr. Daniels grudgingly sat behind a long folding table at one end of the cafeteria. Their task at the end of this long weekend of work was to discuss Thursday's incident and convey the new security strategies that would be implemented immediately for the students of Low Field as they returned to school on Monday.

Each of them took a turn at the podium and made individual remarks. The superintendent welcomed the crowd and uttered the
typical clichés regarding the importance of insuring the safety and
well-being of the students; he assured the crowd that school security
would now become the district's top priority. The Chief summarized the latest facts of the investigation, the deputy accounted for
his actions as they unfolded that unfortunate, historic day, and the
principal expressed his gratitude for the quick and heroic responses
from students and staff that helped prevent the unfortunate incident
from having tragic consequences. Parents and attendees were invited
to make comments or ask questions. Most of them were inane attacks
aimed at the school district personnel and leadership, largely meant
to provoke more criticism rather than spark improvements:

Q   "What good is a Sheriff Deputy standing in the road
     directing traffic for the buses when someone's in the
     parking lot with a gun shooting our kids?"

Q   "Where was the principal while this was happening? I
     heard he was sitting in his office looking at his computer."

Q   "Why aren't teachers assigned to be outside during
     dismissal supervising students? Or why don't the bus
     drivers watch for problems while the kids are exiting
     the school instead of sitting in their busses with the
     engines running while they talk on their cell phones."

C   "If you think you're going to put another levy on the bal-
     lot, I'd think again. If you people can't protect our kids, I
     don't think you need more money from this community."

Q   "Why don't we ever see an officer from the Township at
     the school except at sporting events when they get extra
     pay?"

Q   "Why are students allowed to drive to school? I think
     everyone should have to ride the bus; half of them are
     empty anyways."

Q   "Why aren't there after school programs for the kids so they can get extra help and do their homework instead of running the streets?"

Q   "Where are the teachers? Why are none of them at this meeting? They work less than seven months during the year; I'd think they could be here."

C   "I heard they're not here because they're having their own meeting at the elementary school."

C   "The state should disband this district and cut it up like a pie so each piece could be consolidated with the other little ones around here."

Q   "Why do we have a security system that doesn't protect our kids from crazies with guns?"

C   "You people make too much money; seven months, holidays, snow days. Someone needs to be fired."

And so on...and so on until finally Superintendent Collins announced there would be three final comments before the meeting was adjourned.

Initially, Mr. Collins and Chief Hadley responded to the crowd, however, as their statements were met with more unreasonable animosity, they retreated to a position of simply encouraging the people to vent without challenging or agitating the mob by debating the opinions of the frustrated citizens. An underlying tension between the schools and the community had festered for decades. The slightest provocation was all it took for the smoldering anger of the people to erupt, and situations like this one gave them an unchecked opportunity to voice their scorn for the history of wrongs perpetrated against the citizens and students of Low Field throughout the ages. Open meetings like this were sometimes necessary, but were always unproductive. The forum provided a floor for the ugly, rude and hateful emotions of the people to be aired once again without the decencies of self-control.

16

A T THE VFW Hall the teachers' union held a discussion about school safety. The local president, Keith Byler, led the meeting. He had been a teacher in the district for over twenty years and prior to that was a student and graduate of Low Field. His spirited conviction to the merits of unions was rooted in the area's strong labor tradition and he brought the same passion and strong approach used in those settings to his leadership role with the teachers of Low Field.

"We all know these are dangerous times throughout the world and our school is no different from any other place where people gather. We could be attacked at any time and don't think it would never happen here. That's the mistake the people of Columbine, Sandy Hook and countless other places have made. I called this meeting tonight so that all of us could share our thoughts and ideas about last Thursday's shooting and develop our union response to that terrible incident. The superintendent, the administrators, the board of education and the law enforcement officials of the community have their ideas, but we are the front line against violence. We're the instructional staff responsible for the education of these kids but we're also responsible for their well-being and protection. We also have an obligation to protect ourselves and our families from people who might want to harm us with violence. So, I'd like to begin this meeting by opening up the floor to hear what all of you have to say."

The discussion bounced around the room with random free-fall comments from teachers throughout the district. Keith asked the union officers to post their remarks through a laptop software program that was being projected on the wall.

"Our security system sucks. What good does it do to just have a video to look at after a fight?"

"And that buzzer system we have on the front door is just like Sandy Hook's. What good is that?!"

"I think it's great that we have the resource officer in our district, but he's only in one school at a time and anyone can tell from where the cruiser is parked exactly which building he is in."

"I'm glad we have the doors locked now-a-days and there is a system in place for visitors to contact the office before they're allowed into the building. I mean things are much better than they were, but let's face it, the glass is not bullet-proof and if someone really wants to get into the building, there's really no way to stop him."

"We need bullet-proof doors with locks that work on our classrooms."

"And bullet-proof glass on the low windows that are at ground level, too."

"We have to be ready for anything and everything; schools are a war zone ripe for invasion."

"Yeah, I'd like to see a few teachers in each school armed and ready to protect us and our students."

"There are a lot of guns in this community. A student could easily bring one into the school any day, so I think metal detectors are necessary."

"I'd like to see a cop in each building all day, every day."

"We probably shouldn't take the kids out for recess anymore. A person could be in the woods with a rifle and we'd never know it until it was too late."

"No backpacks or long coats."

An hour later a committee was formed to compile the ideas and make recommendations to improve school security. Additional thoughts and comments could be emailed to Keith anytime in the next week and the committee would meet the following weekend. Keith already had conceived the plan—he wanted as many teachers as possible to be trained and carry live fire arms in their classrooms.

17

ATTORNEY MORRIS WAS the well-dressed man Colton remembered from some years ago when he stopped at the farm to see his father. The young boy had never been that close to such as expensive, black luxury car. Colton didn't know how to pronounce the make of the vehicle and the leather seats smelled like his ball glove when he unwrapped in on Christmas morning. Morris was large man with snow white hair and a dark gray suit; he reminded Colton of a western mountain range— expansive gray from the ground up and a touch of white at the peak.

They sat in a barren conference room of the county jail, facing each other from opposite sides of the steel table. Colton wore an orange jump suit with stenciled letters and the size XXL on the back. The room reminded him of the countless scenes in police shows that provided background noise while his mother made dinner. The lawyer continued to look down at the papers he turned as he spoke.

"Let's see, Colton, the video from the surveillance camera identifies you at the scene; there are statements from over twenty-five eye witnesses that corroborate your altercation with Mr. Roberts-Scott; the gun-powder residue test confirms you fired the gun that was used to shoot the two students and that was removed from your hand by a sheriff deputy; and I'm guessing the ballistics report will connect your gun to the bullet that was removed from the girl, Abby Olson, who is currently in the hospital with paralysis below the waist. Do I have that right so far?" asked the attorney.

"I guess," Colton muttered softly.

"Yet, your mother tells me you're innocent; that what happened at the high school the other day somehow wasn't your fault. Now how can that be?" asked the attorney with skepticism.

"I was attacked," Colton stated.

"Oh, you were attacked; how so?"

"That trash hit me with his truck door so hard it darn near killed me when I hit the pavement. And then he backed up and I thought he was going to run me over," said Colton.

"The statements I've read from the eyewitnesses say that you were arguing with the people in the truck and then Mr. Roberts-Scott hit you with his door before he sped off. So he initiated the physical confrontation. Is that correct?" asked the attorney.

"Yes sir, that's what happened," said Colton nodding his head in approval. "He started the fight by slamming his door into me."

"So then you drew a gun in a school zone and fired shots at a truck that was surrounded by a crowd of people," continued Morris realistically.

"I don't remember that part," stated Colton.

"You don't remember that part," repeated the attorney. "What do you remember, Colton?"

He paused for a moment and then offered, "I remember having a bad headache in the parking lot. Then I was talking to Daron and Kelsey near his truck and I remember getting really pissed off. And then he hit me with the truck door and I must have gotten knocked out. That's it. That's all I remember until I was in the back of the ambulance."

"Do you remember firing the gun?" asked the attorney looking gravely into Colton's eyes.

"No."

"Colton, do you know it's against the law to have a gun on school property?"

"No."

"Why did you bring a loaded gun to the school?" Morris continued.

"I didn't know the gun was loaded," Colton explained. "I didn't want to leave it in my brother's jeep so I tucked it in the waist of my jeans." I thought I had taken the clip out earlier. A friend of mine and I were done shooting ground hogs earlier in the day."

"Shooting ground hogs?" asked the attorney continuing to verify the chronology of Colton's day. "And you thought the clip was not in the gun?"

"Yeah, we ride around farm land looking for ground hogs in fields and we practice shooting with our handguns. The farmers already gave us their permission to kill them and there is no closed season on woodchucks so we can shoot them all year round, except on Sundays. Anyway, when we were done I thought I put the clip in my gun case. I'm real careful when it comes to things like that. Then Travis dropped me off at the school because he had to take his truck to Pruitt's service center to get his oil light checked. So I told him to just drop me off and I could get a ride home with my brother."

"Ok, you said you remember arguing with Daron and Kelsey in the parking lot. What was the argument about?"

"Their dating relationship. I heard he was going to be her date at homecoming and I wanted to talk her out of doing that but when I first went up to the truck she wasn't there yet. So I tried to talk to him; he was cool at first but then we started to argue some. Then when she got out to the truck it just got out of hand."

"What was said in that conversation?" asked the attorney.

"I just told her not to go with him. That he was no good for her and that he was going to ruin her. That was about it," Colton explained.

"And…?"

"I don't know; they were both getting loud with me and then he said something about kicking my ass, and I just got really pissed off and my head hurt; it felt like it was getting squeezed in a vice," recalled Colton as he rubbed his forehead looking down at the dented metal table top.

"And you pulled out the gun you were carrying in the waist of your pants," the attorney offered.

"No, I don't remember that. I thought he was gonna get out of the truck and we were going to fight, but he slammed me with the door. And then I don't remember. Everything just went black," said Colton quietly.

"Because when you got knocked down you hit your head?

"I suppose so, but I don't know for sure," lamented Colton. "When I get mad, sometimes everything just goes black and I can't remember."

"How long has this been happening?"

"A year or so."

"Did you ever go to a doctor and get checked out? Tell a doctor about this problem?"

"No. The team doctor, Dr. Curtis, always used to check on me. He told me I might have problems later on, but I didn't think it would turn out like it did," Colton confessed.

"What do you mean when you say, turn out like it did?" Morris asked.

"I received college letters for four years, but none of them would offer me a scholarship after my senior year."

"You think it was because of your concussions?"

"I guess; the word must have gotten out on me," Colton explained. "I missed two or three games my senior year when scouts were there. I mean they talked to me and my dad but we could tell they weren't as high on me; a few even left at halftime of our last game. My mom says I'm hard-headed in one way, but soft-headed in another. It sucks. Now even the Marines don't want me."

"What do you mean?"

"I enlisted after graduation. Everything was going great until I had a few problems with my head in basic training. It was nothing serious, but I kept getting headaches and getting sick. Finally they put me in the hospital and then they said I failed their physical and they discharged me," Colton said looking at the attorney.

The attorney closed the folder and shoved it into his brief case. "Ok Colton. I'll be in touch."

"That's it?"

"Yes. That's it."

"But when can I get out of here?" asked a concerned Colton.

"I don't know if you will, but I'm working on it."

"You've got to get me out of here, man. My head hurts all the time. I'm not cut out for this. I need out now!" Colton pleaded, his voice rising and falling with emotion. "Now."

18

DARON'S MOTHER BRENDA Roberts got pregnant in March of her high school senior year at St. Luke's Academy of Akron. She was a cheerleader and honor student. Brenda was a self-motivated person who took pride in her unwavering quest for perfection. Earning good grades was appreciated and rewarded in her family, and she would stop at nothing to please her parents with the distinctions she won for academic excellence. Also, she had personal aspirations for the future—earning recognition for her intelligence, securing a nursing job that paid well and pursuing an independent lifestyle in another part of the country were the three goals she set for herself as she planned for college. Then she met Douglas.

He was a basketball star—a gifted athlete with an engaging, kind personality. Better yet, he was humble. His smile was genuine and easy. Everyone liked and cheered for him. He brought positive attention to the school not only because they won games, but by the way he was able to endear himself to the people of the school. Douglas Scott was a perfect example of how an underprivileged kid from a rough section of Akron could benefit, in fact flourish, in the environment of a Catholic education. Their outreach program to increase diversity within the student body was a success and he was living proof of it.

A bonus to the program was that Douglas was a minority with light brown skin. He was a child of an interracial marriage and he looked like any other boy on the team. The texture and curl of his hair was the only clue that there might be a mix of races in his genes.

But it was a non-issue for the supporters of the school. Douglas was a great offensive player with unselfish instincts. He was blessed with almost a perfect body to excel at the sport—six feet, four inches tall with a slender build and the sinewy muscles of a great athlete. His extraordinary coordination and quickness allowed him to easily dominate opponents with his powerful, smooth moves with the ball. The basketball team earned recognition and praise throughout the state, one week being ranked in the top ten of the coaches' poll. He played hard, respected his coaches and was a natural born leader amongst his peers. His success was invariably linked to the school's success, making everyone proud.

Only after Brenda and Douglas had been seen together at a few after-game parties and then hanging out together more and more in school did the undercurrent of hushed opinions become more prevalent, first among other students and then among concerned adults. Fortunately Daron was born months after both of his parents had graduated and his mother's pregnancy was hardly apparent under her graduation gown.

Douglas was finishing his first semester at Northern Indiana State when Daron was born. The scholarship was generous, the calculation being a blend of his basketball talents and the economic shortcomings of his family. But it was obvious during the fall practice sessions that he was too far from home and playing for a coach with an incompatible personality and style. At the beginning of the regular season, the coach informed him that he wasn't selected for the traveling team and his scholarship would most likely be terminated in the spring. He quit school in December and returned home to Akron determined to get a job and to marry Brenda.

In his heart, he believed the roadblock was temporary. Possibly he could play for a different school the following year. Brenda and he could find a college that would be right for both of them and she could start taking courses too. They could work out a routine with the baby and support each other, scheduling classes for different times that didn't conflict with his practices and games.

In the meantime, he would work and save money for their future. He got a job on the dock at one of the local rubber plants loading tires onto semis. The work was hard but he enjoyed not having any pressure on him for the first time in a long while. The pay was good and he was getting stronger from the work. Even the knee that he had surgically repaired the summer after his sophomore year in high school felt better. He made friends. There were other young guys working on the dock and he started to hang out with them sometimes after work.

His high school coach sent letters and made phone calls in his behalf to some of the coaches who had expressed an interest in Douglas the previous few years. It was important to keep his skills sharp so he worked out with the St. Luke's team and played in pickup games at the YMCA and Goodyear Park whenever his work schedule allowed. Then out of the blue one day, a friend from work approached him with an opportunity.

"Look Douglas," his co-worker said, "the truck comes in tomorrow after midnight with some extra boxes on it. All we have to do is unload them and stack them around the corner of the building so that Mac can't see them."

"I don't know, man."

"It will take five minutes. One of us can go in to talk to Mac about the shipping order and keep him busy for a few minutes while the other moves the boxes. Five minutes tops—for $300.00 apiece. That kind of opportunity doesn't come around too often. You know what I'm saying?" the young man reasoned.

"Yeah; it's still risky, man," Douglas said shaking his head.

"$300.00! You'll have to work a month to make that kind of money."

"I don't know, man, it's not my style. What if something goes wrong?" pondered Douglas.

"What's going to go wrong in five minutes? Hey, it's you're call, but I can't do it without you."

Douglas pondered the option for a moment and then fighting his instincts said, "Ok, I'm in."

They slapped hands together and his friend said, "Cool. That's a decision you won't regret."

"I hope not."

The other man touched him on his chest and said, "No one will ever know about this; this is just between you and me, brother."

19

Daron's mom, though only in her mid-thirties, looked even younger than her age. She was attractive, competent and smart. Her employment record was checkered when Daron was young but for the past seven years she had earned several promotions in the branch office of the Akron bank she worked at before they moved to Low Field. Now she had her own desk and a new title, chief loan officer. Since the shootings, however, her face was grave and the dark circles under her eyes expanded. She had been an emotional wreck since she found out that Daron was involved in the school disaster. Her emotions fluctuated between crying privately to ranting and screaming at Daron ever since they returned home Thursday evening from the police station. When the two officers knocked on the front door of the trailer she jumped and threw a book at Daron. They secured his signature on a document he forgot to sign and left.

"You know this whole trailer park just saw that police car at our house," she added to her series of complaints.

"Ma, I told you I'm sorry," Daron said. "I didn't do anything except get me and Kelsey out of there. Colt was the ass with the gun."

"Don't talk. I don't want to hear any of your excuses, not now or ever!" she stated with conviction. "You know how hard it's been for us to get a place out of Akron so you could have a fresh start and now you've messed it all up for us. These people will want to run us out of town."

"Then they're stupid," he said, "because I didn't do anything wrong. Low Field sucks anyway and we should move out of this Podunk town."

"No. I'm not going to let you make the same mistake your father and I made. You are going to graduate from high school and go to college. I want you to have a better future. Finish this year and then you can go away to school," she said.

Daron's head dropped. He had already heard about the principal wanting to kick him and Kelsey out of school. His mom had no idea what was coming next.

"I'm almost eighteen and I was thinking about quitting school anyway, or transferring to some other school. This town is crazy and full of backward hayseed people," Daron said pausing. "And I might as well tell you now, they're kicking Kelsey out of school and I'm probably next."

"What! Where did you hear that?" his mother asked incredulously.

"Kelsey. Her mom got a call from Mr. Daniels saying she was suspended for ten days and that he was recommending that she be expelled for the rest of the year."

"Oh my god; what a mess you've created," Brenda said holding her forehead in her hand.

"Mom, I didn't do anything," pleaded Daron in vain.

"Quit saying that. You wouldn't be in the middle of this mess if you didn't do anything. You sound like your dumb father—I didn't do anything," she said mimicking her late husband's ghostly statement. "Words from a fool."

The phone rang. It was the high school principal, Mr. Daniels. They talked back and forth for a moment and then he delivered the expected blow.

"Why are you punishing these children so harshly? I realize that, but neither of them had a gun nor did they do anything except defend themselves by getting away from an adult with a gun. So why is Daron being expelled? I guess I could understand a few days of suspension and not being allowed to participate in homecoming, but I think any punishment beyond that is excessive on your part. Oh yes, I will appeal your decision to the superintendent—you can count on that," Brenda promised.

She heard an engine and when she looked out a window she saw Daron's truck spewing a trail of dust and smoke as he exited Harmony Trailer Park.

20

Jim Collins had been the Low Field Superintendent of Schools for the past six years. He knew the lay of the land—the weakness and strengths of people, the connections and politics of the community and the uphill struggles he would have to battle if his plans for improving the schools were ever to come to fruition. The incident of two days ago was a major setback for both him and the district. The grave cloud of negativity it cast over the school district's image and its relationship with the community would take months, if not years, to surmount.

New security safeguards were mandated for both buildings when the students and staff returned to school. Off-duty police officers were hired by the district for the hours that coincided with the beginning and ending of the day. Several patrolled the parking areas and two others screened every person entering and leaving the buildings. Long tables were placed inside the one designated entrance for each school allowing for random backpack and coat checks by the part-time and full-time officers now assigned to each building. The show of force was impressive but the new procedures proved cumbersome and caused a lengthy delay in the start of the school day in both buildings.

Collins got up from doing paperwork and returning phone calls and opened the office door. During the day he would occasionally escape the confines of his office by taking a walk through the elementary school, where the board offices were located, simply to see students and staff or to use the male staff restroom. These strolls *next door* as he called them would help clear his head and maintain a connection to the vibrancy and purpose of a school. His secretary, Laura Jansen, stopped his exodus with a handful of messages.

"Kelsey and Daron's parents have each called twice to appeal their expulsions," she noted.

"Expulsions?" he asked aloud.

"Steve suspended them for ten days and told them they were expelled after that unless they met with you and you reversed his decision."

"Would you please call them back and schedule appointments for the end of this week?" he asked. "Wait a second, please. I need to check something."

He returned to his office and confirmed his upcoming appointments. During the fury of the crisis, he and Steve had agreed upon immediate suspensions for Kelsey and Daron but in his mind their involvement in the overall incident did not merit expulsion.

"Actually L J, Monday and Tuesday of next week work better if they are available," he clarified from his office. "I can stay late if they need to come in after work."

"Okay."

She was already on the phone returning a call to one of them when he slipped past her desk and out the door. Taking these walks had become a necessary diversion from the stress of his duties. Lately, however, it seemed like he needed the release more and more frequently. The first few years he was in the district, walking through the buildings was positive and invigorating. He would talk to employees and students about their days. Usually the conversations and interactions would leave him refreshed about the goals and changes he was attempting to accomplish through his work with the school leaders and would bring a smile to his face. Lately, however, the people he encountered would only add another layer to the burdens of his position. It seemed as though no one made good decisions or had any common sense. The collective culture of the schools was slipping back into an aura of divided selfishness; something he knew meant the closing of his window of opportunity for improvement. He stopped in the cafeteria to buy a snack before returning to his office.

"Good morning everyone," he said smiling at the three women toiling over steaming pots. Their hair was pulled back and covered with a variety of accessories and their hands were coated by plastic gloves.

"Hey boss," one of the women returned.

"Let's see, healthy choice or junk food this morning," he asked rhetorically.

"We don't have any junk food," shot the kitchen supervisor defensively.

"Chips?" he asked pointing at the vertical rack of offerings. "Donuts?" he continued pointing at the row of packaged breakfast items.

"They both have vitamin supplements and meet the state's requirements for healthy snacks," she contested.

"I know Carol," I'm just needling you. "You're so easy."

She smiled back at him as he extracted a dollar bill from his money clip and set it on the small register on the way out of the kitchen.

"I'll just go with a banana this morning; need the fiber, I guess," he said leaving. "See you all later."

A quick exit was necessary or Carol would trap him discussing everything that was happening in her job. His typical response to these kinds of veiled complaints was, "That's why we have you here. Think of it as job security."

Upon his return to the board offices, his secretary handed him more messages.

"L J, would you please call Steve for me?" I need to speak with him if you can track him down.

Jim closed the door behind him as shelter from the world and he needed privacy for the upcoming call with the principal. She buzzed in.

"He's on line one."

"Thanks."

He picked up the phone and said, "Steve, how are you?"

"Fine. What's up?"

"Tell me about your thinking regarding the suspensions of the kids involved in the shooting."

"I expelled them both for causing the shooting that put two of our kids in the hospital. We're lucky no one's dead," Daniels stated.

"I realize that as bad as this situation is, it could have been worse, but what have we talked about in the past about your authority to expel students?"

"Well, I meant that I suspended them both for ten days with a recommendation for their expulsion."

"Yes, that's the proper procedure, but I wish you had discussed this with me prior to taking action."

"Why? They both need to be gone for the rest of the year," he continued unequivocally.

"Because your decision is so extreme that they are backed totally into the corner and now it's on me. You just shifted the problem to my office."

"Not if you uphold my recommendation," the principal simply stated. "Just tell them that they're out."

"Yeah, that's the problem. What if I don't agree that they be expelled for the rest of the year? Because we didn't discuss the options and unify our thinking beforehand, now we're going to be disconnected if I don't agree with your decision. That's a problem for both of us. We need to be on the same page when it comes to the big issues, and I like the option of expulsion only after we have exhausted all the other options, not as our first option," the superintendent reasoned.

"I don't understand, Jim. There was a shooting at my school. Two kids almost lost their lives; in fact, one might never walk again and you don't want to expel these kids?" Steve asked.

"My first instinct is to say, no," replied Collins. "That's why I wish you had called so we could discuss your thinking before you issued the suspensions."

"Well, I guess I am on a different page then," stated Daniels. "Look, you and the board give me shit about running a tight ship. You all say you want a disciplined school, and then when I discipline kids who do something really bad, you don't agree and want to give them another chance and then another chance." The principal paused momentarily and retorted, "Just overturn the suspension and send them back. That will help with discipline. Then all the other kids will see that even if they cause other students to get shot, nothing will happen. That will be great."

"Look, I don't know how this is going to turn out. I just wished you would have discussed the situation with me before you dropped a sledge hammer on these kids and their parents."

There was an awkward pause before the principal continued, "I'll probably lose my job, but I'm just going to say this. You know, there are bad kids in a school just like there are bad people in the world, and the good kids need to see the adults punish the bad kids when they do bad things."

He continued, "Here's the way I see it—every year, some kids need to get expelled; one year maybe only a few and then in other years maybe a dozen—it keeps the balance in the school. It sends the right message to kids—the boarder-line kids. The message is clear—if you screw up, something will happen to you. They will get disciplined. It helps them stay straight and keep out of trouble. If we don't have that kind of punishment and discipline in this school, all hell will break loose. And in the hierarchy of school offences, if the two students who were in the center of a school shooting don't get expelled, then what does it take around here? Murder? Literally, it looks like a student would have to actually kill someone to be expelled. I really don't understand you," he said exasperated with the situation.

"Whoa, wait a minute. To some extent I understand your point," countered the superintendent. "Tell me though, are Kelsey and Daron in trouble often? I've never heard you even mention their names except in a good context, but I don't know your history with them. Seriously, are they troubled kids?"

"No. I mean a few small things but they haven't been in a lot of trouble this year," admitted the principal, "but this was a major issue and something big needs to follow."

"You have to consider the full picture, not just a few minutes in time. We have to be a haven of fairness and protect all of the students, even when they make mistakes or become involved in something that quickly spirals out of control."

"You know Jim, whatever," said Mr. Daniels with an air of apathetic resignation in voice. "It will be what you decide anyway. Now you can put them back in school next week and make me look like a fool again. You're the good cop and I'm the bad cop. But I don't want you and the board saying I don't have discipline in my school. It's on you if those kids come back in this building and I'm going to let the board members know that I want them expelled."

"Okay Steve, it sounds like you're done listening," said Collins, "but let me say this; I honestly don't know what I'm going to do about the suspension. I'll meet with the parents and the students and weigh all the facts before I make a decision, like I always do."

"That's great for you, but I don't have that luxury. My decisions need to be swift and decisive. I can't namby-pamby around mulling over what to do and run this high school giving kids fifty chances to screw up before something happens to them. People want action on my end and that's what I give them."

"One more thing before I let you go. I've been thinking about Colton's brother Clayton," said Collins.

"Yeah, what about him?" asked Daniels.

"Nothing in particular, but I was just wondering if he's getting flak from other students or if he's got any personal issues because of his brother's situation."

"No, I saw him yesterday and he seemed fine," responded the principal.

"Alright, just a thought but you might want to keep an eye on him. I'll talk to you later," concluded the superintendent.

There was a click on the end of the line when Daniels hung up the phone. Jim Collins hung up and dropped his forehead in his hand. His mind swirled with the issues of right and wrong and compassion and empathy for all students. Maybe he analyzed these situations too carefully. Maybe things weren't as complicated as he thought. He saw gray when others saw black and white. Maybe he was too soft; not decisive enough for today's world. Or maybe it was just time for him to move on.

21

On Saturday, Will's doctor examined his wound and studied his bedside medical chart. Will was still taking pain killers but the results from the most recent MRI showed no complications from the gunshot. In fact, his vital signs were all normal so the doctor said he could be released from the hospital on Sunday. A physical therapist brought him a pair of crutches and taught him how to properly use them. The doctor recommended the use of crutches for at least three to four weeks and probably for the entire eight-week rehabilitation period. He did, however, give Will permission to experiment walking without them for short periods of time in order to test his strength.

His leg still hurt but his spirits were up, and although it was unrealistic, he believed that he would be able to tee it up on Wednesday at The Old Quarry Golf Club in the Ohio High School Athletic Association's District Golf Tournament—the last stop before the state tournament. His coach had sent him a text late Friday afternoon saying that, although the OHSAA would not grant him a waiver from playing in the tournament because of the shooting, he was granted a special dispensation for the event—if he was able to compete he would be allowed to use a pull cart instead of carrying his bag in the tournament round.

Will asked the attendant who was wheeling him out of the hospital after his discharge to stop by Abby's room. His mom was with him. She had brought sweat pants and a hoody for him to wear home while his father brought the car from the parking lot to the emergency

room drop-off doors. After gathering his personal effects and signing his release papers, Mrs. Harper walked beside the wheelchair as
they rolled slowly toward the elevator. She agreed with her son that
it was a good idea to pay a brief to visit Abby. He wanted to see her,
say hello and wish her well. After all, they now shared a bond like no
other two students in the history of Low Field High School—both
having been shot on school property.

Abby's condition, however, wiped the smile from his face and the
joy from his heart. She had so many tubes and cords strung from her
body to bags and machines that he was absolutely stunned. Her mom
jumped up from the straight metal chair; her daughter's eyes were
closed to the world.

"Will, it's so good to see you," said Mrs. Olson.

"Wow, Mrs. Olson, I'm so sorry. I had no idea," he stumbled to
say. "Is Abby okay?"

"She's sleeping. The doctors say she's stable. They want to do
one more surgery next week after the swelling goes down near her
spine to see if they can repair the nerves that were damaged by the
bullet," said the girl's mother holding back her emotions.

Will got up from the wheelchair and walked to Abby's bed side.
He stared at her motionless body and helpless face. An overwhelming feeling of sadness stirred his soul. Oh my god, he thought. If this
was me I'd want to die. He shook his head and squeezed Abby's limp
hand being careful of the IV that was taped to the back of it.

"You get better Abby. Don't let this mess take your spirit away.
You keep fighting; keep fighting," he whispered.

He stepped back visibly shaken and sat back down in the wheelchair.

Her mom touched his shoulder and said, "Thank you for stopping
by Will. This was very nice of you. I'll make sure Abby knows you
were here."

"Sure. I'll come back and see her next week," he said.

The elevator ride was a blur. Will's thoughts swirled around what he had just seen. He felt guilty for being grateful it was not him lying in that bed. When they reached the exit he was unexpectedly facing a television reporter and cameraman.

"Will, how do you feel?" asked the reporter holding a microphone close to his chin.

"I'm fine, thank you," replied the boy.

His father had pulled the car up to the sliding doors. Astounded by the boldness of the reporter he brusquely stepped between his son and the reporter. He put his arm around Will and helped his son stand and shuffle toward the car.

"Will, do you have a comment about the shooting?"

"No sir," Will said without making eye contact with the reporter or the camera. He maneuvered his stiff body into a position where he could get into the back seat of the car without hurting his leg. He winced with discomfort. Once he was in position to ride home, his father helped him secure his seatbelt.

The reporter asked, "Will, just one final question, when will you return to school and will you be able to play in next week's district golf tournament?"

There was a pause as he gathered himself. His mother stepped forward toward the reporter and cameraman holding up her hand and getting ready to speak.

"No, it's alright mom. I want to say something," said Will.

The camera man ducked down and pointed the camera at Will who was sitting sideways in the backseat with his leg stretched out.

With remarkable poise and eloquence Will said, "I do feel better and I know after visiting Abby Olson on my way out of the hospital a few minutes ago that I'm a very lucky person. I really don't know what caused the shooting a few days ago but I'm going to do best to put this all behind me as quickly as possible. We really need to pray for Abby to get better. Please everyone out there keep Abby in your thoughts and prayers. She deserves to get better; she deserves to have a normal life. I don't know what else to say other than if I'm able to play this week in the district tournament, I know I'll be playing for Abby. Let's hope she gets better very soon."

His father carefully closed the back door of the car. Both parents got into their respective sides of the front seat and slammed their doors shut. Mr. Harper pulled the car away from the hospital turn-around and Will waved the Low Field *"L"* with his left hand to the camera out the back window.

22

TWENTY OF THE forty-one teachers in the district volunteered to attend the training session and apply for a concealed carry gun permit. Four others expressed a willingness to go through the training but only for a show of solidarity; they really didn't want the responsibility of actually having a gun at school especially with the possibility of being called upon to use it. The union unanimously approved to pay for the training. In the teachers' lounges at both buildings, sentiment for the movement was strong in spite of the ensuing uphill battle to gain the required Board of Education approval for the exception to the state law. At lunch many teachers huddled around a single table and the discussions were hyped with emotion.

"This will be a game changer, as they say," one teacher proclaimed.

"The board will have to approve at least one person beyond the SRO after so many of us get the permits. In fact, if they are smart they'll approve a bunch of us to carry guns. Maybe we should construct a plan based on the different areas of the buildings. You know, to create blanket security," said another.

The conversation continued with enthusiasm as the teachers willingly expressed their comments without hesitation.

"We'll be the first district in the state with armed teachers—maybe the whole country. This is going to bring us recognition and respect."

"It's about time someone gets serious about protecting teachers and students from random attacks."

"Maybe the shootings were a Godsend."

"We've got to develop a protocol for safeguards, though. I mean we need the guns to be readily accessible on one hand, yet very secure on the other."

"And they need to be kept in good working condition and ready to use at a moment's notice, as do everyone's shooting skills. Maybe the board can create a shooting range for us to practice at once a week or so. I think police officers are required to shoot at least once a month."

"We should see if the principals would get trained, too. That would be powerful. I mean, how could the board say no then?"

"Maybe the secretaries? At most of the school shootings in the past, the secretary was the first person to know there was a problem."

"That's a good point; our doors and offices were built in an era when none of this was an issue. They couldn't stop anyone who really wanted to get in, but the main office is located close to the front door in both buildings."

"They probably won't go for it, but it would be nice to have members of both unions and the principals all willing to be trained. That would really pressure Collins and the board."

"You're damn right. And sometimes that's what it takes to get things done. Pressure breaks pipes, as they say."

"I can ask Steve. I have a prep period after lunch."

"We better wait until Keith gives the okay. I heard he was calling the national office today to ask for their legal opinion and see if they'd support us, and I think the committee is supposed to meet again this weekend."

"You know who we should also start calling, parents and influential community members."

"That's a great idea; I think the parents are going to love this idea."

"You got that right. They're going to thank us for this one. Finally someone is truly assuming the responsibility for keeping their kids safe."

23

O N Sunday afternoon, Mr. Daniels made two phone calls from home. He told his wife he was going to take the dog out for a walk to the thick woods at the back of their property, something he did regularly. Once they were far enough back to be out of sight from the house, he checked his cell phone reception for a signal and dialed one of the numbers he had stored on Saturday morning while he was finishing paperwork from the hectic week at the high school.

"Mrs. Boyd; it's Steve Daniels from the high school," he said nervously.

"Yes," she replied still angry at him but hopeful that he was calling with a compromised position on Kelsey's suspension.

"I'm sorry to bother you on a Sunday, but it's important."

"It's okay," Stephanie said, "what can I do for you, Mr. Daniels?"

"Well, I've been thinking about our conversation from the other day, and um, I feel terrible about Kelsey being expelled from school," he said in an attempt to lay a calm groundwork for the conversation.

"Yes, so do I," Stephanie replied anxious for him to get to his point.

"Well, I might have thought of an option for you."

"What would that be?" she asked.

"Have you ever heard of the charter school, Classrooms Without Boundaries? It's an electronic alternative school licensed by the state department of education where the students get a computer from and take their classes at home with teachers and lessons online."

"Yes, I think I've seen a commercial on television about it but I thought it was for people who home-schooled their children."

"It is a popular option for home-schoolers, but the school is also open to any student in the state as well. That is, unless they've been expelled, and that's the reason for my call. You would need to enroll Kelsey in the program today or tomorrow. I can hold the suspension paperwork from getting to the superintendent's office for a few days and nothing would ever show on her records about her suspension or expulsion. Classrooms Without Boundaries would enroll her in their program, and she could continue taking the same classes she has now, only at home. The important thing is that she could graduate on time in the spring and get into college, and the expulsion would never be recorded on her high school transcript. That's really important for the future.

"I don't know Mr. Daniels. I mean your idea sounds better than her being expelled and sitting around home with nothing to do, but I don't know. This seems pretty drastic. Why do I have to decide today or tomorrow?"

"I know it seems rather sudden because once the superintendent signs the expulsion papers, that school is not allowed enroll her and we don't have any options other than continuing on the path to expulsion. That's why you have to move quickly. I felt really bad about Kelsey's situation and I was trying to help you all get through this in the best way possible. I can text you the phone number for the school or you can get all the information at their website."

"Alright, Mr. Daniels," she said, I'll talk to Kelsey and we'll check the website. Thank you, I guess."

"Sure, no problem," he said. "Give me a call if you have any questions. Again, I don't mean to pressure you, but you will have to move quickly. I just feel bad for her; trust me this is the best option."

Daniels's next call was to Daron's mother Brenda Roberts. Their conversation was similar to that of his previous call. As he walked back to the house, he felt better about the situation. He was hoping both parents would follow his advice and enroll their kids in the alternative school immediately. Why wouldn't you, he thought. It was a simple way to avoid all the negativity of an expulsion and it would keep their kids in school and on the route to graduation. Not to mention, it cut the superintendent out of the process.

On Monday morning, he received phone calls from both parents informing him that Kelsey and Daron had withdrawn from Low Field and enrolled in the electronic school. He was not surprised. What did surprise him were the additional eleven students who also withdrew and enrolled at Classrooms Without Boundaries. One of the local churches coincidentally had sponsored a guest speaker from the charter school over the weekend espousing the quality, efficiency and safety of the school, and a host of parents bought into the argument. Student safety had become the number one priority for families.

Moreover, the shooting had occurred just days before Catholic Schools Week. Area parochial schools annually promoted their services and programs in an attempt to attract new students for the upcoming school year. Parents and students were invited to visit and tour the schools. During the week long activities, they showcased their best attributes and the outstanding achievements of their students. Ironically, this year they announced an exception to their usual enrollment timelines and were welcoming students to apply for immediate admission at the mid-term. The strategy was originally developed to counteract a sharp decrease in their enrollment numbers because of tuition increases; but, because of the Low Field shooting, even more students were considering an abrupt transfer to the Catholic schools at the beginning of the second semester of the present school year. The financial blow to the district was mounting significantly.

24

KELSEY'S MOM DISCOVERED the front yard prank when she was leaving for work. The low shafts of diffused sunlight illuminated the climbing mist in a dancing range of colors painting a surreal landscape in her unsuspecting eyes. Toilet paper hung like soft white noodles from two of the large maple trees near the road. Rolls and rolls must have been used to achieve such a density. Initially she recalled participating in a similar hoax when she was in high school; but, what took her thoughts to a deeper, sicker feeling was the decoration on the mailbox at the end of the driveway. A dunce cap had been taped to the top of the mailbox and a white sheet had been thrown over the structure. A crude letter K had been spray painted in black on the sheet. Stephanie weighed her options while driving to work and once she arrived she called the Low Field Police and reported the hate crime against her family.

She sent Kelsey a text: *Do not touch anything outside police will be there to investigate*

Daron was up early, too. Usually he and his mom left home about the same time during the week on their way to school and work. It felt odd to watch her leave while he sat watching TV in his pajamas.

"Remember to go to the school this afternoon to empty your locker and return your textbooks," she reminded him. "Mr. Daniels is expecting you around 3:30."

"Okay mom; I'll remember," he assured her.

"And clean your room today—you promised me you would make room for the new computer so you can do your schoolwork. Don't just sit around all day. This isn't a vacation."

"Alright, I will," Daron said.

After having breakfast, he sent Kelsey a text: *Hey want to go for a ride*

She didn't answer so he took a shower and got dressed for the day. He straightened his bed covers and was picking up the array of dirty clothes scattered about his room when she finally texted him back:

Can't go out house got tpd
What happened
Toilet papered
Oh I thought we could go visit Abby c how she's doing
Probably not a good idea
Why
Her parents blame us
Really should blame Colton
I know but I cant go anyway
Whats up
Im not allowed to c you
Oh

Daron was furious and in disbelief at the reaction he and Kelsey were receiving after the shooting. He grabbed a warm-up jacket on his way out and slammed the door of the trailer. He needed to take a ride and think. As he came around the front bumper of his truck he almost stumbled over a yard statue that was leaning against the driver's side door. It was a three foot high statue of a black man in a red jacket holding a lantern. The man represented a stable hand waiting for the arrival of the property owner's carriage a century earlier, but in today's society Daron had always thought of these statues as decorative symbols racists would post near their front walks so blacks knew something about the people on the other side of the front door. In disgust he knocked it over with his right foot, opened the truck door and then yanked it shut with a bang.

His mind was racing with hate and anger for the people of Low Field as he drove toward Akron, his real home. Back in his old neighborhood he went to the small city park where he had spent so many hours as a child climbing on the playground structures and playing ball when the weather was warm and then sled riding in the winter. He hadn't kept in touch with his friends from elementary school, and he wondered how they were doing. Race issues were different here, more direct and in the open. Pervasive poverty and the culture clashes for power created a commonplace irritation among the races that never seemed to be at peace. Moreover, the inherent desire for elite stature in the neighborhoods created personalities and interactions based on an artificial bravado that permeated the fiber of the streets. The attitude of toughness and dominance was so pervasive that failure to embrace it was not an option.

But not for little kids; he remembered drawing a picture in first grade and coloring the faces of the people various shades of brown and white as his initial awareness of the difference in peoples' skin colors. He wondered where he fit in.

When he asked his teacher about it she said, "People might look different on the outside Daron, but on the inside we're all the same."

That evening, when he asked his mother about his color, she hugged him and said,

"It's complicated, honey. Don't you worry about that right now; just know that mommy loves you," she said reassuringly.

As a young man on the precipice of adulthood, Daron never had a deep conversation with his mother regarding racial bias and inequality. Now more than ever he felt alone, uncomfortable in his own skin. She would certainly have a unique perspective on the issue—the time had come for him to hear her views of the complexities of race in today's culture.

He left the park with a sense of calmness, and he was hungry. He got some drive-through lunch and headed out of town. Maybe Will would be at the golf course practicing this afternoon. They had been in a few classes together in the past few years, although they didn't know each other more than to say hello. Daron wanted to see him, to apologize for what had happened and see how he was doing. When he got to River's Edge Golf Club, Will was sitting on the rear bumper of a car. The trunk was open and a man, probably his dad, was helping him put on one of his golf shoes. Daron parked and walked over.

"Hey Will, how are you feeling?" Daron asked sheepishly.

"Hey, not so good today," Will answered honestly.

"Are you going out to play?"

"That's the plan, but I'm not sure yet. This will be the first test for the new golf swing. I was thinking if it works I'll call it my bulletproof swing," Will joked half-heartedly.

"Look, I'm really sorry about what happened last week," Daron sincerely apologized. "I had no idea Colton had a gun and would start shooting like that with so many people around. Everything happened so quickly; I just couldn't believe it."

"Yeah; well, I figure I was in the wrong place at the wrong time."

"I'm really sorry man."

Daron reached out his hand and Will accepted the apology with a grasp.

"Not your fault, I suppose. I just hope I don't fall on my ass out there."

"You won't Will; you're too good. Go out there and represent," Daron said.

"Thanks Daron. I'm gonna try."

His dad returned to the car with a pull cart and began strapping Will's bag to it.

"Dad, this is Daron. Turn the bag the other way please; so it's on its side," Will said.

"*The* Daron?" asked his father.

"Yeah, *the* Daron."

The moment was awkward for everyone. Daron started to walk away. He turned and said, "Hey, I'll let you go man. Again, I'm truly sorry for what happened. Good luck this week. I'll be rooting for you."

"Yep, thanks."

When Daron arrived at the high school all of the students were gone, except for the football and cross country teams. Daron could hear occasional whistles and voices coming from the football field. He passed a few teachers in the hallway on his way to his locker.

One of the teachers stopped him and asked, "What are you doing here, Daron?"

"Just here to clean out my locker," Daron explained holding up his hands in innocence.

"Does Mr. Daniels know that you're here?" the teacher continued.

"Yes, he knows; I'm going to the office next to turn in my books. Daniels is getting what he wants—me out of this school."

"Good."

Daron could feel himself getting tense and hot. He wanted to call the teacher a jerk or punch him in the face, but he just kept his head focused on the contents of the locker and made quick work of it. In the office, the principal stacked Daron's books on a table and wrote a brief note that he placed inside the cover of the top book. Their interaction was brief and pointed.

"Thanks for taking care of this Daron. Good luck to you," Daniels said.

"Yeah. Hey, would it be okay for me to go up and say goodbye to Mr. Neale? He's a great teacher. He helped me out a lot since I moved to Low Field and I'm really going to miss talking to him," Daron said.

"He was sick today," replied the principal.

"Oh."

They both turned and walked in different directions from one another.

That evening at dinner, Daron told his mother that he needed to take a trip. He wanted to go see his grandparents in Florida. The computer and printer from the charter school wouldn't be delivered until later in the week. She could let him take the truck or put him on a plane, but he needed to sort some things out for himself, far away from Low Field, Ohio, and as soon as possible before he snapped and did something he might later regret.

25

A LIGHT DRIZZLE WAS falling the morning Colton was taken to the
county courthouse for his preliminary hearing. The air was chill-
ing to his bare arms. They were cuffed in front of him exposed by
the short sleeves of the orange jump suit. He was never so embar-
rassed in his life. It was like the night he threw five interceptions
against Glenwood.

Before they left the field at the end of the game, the coach looked
him in the eye and said, "Keep your chin up. Sometimes things don't
go like you want them to; that's part of life. No excuses. You're the
leader of this team; act like it."

The words came back to him in a flash so he lifted his head and
looked straight ahead as he shuffled past the reporters and cameras
flanked on either side by a sheriff deputy. The doors to the courthouse were monstrous; the biggest doors he had ever seen in his life.
It looked like a castle to Colton. The huge limestone structure was a
daunting, century-old building meant to maintain and preserve jus-
tice in the county. He was sad to be joining the historic litany of
forgotten, tragic stories that had come before him.

When his name was called, he and his attorney walked to a wide
podium before the judge. They stood side by side as the charges were
read and Colton was asked to state his plea.

"Not guilty sir," Colton said meekly.

His attorney asked the judge for permission to make a statement.

"Your honor, my client pleads not guilty because he has a recurring untreated medical condition that causes him to temporarily black out and lose control of his mental faculties. I would like to point out that he has never been in front of a judge and has no juvenile or adult record—in fact, this is his first arrest. He graduated last spring from Low Field High School with a proud, unblemished career as a top student-athlete of that institution. I ask the court that he be remanded to the custody of his parents so he can get the medical treatment he needs. Also, your honor, my client is not a flight risk and posting bond would be a hardship on him and his family."

The judge read through several documents, paused and then looked up over the tops of his glasses and said, "Duly noted counselor. The defendant will be remanded to his parents' custody and placed on house arrest with a monitoring device. The defendant may only leave that residence for medical appointments. Bail is set for $5,000. He is ordered to reappear in this court in 90 days. Case dismissed."

He hammered the sound block with his gavel.

Colton made no comments as he crossed the street to the county jail. One of the deputies removed the handcuffs and shackles and returned him to a cell while his family made the arrangements for his bail money. Later, the deputy returned his clothes to him and opened a dressing room for him to get dressed. He signed for his personal effects and met his parents in the underground garage, where a deputy had allowed his father to move their car. His parents and the attorney stood seriously in discussion.

"Write down a timeline of his injuries the best you can recall. Make notes of what happened, what condition he was in, any medical attention he received, what the doctors said, all of that. Basically every injury involving his head and everything you can recall about each incident," said Attorney Morris. "Oh, who is his doctor?"

Colton's mom answered, "Dr. Curtis. His office is in Medina."

"But now I'm covered by my GI benefits. They told me I can go to a VA Hospital," Colton offered.

The attorney agreed, "That's probably a good idea. There's one near Cleveland. You folks should call Dr. Curtis and he will advise you about how all of that works."

"Okay Alan, my wife and son will write down everything about his concussions. I have to take a load to Missouri and then bring one back the rest of this week so I won't be much help, but she's got a good memory for that kind of stuff and she keeps good records for the family," Roy said.

"Oh, and make a list of the colleges or coaches that wrote or called about him playing football for them and what they said when they were recruiting him and then what they said later—if you have any letters from them that would be helpful. And I need to see all of his correspondence from the Marines and his discharge papers," said the attorney.

A buzzer sounded and an electronic lock made a mechanical sound. Colton came out from the other side of a steel door.

"Colton, I was just talking to your parents about our next steps—we need to meet in my office in a few days," Morris said. He looked back to Mrs. Caldwell and said, "Bring all the things we talked about, okay?"

"Yes. I'll sit down with Colton and go through our things and bring everything we find about his condition," Mrs. Caldwell answered.

"Good; just call my office for an appointment. We need to meet in two days, three tops."

The family got in their vehicle and drove past the media before they had time to realize Colton was a passenger. The ride was quiet, almost awkwardly so.

Finally his dad spoke, "Colton, I was thinking that maybe you should come out and ride in the cab with me on some trips for a while. You know, get out of town and clear your head."

"He has to be here for his meetings with the attorney and his doctors," his wife objected.

"Of course. We'd have to make sure you're back for any appointments; maybe in a week or two," his dad said agreeing with his wife.

After a few minutes of quiet, Colton finally responded, "Yeah sure dad; that would be good."

"Good. Don't worry son, we'll get through this, one way or another," Roy said. "My pa used to say, you can always clean up a mess; some just take more effort than others."

When they finally arrived at home, Colton felt sick; he was anxious and muddled over his predicament. He changed into running clothes and told his mom he was going out for a run.

She said, "Be careful and put on your reflective vest."

"Okay mom; be back in an hour or so," he promised.

Colton jogged lightly down the long country road that went in north and south directions from the end of his driveway. His stride started choppy and short but within a half mile he was stretched out and breathing as smoothly as his effortless, controlled gait. The cool afternoon air filled his lungs and the engine of his heart rate pumped his blood more vigorously throughout his sweating body. He got lost in his thoughts and the crunching of his shoes in the gravel on the road's berm. Suddenly he appreciated his freedom and his life more than ever before, having regained what had briefly been taken from him.

If only there was a way to make amends for what had happened. Even though he couldn't clearly remember his own actions, he was sorry, genuinely sorry. Low Field High School represented the best days of his life. He would do anything to undo the injuries he inflicted on the two students and to remove the blemish on the school and the community for which he was now and forever responsible. His head hurt. The throbbing and pulsing on the sides of his head were distorting his face in pain. His vision narrowed more so he quit jogging and started to walk. He stopped and leaned over, placing his hands on his knees to steady himself. His body softly swayed back and forth several times before he passed out—his dead weight falling with a thud in the wet mud near the berm. His head and torso rolled with the slope resting in the drainage ditch that ran parallel to the road.

26

SIMULTANEOUS WITH THE surreptitious movement among some of Low Field's teaching staff to become armed guardians of the school and its students, there was a second group of the teachers banning together to raise funds in support of Abby Olson's medical treatment and recovery. Hundreds of ribbons in the school's colors of red and white had been cut and formed into the common loop with tails, the international symbol for cancer awareness. Her initials A and O were stenciled on each tail of the ribbon in her honor. It was their talking point to discuss the plight of the talented art student who had the misfortune of being in the line of fire that fateful day in October. The ribbons were to be sold at the Homecoming Game; but, when the announcement came of its postponement to the final game of the season, the group of teachers and parents mobilized their efforts accompanied with posters and baked goods to locations in front of the diner, the local pharmacy and the grocery store in Low Field.

Funds were being raised to help the girl, a victim of a senseless act. The generous nature of people wanting to right a wrong stirred and unified many people in the community. A get well card the size of a piece of dry wall was moved to various locations and people were encouraged to send a message to the recovering teen. Within days the massive card was delivered to her hospital room and a second card was needed. Moreover, the teachers got permission from her parents to publicize her school email address so that when she was able to open her account she would be faced with the overwhelming show of support from fellow students, neighbors and residents.

One of her friends advanced the idea even further demonstrating the far-reaching power of social networking at its best. The posting of her ordeal on student's Facebook pages triggered the creation of a specific page dedicated to Abby with updates about her story and on-going medical status. The likes from this initiative unexpectedly prompted thousands of responses from well-wishers of every state, and remarkably, from people in six different countries around the world. Photos from the horrific scene in the parking lot were paired with candid pictures of Abby with friends just being normal kids. Additional photos from the hospital as well as postings of her art created a collage of a talented young artist facing a grave medical condition, drawing sympathy from countless people and connecting them to her situation in real time. Mrs. Nash, her favorite art teacher at the high school, and her mother collected their favorite ten paintings and drawings for the page. They photographed the works and helped Abby's friends post them on Facebook. People spontaneously offered to make donations to offset her medical expenses.

A museum in Akron inquired about the possibility of hosting a special exhibit of her works and one person offered to buy her prize-winning painting that was just returned from the summer show in New York for two thousand dollars. A graphic arts teacher from another school district offered to print a limited series of numbered posters of the work, as well, which were to be sold to offset the families growing medical expenses that would continue long after she left the hospital. Furthermore, a limited-edition t-shirt was created with the artwork stenciled on the front. Her father, with the help of a friend in a local bank, quickly established an account to collect donations and deposit funds that were raised through the efforts of concerned, helpful people who stepped up to help the family.

When the call came from a curator at the Cleveland Museum of Art with the request to display *Winter Solstice*, her parents' emotions soared. The museum was Abby's favorite place to spend a day studying the works of the masters she admired. As a family, they had taken dozens and dozens of trips to the museum so Abby could spend hours scrutinizing her favorite works from the institution's outstanding collection.

The dizzying events of the past week had turned her mother's complexion the same pallor as her daughter, a lifeless shade of ashen gray. Nothing had prepared her for this aspect of motherhood. Abby was Mrs. Olson's only child and the center of her world. In fact, she and her husband had originally moved to Low Field Township so Abby could have a horse. Riding was the thing she loved most as a young girl, and, like many parents of their generation, they would do almost anything in their power, sometimes to a fault, to indulge their daughter by granting her wish to own a pony. Now, nearly a week after the trauma, Abby remained groggy, going in and out of sleep, rarely acknowledging their presence. The repeated days of sedation and surgeries kept her far from her parents' reality. Now, as their daughter lay in the hospital bed, helpless and distant, they felt powerless to impact her life.

After the third surgery on Monday, the doctors announced that they were cautiously optimistic that the nerves would respond and make a significant difference in her recovery. As the swelling decreased during the first few days of the following week, they checked on her with increasing regularity, knowing if there was to be any advancement in her recovery it would happen sooner, rather than later. On Wednesday afternoon "Abby's miracle," as her mother had phrased it, showed signs of possibility when Abby felt the doctor's pen when he raked it up and down the sole of her foot. A few hours later, she wiggled the toes of both feet to cries of celebration from everyone in her room. A small smile curled Abby's lips even though her eyes remained closed.

At the same time that Abby's response was causing jubilee on the third floor, the person who had created her crisis was being admitted into the emergency room below. A passing driver on the desolate road caught a glimpse of the reflective vest and decided to pull over. He called 911 and covered Colton's limp body with an old blanket from his trunk. The Good Samaritan stayed with the boy until the ambulance arrived and the EMTs began medical treatment. While he was being transported to Akron, Colton regained consciousness and was able to identify himself to the man sitting with him in the back of the vehicle. His mother arrived at the emergency room expecting to add yet another layer to what had already been the worse days of her life.

27

A GENERAL LEVEL OF distrust existed between the teachers and the principal at Low Field High School. Some of the problem was simply a result of personality differences, but there was also a long history of internal conflicts over the principal's decisions that were not viewed by the staff as favorable to their selfish interests. Additionally, some of the conflict was a result of the obvious dissonance between administrative personnel and members of the teachers' union. This inherent friction existed in almost every school, in fact, in almost every workplace, between the employees and their supervisor.

One of the teachers at the high school, Mark Humphrey, did have a reasonable relationship with Steve Daniels. In the past the teachers played on Steve's need to be liked so they manipulated the principal to go along with ideas and positions that were primarily balanced toward their own interests instead of the common good of the students or school district. Humphrey approached the principal about the idea of arming staff members as a proactive deterrent to future violence that would be noted as a positive honor for him as the educational leader in the building.

Daniels smiled and said, "I'm all in. That's a great idea. And I already have a concealed carry permit."

"Good, we finally agree on something of importance," said the teacher.

"Actually Mark, we agree on more things than you probably think. You have to remember I'm under a lot of pressure here. The superintendent calls the shots. If I disagree with him too often, I could be out. I mean, I still have two kids in school and I have to keep my job," said the principal.

"I know Steve; you're in a tough position."

"That's right; but on this one, I have a feeling the board will be with us. I doubt that Collins will want us armed, but I know the board members pretty well, and I think Lee and John will concur with our position so all we'd need to do is to convince one more," stated a confident Daniels.

"We believe it's the best way to truly protect the students and the staff from a horrific incident. Let's face it, we were lucky the other day, but it served as a wake-up call for the staff," said Mark.

"In fact, I think this might be the thing we need to finally get rid of Collins. I can call the board members this afternoon," the principal offered.

"No. No, we're not ready for that yet. We just wanted to see where you stood on the subject."

"Well, you can tell Keith that I'm all in," he said unequivocally.

"Ok. I'll pass it on. Thanks Steve."

In the afternoon, Daniels closed the door to his office and made phone calls to the two board members. One of them was John Fitzpatrick, the board president, who was traveling for work but took the call on his cell phone. Steve explained the reason for his call. Fitzpatrick hesitated, heeding the superintendent's caution to be wary of calls directly from the principals without his advanced notice.

John responded slowly, "I don't know, Steve. I happened to read an article recently in an NRA publication that made some good points on the issue, but board policy has to be reasonable and prudent and consider a lot of points of view. I'd want to take a long, careful look at all of the implications first and probably run it by the school attorney. What's Jim opinion?"

"We don't know yet," admitted the principal.

"Well, even though I'd consider a discussion and review of the issue by the board, any recommendation would obviously need to start with the superintendent," Fitzpatrick responded.

"Sure. I was just checking for your quick opinion John, and I wanted to keep you in the loop with what we're thinking about. We'll keep in touch with you about this; you take care."

"Yep, you too. And Steve, talk to Jim," said the board president.

One of the new protocols for dismissal following the shooting was an idea suggested by the faculty. The principal and teachers manned quadrants of the parking lot before the students were permitted to exit the school. The all-clear sign was given and students poured through the doors like a flood of youthful humanity.

Keith Byler and another teacher stood talking in the student parking lot. They observed the upper classmen toss backpacks into cars, slam doors and ignite engines causing blasts of loud music as they jockeyed with each other for exiting positions. Near the buses, Steve Daniels caught Keith's eye. Daniels was making a pistol symbol with the thumb and index finger of his hand. An alerted Keith scanned the lot in a quick, hard panic, lifting his palms up in a questioning gesture. His eyes were wide and his look intense as he scanned the area in an attempt to locate the object of Daniels's signal. Daniels shook his head *No* and waved both palms at the teacher. Daniels then held up an index finger as a sign for *wait a minute.* The buses and cars left the lots within a few minutes and the two men closed toward each other to talk.

"Why did you make the gun sign?" Byler asked with agitated concern.

"Sorry; I wasn't thinking."

"Damn, Steve, I thought you saw a gun," the teacher complained.

"No, I spoke with Mark this afternoon and I just wanted you to know I'm good with your concealed carry idea."

"Yeah, he told me," said Keith.

"Well, we have one board member who's okay with the idea too," boasted Steve.

"What do you mean?" asked the union president.

"I called Fitzpatrick and he's good with it," Steve said.

"Why did you call John?" asked Keith incredulously. "The idea is still pretty much in the discussion phase. We really wanted to be more organized before we try to move forward."

"Listen, if you're going to get anything done in this district you have to go through the board anyway. And this can't wait for months of committee meetings and deliberation and discussion. We need to protect these kids and the staff so the sooner the better," stated the principal.

"I appreciate your enthusiasm, but we were thinking we'd get the teachers trained first and then see if you and Fran were good with the idea before we approached Jim. You're getting the cart way in front of the horses, as usual," Byler said with increasing frustration.

"Trust me; we'll have a better chance if we get our ducks in a row before we take it to Collins. If we have board members in our pocket, he's more likely not to resist us. If we don't get a base of support upfront, I'll bet he says no to the idea. The guy's too soft and he's always worried about what the community will think and fifty other issues instead of just getting things done. We need to get this done now."

"I don't agree, Steve; I wish you hadn't started calling board members first. If Jim finds out that we're trying to do an end run around him by going directly to the board, I don't think he'll be too happy, or supportive," reasoned Keith.

"Don't worry about him. I think the board has lost confidence in him anyway. It's time for us to make our own way around here and do the things that need done, with or without him," declared the principal.

"No, Steve. I don't like this. You always need to be in the driver's seat calling the shots. This is our idea, not yours; we don't need you to sell it to anyone. Don't call any more board members," screamed Byler, pointing a finger at the principal. "We need to get the teachers trained first and then figure out the best way to move forward. We'd like to work together on this and stay on the same page, but, if you're going to take your usual 'bull in a china shop' approach, we'll do it without you. Do you hear me?"

"Okay," said the principal shaking his head as he started to walk away. "You let me know."

The two large men, both former collegiate athletes, parted and walked in different directions—the principal flushed with anger and disappointed that his efforts were not met with more gratitude and enthusiasm and the union president disgusted that the principal was now involved with their plan.

28

KELSEY'S COMPUTER AND printer arrived within three days of her enrollment in the alternative school, Classrooms Without Boundaries. The electronic hook-up, registration and log-in were quick and effortless. In less than an hour she had enrolled into the same classes she was taking at Low Field and began the process of getting caught up in all four courses. Her first impression was very positive. She was able to access the study guides and the chapter tests without difficulty and even entered a chat session with an online teacher just to see what it was like. This program would definitely take more self-discipline than being at Low Field where you were forced to learn, day by day, period by period, one spoonful at a time, but the unstructured nature of the program had its advantages, too. The path to the finish line became clear to her within the first afternoon, and, in the enthusiasm of the day, she actually started to map out a plan where she could complete the courses by March or April and perhaps even graduate early.

She tried to text Erin and a few of her other friends but didn't receive any responses. Maybe they were done with her, walling her off from them because of the shooting or possibly because she was no longer their classmate. She wondered if one of them had something to do with the toilet papering of the trees and the racist mailbox decoration. It made her queasy just to think about someone planning and actually doing the prank in the wee hours of the night. She felt the same way her mother did about it—their privacy had been violated. This was her home, her sanctuary from the world. Now her reputation in the community seemed blemished and tarnished. But maybe she was just making too much of the incident. Then again, the symbol on the mailbox was serious and unsettling. How stupid were people? My god, she thought, it's the 21ˢᵗ century. Please, wake up and get over your dumb racist thinking.

After school Erin and Samantha stopped by her house to say hello and see how she was doing.

"I'm so glad to see you guys; I missed you so much," said Kelsey hugging her friends. "I thought you must have deleted me from your phones."

"Dah, you know we're not allowed to carry our phones at that lame school. What, you've been out for three whole days and you already forgot that?" Erin laughed.

"God, I can't believe that. I'm so dumb," Kelsey said tapping her head.

"You're just stressed," Samantha said. "So tell us about the electronic school—should we do it too?"

"Are you kidding?" Kelsey asked seriously. "That would be awesome. We could all quit Low Field so they lose even more money. Maybe they'd have to close the place if enough of us joined the charter school."

"That would be so funny. I'd love to see the look on Daniels's face if a bunch of us quit."

"I heard some kids are transferring to that Christian school because of the shooting," Samantha said.

"Oh, that's so cool," said Kelsey.

Erin grabbed Kelsey by the arm and started to walk with her towards her bedroom. She said, "So show us the computer and the deal. How do you take your classes and do homework?"

"Well, I just got everything set-up today, but so far it looks easy. I even think I'll be able to graduate early."

"Get out," said Erin.

"That's awesome," Samantha agreed. "Hey can you Skype on this? God you'll be talking to boys all day long."

"Don't be stupid," Kelsey said. "But, yes, you can Skype and I already did my first chat with a teacher online about some BS and it really seemed cool. And the classes are what they call, self-paced, so you can do as much or as little as you want to. You just have to log on sometime each school day and either read for a while or take a chapter test or something like that."

"Wow; that's so cool. I'd love that instead of sitting through those boring classes and being hit on by smelly teachers and ugly guys."

Erin got excited and said, "There's other news. Abby's getting famous for her art now and they were saying in school today that she wiggled her toes yesterday. They think she'll probably get better."

"And Will's going to try to play in the district golf tournament with a gunshot wound in his leg," Samantha added.

"Yeah, I saw that on TV last night," Kelsey said. "I can't believe that, can you?"

"No; but it looks like things are working out for everyone. You don't even have to go to school anymore; I am so jealous."

"You're so lucky Kelsey. Maybe some good things will come of Colton's stupidity," said Erin.

"Oh, did you hear about him?"

"No, what?" asked Kelsey attempting to seem disinterested.

"He went to court and he got let out of jail on bail but he has to go back in a few months. Catch this, he's saying he doesn't even remember shooting the gun at you guys. Can you believe that guy? What a pair he must have," Samantha continued.

"Oh, wait, it gets better; I heard his family is going to sue the school district for millions because of his football concussions."

"You're kidding," stated Kelsey.

"No. They're saying the only reason he did the shooting and didn't get a college scholarship or have a career in the Marines is because he played football in high school. And the school didn't provide the proper medical treatment. So they're blaming the school for everything."

"And he's in the hospital, for your information," said Erin.

"God, now what happened?" Kelsey asked.

"When he got home from jail he went out jogging and passed out or something." Samantha said. "Some guy found him on the side of the road and called 911. Now, he's in the hospital, and they don't know what's wrong with him."

"I'm so glad you guys stopped by. I don't know what I'd do without you," Kelsey said hugging her friends again.

"Remember our math skit in middle school—we're forever *the power of three!*" exclaimed Erin.

"Always will be," Kelsey agreed.

The girls did a group hug similar to a football huddle.

"You guys should stay over tonight. I'll make Wyatt buy us ice cream and junk food. Do you want to?" Kelsey asked.

"I can't; sorry."

"Oh come on Sam."

"Sorry, I have the ACT tomorrow morning; third time's a charm, right?"

"Oh, well that's an acceptable excuse."

"Erin?"

"I'll call home and ask my mom. Can you get a ride home, Sam?"

"Wyatt, the vampire, can take you!" smiled Kelsey.

They burst into laughter.

"Not Count Wyatt!" Erin screamed.

The laughter continued as the three shared the innocence of youthful friendships.

29

COLTON HAD A blood clot in his brain. Anti-coagulants were prescribed and he was placed in the intensive care unit so his vital signs could be more closely monitored by the staff. The daily headaches weren't as severe, but now he experienced occasional dizziness and intense bouts of depression. The doctors insisted on keeping him in the hospital for constant observation for at least three days. His mom was waiting to see him in his room when they brought him back up from yet another CT scan. They had talked in private for the first time since his release from jail.

"Colton, you made a big mistake with that gun. What were you thinking?" she asked bluntly.

"I don't know, mom. I had Travis drop me off at the school on our way back from his uncle's place and I don't even remember having the gun on me. And then things just got outta hand, real quick," he said pausing, "and I honestly don't remember what happened."

"Colton, remember what I told you when you turned eighteen?" she asked. "The law doesn't forgive you for stupid mistakes any more," she said.

"I know. I'm sorry if I let you down."

"You've got to get a plan for life, Colton. I know you've been disappointed with the way the last few months have gone, but you need to forget about that girl and get going on a career of some sort once we get this situation in the past," she advised.

"You know what I'd really like to do, mom?" he asked.

"No, what?"

"Be a cop; or maybe a coach and a teacher. But I'm afraid I messed up my chance at that too," he said.

"I don't know. When we go the appointment with the attorney, why don't you talk to him about your future? Or maybe go up to the church and see Pastor Mike some time. You should get some advice from someone who's made something of himself—someone who's respected by people. I want something better for Clayton and you, and you're dad isn't the right man to put you on a good path," she said.

"I know mom; I'll go talk to Pastor Mike or maybe Coach Adams."

"They're both good men; they can help you," she agreed. "You get some rest now."

She sat next to the bed in a straight metal chair and held her son's hand. She watched him fall asleep like she had years earlier when he was a young child. She was worried about him but didn't know how to help him develop a meaningful career and life plan. After he fell asleep she quietly gathered her coat and purse, leaned over and kissed Colton on the forehead. Then she left the room, never to see her son again.

30

THE MORNING OF the district golf tournament in a Cleveland suburb, Will was startled from sleep by the hotel wake-up call. The previous night, in the blackness of the strange room, he had gotten out of bed over and over to walk around the small room, unable to sleep, his leg throbbing with pain. The doctors had written a prescription for pain killers. His mother had placed six of the pills in a small plastic bag. They were in a pocket of his suitcase, but he maintained her old-fashioned notion about not using medicine or taking pills unless the situation was beyond dire. Furthermore, the doctors and nurses at the hospital had warned him so many times about taking no more than the recommended quantities of the pain killers that he became very concerned about the possible side effects of the medicine as well as the unintended possibility of addiction that accompanied the use of the drug. He planned not to take even one of the pills—no matter how much his leg hurt.

After taking a shower, he put a fresh bandage on the wound and got dressed. Realistically, Will had serious doubts he could play well enough to qualify for the state tournament. The past two days had not gone well. Monday he played nine holes at River's Edge. It took him almost three hours. Walking was difficult, and even with his dad helping him find his golf ball following errant shots, he barely finished before darkness overwhelmed the daylight. At times he hit the ball reasonably well despite his newly developed swing flaw of hanging back on his right side during full swings. He knew it was his body's subconscious manner of protecting his left leg. His ball striking would be compromised but his short game skills and putting ability gave him a shred of hope that he might post a low enough qualifying score in the penultimate tournament. During yesterday's practice round, however, he had to ask his playing partners to continue on without him after playing only four holes so he could rest. He waited while the next five groups continued to play through in succession until there was finally a gap between two groups that he used to insert himself into the flow and continue his round.

The course was built on a piece of property with gentle hills and undulations which made his walk even tougher. When healthy, he walked with long strides, being almost six feet, two inches tall. He liked to carry his clubs and walk the course when he played competitive rounds. Normally, the feel of the ground and the steady, methodical pace of play he gained through walking the course helped him develop a natural rhythm and tempo. He used the time walking between shots to be his own swing coach and stay focused on the task at hand. His mental toughness and ability to make good course management decisions during a round was one of his greatest strengths as a player. For the district tournament, the OHSAA had approved his use of a pull-cart instead of carrying his clubs but the gesture had only limited benefit. With his gait much shorter, he noticed his walking resembled the up-and-down motion of hobbled stride. His overall strength was reduced from the injury. He managed to play all eighteen holes, but the practice round took him an excruciating six hours and thirty minutes to complete instead of the customary four hours.

As his story spread at the local and state level, Will received praise on the one hand for his determination and courage. For others the decision to play was immature and foolhardy, something his coach and parents should simply forbid him to attempt out of concern for his future. He was a student who had been shot in the leg one week ago who was now attempting to qualify for the Ohio High School

State Golf Tournament—a monumental task in everyone's eyes. The Low Field golf coach had requested a special dispensation for him to be automatically advanced to the state tournament because of the extraordinary circumstances and timing of the shooting, but the state refused to grant the advancement to the next round citing the closest similar example to his situation. An injured or sick student who was unable to compete in any stage of the progressive tournament was forced to withdraw without moving on to the next round of the event. They expressed sympathy for Will's dilemma, but refused to set a new precedent because of his condition. It simply would not be fair to the other competitors throughout the state.

Will understood their position and actually preferred to qualify on his playing merits rather than being advanced through a special medical exemption. His motivation was as focused as a prizefighter. The district and state tournaments represented the most important benchmarks of his progress toward fulfilling his ultimate goals— playing golf at a Division I college and hopefully after that, playing professionally.

The doctors at the hospital had recommended he not play for the remainder of the season. For one thing, they said his leg should not be subjected to the dynamic torqueing that was required to rotate through his full swing shots. Moreover, they cautioned him, and his parents, that attempting to walk the course so soon after the trauma of the gunshot wound to the upper thigh muscles was asking for possible serious complications to the proper healing of his left leg. The gamble of playing this week could, in fact, create permanent damage in the leg if it was not allowed the necessary time and rest for a full recovery. They repeatedly pointed out the dangers of making a very short-sighted decision. Regardless, he decided to tee up a ball and play.

His round started poorly. Being one of the three sectional champions that progressed into the district tournament, he was in the last group off that morning. He blocked his drive on the par 4 far to the right of the fairway deep into a wooded area and towards a line of out-of-bounds markers. His provisional ball was slightly better but also ended up to the right of the fairway. After searching for several minutes, he found the second ball in the thick rough nestled down in a patch of high wet grass. Will's father informed him that his initial drive was indeed out of bounds so he declared the provisional ball to be in play. He proceeded to chop his next shot out of the rough with a wedge, advancing the ball merely sixty yards. His fifth shot was not hit solidly and was also blocked to the right. It finished on the fringe some seventy feet from the hole. After three putts, he left the green with an eight. He was both shaken and demoralized by the terrible start. Before he hit his tee shot on the second hole, he took two of the pain killers, washed down with a long drink of bottled water.

He made a bogey and a double bogey on the next two holes. On the fourth tee he was already eight over par but the pain in his leg had subsided. His five iron to the 180 yard par 3 was his best swing of the round, the ball stopping twelve feet from the pin. He two putted and made what would be his only par of the day. Bad swings and poor play around the greens compounded his scoring problems. When he walked off the ninth green seventeen over par, shooting a 53, it was his worst nine hole score in years. Near the clubhouse, he was limping badly and his coach and his parents urged him to withdraw from the tournament because of his injury. They expressed how proud he had made them by even teeing it up that day and assured him there was nothing but honor in the way he had staunchly represented himself, his school and his community by playing in the event; but Will refused to withdraw.

The back nine was as disappointing as the front nine. He probably should have quit, but it was not in him. The day, however, taught him several important insights into himself—he truly enjoyed the competitive nature of playing golf at a high level and he wanted golf to be his future, now more than ever. On the sixteenth hole, he removed his six iron from his bag and started to use is as a makeshift walking cane. One of his playing partners offered to pull his cart and clubs for him, but Will refused the help worried the gesture of offering Will assistance might jeopardize the player's round and future eligibility for the state tournament.   Their group had fallen back out of position from the group in front of them by several holes, but the tournament director, aware of the dilemma and special circumstances causing the delay, ignored the complaints of some coaches to penalize Will or the group for slow play.

A crowd of over two hundred spectators and golfers watched from the clubhouse veranda and behind the eighteenth green as the final group climbed the steady slope of the final hole. Will lagged more than 75 yards behind his fellow competitors pulling his cart with his right hand and balancing his distraught body with the six iron in his left hand.   They marked and cleaned their balls in preparation for their putts on the last green as Will gamely limped over the final crest and onto the putting surface. One of them leaned his putter against his leg and started to clap for Will. The act spread like an electrical circuit throughout the crowd of people. At this point, Will was soaked with sweat, exhausted both mentally and physically and his leg hurt more than ever.

He stopped what he was doing finally sensing the applause was for him. The shock of recognition made him look up slowly scanning the cheering spectators. He was stunned and his body involuntarily shook for a moment. He raised his right hand in acknowledgement and appreciation of the gesture and then refocused his attention on the upcoming putt, a quick eight footer for bogey. After the other two competitors finished their rounds, Will stood tensely over the ball and made his best stroke of the day, rolling the ball with perfect pace into the low edge of the hole. There was an eruption from the crowd. It was as if by holing the putt he had just won a major championship. The ovation and applause continued while he limped to the cup and removed his ball. Will looked up, smiled and lifted his arms in mock triumph. He nodded and waved thanks to them as his eyes filled with tears. Never before had he felt at once so happy and yet so disappointed. His mom and dad hugged him as he left the green and his coach shook his hand. The tournament director was waiting in a golf cart to give him a ride up to the scoring area in the clubhouse.

He shook Will's hand and while they made the short ride up the cart path he said, "Will, I've been a golf professional for nearly thirty years and I've seen a lot of great things on a golf course—holes in one, a double eagle, weddings; but I've never witnessed anything like what you just did.

"Sir, I think I just shot 110," said Will with a disappointed smile.

"And that was probably the worst day you've ever had on a golf course in a long time."

"Pretty much," Will agreed. "I probably finished last."

"Yeah, I think you did," said the older man lightly punching him in the arm.

They both laughed lightly. The golf professional drove the cart up the sidewalk and stopped it close to the door so Will could walk the shortest distance to the scoring table.

The golf pro looked him in the eye and said, "Will, I know you're disappointed in today's score but over time I hope you'll think differently about what you did today. You carried yourself like a champion out there and that's far more important than winning a golf tournament. You did the game of golf proud today. Thank you for that young man."

They shook hands firmly looking squarely in each other's eyes.

"Thank you; you're probably right but I just can't believe that I'm not going to state next week. That's all I've wanted for the past two years," Will said.

As Will struggled through the heavy clubhouse door and up the stairs to the scorer's table he said to himself in a soft voice, "Colton took that away from me."

31

A FTER TWO DAYS, the Low Field Police Department still had no leads regarding the hate crime on the Boyd property. The theft of the statue had also been reported, and after interviewing Stephanie and Brenda, they assumed the two cases were related but were unable to find any evidence to connect the two acts. Members of the FBI's Cleveland Field Office were called by the local authorities and traveled to Low Field to investigate the two scenes. Unfortunately, the agents determined that the incident was an isolated, local matter and not related to any national organizations. They filed their reports and abandoned their investigation. For the time being, the crime would simply join the pile of cold cases for the local authorities to monitor, that was until they received an odd and somewhat disturbing tip.

An agent from the FBI Cyber Division who specialized in computer criminology and counter terrorism was reading extremist political blogs when she spotted a post later in the week bragging about the incident. It was crude and showed the author had little if any sophistication of internet anonymity. The person posted a photo of the mailbox on a conservation site, *Freedom Fighters*, that was actually a bogus website run by an undercover operations unit to help monitor homeland anti-government and terrorist activities. It was a simple process for the investigator to determine the point of origination of the post—a library computer in Watson City, the town due north of Low Field.

Time-and-date stamped surveillance video and computer usage logs from the library showed the positive identity of the bloggers. An arrest warrant was prepared for the pair—Roy Caldwell and Clayton Caldwell. Chief Hadley sent a pair of his patrolmen to the Caldwell farm to arrest the two and bring them into the station for booking.

His final words to the senior officer were, "Be direct, be careful and be quick about it."

The barking and excitement of the dogs signaled the police car's progress up the Caldwell's driveway. The officers knew of the potential for trouble at the Caldwell residence—they had been called to the house for domestic disturbances many times over the years. Roy Caldwell had a reputation as a violent, ill-tempered man. They didn't see anyone outside but started recording their actions via the cruiser's dash camera as a procedural matter.

Mrs. Caldwell glanced out the kitchen window and quickly hid the small whiskey bottle on the top shelf of a cupboard behind a boxed cake mix. She gulped the rest of her drink and rinsed the glass. Mr. Caldwell was in the barn getting some bales of hay down from the loft. He was headed out for a three-day trip starting the next morning, and he liked to have the feed down near the stalls so his boys would have no excuses for not feeding the livestock while he was gone. It was his usual routine to take a pistol to the barn and shoot rats hiding in the hay if he saw any. The crack of a gunshot stopped the police officers in their tracks, confused by the sound from the barn. A second volley sent them scampering for cover behind the cruiser as they drew their guns and called in to the dispatcher.

"Get down! That's gunfire. Dispatch, this is Deputy Somers," he reported frantically. "There's gunfire at the Caldwell farm on South County Line Road; send back-up."

Somers motioned to the other deputy to go around to the other side of the house. He advanced toward the barn, hiding beside a rusty pickup truck. He found a secure spot, knelt on one knee and shouted into the air, "Roy Caldwell. It's Deputy Somers. We need to talk to you."

Roy had lost most of his hearing over the years from driving big diesel trucks and working around farm equipment but he could hear someone's voice coming from outside the barn. He stepped out from behind the weathered, gray door of vertical boards. He was putting the pistol in the side pocket of his long jean jacket when he saw the police car. He stopped and looked around but couldn't see anyone. He instinctively held the gun down at his side. The back door of the house opened and his wife called out to him.

"Roy," she screamed, "the deputy needs to see you."

"Well, I'm right here. Where the hell is he?"

"Mr. Caldwell, put the gun on the ground," said the officer

Roy could now match the voice to the deputy's location beside the truck. Somers had his gun trained on Caldwell.

"Sir, I said put your gun on the ground."

"I was just shooting rats in my barn. What's your business on my property?"

"I need to talk to you, Mr. Caldwell," the young officer said firmly.

"What? Why are you here?" demanded Roy, still confused by their presence. "I'm asking you to state your business."

"I need you to put your gun down so we can talk."

His wife screamed at him from the porch, "Roy, put your gun down!" She turned to the officer and informed them pointing at her ear, "He's hard of hearing."

Caldwell released his grip on the gun holding it only with his thumb and index finger. Slowly he walked over to a rusted cooler and set the gun on its top. He stepped away from the barn and headed toward the back porch. He sat on the step. Both officers moved quickly towards him, their guns pointed menacingly at him.

"Put your damn guns down," Roy said with agitation.

The officers stepped closer. Somers lowered his weapon and removed some papers from his front shirt pocket.

"Roy," said Somers, "we don't want any trouble but this is a warrant for your arrest."

"Arrest? For doing what?" asked Caldwell.

"Why are you arresting him?" demanded his wife.

"Ma'am, stay where you are," said the deputy pointing a finger at the woman. "Mr. Caldwell, the arrest warrant states the charge of criminal trespassing, contributing to the delinquency of a minor and for hate crimes."

"What?" Mrs. Caldwell asked.

"What the hell are you talking about?" said Roy.

"You need to come to the station with us now, sir. Please place your hands on your head and stand up." Roy Caldwell complied and Somers swiftly handcuffed his hands behind his back.

As they led him to the cruiser and helped him into the rear seat, Caldwell called out to his wife, "Call that damn attorney again."

"Where are you taking him?" she asked

The deputy shouted his response to the woman, "The Low Field Police station, ma'am."

"I can't take any more of this upheaval. He didn't do anything and neither did my boys. You all just have it out for us," complained Mrs. Caldwell, increasingly upset by the situation.

"We're just taking him to the station so he can talk to the Chief,"

As they were assisting Roy into the back seat of the cruiser and calling in a status report, she walked calmly from the back porch toward the barn. Her hands were shaking as she picked up the pistol from the cooler just as the back-up car sped up the dirt driveway, siren blaring and dust billowing in its wake. Mrs. Caldwell turned and walked toward the two cruisers with tears running over her tired cheeks. She fired shots in rapid succession. The officer in the second car slammed on the brakes of his cruiser, stopping the vehicle at an angle so he could use it as a protective barricade from her assault. The bullets she fired exploded into the unpaved driveway and flew wildly above the cruiser. Without hesitation the back-up officer crouched beside his car and reflexively fired one kill shot, striking her directly in the heart. Her small body lurched backward and fell to the ground, the gun firing one more shot through the kitchen window, bursting shards of glass through the pale sunlight of the October afternoon. In an instant, the noise evaporated into a shockingly solemn silence.

32

"MR. FITZPATRICK IS on line one for you," Laura Jansen buzzed into the superintendent.

"Thanks L J."

John Fitzpatrick was serving in his third term on the Board of Education, this year as the board president. Having been on the board for over nine years, he knew the history of the district's staff, families and problems in great depth. John had worked as a controller in the mid-west regional office of a tool supply company before his third heart attack prompted an early retirement. The superintendent respected his opinion because of his vast experience in dealing with many similar issues in his career. Jim valued the opportunity to discuss and sometimes argue important issues in confidence with John, knowing the result would benefit them both when they were called upon to be spokespersons for the school district. When they were faced with situations that required comments to the public, the many hours they had engaged in informal debate made their opinions better informed and prepared them for the unexpected counter attacks from the opposition.

"John, how are you," Jim asked.

"I'm fine Jim," replied John. "You got a minute?"

"Sure, I was just checking emails; happy to take a break," Jim replied.

"Well, I heard Will played in the golf tournament yesterday," John commented.

"Yeah; he didn't win the tournament but I heard he won a lot of fans."

"Amazing kid. I spoke to his dad last night. He said Will's leg was really hurting when they got home. They planned on icing it last night and I guess he has a check-up with the doctor today."

"He's a special kid," said Jim. "I'm really disappointed for him. I wish I could find the silver lining in this incident, but I can't."

John agreed, "We've just got to make sure he doesn't miss out on his dreams because of this mess."

"I agree. Do you have something in mind?" asked the superintendent.

"No, unfortunately I don't, but like most things, where there's a will, there's a way—no pun intended," he laughed. "I mean we just have to give it some thought. If we put our minds to it, we'll come up with something."

"Yeah, and I heard Abby had a breakthrough," said Jim.

"Yes, that's fantastic," John echoed. "The last thing I heard was that she was regaining the feeling on her left side and a little on the right side. Have you heard anything this morning?" asked the board president.

"No, actually it sounds like you've heard more than me," answered the superintendent. "It sounds great. I know the staff has really done a nice job of getting community support for her this week."

"Yes and they should be commended for their efforts. They might have really helped Abby get through the worst of it. Maybe we should announce some of this at the board meeting?" John asked.

"Sure, I agree. I'll make sure we do an update on the kids and thank the staff on the agenda."

"Hey, what have you heard about Mrs. Caldwell?" John inquired.

"What a tragedy," said Jim. "I haven't spoken to Harlan yet, but someone said it's being called a suicide by police, but I'm suspicious. Obviously, right now we're really concerned for the boys. I guess

Clayton is staying with his grandparents for the time being. I think Roy's in jail and Colt is still in the hospital as far as I know."

"Any announcement about funeral arrangements yet?" asked John.

"Not that I've heard, but I'm sure Laura will find out and I'll have her call or email everyone as soon as we know something," offered the superintendent.

"It's unbelievable," John said. "What a tragedy for those boys and that family." He paused for a moment and continued, "Jim, have you been told about this idea the staff has to get trained for concealed carry?"

"Yeah, just heard about it last night—from my wife," Jim said.

"Funny how word gets around in this district," John said. "Instead of Keith just making a phone call to you or scheduling a meeting to sit down and discuss the idea, you have to find out through the rumor mill.

"We're like one big, dysfunctional family in this district," laughed Jim. "And old habits are hard to break. I think we've improved our professional communication and procedures, but as soon as we move on to some furtive issue, the old patterns return like water running downhill. I swear that statue of Sisyphus you gave me a few years ago will be my legacy here in Low Field."

"Don't feel you're alone in the struggle. The place has been like this my whole life here. At least we've made it better than it was," John offered. "But who knows what will happen after we're all gone."

"So, to get back to your question, what do you think about staff members carrying guns?" the superintendent asked. "Oh, before I forget, I need to tell you that I've received calls from two attorneys regarding law suits that are being planned by several of the families and, most likely, will be filed against the district because of the shooting. I've already put our attorney on notice about the situation, just so you know."

"What did he have to say?" asked John.

"He wasn't sure but he remembered historically that in several other school shootings there were substantial settlements that went against the district so hopefully that insurance we pay for each year will protect us from personal damages. He's going to research it for us when I get something in writing, and I'll update the board at the next meeting."

"Damn, there's always something," said the board president. "So, what's your opinion on the gun issue?"

"It sounds like one of their usual attempts to get their members unified so they can make one of their grandstand plays with their supporters at an upcoming board meeting," Jim said. "From what Kathy heard, they've got about twenty teachers who've agreed to go through the concealed carry training and get permits. I guess they also talked to the principals, soliciting their support."

"I've thought about this issue pretty carefully since the Sandy Hook tragedy. My first thoughts were absolutely no way do we ever want to put more guns on a school campus. You know I'm a big supporter of the Student Resource Officer Program that we started here, but we all realize the shortcomings of having only one officer on duty to patrol two schools."

"Sure; I know you've thought we should have a full time police officer in each school," said Jim.

"I think it's one of those we're damned if we do, damned if we don't kind of issues," said John, "but I do believe it's a necessity in today's world. There is always going to be a limited supply of money, and sometimes the community thinks we're at cross purposes with other governmental entities like when we subsidize the salary of the SRO or pay off-duty officers to attend football games. I mean, everyone wants the kids to be safe from random acts of violence, and yet the public is quick to judge the expenditure of taxpayer funds to provide a reasonable level of security," reasoned John.

"So, we have to make our own, hard decisions when it comes to these kinds of really tough issues, right?" Jim asked somewhat rhetorically.

"Yes, I agree. So, I reconsidered the whole issue, trying to be open-minded and trying to see other people's points of view; but, I guess the point I keep coming back to is that I don't believe putting more guns, in the hands of people on school grounds, teachers, mind you, who are untrained in the use of violent, lethal force as a means to stop a person in the midst of a crisis situation, is the correct answer. Stopping violence by condoning an environment with a greater degree of weaponry is not something a teacher is prepared to do, even if the person passes a class on concealed carry and agrees to be armed. I think the possibility of aiming and firing a gun at another person is such a contradiction in the heart of a teacher that most of these people are not psychologically prepared to engage in that action. I'm afraid we're setting the stage for a disaster," said the board president.

"Okay, I understand your perspective, but you're jumping to the point of the argument of preparedness and the willingness of the individuals to carry out the ultimate act of being armed. But what if that never happens?" Jim debated. "For the sake of argument, before we get to that point I think it's worth asking the question as to whether or not arming random staff and publicizing that policy as a deterrent is a more effective way of preventing the random gunman from even stepping foot on the school grounds. I mean it's kind of like the large, barking dog in the house. Do we stop that person from bringing a gun into one of the schools just by creating the scenario of multiple, unidentified and prepared defenders in both buildings?"

"I know, but think of the real world," countered John. "Everyone knows there are police officers minutes away from anywhere, but it's not enough to stop crime or violence. And cops sometimes have to use their guns, whether they plan to or not."

"It's a complex issue, John, but as of today, I agree with you that arming a bunch of teachers is not our best solution," Jim concluded.

"Right, but maybe the board should discuss it?" asked John.

"Well, we could do that at the next board meeting or hold a special board meeting that's open to the public. We could allow a limited number of speakers or open the floor for questions. Maybe have Chief Hadley and Deputy Perry on the agenda as well—hearing their perspectives might be helpful and serve as a way to preempt the teachers before they get too far down the road with their plan," Jim suggested.

"I like that idea, but we will need to put a time limit on each speaker, even us. Let's try to do that before the teachers make one of their show-of-force plays at one of our regular meetings. We might want to hold a special meeting and have the union discuss their ideas out in front of the public; let them be on the hot seat for a change?" John said.

"Okay; I hate to have another one of those kinds of town hall meetings but we might want to do that regarding this issue. I'll call the other board members today and tomorrow and get them up to speed on what we discussed. We should probably start with some dates; let's see, the regular board meeting is two weeks from tonight. Do you want to try for next Wednesday or Thursday evening?" Jim asked.

"Yep; either one of those nights is good for me. Do you think that gives us enough time to pass the word to the community, though?"

"You're joking, right?" Jim asked. "A powder-keg topic like that will be a standing-room-only event even if we announced the meeting an hour before it starts. Seriously, though, I can write a press release to the media and we can let parents know through the phone message network. Let's see what the other board members think and I'll have Laura give you a call on Friday.

"Sounds good, Jim," said John. "Take care."

"See you," Jim said.

Mr. Collins hung up the phone with a sick feeling in his mouth. Many times during his tenure at Low Field, he agreed to host a public meeting regarding a highly charged issue or *hot topic* as he thought of it. They were always messy and stressful. Jim knew the importance of inviting people to forums like this and allowing them to express their opinions regarding school issues. Oftentimes, however, these meetings did little to accomplish the main goal of establishing some sort of common ground among the diverse perspectives of local taxpayers. The proposed rational discussion usually manifested itself into an illogical interpretation by many residents, pitting the goals of the schools against the vision of the community. Most often, the outcome further polarized the peoples' diverse opinions in opposite directions. It was an unfortunate trend, decades old, that continued to this day and divided the residents into one of two distinct groups—those people with the determination to support the schools through the good times and the bad times, and those with the agenda, tenacity and willpower to destroy the school district at any cost.

33

T HE TEAM OF neurosurgeons who had performed the last two operations on Abby's abdomen was joyous with the news that she
was regaining the feeling and movement in her legs. Following the
initial trauma to her spine from the gunshot, time was of the essence.
The first surgery was performed to determine the extent of the damage caused by the bullet and to stabilize her medically. When she
woke up in the recovery room, there was a hint of further problems
when the nurses reported her incontinence. The following morning
the paralysis below her waist was discovered, confirming the doctor's
concerns of nerve damage to the area.

A specialist, Dr. Kutar, from the Cleveland Clinic volunteered to
assist the team of surgeons from the Akron area with the diagnosis
and with any subsequent surgical procedures. A second CT scan was
done before the weekend and the doctors conferred through several
conference calls about the results. The doctors viewed the images
simultaneously via a medical software program that allowed them to
see the same results at different locations. The determination was
made that Abby's wound caused a fourth-degree injury with severe
damage to the cauda equine region of her spinal nerves, requiring
a quick medical response in the form of a very delicate operation.
Dr. Kutar drove to Akron to assist with the Saturday surgery which
spanned over nine hours. Her parents were informed before the procedure that there was less than a 50/50 chance that the surgery would

be successful. They hoped the pessimistic number was deliberately stated low to keep their hopes down.

Actually, the doctors had inflated the prognosis in hopes that Abby's parents would present a positive attitude to her when the family discussed the possibilities before the surgery. The odds of her ever walking again were essentially much lower. So, when the good news spread through the hospital and medical community about Abby, Dr. Kutar, who was also a Hindu priest in his community, went into his office and privately paid homage to his god Vishnu for giving the team of medical professionals the spiritual guidance to help the young woman. Such was the extent of the miracle.

For the better part of the past week, Abby's parents had barely slept, oftentimes slouched uncomfortably in the chair at the foot of her bed. They took turns running home taking care of the mail, talking to people at work and refreshing themselves with a shower and clean clothes. Their spirits never outwardly waned for their only child's recovery. The support they received from the community and from well-wishers all around the country and the world truly moved them to keep up a brave and optimistic demeanor for their daughter. At the end of an arduous week, Abby's hospital room had the appearance of a florist and card shop thanks to the outpouring of flowers and mail from concerned neighbors, friends, students and family.

Abby, on the other hand, had descended into a deeper level of depression, grimly concerned about her future. Her tall, thin frame had become even thinner with only IVs to keep her nourished since the traumatic injury. The smell of cooked food brought in regularly from the hospital kitchen made her nauseous. She had started to reconcile herself to the possibility that she might never walk again. Her ability to do her art would exist, but with obvious limitations. Her creative instincts were heightened, however. The incident had created the idea for a series of works about the shooting that she had tentatively titled *Chaos*. In her vision, all three were dark, painted almost exclusively from heavy tones of purple, red and black—quite different from her usual brighter, more buoyant pastorals. As she envisioned the new works, the first painting would depict the dark hole she saw herself being sucked into when the shock of the bullet pierced her skin. The second was a reflection of the corpse-like pose she was repeatedly forced into while lying on the operating table with tubes and masks sustaining her vital functions, and the third was an abstract snapshot of her mind on these bleakest days of her young life. The sketchy image was at this point a dreamlike Dali-inspired minimalist work in progress, a totally new and exciting direction for her to consider. Her need to create had not been diminished by her time in the hospital.

When she woke up early Wednesday morning from a drug-aided night's sleep, she could feel a thousand pins and needles in both legs—the response from her legs was even better than the previous day. She touched her thighs and could feel her own fingers squeezing the flesh. She flexed her knee joints back and forth a few inches amazed at the return to normalcy.

"Mom, I can't believe it!" she said with relieved joy.

"Careful honey," her mom quickly cautioned. "The doctors want you to lie very still so you don't damage your spine."

"I know; I actually can't move but I'm so relieved," Abby confessed. "I don't think I could have survived if I had to spend the rest of my life in a wheelchair. I'm so lucky."

"Yes, honey. We're all so lucky," said her mom kissing her daughter's hand.

34

COLTON HAD NO visitors at all the next day and no one returned phone calls or text messages until he got one from Travis.

Hey colt b up to c u soon

Colton sent an immediate text in reply,

Cool thx

Within an hour Travis walked into his room carrying a shake. Under his sweatshirt he revealed a bag like a magician with a burger and fries and handed it to Colton.

"Oh wow, thanks T; you're the best," Colton said with a big smile.

"No problem. How's your noggin, dude?" Travis asked.

"I feel pretty good today; no headaches or any pain, yet," said Colton.

"That's good; no pain, all gain," quipped Travis.

"Yep," Colton replied with a mouthful of French fries.

"Hey, Tammy called and I gave her your phone number," Travis said. "Has she gotten ahold of you?"

"No, but I haven't had my phone for about a week. My mom just brought it to me a day or so ago," Colton explained.

"Well prepare yourself Colt. That girl has her eye on you and I don't think she's going to be stopped by your lame attempts at avoiding her," joked Travis. "I mean the whole jail thing and hospital thing are fine but you're going to have to come up with something better if you hope to avoid Miss Tammy."

"Man, I wish Tammy was here right now instead of your sorry butt," countered Colton.

"You can talk crap but just remember, you've been warned. Your old friend Travis warned you," Travis said.

"Thank you," laughed Colton.

"Hey I want to ask your opinion on something," said Travis.

"Sure."

"I've been thinking, if I ever get famous I'm thinking about legally changing my name to a one word name; you know like some musicians and athletes do and I wanted your opinion," said Travis.

"A one word name?" Colton asked. "Like Prince?"

"Exactly; think about Madonna or Socrates or Superman. What do you think?" pursued Travis.

"I think you're crazy," Colton answered. "In fact, that would work pretty well for your one-word name, *Crazy*."

"I think that's taken," said Travis rubbing his chin.

"Crazy's taken?" Colton asked.

"There's some guy who calls himself Ludicrous," explained Travis. "Doesn't that mean crazy?"

"What, do I look like an English teacher?" joked Colton.

"Well I think it has potential and I'm going to keep working on it," said Travis. "People with revolutionary thoughts always have detractors and I'm not going to let you be a wet blanket on my great idea."

"Oh please don't let me be the voice of reason that derails your great idea, Crazy," Colton said smiling and shaking his head at his friend.

They continued to laugh and talk about insignificant matters for a while. Travis knew about the events at the Caldwell farm earlier that day. The gravity of the event weighed heavily on him and he felt deceitful concealing it from his friend. He artfully kept Colton in a lighthearted mood and attempted to verify whether or not Colton knew about his mom. Within a few minutes it was clear to him that Colton had not been informed of the tragedy. Travis considered himself unequipped to bear such personal and tragic news to his best friend. It would amount to another body blow to Colton, who was already reeling from recent events. Cowardly, he decided to avoid the topic altogether figuring Colton should receive that kind of information from a family member.

"So, what's your doctor saying about why you blacked out?" asked Travis.

"They think I have a blood clot. So they put me on blood thinners a few days ago and they're just watching me and doing some tests to see if the pills are working."

"Good. When are you supposed to be released?" Travis asked.

"I don't know for sure; they were talking about transferring me to the VA Hospital in Cleveland but the doctor came here," said Colton. "He thought I might get out in a day or so. That's all they've told me."

"Oh. Have your parents been up to see you?" Travis asked not believing the words had actually come out of his mouth. He punched himself silently in the mouth.

"No. I haven't heard from them or Clay since last night. They'll probably come up later," said Colton confirming his unawareness of the situation.

Two of the Low Field deputies walked into the room with a nurse.

One of them looked at Travis and said, "We need to have a moment with Colton in private. Would you mind stepping outside, please?"

"Sure," said Travis. He closed the door behind him as he stepped into the hallway.

"Colton. We're here because we have some bad news."

"What's that?" Colton asked.

"There was a shooting at your parent's farm this morning," said the older deputy.

"What! What happened?" asked a stunned Colton.

"We can't discuss the details at this time because there's a current investigation of the incident, but we're sorry to inform you Colton," the deputy paused and stepped close to the bed before saying, "your mom was shot Colt—she's dead."

Colton's hands grabbed the sides of his head, "What! No. What are you saying? My mom? How? What happened?!" he shouted.

The nurse and the officers softly restrained the struggling boy. His face flushed from the news. One of them simply said, "We're sorry, Colton."

Colton writhed in his bed—his head stretched back, his hands over his face. Emotion like he had never felt before overwhelmed his entire being. His body shook as he sobbed. After a few moments, he turned to the side with his head down in his chest. He pointed to the door.

"Get out," he screamed. "Go."

The nurse remained in the room with Colton and another nurse rushed in also to provide assistance to the patient. Travis stood in the hallway with the officers. No words were exchanged but they maintained their positions together supporting Colton but with different agendas. A third nurse appeared from a central station and entered the room carrying a small cup with some pills and a glass of water.

"My head hurts," Colton moaned.

"Where exactly?" asked the first nurse touching his hands before gently pulling them back from his forehead. "Show me, Colton."

"My temples; on the sides and behind my eyes," he explained.

"Okay. I'm going to get something to make you feel better. I'll be right back," she said stepping briskly out of the room, then jogging down the hall.

The others tried to calm Colton and get him to lie down again. The nurse quickly returned carrying a plastic bag filled with a clear liquid. She hung the bag on the stand and started the new IV. A saline and sedative solution was necessary to help him relax. Death was nothing new to her; unfortunately, it was an everyday part of her work. Over the years she had witnessed so many shocked responses to the news that a friend or family member had died that she was now numb and prepared for the sad reaction of astonishment. The necessary words and treatments were so ingrained in her being that she instinctively and calmly carried on doing her best to comfort the grieving people.

For a young person like Colton, being told of the death of his own mother was the most powerful sense of loss he could possibly experience. The pained expression on Colton's face showed that his grief was both deep and complex. The nurse knew that the shock of receiving such horrific news would most likely send him into a state of confusion for days. His grief would carry his thoughts and feelings to a very dark place. The gravity of such stunning news could also trigger profound depression and an overwhelming sense of purposelessness in his life. His recovery was now seriously compromised. She needed him asleep so she had time to discuss this significant complication with his doctor. The nurse surmised his worse days were yet to come.

35

DARON SPENT THE days waiting for his computer to arrive from the e-school hanging out back in Akron. He took his worn basketball to the park near his old home and the sounds of the ball dribbling and hitting the backboard seemed to draw people to the court like a unique category of specialized music. Most of the players who showed-up were either guys who had graduated and had nothing to do or were drop-outs who had lost a human connection with school and saw no advantage in persisting to accomplish a task in which they saw no value. Daron knew a few of them from growing up in the neighborhood but he never saw any of his closest friends from elementary school. He hoped they were doing okay but chose not to ask the others about them.

Cars full of guys would occasionally stop and watch the games. Some would leave for a while and then return with either drive-thru food or forty ounce bottles of beer in form fitting brown bags. Daron liked the soft buzz he'd get from drinking on an empty stomach while he sat out several games. He also enjoyed the camaraderie of just playing ball and being with a bunch of guys—it was a relaxing way to pass time, and they were fun, always cracking on one another, posturing with false bravado and just laughing. He got invited to go shoot craps in the projects, but decided he better drive back to Low Field before his mom got home from work.

His mom's car and a police cruiser were already at the trailer when he got home.

"Where have you been, Daron?" she asked scornfully. "And why didn't you take your phone?"

Daron replied, "Sorry, mom. I forgot it today. Why are they here?"

"We needed to talk to you and your mother about the statue," one of the deputies offered.

"I thought we already covered this a few days ago," his mom said. "Why are you really here? There must be a reason two of you drove out here rather than just call me."

"Well, we know now who stole the statue and put it near your truck—it was Clayton Caldwell and his dad," said the other officer.

"What?" Daron said with a surprised look.

"Mrs. Roberts, because of the serious nature of this incident, the chief asked us to stop by to see if you would like to file charges against them."

"For what?" asked a puzzled Brenda.

"For committing a hate crime against your family," said the officer.

"A hate crime?" she said still somewhat stunned by the information. "No. I don't know. I'm going to have to think about that."

Daron spoke up and asked, "Can I file the charges? I'll gladly file charges against those bone heads."

"Are you eighteen yet?" asked one of the officers.

"Whoa, Daron;" cautioned his mother. "We'll need to discuss this. Officer, can I get one of your cards? We'll talk this over and I'll give you a call tomorrow."

"Sure; here you go," he said handing one of his cards to her. "That's my cell number so it will ring right to me whenever you call."

"Thank you," said Brenda Roberts opening the door of the trailer for the officers.

After the two police officers had driven away, Daron's mom called him back to the kitchen.

"Where did you go today and why do you smell like you've been drinking," she stated directly.

"Mom, I went to Akron. I drove around the old neighborhood and ended up playing in a few pickup games of basketball. I was thirsty and all they had to drink was beer so I had one; it's no big deal," he reasoned.

"Yes it is, Daron. You're only seventeen. Where were you and who were you with?"

"I drove back over to Goodyear Park. I was just shooting hoops with some guys. You know, getting some exercise and having some fun and I drank one damn beer; I swear I had one damn beer," he said loudly.

"Don't you raise your voice or use that language with me, young man," yelled his mother.

Daron started to walk back to his bedroom and said, "Sorry, I had one beer."

"Don't walk away from me; why would go there, Daron?" she continued.

"God, I don't know mom. I just got bored waiting around here for the computer and wanted to take a ride," Daron replied.

She shook her head in despair. She realized the significance of his day more than he did—Akron still felt like home to him. It was where he felt most comfortable. In spite of spending the past three years in Low Field, his roots were still in the city.

Brenda sat down at the kitchen table and said, "Listen, I don't know if this new schooling arrangement is going to work for me. I can't go to work and be constantly worried that you're not here doing your school work."

"I know mom. I just went to Akron today because I was bored and tired and confused. Once the computer comes, I'll be busy and things will be better. I just needed something to take my mind off of all of this mess," he said.

"I might have to take your truck keys, or sell your truck," she said almost thinking out loud.

"No; just take the keys. That's fine," he offered. "You don't have to sell my truck."

"I can't believe how this mess has unraveled our whole lives. Now the police want us to file charges against a boy whose mother just got killed," she said.

"We should file against him," he said with conviction. "That whole family is a bunch of racists. Who cares if his mom got offed? The way I see it, there's one less racist to spread their bullshit—sorry, poison."

"Daron, think about what you're saying," she said shaking her head and wincing. "Colton and his brother have grown up with parents who might have backward ideas about race relations, but we don't know that. If anything, you should feel sorry for them, not hate them. And those boys just lost their mother, Daron. Think about that. Their mother is gone forever."

"I know, and that's too bad about Mrs. Caldwell, but why I should feel sorry for a bunch of racists who hate me?!" Daron said rhetorically. "Nobody feels sorry for me and I don't even remember my own dad. No one cares about that."

"That's not true. You know I'm always here for you," his mom said with a hurt expression.

Daron quickly said, "I didn't mean you, mom. I know you are and I know you care, but nobody else even knows or cares that my dad's been dead just about my entire life. That's not fair."

"Life isn't fair. We all have burdens to bear," she said.

"I know, but I'm mad at them, the Caldwells," he admitted. "They're causing trouble because my dad was black and I don't even know my dad. And I'm mad at dad for never being there for me—for us."

"They don't know anything about us, Daron, and unfortunately they haven't taken the time to try to get to know us. Remember that any time you rush to judgment about another person. You should always give that person the benefit of the doubt until you get to know them and that takes time. They made that mistake but I want you to be a better person by not holding it against them," she said.

"But they assume so much about things they don't even know anything about," he said.

"It happens all the time," she explained. "Even when we were young, your father used to say about people who held a racist ideology that he felt sorry for them because they were ignorant about black people. They didn't understand that all of the people in this country are the same. We all came from someplace other than America and we all want similar things—a chance to make a good life for ourselves and our families. It's as simple as that—Americans all really want the same things. We just get caught up in politics and culture and religion and money and we lose sight of the important things we have in common."

"Dad said that?" Daron asked.

His mother laughed lightly, "Well, I'm probably making it sound better than the way he said it, but yes, we used to talk about those kinds of things all the time. I mean, there weren't too many interracial couples when we were growing up. Your dad benefitted from being around white people when he transferred to the parochial schools in middle school. They were kind and good to him and it helped him develop a more complete perspective about racial differences. That's one of the reasons I wanted us to move to Low Field. I thought it would help you to live in a white neighborhood; so you could understand both cultures."

"I don't know if it worked out so well," Daron said. "It seems like we moved to the Deep South in the 1950's coming out here. It seems like no progress has been made in Low Field, like it's stuck in a time warp."

"Change comes slowly and you're one of the first black students to ever be in this district," his mother said. "What you're experiencing is probably what every person who's ever tried to break through the color barrier goes through. Some of these people view you as a threat."

"How am I a threat?" he asked incredulously.

"You're a threat to their way of life. Most people resist change even if there's no good reason to oppose it. The fact that we're in Low Field threatens their comfortable way of life. If we were gone, everything could stay the same and they wouldn't have to change their attitudes. What they don't understand is that change is inevitable; nothing stays the same, so why not embrace the energy that comes from change and make your life better by using change to improve your life? You're just one more person helping to end racism in this country, but, as you're finding out, that's not an easy thing to do."

"Until a week ago I didn't think about it much. I mean I knew it was there but it was kinda like a shadow, in the background. I knew everyone looked at me differently and treated me a little differently than the other kids but it really wasn't a problem until Colton flipped out on me," he said.

"Daron, racism got your dad killed," his mom stated.

"How's that?" he asked.

"This is just my theory, but I always believed that the incident on the loading dock when your dad first got in trouble was a set-up. A man from the church I attended as a young girl was the plant manager and his son played basketball with your father. That's how he got his job at the rubber facility, but my father also knew this gentleman because they volunteered to work at the same mass on Sunday mornings. They passed the collection plates and counted the donations for that mass," she explained.

"Okay, so what's that got to do with dad getting killed?" asked Daron.

"Well, I've never wanted to tell you about this but my dad was furious when he found out I was pregnant with you. And I think he was looking for a way to cause problems for your father. So after you were born and we came home from college after that first year, he needed a job and he got hired at Goodyear. I've always thought my father spread some of his own prejudice with the plant manager and they deliberately tried to get your father in trouble."

"You're saying grandpa got dad killed," Daron said. "But I always thought it was just some dumb scheme with another guy dad had grown up with."

"That's partially true. Your father did know the other guy who was working on the loading dock at the time, but I always thought he got paid-off to trick your dad into unloading the stolen tires from the truck. When they got busted, your dad was arrested and charged but somehow the other guy got his charges dropped," she explained.

"What? That's bullshit; sorry. So you think grandpa deliberately got dad in trouble?" he said.

"He probably didn't intend for your dad to get into such serious trouble, but that's what I believe happened. And I'm sorry to have to tell you that," she admitted. "I think it was my father's racist attitude that came out and he wanted a way to pay your dad back for getting me pregnant."

"But you told me dad got out of jail in a year. Why didn't you guys just get back together then?" Daron asked.

"We tried a little, but your dad wouldn't leave well enough alone. I talked to him over and over about just moving away, but because of the criminal charges he had lost any opportunity he had to play basketball or to attend college. He believed he had been set-up and that his life had been ruined, and he wanted revenge. One night he confronted the guy whom he was working with on the loading dock. They got into a fight and he stabbed your dad and left him in the park that night. He bled to death. Everyone left the park; no one called for an ambulance until a few hours later and it was too late. The guy admitted to stabbing your dad, but he got off because his friends testified he did it in self-defense."

She was shaking her head back and forth throughout the retelling of the story while dabbing away small pools of tears from her eyes.

"Mom, did you love him?" Daron asked.

"Of course I did honey."

"Why didn't you do anything about it then?" he asked.

"Daron, you think the racism you're feeling is bad now but you can't imagine how hard it was on us back then. The civil rights movement was somewhat successful; protests against the Vietnam War as well as the women's movement had also changed things in America. So, the pendulum had started to swing back in the opposite direction but the change was just beginning. The same prejudices against blacks or women were still there, but they were driven deeper below the surface—just like they are today. I keep hoping that people like the Caldwells are gone, but they're not. What you're going through today is not much different than what your dad and I encountered twenty years ago. I don't know if we'll really see the end of racism in our lifetime, and I'm truly sorry that you have to live with it," she said.

"Tell me about it. Every time I look in the mirror I see a black kid but it was never like that before. Now I can't stop wondering what others are thinking about when they look at me," he said. "I think it's making me paranoid."

"Daron, you can't worry about what others think; you just have to know that you're the future of America. A hundred years from now, everyone in this country will not only be a mix of ethnic backgrounds, but also a mix of racial backgrounds. In fact they already are if you study anthropology and go back far enough in history. Racism will only fade to the point of non-existence for most people when it directly impacts them and their children and grandchildren. You are a living example of what will cause racism to disappear in this country, but that, I'm sorry to say, will take a long, long time. I hope your children or their children never have to have this conversation."

Daron looked up at the ceiling and then down at the table and blew out a breath of exhausted understanding.

"So, even my own grandfather is a racist," he said shaking his head.

His mom looked at him and said, "I'm afraid so, and that's why I didn't call them to ask about you visiting."

36

STEPHANIE BOYD DROVE Kelsey and her friend, Erin, to Cleveland for a special day of shopping. They needed to re-connect and have a good day of simple fun. The day represented a fresh start, of sorts. There had been too much drama the past few weeks and all of their life compasses needed to be realigned, their collective slates wiped clean, their batteries recharged. Two of their favorite places to shop were located in a wealthy suburb, a mall with a pair of high-end, upscale department stores and The City Centre, an outdoor, shopping experience designed like a city with storefronts facing a series of streets. The rows of elite retailers and famous designer labels only existed in a few locations in the mid-west. They enjoyed seeing the exclusive shoes and clothing in person that they could only otherwise view through images in magazines and websites. Nowhere else could they view and touch these fashions directly unless they traveled many hours to a metropolitan area such as New York or Chicago.

They had a great time browsing in a computer store, a bookstore and one specialty store after another. They also tried on clothes at some ultra-chic stores—the places where the rich and famous and Hollywood stars shopped. These were the stores that set the seasonal fashion trends for the entire country. They carried the most up-to-date and trendiest items that appeared in the media, unlike the customary, everyday choices at the more moderate discount stores and neighborhood malls in the depressed communities around Akron. The prices seemed outrageous to them, so they didn't buy anything

before going to lunch. The talked and had fun. Kelsey had completely forgotten about her recent problems. Her mom was happy to
see her daughter and Erin just having fun again.

They decided to stop at The Urban Look before they left for
home. The stark, industrial feel of the store reminded them of a
movie set. It had a great vibe and cool music. Even the clerks who
worked there looked like they were having fun. They wore funky
hats and clothes and their personal looks set them apart from traditional store employees. Outlandish tattoos, hair styles and piercings
were common among them and stretched the normal boundaries of
young Midwesterners.

The fall/winter apparel line was in-stock and both Kelsey and
Erin found items they wanted to try on. Even though Christmas
was well over a month away on the calendar, some items were already
on sale with their costs significantly reduced. They were talking to
each other through the walls of the fitting rooms when the music
stopped. An eerie quiet stopped everyone in the store for a momen-
tary pause. A problem nearby had caused people to run in pandemonium. Gunshots had been fired at the store directly across the street
and the employees reacted quickly.

"The store is on lockdown!" the employees started to yell.

People instinctively screamed and ran behind displays in panic.
They banded together looking for friends and family members—
Stephanie Boyd dropped an item and started running for the dressing
rooms. The young store manager, who looked like a college student
or artist, fumbled with a set of keys near the main doors to the street.
He gave up and quickly ran toward the back of the store to acti-
vate the emergency security system. A metal grid-like garage door
lowered from an elevated box covering the entrance of the store and
mesh screens descended over the windows. The gunman, a young
white man in his twenties, dressed in camouflage pants, a black hoodie and carrying a back pack ran into the store before the gate closed to
the ground. He fired two rounds from a military-style rifle into the

ceiling. The shots echoed like fireworks within the confines of the store walls and ceiling tiles.

He screamed, "Everyone on the ground! Now!"

People cowered behind shelves and mannequins and some continued to run and scream. He fired several more warning shots to get everyone's attention.

The gunman repeated his command, "On the ground! And shut up!"

A sales clerk ran toward the back of the store carrying a cash register drawer. The gunman fired at the employee and the bullet knocked the money from his hands. Coins and paper bills cascaded through the air making a loud noise as he lost his balance and thudded into a wall. The gunman walked calmly toward the man's body, lying near the hallway that led to the dressing rooms and the storage and delivery areas of the building.

Kelsey and Erin had formed an idea of what was transpiring in the main part of the store and crouched in corners of the dressing rooms, texting each other frantically. The gunman, alerted by the quick exchange of jingles and vibrations from the phones, kicked the door open to the first dressing room. Kelsey was sitting up with her legs curled in front of her on a bench. She pulled her coat off a hook and held it in over her bare legs. Four or five pairs of jeans she had been trying on were scattered on the floor between her and the man. He pulled the coat down and stared at her. She glared back at him, never more serious in her life.

He pointed the gun at her head and slowly moved from side to side looking at her from different angles. She couldn't believe this was happening; all in a matter of seconds her life was again flipped upside down. He leaned the rifle in the corner, slipped off the backpack and walked toward her. In an instinctive rush she kicked him in the crotch with as much power as she had in her body. The kick struck the man perfectly and a loud moan welled from deep inside of him as his body buckled.

She lowered her shoulder and rammed into his bent-over body knocking him hard into the mirror at one end of the dressing room. Reflective silver fragments of the mirror rained down on the man lying on the floor. He reached for her leg as she grabbed her purse and fled past him and out of the dressing room, jumping over the bleeding body of the store manager. Her mother yelled for her. The gunman stood slowly, sick to his stomach. After a minute he slipped one strap of the backpack over his left shoulder and grabbed the gun. He made up his mind to add her to the victim list. He stepped back into the main part of the store scanning both left and right with his gun aimed and ready to fire at her. The gunman stepped over the young employee and fired two merciless kill shots at close range. Witnesses gasped at the senseless brutality.

A security officer who was monitoring the store video surveillance cameras when the incident began had watched the proceedings unfold through the cameras as he hurriedly pulled a bullet-proof vest over his shirt and got his handgun from a locker. He entered the main customer section of the store quietly from a metal door in the far corner of the room. His years of training and gun-range practice with paper targets paid off as his first two bullets struck the gunman in the chest, one inch apart. The impact knocked him off balance and his trigger finger instinctively reacted, firing an errant shot high into the front wall of the store. The security guard's third shot struck the man in the center of his forehead just below the edge of his stocking cap killing him instantly. The people witnessing the surreal event issued a collective inhalation and continued with panting breaths and shocked emotion. A cloud of gunfire smoke filled the quiet store. The security officer, a fit young man whose hands were shaking, spoke decisively into a radio microphone attached to his jacket.

"Suspect down," announced the security officer. "I need back-up and an ambulance to building 7-north. Repeat, suspect down. Request back-up and an ambulance to 7-north. Do you copy?"

An employee de-activated the security coverings to the store's doors and windows. A small army of law enforcement personnel faced the store and, as soon as they could, burst through the doors with their weapons in ready position. The patrons had their hands raised and many pointed to the area of concern near the hallway.

The stunned patrons of the store, slow to acknowledge what they had just witnessed, stood and gathered themselves and their belongings. They hugged family and friends and slowly acknowledged, somewhat is disbelief, that the situation was over and they were okay. Several of them started to clap for the security guard and immediately the others all burst into spontaneous applause as if they had just seen a sudden, surprise ending of a Broadway play. They called out their appreciation to the heroic security guard who had saved many lives by taking one. Mrs. Boyd wrapped her coat around Kelsey and hugged her hard with one arm.

"Are you okay?" she asked her daughter.

"I'm fine mom," said Kelsey "We've got to get Erin."

Her friend was hiding in the corner of the dressing room. Kelsey gathered her jeans from the adjoining dressing room and tugged them on. She knocked on the door of the room Erin was in. Erin heard Kelsey's voice and opened the door.

Kelsey said in a reassuring voice, "Erin, its okay. You can come out. It's all over."

The girls hugged and Erin asked, "What in the world happened?"

"This time I kicked the guy with the gun in the balls," Kelsey said.

37

THE LONG GRAVEL road that led back to the main building at the Fish and Game Club was lined with dense varieties of mature oak, ash and maple trees. Their limbs overhung the edges of the single lane with a canopy of vibrant fall hues. Brush and undergrowth obscured the view into the thick, primitive woods, also rich with low-hanging burnt-orange, sodden-brown and blood-red leaves of fall. The half-mile drive back to the parking area had the eerie, claustrophobic feel of watching a horror film.

Twenty of the forty-two teachers in the Low Field Local Schools who sat in the cabin exhibited an array of feelings from excitement to trepidation about the Concealed carry Class. Keith Byler had brought a few dozen donuts and two boxes of coffee-to-go for the participants. He introduced Bill Henry, the retired police officer who would lead them in the endeavor.

"Welcome to all of you," Bill started. "You are some of the bravest teachers in the state of Ohio and I'm proud to be working with you today. It will be a long day, but, together, we will make the students of Low Field among the safest and most protected children in the country. This morning we will be in the cabin covering the required information and knowledge components of the class and this afternoon we will be outside shooting on the range. Before we get started, a few housekeeping chores—the bathrooms are located in the back corner of the building, there, and we'll break every hour or so for five minutes to stretch or take a smoke break. Lunch will be brought in around 11:30 and we should finish about 5:30, just before dark. Any questions? Good, let's get started."

The class was conducted from a power point presentation created through a collaborative effort of the state and the NRA. The curriculum covered constitutional gun rights, the details of Ohio's concealed carry law, gun fundamentals and safety, and live practice with fire arms on the shooting range. The day progressed from a dry, mundane classroom presentation the teachers were all too familiar with to a day's end climax on the firing range that provided them with a heart-pumping rush of adrenaline.

Absolutely all of them, women and men, young and old, strong and frail, experienced and novice enjoyed firing the handguns on the range. The feeling of power and control was intoxicating, and everyone finished the class with the commitment to apply for the permit and to purchase a weapon, if they didn't already own one. They all vowed to join the F & G Club following the class and to visit the range together on a consistent basis for practice sessions. Some of them viewed it as much as an excuse for a social get-together with the evening ending pleasantly at The Airport Bar and Grill as they did a meaningful advancement of their joint initiative, but for others, the introduction to fire arms awakened something latent and instinctive in their souls—a proactive way to defend themselves against criminals and immoral people in society; in short, an equalizer against evil. In just one day they all experienced dramatic gains in their knowledge of gun safety and care as well as the increased ability to handle and shoot a gun with surprising skill and accuracy.

They thanked Bill and Keith for creating the synergy that made the day possible. This was going to change the environment of the school, and their working conditions, in such a significant manner that they couldn't believe they hadn't considered the idea sooner. Surely the superintendent and the board, with schools being such easy targets for maladjusted people to commit despicable acts against society's most vulnerable citizens, children, had to support the initiative to arm the teachers. Once the policy was passed and the information was disseminated throughout the community through word of mouth and the media, it would provide a sizable deterrent to anyone who ever considered attacking innocent people in the Low Field Local Schools. And, if a person was foolish enough to try, he or she would be met by numerous defenders of the students and staff, all prepared and willing to use lethal force to stop the intruder without mercy.

The teachers were proud of their new-found authority and were eager to continue to move forward with the plan until it was a reality. Their enthusiasm for the counterbalance to unnecessary violence was at an elevated pitch by the time they packed up their cars, exhausted yet exhilarated from their day. Everyone agreed to meet at The Airport for a drink. The teachers' union bought the first round and Keith Byler proposed a toast.

"Here's to the new armed guards at Low Field," Keith proclaimed. "May we always be ready to defend ourselves and our students!"

"Here, here!"

38

A CELL PHONE VIDEO of the store shooting went viral within a few hours. A young woman had been sending a text message when the lock-down announcement sent the store's visitors into a panic. She quickly started recording the incident while squatting for protection beside a display cabinet. As luck would have it, her position in the store was the perfect location to film the horrific three minutes that followed. The gunman actually moved from the far entrance to the store directly at the camera as he advanced closer to inspect the manager he had shot. His identity, intent and even the expression on his face was unmistakably clear in the amateur video.

The gunman disappeared from the camera's view briefly when he entered the dressing room, but returned to a spot barely a dozen feet from the videographer after killing the innocent worker who lay on the floor. Inadvertently, he positioned himself in perfect proximity of the camera when the climactic bullets from the security guard's gun ended the terror spree and his life. The video was even used by investigators after they downloaded it from the internet the next day. The store surveillance cameras captured the incident in its entirety but from an overhead perspective that did not possess the clarity and emotion of the customer's video. The natural instinct moviegoers demonstrate by willingly suspending their disbelief while viewing fictional violence, knowing that it is an imaginary trick of cinematography, is absent when watching similar raw footage of actual violence.

The internet video fascinated thousands of people, near and far, because it was real life, and death.

Once again a shooting in Ohio dominated the national news. It was nothing anyone in the state wanted to be known for, except the perpetrators of the violence. The imitators and sheep-like criminals who follow the leads of others, regardless of the ethical nature of the act, made the likelihood of copy-cat offenses an especially worrisome problem for law enforcement personnel following a highly publicized incident. Officials knew the only connection between the school and store shootings was the desire for notoriety by the second shooter. A distorted form of jealousy and competition sometimes bonds individuals to emulate one another in these cases. Police throughout the state continued to work in a heightened sense of alert while they patrolled and monitored their communities.

For Kelsey Boyd the after-effects of the experience caused a depression that made her feel both emotionally and physically sick. Immediately following her instinctively brave action to fight the store gunman and then flee from him, her body was charged with positive energy from the adrenaline that had pulsed through her system. But, in the days that followed, a quiet sense of fear regarding what might have happened that day resonated in her psyche. Her mind was full of unsettling thoughts that kept reoccurring and playing out with different, terrible endings. Her mom persisted in trying to put a positive spin on the event, but to no avail.

"Kelsey, you learned a lot about yourself by your actions. You're tough and you have a strong fighting spirit. When confronting the most serious danger a person can face, you decided you were going to survive no matter what," her mom said with encouragement. "Your reaction was perfect. You helped stop him and you probably saved many lives."

The comments were well intended but didn't make Kelsey feel any better. For all intents and purposes, the last two times she left the house she faced life and death situations. It was all too stressful for her to comprehend and deal with in a matter-of-fact, rational sensibility. When would it end? When would her life return to some resemblance of normalcy, she wondered?

In her bedroom, Kelsey turned on her computer and logged into her Contemporary Studies class of her online school. Within minutes she got immersed in the readings. Hours passed and she refused to allow herself to take a break, knowing it would just reopen the doors of her memory, returning her to the events of the past few weeks. Instead she read assignments, completed the study guides and passed the unit tests one section at a time until she finally collapsed late in the evening, falling asleep without eating dinner or getting ready for bed.

Stephanie listened to the message on the answer machine from the police deputy. She was alarmed to hear that the police had discovered the acts of toilet paper and mail box vandalism had been the work of Clayton and Roy Caldwell. She wanted to tell Kelsey, but her better judgment made her wait. Mrs. Boyd understood that Kelsey needed the time and space to work through the aftermath of her recent ordeals on her own terms. She looked in on her daughter once that evening to see how she was doing with her homework and, seeing Kelsey asleep, she left her alone to battle the demons in her memory.

39

THE INFORMATION DESK attendant instructed Travis to pick up Colton near a door around the corner of the hospital's emergency room. The large space was the first parking spot outside the exit, a space usually saved for an important visitor or reserved for the disabled. A sign designated the area specifically for people to *drop off or pick up patients*. When Travis got to Colton's room, a nurse was reviewing discharge instructions with his friend. She gave him a prescription bottle and the papers. The two exchanged a fist bump and Travis handed Colton a bag containing a neatly folded pair of jeans, a t-shirt and a hoodie.

"Remember to call your doctor later today to schedule an appointment, Colton." She continued, "He needs to check your blood work and examine you every week for a while; okay?"

"Yes, ma'am. Thank you."

"You take care, Colton," said the nurse. "Mr. Tucker is our attendant today and he will take you downstairs in a wheelchair; it's a hospital requirement."

She motioned to the young man in hospital scrubs to position the wheelchair for Colton. She touched Colton on the shoulder as he left the room and the three men got on the empty elevator.

The attendant spoke. "Well no more excitement for you from now on, you here?"

"I'm with you on that," Colton said. "No more surprises."

They took the elevator down to the exit. Colton shook the man's hand.

"Thanks," Colton said to the attendant.

"Sure. Good luck to you."

They were driving to Low Field. The truck windows were cracked and Travis was trying to find a clear station on the radio.

"So, how are you doing?"

"Honestly Travis, I don't think I've ever been worse," confessed Colton.

Colton and he had been friends since grade school. Their usual routine was to talk about girls, guns and games, but today was very different. Colton was in the truck but it was obvious to Travis that his mind was somewhere else, far away. Travis couldn't imagine what his friend was thinking. The silence was awkward but he respected that Colton was reconciling himself with his new reality—the terms of which unimaginably sucked.

"You hungry? There's a drive-thru just past the light," Travis offered.

"Sure; sounds good."

They got their order and arranged it the way they always did sharing the cup holders and balancing the open wrappers on their laps as they ate. The bags were on the floor between their feet, ready for the imminent waste wrappers and used napkins. The road became more rural, changing from a constant succession of stores to single houses, increasing separated by more green space. The reception of their favorite country station was strong and clear, but Travis kept the music turned down so Colton could be at peace with his thoughts.

Colton broke the silence by asking his friend, "Do you know where Clayton and my dad are?"

"Last I heard Clayton is staying at your grandparent's house and I think your dad is still in jail," replied Travis.

"Good god. What were those two dumbasses thinking?"

"I don't know, man," said Travis. The only thing I can think of is they were trying to get back at Kelsey and Daron for you."

"Some help. Travis, would you mind stopping at my grandparent's place?" asked Colton. "I need to see Clayton."

"Okay, no problem," Travis replied.

The miles went by as silently as the conversation between them. Travis decided to just sit back and listen to the radio. There was no point in forcing the issue with Colton; he would talk when he was ready. Treat others the way you would want to be treated he thought.

"I'm sorry Travis. I know you've got better things to be doing with your day than driving me around," Colton said.

"I've got all day Colt. We can go wherever you want to go."

"Thanks. You're my best friend. I appreciate your help," Colton replied.

There was a heartfelt pause and then Travis said, "Yeah, but don't get all broke-back mountain on me now. I don't want to cry in front of you."

"Okay you stupid prick," laughed Colton.

Colton lightly smacked the brim on Travis's cap knocking it off his head. They both smiled and sat back in their seats, relaxing for the last few miles to Colton's grandparent's place.

Colton turned up the radio a bit and said, "Man I hate to say it but I could really use a good-old Randy Travis song right now."

40

WILL HAD PLAYED high school golf matches against Luke Redmond six times over the past three years. Since their sophomore years, both boys had represented their respective schools as the number one players. Luke attended Harrison Hills, one of Low Field's biggest conference rivals. Will held the edge four to two in their head-to-head nine hole school matches but the scores and matches were always close. Many times the winner was determined on the final hole. This season as seniors, they split their two dual matches, each player winning on his home course, but Will had won the most important event of the season, the eighteen hole sectional tournament individual medalist honors a few weeks ago over Luke who finished as the runner-up. As a result both qualified for the district golf tournament the following week. The field was made up from the lowest individual qualifiers from the area's four sectional tournaments the previous week, as well as the top two teams from each of the sectional competitions. At districts, Luke played his best golf of the fall, shooting an even par 72 to win the individual medalist honors which qualified him for the state tournament in Columbus. It was the same district tournament Will courageously played shortly after the shooting at Low Field.

Since being paired together in a summer tournament, they had started to exchange emails and text messages out of mutual respect for one another. They wished each other good luck before matches, kept in touch regarding their match results during the season and compared notes about course management strategies for unfamiliar venues that would benefit each other in upcoming matches. After Will had been shot, however, the emails became more personal and their friendship grew stronger. They started rooting for each other as if they were teammates. Being the two best golfers in the area bonded them together on a level that exceeded school loyalty and transcended high school golf—they were serious players who aspired for more from golf than simply a few high school memories. They talked about college teams and coaches and they shared their personal goals and dreams for the future with one another. So, even though Will didn't qualify for state, it was natural that he wanted to attend the tournament and support Luke.

Rocky Creek Golf Club, a new course north of Columbus, was hosting the tournament this year. Luke had sent Will an email the night before describing Thursday's practice round as a nightmare. Wind gusts of over 40 miles an hour and a high temperature of only 44 degrees made play that day almost impossible, and the greens were rolling so fast that Luke estimated he had 3-putted as many as eight times during the round. The course was hilly and errant shots resulted in difficult recoveries because of the severity of the drop-offs on one side of most fairways and deep collection areas around the greens. The land was open and exposed to the elements. Luke made the comment to Will that the architect *must have been on crack* when he designed the course to make the majority of the eighteen holes so difficult. Luckily, Will's leg was feeling much better just one week after the district tournament, and he looked forward to once again being on a course, even it was only to watch Luke play his first round from the comfort of a golf cart.

Will and his dad got up early and drove to Columbus the morning of the first day of the two days of competition. On the way they passed countless miles of farmland divided into neat squares and rectangles of crops, stretching on either side of the highway, in uniform heights and different hues of dying brown. An occasional water tower stood tall above the fields. Each one reminded Will of an oversized golf ball on an enormous tee. The drive seemed longer than it actually was because of Will's anticipation of the event and his desire to connect with his friend before the round. Luke was in one of the early groups that morning. They arrived too late to talk to him on the practice range while he warmed-up. Will spotted Luke on the putting green and decided to wait for him in an area he would walk past on his way to the first tee box. Will wanted to say hello and wish him well before Luke's name was called by a tournament official to start his round.

"Hey, you made it," Luke greeted Will.

They shook hands and bumped chests together. Luke continued, "Thanks for coming."

"Wouldn't miss this for anything," Will said.

"Well, I hope you brought your hiking boots because this place is a beast to walk. There are a few places, though, where you can see quite a few holes without having to walk the whole course. You'll see what I mean when you get out there," Luke informed his friend.

"It's not a problem; my dad got us a cart," Will said pointing to his father who was sitting in a golf cart on the concrete path near the first hole. "How are you swinging today? You okay and ready to go?"

"Yep; had a good warm-up, but this place is about survival," Luke said. " I don't think anyone is going low here—in fact, right now I'd bet over par wins."

"Well, that plays into your strength," said Will. "Just make a bunch of pars and let everyone else fall back."

"That's exactly what I was thinking—be patient and play solid, conservative golf, at least for today. Hey, lots of coaches here—keep your eyes open," Luke said to Will.

"Go get 'em, Luke."

When they introduced Luke on the first tee, Will gulped with emotion. He was happy for Luke but at the same time, jealous that his name wouldn't be called this day. Luke's opening drive was struck solidly and landed in the center of the fairway. Will and his dad followed the group, riding slowly down the cart path. After the first two holes they found a vantage point where they could see Luke play the next few holes. They sat at a high point between several holes and watched him make all pars on the opening four holes. Luke continued to pay solid, steady golf and he made the turn at one over par.

Weather conditions worsened during Luke's playing of the back nine. The wind freshened and a light, misty rain made it necessary for the players and spectators to open their umbrellas. There was a shelter behind the twelfth green that Will and his dad decided to use as their viewing base for the initial holes on the back side. Many other people had the same idea. Will was using a pair of binoculars to watch Luke putt out on number eleven. A man who had seen the Low Field Golf embroidery on Will's fleece pullover walked up to him.

"Excuse me, are you Will Harper?" the man asked.

"Yes sir," answered Will.

"I thought so," he said. "I'm David Hughes; I'm the golf coach at Pine Grove College near Cincinnati."

"Hi; nice to meet you," Will replied. "This is my father, Tom Harper."

"Hello; pleasure to meet you," said Will's dad.

The coach turned back to Will and said, "Congratulations on your win at the sectionals Will. That was really well played."

"Thanks."

"I was very sorry to hear about the shooting," said Coach Hughes. "How are you feeling?"

"The leg is healing okay," Will said, "but I'd feel better if I was out there."

"Sure. So tell me, have you made a commitment to play in college yet?"

"No sir."

"Well, I don't know if you'd be interested but I've got one opening for next year's team and it has a partial scholarship attached to it. PGC is a Division III school of about 1,500 students. We offer lots of four-year degree programs and we play both a fall and spring season, mostly conference play in the five-state area," said the coach. "Here's one of my cards. You're welcome to come down and visit if you'd like—just give me a call a week or so before and I'll make the arrangements."

"Thank you," Will said. "Are you going to be here tomorrow?"

"I'm not sure. I'm meeting with a few players tonight," the coach admitted. "I might be here tomorrow or I'm not sure."

"Okay. Thank you," said Will. "I'll talk with my dad tonight about visiting and let you know."

"Sounds great," said Coach Hughes. "Nice meeting you, Will; Mr. Harper."

When Will finally cleared the excitement from his head and tried to spot Luke, he realized enough time had passed for Luke to have played right past them. He was now on the fourteenth hole. It was raining heavier. They decided to wait for the rain to let up and then make their way back to the clubhouse where they could watch Luke finish the last two holes. While they were on their way, they passed the Ohio State Coach.

"Hi Coach, I'm Will Harper from Low Field High School near Akron. We met at the AJGA tournament in Dayton last summer; I mean two summers ago," Will said nervously.

"Hi, nice to see you, Will," said the man.

The coach kept walking, obviously not interested in spending any more time than had already transpired exchanging greetings.

"Wow, that sucked," Will said. "He blew me off like I was nothing."

"Pretty rude but that's his reputation," said Mr. Harper. "He's only interested in players who he thinks can help him and his program. He's probably looking at recruits for two or three years out; it's not worth thinking about, Will."

They shook the rain off of their jackets and umbrellas and found a spot to watch Luke putt on seventeen and to play the eighteenth hole. Only a few groups' scores had been posted on the large score sheets taped to the windows in the restaurant. The tables and chairs were filling up with soggy spectators trying to dry out and get warm.

Luke pared the final hole of his round and put his soaked bag under a covered porch with those of the other players before entering the tournament scoring area. He and his playing partners exchanged scorecards and checked them for accuracy before signing them. They stood and shook hands. Luke talked to his coach, then they and his parents came into the restaurant area.

"How'd you end up?" Will asked shaking Luke's cool, damp hand.

"79; a tough, grinding 79," Luke said. It was pretty nasty out there."

"Actually that's probably going to end up being a pretty good score today," Will said. "I mean that was an ugly weather and nobody that I've seen was even close to par."

"Wow, you're right," Luke said scanning the large score sheets for results. "79 is tied for low round so far, but there are still a lot of guys out there."

"That's good playing, Luke," another player said to Luke as he shook his hand.

Luke's mom and dad approached the table.

"Luke, do you want to stick around here or head out and find some place to get dinner?" she asked.

Luke thought for a moment and said, "Um, let's get out of here."

"Would you fellows like to join us?" asked Luke's father.

Will looked at his father and nodded yes silently.

They looked at Luke's parents and said in unison, "Sure, thanks."

41

AT ONE TIME, when Colton was little, his grandparent's place used to be a working farm. His Grandpa Clyde had a regular job at a small machine shop near Watson City but also carried on the traditions of the family farm for many years. He used to like to walk with his grandpa and their dog Lucky to check the great expanse of corn plants that grew in neat rows throughout the wide, rolling field that stretched far behind the barn. If he was there at feeding time, his tall, thin grandfather would have him climb on a wooden section of fence near the barn and ring the bell signaling feeding time to the animals. He would watch the small herd of cattle that usually grazed lazily in the fenced area that ran for many acres along the two roads that framed the southwest corner of the property move together with slow purpose toward the muddy side of the barn that sheltered a long feed trough. His grandpa would talk to the large animals as if they were his children, and Colton would laugh at the cows when they passed gas or went to the bathroom matter-of-factly and without concern of where they stood.

One year his grandparents didn't replace the herd that was taken to market and then sold most of the acreage of both fields to a neighboring farmer to the north. The fence slowly disappeared over the years and both fields were combined into a large hay field. Occasionally, the new owner would plow and plant the farmland with a more profitable crop. Colton and his brother enjoyed those years because the planted field made the property that surrounded their grandparent's house and out-buildings once again look like a working farm. A faded photograph of their mother's homestead hung proudly above the fireplace mantle in their living room. For Colton, the picture conjured happy boyhood memories of sledding, horse riding and holiday feasts at his grandparents.

Travis pulled down the driveway to the wide parking area between the house and the barn. Colton got out of the truck and petted the dog that barked a greeting to them. He waived to his grandpa who bounced back and forth on the small riding mower along the edge of his now two-acre farm. Travis said he'd wait outside. Colton knocked and went in the side door of the house.

"Hello? Grandma Clare, it's Colton," he said loudly.

"Hi, honey; sit down," she said, "I'll get you something to eat."

His grandmother had suffered a stroke a few years back. Her face never regained its simple, hardened symmetry, and she pulled her left leg slightly, like a broom, as she walked. His grandpa hung his coat on a hook in the back hallway. The couple, now in their early eighties and exhausted from a hard life, sat at the kitchen table and talked with Colton.

Clayton had been staying with them for the past few days after he had appeared in Juvenile Court and the judge remanded him to their custody for the time being since his father was in jail. Clayton had returned to school for the first time since last week, but they expressed concern about him because he hadn't said much of anything since learning of their mom's death. Like everyone, he was in shock, but he was the youngest in the family at seventeen, so his unwillingness to express his feelings outwardly was disconcerting to them. During supper he wouldn't converse. He just ate quietly, maintaining a forlorn, depressed look. His grandma had called the high school and talked to the principal about the situation, and he assured them the counselor would spend some time with Clayton at school today. Moreover, Pastor Mike was coming by before dinner to talk to them about the funeral arrangements and he offered to talk to Clayton as well. They all cried for a while as they talked and tried to make sense of their family tragedy.

"Travis's going to drop me off at home and I'll go see the lawyer this afternoon," Colton said. "I'll try find out what's going on with dad too. I'd like to talk to him, if they'll let me."

"His court hearing is either this afternoon or tomorrow; I don't remember which," said his grandfather. For the past few years he had trouble remembering things.

"Well, I'll see what I can find out and I'll stop back later to see you and Clay," he told them.

His grandmother said, "Come for dinner, Colton—about five o'clock, but I can hold it if you're running late so take your time."

"Okay, I'll be back as close to five as I can," he said.

They stood and he hugged both of his grandparents. He blotted his eyes on the sleeve of his jacket and shook his head from side to side.

"Love you," his grandma said touching his cheek with her frail, boney hand.

"Love you, too."

42

ATTORNEY MORRIS'S SECRETARY told Colton that his father's arraignment was scheduled that afternoon between 1:00-4:00 in the east courtroom of the Low Field County Courthouse. Judge Stevenson was to hear the criminal case and Attorney Morris was already at the courthouse. Travis took Colton home and he quickly changed into dress clothes. They hustled downtown in hopes of seeing his dad. Colton passed through the screening station just inside the doorway and caught a glimpse of the attorney standing in the wide hallway outside the large, oak courtroom doors. Colton walked briskly to the man.

"Hey, Mr. Morris," Colton said, "is my dad here?"

"Not yet," answered the stately attorney. "The officers will bring him over from the jail when his case is the next one to be heard by the judge. How are you feeling Colton?"

"I'm better," responded the young man. "Are you going to be able to get him released? I mean we need to have my mom's funeral, and he should be there."

"Yes I know. I'm sorry about your mom, Colton. Today the plan is to have your dad plead guilty to a reduced misdemeanor charge and ask the court for his immediate release, possibly with a fine and probation or community service. Something other than jail time because of the family's situation. Hopefully the judge will agree," he said.

Mr. Caldwell appeared in the hallway wearing the standard bright orange jumpsuit. He was escorted by a sheriff deputy dressed in grey slacks, a black shirt and wide-brimmed black hat. The uniform was embossed with gold lettering, pins and badges that reflected the overhead light like glittering stars. Colton, visibly agitated with rising emotion, approached him causing the officer to pause not knowing his intention.

"Dad, what were you thinking? Are you crazy?!" said Colton.

"Shut up, Colton," said his father sternly. "This is not the time or the place."

The deputy raised his hand with a stop gesture and glared at Colton.

"Not the time?" Colton continued loudly. "Mom's dead, Clay's a mess and this isn't the time. We can't even plan her funeral because you're in jail, for god's sake. What a mess you've created!"

"Colton, that's enough," barked his upset father.

The attorney stepped up to them. Colton's head started to hurt.

"Colton, why don't you take a walk so I can talk to your dad?" suggested Attorney Morris. "You can sit in the courtroom during the arraignment and then we'll meet out here afterwards."

A few minutes later inside the courtroom the attorney and defendant were called in front of the judge.

"State your name."

"Roy Caldwell."

The judge looked down and read the court documents in his hands and then said, "You have been charged with two counts of criminal trespassing, two counts of hate crimes, two counts of contributing to the delinquency of a minor and one count of illegal use of the internet."

"Your honor, if I might," asked Attorney Morris.

"Yes, go ahead," granted the judge.

"Your honor, my client acknowledges his participation in these offenses; but these irresponsible acts were performed by a man whose family is mired in extraordinary emotional turmoil which, in this case, impaired his judgment. Please note that neither of the victims chose to press charges in this matter. It is my opinion that the police overstated the allegations. I'm therefore asking the court to consider reducing the charges against my client to a misdemeanor offense of criminal vandalism, and in exchange, my client is willing to plead guilty and to make full restitution for any damages as well as serve probation or perform any community service that the court deems worthy in this case.

The judge paused considering the attorney's request.

Attorney Morris added, "Excuse me your honor, it's also important for me to inform the court that, tragically, the defendant's wife was killed less than two days ago and that he has two sons living at home. The three of them need to plan a funeral for Mr. Caldwell's wife and the boys' mother. This is a family in pain. They need time to grieve and support each other. So, again, based on my client's record of only one prior case many years ago, I respectfully ask that the court consider my request for a reduced charge."

The judge looked up from the papers in front of him, lowered his glasses on his nose and looked sternly at the haggard man clad in orange.

"Mr. Caldwell, do you understand the serious nature of the charges that have been brought against you and the problems you've caused for your family?" asked the judge.

"Yes sir."

Judge Stevenson continued, "I don't know what bad judgment led to your involvement in the charges that have been brought against you here today, but let me say sir that I hope you recognize the possible ramifications this arraignment could have on you as an individual and the detrimental impact a guilty verdict could have on your family. If the court were to grant you leniency by accepting your plea to a reduced charge, it would be the court's hope, sir, that you would use the opportunity to spend your time more wisely, both providing for your family and supplying a higher quality of fatherly guidance to your sons. Do you understand what I just said?"

"Yes sir."

"Do you have anything to say, Mr. Caldwell?" the judge asked.

"Only that I understand what you said and that I apologize for what happened, your honor. It will never happen again," promised Roy.

The judge paused again contemplating his course of action. He took only several minutes but the time seemed much longer.

"Let the court records reflect the original charges against the defendant. Because of the special circumstances surrounding this case and the defendant's offer to plead guilty to a lesser charge, the court is willing to reduce the charges to two counts of criminal harassment with a $3,000 fine and two years of probation," said Judge Stevenson. "Mr. Caldwell, how do you plead to the charges?"

Roy whispered something to his attorney who nodded and then he simply said, "Guilty."

"Based on the defendant's plea and given the unusual state of affairs surrounding this case that have been enumerated by the defense, the court finds the defendant guilty of two counts of criminal harassment and sentences the defendant to two years of probation and fines the defendant $3,000. Case dismissed, and my sympathies to your family," said the judge.

The gavel ended the brief hearing with a loud crack.

43

L UKE WAS TIED for sixth place at the conclusion of round one. After dinner they met back in Luke's hotel room and the boys checked the OHSAA website to see the players' scores from today and the list of tee times for tomorrow. Luke's equipment was spread around the room—his clubs leaning against chairs and walls, his rain suit and clothes hung over lamps, his umbrella open in a corner and his shoes and the contents of his bag stacked on the window heating unit, all drying out. The friends had a good time reviewing the day's round and spending time together. Around 9:30 their dads came up to the room. They agreed to meet downstairs in the lobby for breakfast at eight which would leave enough time to check out and get to the course early enough for Luke to properly warm-up before his 10:15 tee time. All four were exhausted from the day and slept well, in spite of the saggy hotel mattresses.

The morning sun had burned off the early fog from the hollows in the undulating countryside around the golf course. On the driving range, it didn't take long for Luke to find a smooth rhythm to his swing, and he struck shot after shot solidly and with precision. He talked with his father and Will while he worked through his bag to his longer clubs. His coach and another man approached Luke as he completed his full swing warm-up and was returning his clubs to his bag. The fit, younger man had the look of a golf professional and introduced himself as the assistant coach at Mid-Valley State.

"Nice to meet you Luke; that was a solid round yesterday given the conditions," the man said.

"Thanks."

"Well, the weather's a lot better today, so you should have more fun out there. Your golf swing looks very great."

"Thanks coach," Luke said. "If you really want to see a great swing, you should watch my friend Will swing a club." Luke gestured to Will with his thumb.

"Alright, hi Will, I'm Kevin Mitchell," said the coach smiling and shaking Will's hand, "but it doesn't look like you're playing today."

Luke quickly inserted a comment to spare Will an awkward explanation, "He should be playing. He beats my butt most of the time, but he ran into some bad luck. I'm going to the putting green to hit some putts; nice to meet you coach."

"Hey, play well bud," said Will. "We'll be out there."

"Yep I'll look for you," Luke said.

Luke and his two-person entourage gathered his equipment and left for the putting green.

"So where are you from Will?" asked Coach Mitchell.

"I played for Low Field," answered Will.

"Low Field; where's that?" he asked.

"It's just north of Harrison City, where Luke's from," explained Will. "Our schools are in the same conference."

"Okay, well, I'll tell you what; here's one of my cards with my email address. If you're interested in MVS, why don't you send me your stats and tournament results for the past few years and I'll take a look at them," offered the coach. "And if you or your coaches have any videos of your swing that you can email to me, that would be helpful too."

"Sure, I can do that," said Will with nervous excitement.

"Great. It was nice to meet you and I'll look forward to getting those emails," said Coach Mitchell.

The coach shook his hand and walked further down the range. He stopped and watched another player and chatted with his coach. Will's dad whistled and waved for him to join him on the way to the first tee. Will was excited. Mid-Valley State wasn't too far away and their golf team had a strong tradition of winning. It was nice of Luke to shift the coach's attention to him. Colton's act of violence had robbed Will of one of the most important opportunities of his life, but, maybe Luke had given him one back. For the first time all week, his anger about the shooting was replaced by something positive—a chance to prove to himself and to others that he could play the game at the next level, college.

Luke got off to a rough start bogeying the first three holes in succession. He started pressing, trying to make up the strokes too quickly and three putted from fifteen feet on the fifth hole. Will tried to calm him down by saying the word *"patience"* loud enough for Luke to hear as he walked past them to the next tee. Luke was getting frustrated with himself but Will knew he would only further complicate his woes if he played too aggressively. The pins were tucked into corners of the greens and the set-up from tee to green was very difficult.

At the turn, Luke had fallen back to the middle of the field, having shot a mediocre forty-one. It just wasn't his day. The timing of his swing was off just a little, and he was missing shots both to the right and the left with his driver and having to hit approach shots from the heavy, wet rough that hadn't been cut for days because of rain. Almost half the field of other players passed him on the leaderboard. By the day's end, Luke had only hit five greens in regulation and his short game wasn't sharp enough to save his round. He shot a disappointing eighty-three and finished the state tournament in thirty-seventh place.

He was visibly upset when Will approached him after his round.

"God, I can't believe I played so badly today," Luke said angrily. "I just sucked today!"

"Hey, it happens; you know that," Will said knowing his words were of no benefit. "It can be a brutally cruel game."

"My only chance at state and I blew it," Luke complained.

"Hey, at least you had your chance."

"Sorry," Luke said, "I didn't mean it that way, Will."

"No, I didn't either," said Will. "I mean you should be proud. You're one of the best golfers in the state of Ohio. Don't beat yourself up over today. You just didn't have your best stuff. You know it happens to everyone; even the best players in the world struggle from day to day."

"I know," Luke said, "but it still sucks."

"Hey, I'm proud of you. You represented your school and our conference in the state tournament; there's something to be said for that. When you're an old man, you can talk about your glory days playing in the state golf tournament," Will said.

"Yeah, I guess so," Luke said forcing a smile.

"In fact, you'll probably tell your grandkids that you almost won the thing," Will joked.

Luke shook his head and laughed, feeling better. The boys' fathers were talking in the parking lot. Will's dad called to them.

"Hey Will, you about ready to go?" he asked.

"Sure. Hey Luke, congratulations on playing at state," Will said as he softly slapped his friend on the arm. "I'll send you a text or email you. I might need your help taking a video of my swing for that coach from Mid-Valley; maybe we can get together next week?"

"Cool. I was thinking about breaking all of my clubs but maybe I'll wait until winter," Luke said with a smile.

They shook hands and headed to their respective cars. Will's gait remained slightly hobbled and he had to lift his left leg as he positioned himself in the front passenger side of the vehicle. Their dads also shook hands.

"Safe travels," said one father.

"You the same," said the other.

44

T HE BOARD OF Education President, Mr. Fitzpatrick, returned the superintendent's phone call near the end of the school day. Jim Collins had just finished drafting a Press Release announcing the upcoming Town Hall Meeting and was anxious to have his secretary fax it to the respective television and print media before the end of the work day. Laura buzzed him:

"Mr. Fitzpatrick is on line two," L J said.

"Thank you." Jim said, "Hey John, thanks for getting back to me."

"Good afternoon Jim," John said, "how are you?"

"Pretty well thanks; I needed to talk to you about a few things. First of all, everyone's schedule is clear for the Town Hall Meeting next Thursday so I just wanted to verify the agenda with you, if you have a minute," said the superintendent.

"Sure."

He read the Press Release over the phone. The stated topic for the meeting was *Low Field's Response to School Violence: An Open Forum*. They discussed the proposed agenda—a series of speakers making brief remarks limited to five minutes each that included the two of them, Chief Hadley, several parents, the Student Resource Officer and Keith Byler. Then the floor would be open to the public for comments and/or questions directed at the panel members. Either Jim or John would serve as the meeting's moderator.

"Sounds good," said the board president. I think we should arrange for a few off-duty deputies to be there for security purposes."

"I agree," said Jim, "in fact I already asked the chief to have several cruisers parked in visible areas of the parking lots and to have one of his people positioned outside too."

"I like that," John agreed. "We'll probably have a big crowd and, as you are well aware, these types of meetings can easily get out of control."

Jim laughed, "Yeah, I can't say I'm looking forward to it, but, frankly, I would like everyone to express their honest opinions and say whatever is on their mind. It doesn't do us any good to script this meeting to go in a particular direction. Let's just get the topic out there in front of everyone and hear the different ideas."

"That's fine. Do you know what direction Keith is going in with his remarks?" asked John.

"No, but we're meeting after school today," Jim said looking at his watch. "In fact, he should be here any time now."

The board president cautioned the superintendent by saying, "I think the emergency levy and the contract stalemate should be off limits during this one, though. Do you agree?"

"Definitely," said Jim. "We'll probably have to work hard to enforce that during the meeting, but I'll make that point and see if I can get an agreement from Keith to stay away from that topic. We don't want to bait and switch the community at this one by turning the meeting into a levy campaign stump. This topic is too important to muddy with our funding problems and contract disputes. And we still have a few weeks to make our final push for the levy renewal before the November election."

"By the way, we need to discuss those cuts you are proposing at the Board meeting. It's important to remind the board members and the people in attendance about the serious problem we have if this levy goes down again," said the board president. "Didn't you say we only have one more opportunity to place the levy on the ballot as a renewal after the November election? And if it fails again the state will come in and take over the district?"

"Well, it's actually more complicated than that, but yes, what you just said is the most probable scenario." The superintendent continued, "We've already lost the second half of the tax revenue produced by the levy this school year and if it doesn't pass next month we will lose the entire amount next fiscal year, meaning the state will force us to make cuts to staff and programs in an equal dollar amount so we can balance the budget. In other words, the budget must be neutral or else we're operating the district through deficit spending and that's against the law. So, the levy is worth two million bucks. And the timelines of the contract force the board to make the cuts in anticipation for next school year before the May election. So, the way I see it, all hell will break loose this spring if the levy fails next month."

"Somehow we have to get that message across to our parents," said John.

"That's very true; but they're a shrinking number of the community, and half of them are mad at us, too. Speaking of that, before Keith gets here I wanted to give you a heads-up that we got a notice of the first lawsuit because of the shooting," said Jim.

"What do you mean exactly?" asked John.

"It's a bit of a surprise but we're being sued by Colton's father on behalf of his son," said the superintendent.

"What? How's that even possible? We should be suing him," said John. "On what grounds is he suing us?"

"We were served with the complaint this morning basically informing us that his attorney has filed a personal injury claim against the district. I scanned the paperwork before I forwarded it to our attorney. In essence it claims that we were negligent in failing to protect Colt from the repeated head injuries he suffered while playing high school football at Low Field which caused his condition to worsen and led to permanent traumatic brain damage," said Jim.

"Do we still have the signed parental consent forms?" asked the board president."

"I sent the Athletic Director an email about it," said Jim. "He doubts that we have them but he's going to check his records after school."

"So what do these injuries have to do with him bringing a gun on school ground and firing it into a crowd?" John asked.

"The way I read the document, they're basically claiming the brain injuries have resulted in a permanent medical condition for Colton that has caused him to lose consciousness when he is under stress or emotionally upset and when that happens his judgment is impaired and he is unable to control his thoughts and actions in the way a reasonable person would. So it gives him a blanket excuse for his actions and basically turns the shooting into our fault," Jim laughed sarcastically. "I mean, it's a lawsuit John; it doesn't mean he's going to win the litigation."

"Wow, I expected some legal response to the shooting but certainly not from the Caldwells," said the board president.

"I know, but let's face it, there's a long way to go on this stuff. We'll be lucky if Abby and Will's parents don't also file a suit against the district," said the superintendent. "This is the first one and I just wanted you to know about it."

"Sure; one more thing to keep us awake at night," John said.

The superintendent stood looking out his office window. He tipped his head to the empty-handed man walking down the sidewalk toward the door of the board offices. Jim said to John, "Keith is coming. If you don't mind I better go."

"Okay," said John.

"Have a good weekend," laughed the superintendent.

45

KEITH AND JIM could have been friends except for the positions they held in the school district's hierarchy. Representing labor and management pushed their perspectives and interests to opposite ends of the spectrum professionally, and the history of bitter conflicts and struggles inherent in the nature of their respective roles created a chiasmic divide between them that neither man could overcome. Over time they had come to a common, unspoken understanding that their antagonistic relationship was just business, nothing personal. They shook hands and greeted each other out of a courteous sense of obligation.

"Thanks for coming," Jim said motioning for Keith to have a seat at the table.

"Sure."

They discussed the agenda of the Town Hall Meeting. As always, Jim stressed his main concern for the timing and pace of the event. Sixty to ninety minutes was the targeted length for the meeting. Therefore, it was paramount for each speaker to limit his or her remarks to approximately three to five minutes, but he also assured Keith that he was free to stretch his allotted minutes so long as was necessary to express his proposal as long as he stayed on topic. This meeting was not the time or place to discuss the upcoming levy renewal or the contract dispute between the teachers' union and the board of education.

Keith looked at Jim and said, "We think the community will love our solution to the school security issue here at Low Field."

"I hope so," said Jim, "but let's face it Keith, they don't seem to love anything we do."

"This will be different; we can save money and make the schools safer," Keith said.

Jim moved uncomfortably in his squeaky chair and said, "Frankly Keith, I find the idea of having a bunch of teachers with guns in our schools to be a frightening proposition."

"I'm sure you do, but I think at least three board members disagree with you," Keith added.

"Remember, any and all policy changes start with a recommendation from the superintendent," Jim cautioned.

"There have been instances to the contrary," Keith countered.

"Oh, is that right?" said Jim.

"Yes that's right," Keith said confidently, "check with your attorney."

"Listen, I'm willing to consider any reasonable idea that can help the district, so don't assume you know what my thoughts are regarding the gun proposal," Jim stated. "I'm really trying to keep an open mind on this issue."

"Good because we've got to get this levy passed. The teachers are working without a contract, and the wage freeze and medical concessions we took for the three years of the last contract have made us fall way behind the average for the county. We are close to a breaking point here. We can't do any more to help without a new contract and an increase in pay," Keith said pointedly.

"Well, if the levy fails next month, the cuts will have to be very deep to achieve the savings the state will demand—it will affect many programs and positions," Jim said.

"You better start by cutting services—services provided by classified staff. The basic premise of a school is students and teachers; not busing and lunch and an SRO and high-priced administrators. Those need to be your first cuts," Keith stated. "And your contract is a public record too."

"I know your point of view Keith," the superintendent said. "We've been through this many times, but let's not turn this meeting into a negotiations session. We're not going to solve those problems today."

"Sure, but you need to know where we stand. The teaching staff does a great job and we love our students," Keith said. "We deserve to be rewarded for our loyalty to this district, not screwed by it. If the levy goes down, you're going to have another strike on your hands."

"Well then, let's get the levy passed. I've got a newsletter going out that has great information from the treasurer and explains the academic improvement we've made as a district," Jim said.

"Are there pictures? I mean pictures of the kids? That's what people like to see," Keith offered. "Whatever publications you create need to have pictures of smiling kids having successes at school."

"Sure, we've got some of that with the financial information," Jim said.

"Good, because people don't read the information," said the union president.

"But we have to provide it," Jim said. "If we don't give them the facts, we get accused of trying to keep secrets from the public."

"Look, we get criticized no matter what," Keith said. "We are trying a few things before election day: there's a spaghetti dinner fundraiser for Abby Frazier this Sunday afternoon and we'll have a levy booth there; we're going door to door with a bunch of middle and high school students next Saturday to pass out literature that we produced; and we have parents handing out buttons and fact sheets at some stores during the next two weekends. So we're doing our part."

"That sounds great," Jim said. "Thanks."

"Yeah, sure. Hey, I'm late for practice. You might consider making personal phone calls to homes about the levy. The administrators and the classified staff need to do something for this levy campaign too," Keith suggested. As he stood he looked down at Jim and said, "If the levy goes down, we all go down."

46

ONCE A MONTH, the charter school Classrooms Without Boundaries hosted a social event for their students and parents. The school's operating license spanned the entire state of Ohio, so on these occasions they divided the state into four quadrants and faculty members traveled to centralized locations in each of the four areas in order to allow the students in that region to come together, meet their teachers and socialize with other students—experiences they missed while completing assignments electronically via a computer in their homes. It wasn't much, but everyone involved in the school concurred that the monthly socials were invaluable components of the overall program. The students said it made them feel connected to the school in a different, yet meaningful way.

Daron didn't go to Florida. Instead, when his computer and printer arrived, he completed the set-up and established a connection with his new school. He immediately set his sights on the goal of finishing the four credits he needed to graduate from high school as quickly as possible. He had spoken to an Army recruiter already and was seriously considering that option if he decided not to attend college right away. School had never been a passion for him, although since transferring to Low Field in the ninth grade, his grade point average was a respectable 3.3 on a 4.0 scale. Everyone had always treated him with politeness in high school, but he never fully related to other students due in part to his failed attempts to participate in extra-curricular activities or sports.

One spring he attended an Environmental Club Volunteer Day and worked cleaning up litter in the Low Field Community Park for the upcoming summer season, but he thought the advisor played favorites with the pretty girls, and in general was an odd person with whom he really didn't want to spend his free time. When he was young, he took piano lessons and demonstrated a talent for music; but, as he got older, peer pressure from his classmates pushed him toward sports and away from the piano. Against his mom's wishes, he joined the football team when they first moved to Low Field, but some players gave him a hard time, seemingly resentful of the attention he garnered from the coaches. Moreover, they made it apparent that they didn't like the possibility of Daron winning a position over someone who had grown up there, so he quit. Another season he signed up for the cross country team. The simple freedom of running had always appealed to him and after working out with the team for a few weeks his conditioning was rapidly improving. He enjoyed the individuality of the sport and he liked training with the other runners on the team. Things were going well until he had the misfortune of stepping in a gopher hole while jogging in a field and nearly broke his ankle. The doctor said it would take six to eight weeks to heal which was almost the entire fall season, so he agreed with the coach that it would be better to allow the injury to heal completely by waiting until the next year to train and run again. He never went back.

The four classes at the charter school he enrolled in were Senior English, Algebra II, American History after 1865, and Sociology/Psychology. Within a few weeks he had already established an effective routine. As soon as his mom left for work, he would log-in to the school's website and work on assignments. He tried to replicate a school schedule by spending about forty minutes on one class, taking a short break, and then continuing on to the others, always in the same order. It was like going to school for a half a day, periods one through four and then having a senior early release for the rest of the day. He was still mad at Mr. Daniels for threatening to expel him because of Colton's stupidity, but the electronic school seemed like it was going to work out as a good alternative.

This was his first social. He tried to talk his mom out of going but she insisted they attend the gathering to become acquainted with other students and the teachers of his online classes. When they were getting out of the car, his mom encouraged him to mingle with other students. The meeting was in the Watson City High School gym. Several of the teachers introduced themselves and welcomed them to the event. Daron and his mother registered and affixed name tags to their shirts. The monthly socials always had a theme and this month's was *Make a New Friend*. Every student had to meet someone new and exchange email addresses with that person. Obviously, Daron didn't view this as being a very difficult task to complete seeing as he didn't know anyone in the school, except Kelsey. While Daron was at the registration table he saw her and her mom standing across the room. They hadn't seen each other since the day of the shooting, and he knew her mom had forbidden her to have any interaction with him, even a text or an email.

He nodded to her and gave a quick hand greeting. Surprisingly, she pulled her mom's sleeve and approached Daron and his mom. They exchanged greetings, and as the two women continued to talk, Daron and Kelsey offered to get everyone a cup of coffee or punch as an excuse to separate themselves from the two women.

"How are you?" Daron asked Kelsey as they walked toward the refreshments.

"Good. Listen, I'm sorry about everything, but my mom's been a paranoid about us being together since the first shooting," she said.

"Oh my god, I heard about the mall shooting. That was unbelievable," he said. "Are you okay?"

"I'm fine. It happened so fast that I didn't have much to think about. Really, it was over in a few seconds and I guess I'm getting used to being in the middle of gunfire," Kelsey laughed.

"That's crazy," he said, "but I'm glad you're okay."

"Thanks. Let's just call a truce on our dating for now and let some time go by. Then we can see. I think it's for the better if that's okay with you?" she said.

"Sure, whatever works for now," Daron agreed.

They returned to their mothers and handed then each a cup of coffee.

Kelsey spoke for the two of them, "We're going to go make new friends."

"Yeah," Daron agreed.

They walked to a group of students who were bunched in one section of the gym talking in pairs and trios. Daron stood near a few students until they gave him a chance to introduce himself; Kelsey did the same thing with a few female students. They both smiled and chatted with ease sensing they were two of the oldest students in the program, as well as the newest. Daron discovered that one of the guys was actually taking the same Sociology/Psychology class that he was enrolled in and that they had spent time together in the same chat room one day. The boy was a fourteen year old senior named Oscar who was also planning to graduate this year from the program. He asked Daron if he had started the ancestry assignment for the class.

"No," Daron replied, "what's that about."

"It's pretty cool," Oscar said with excitement. "The school bought us accounts to YourAncestry.com so once you register and learn how to use the site, you can search your family history pretty far back and create your own personal family tree. In the first hour or so, I was able to get four or five generations back on my mother's side with very little research. I found my great-grandparents and their parents and a bunch of other family members I didn't even know existed. It's fun; you'll really like it."

"That sounds very cool," Daron agreed. "I actually don't know that much about my ancestors beyond my grandparents."

"I didn't either. Everyone in my family said they came from England but I found out that one of my great-grandmothers was born in Russia," laughed Oscar. "She was some old lady from St. Petersburg who gave birth to my grandfather in Germany when she was almost forty years old; wild, huh? It's like straight out of Tolstoy."

"That's interesting. What chapter or section is that in? Do you remember?" Daron asked.

Oscar shook his head and said, "I'm not sure but I think about chapter ten. It's a little after the mid-term exam. I did it a few weeks ago, so I'm not too sure."

"Oh; I just started the class. I'm only on the second chapter," Daron said.

"Anyway, you'll probably have fun doing that one because it kind of sets up the chapters that follow—social assimilation, social mobility, social alienation and some other pretty cool cultural topics. You learn why some immigrants are successful and find their rightful place in our society while others are messed up and are never able to find a cultural niche for themselves. All Americans are from someplace else; some fit in and some don't—I find it fascinating to study," Oscar ranted.

Daron took a step back from the younger student and said, "Sounds interesting. Thanks Oscar. It was a pleasure to meet you face to face. Now we'll know each other when we're in the chatroom together."

Daron walked away from Oscar, having made his obligatory new friend for the evening. His mind was churning about the ancestry tree because he realized that he knew nothing about where either his mom or his dad had come from, beyond Akron, Ohio. Later, during the car ride home, he talked to his mom about the project. She explained what she knew about the people a few generations back on her side of the family and admitted that she, too, was curious to see what he would learn about them as he unraveled their past. Moreover, she confessed that she knew virtually nothing about the Scott side of the family, acknowledging that Daron's Uncle Rafer was the only living relative of his father's immediate family members. She recognized what an unintended void she had created for her son by not knowing more about her late husband's family. Hopefully the project would help them both gain a better understanding of those peoples' journeys and struggles. Daron sensed that she was lost in thought and asked her if she had enjoyed herself and wondered, facetiously, if she had made a new friend at the gathering.

"It was nice to talk to Kelsey's mom again," Brenda said. "She's a very nice person and she's smart, too.

"What did you talk about?" he asked.

'Well, lots of things, but the most interesting topic was the option of filing a lawsuit against the school," his mother admitted.

"Really?" he asked with an amazed look.

"It's worth considering," she said. "First of all, they didn't provide a safe environment for you and Kelsey in the parking lot, allowing Colton, who's an adult, to come right off the street and assault you two with a gun. And, secondly, we think Mr. Daniels might have violated your civil rights by threatening to expel you two from school for no good reason."

Daron rubbed his hands together and smiling said, "Maybe we can get some money."

His mom glanced at him and said, "Maybe we can right a wrong."

47

INDUSTRIAL SIZE, FIVE gallon pots of boiling water bubbled and steamed in the school cafeteria kitchen as workers filled them with box after box of spaghetti. Sauce and meatballs were heating in separate pans under the watchful eyes of several cooks. Other volunteers chopped and fixed small salad bowls with iceberg lettuce, carrots, peppers and tomatoes slices all lightly soaked with Italian dressing. Stacked bags of fresh bread and a large bowl of butter patties balanced on ice cubes were arranged at the end of the serving line so once the customers started to file past, they would receive each item of the fundraiser dinner in a steady, continuous progression, much like the car assembly lines that made a large portion of the state prosperous. A flat, single-layer cake sat on a separate table decorated with the message, *Get Well Soon Abby!*

Two long folding tables greeted the patrons as they entered the school, many still dressed in their Sunday church clothes. At one table two teachers collected the money for the dinner and exchanged meal tickets for dollar bills. The homemade tickets announced the purpose of the fundraiser—a community effort to help defray the medical costs for Low Field senior Abby Olson. The second table held six gift baskets created for a blind raffle, the most popular one being for the 50/50 cash raffle. Tickets were one dollar a piece or ten for five dollars. People filed along depositing their tickets in the baskets of their choice. A large bulletin board followed the second table and a desk with magic markers was left in front inviting the people to sign the board and offer well wishes to Abby. Some drew pictures knowing it was her passion in life while others wrote simple messages followed by their signatures.

Attendance was outstanding, especially during the first two hours after the area church services had let out. The high school art teacher had collected all of Abby's art works that she could find and hung them on large, free-standing display boards at the far end of the cafeteria away from the food line and trash cans. A power point presentation scrolled other paintings and drawings by Abby in a continuous loop on the three televisions hanging high on the walls. Occasionally one of the teachers would turn on the microphone at the portable podium that had been brought into the cafeteria for the event. She would thank the crowd for their attendance and for their support of the dinner and would update the crowd on Abby's medical progress, since the latest developments contained nothing but good news. Near the exit doors another table was littered with informational flyers, buttons and yard signs encouraging the visitors to support the upcoming renewal levy.

Abby had been actually walking a few painful steps at a time in the hospital's rehabilitation unit for the past two or three days. She would stand between a device that resembled parallel bars from gymnastics, weak from the shooting and subsequent surgeries. A therapist walked backward in front of her as a precaution. She was amazed how much leg-strength she had lost in so little time, but as her appetite improved she felt better and was anxious to push her body.

One of Abby's favorite teachers from middle school was a close friend of her mom. They spoke to one another almost daily since the shooting. The teacher knew from the conversations that Abby's parents were likely to file a lawsuit against Colton Caldwell and possibly the school district, knowing their insurance would never cover all of her medical bills, let alone provide compensation for the pain and suffering she had endured as well as protect her from the possible long-term physical complications she might experience as a direct result of the gunshot trauma. They hoped her youthful age would help her recover and allow her to live a relatively normal life, but there was no way to be sure if she would experience adverse mental and physical quality of life issues in her later years. The teacher told Mrs. Frazier about the fundraiser and was happy to hear that Abby might be released from the hospital within a few days, of course with the realization that she would be required to complete an intensive rehabilitation regimen for many, many weeks.

The dinner was scheduled from noon to 4:00 PM. At 3:30 Abby's mom phoned her friend to inform her that there was great news— Abby had just been released from the hospital and they were on their way home with her. The teacher begged them to stop by the school, even if Abby had to stay in the car so the people could see her and wish her well in person. The teacher couldn't resist the temptation to spark the crowd with the news of a possible appearance of the family.

"Ladies and gentlemen, you are here at the right time because we might have a very special visitor before 4:00," she announced. "Please have a piece of cake and relax for a few more minutes."

Shortly before the conclusion of the fundraiser Abby entered the cafeteria through a backdoor in the kitchen. She was sitting in a wheelchair flanked by her mother and pushed from behind by her father. All three looked exhausted with dark half-moons under their eyes. Several people gasped and screamed:

"Look, its Abby!" one of them screamed.

Every one of the hundred remaining supporters stood, clapped, screamed and whistled. Abby and her parents smiled and beamed with heartfelt appreciation. Several of the teachers ran up to see the trio, hugging and kissing all three. All of the people had the same looks on their faces as if they were watching a bride enter a church on her way up the aisle to be married. One of the workers brought the microphone over to them. Abby's mom accepted it and cleared her throat as the clapping subsided.

"We can't thank you enough for your well wishes and generosity during the past few weeks. It has been an awful time, but all of the community support has truly meant so much to Abby, Lyle and me that no words are adequate to express our appreciation," Mrs. Olson said. "Thank you all very much for your kindness. We will never forget how you have been there for us. Honey, would you like to say anything?"

She handed the microphone to her daughter who simply said, "Thank you all; it's so wonderful to be out of the hospital."

48

A COLD STEADY RAIN fell in the early morning hours of Mary Caldwell's funeral. The precipitation was accompanied by a brisk wind that separated many of the stubborn bronze and russet-colored leaves from the old tall trees near the church creating a damp, leafy patchwork that stuck to the soles of the visitors' shoes. The bright garnet and golden maple leaves of early fall already had been gathered by diligent rakes and burnt in piles that sent the familiar gray plumes of smoke and the aroma of autumn spreading through the neighborhood near the town crossroads where the tired, century-old Presbyterian church sat in need of a new coat of paint.

Mary had attended the church since she was a young girl, although in adulthood less regularly than she would have liked. Her faith, however, was steadfast and strong until the end. She was the only daughter of Clare and Clyde Brown. They were proud people who, like most parents, envisioned a big, significant life for their daughter. As a child she was vibrant, willful and energetic; and she had a precocious mind. When she first learned to talk, she could recite nursery rhymes and poems while bouncing in her play pen in the kitchen at her mother's side. By three she would sit quietly in her small rocking chair reading her children's books to herself.

Her mother would say, "Read the story aloud to me, Mary."

And she could, one book after another, with little help. They played school together during the day and Mary learned to write on a child-sized chalkboard and desk that was set up in a vacant corner of the kitchen. After dinner Mary would sit on her father's lap in his bulky, leather recliner and they would read her wildlife magazines. She would amaze her father with the array of information she could discuss even before she was old enough to attend school.

In the summers, Mary and her mother would spend hours and hours together outside in a fenced-in area they referred to as the backyard. The sandbox and teeter totter were Mary's favorite places, but she would also help her mother pick weeds and bang the hard soil of the garden with the hoe her dad had cut down to her size. On winter days, she would get bundled-up in her snow suit, mittens and boots and run freely behind the house creating snowmen guards to protect her make-believe kingdom. Her dad would keep her castle warm by burning wood in the old stove that sat in the front portion of the barn, and she would occasionally join him for a respite sitting in a youth lawn chair and drinking hot chocolate.

As she grew older, so did her capacity for compassion and empathy for others. She looked out for all the children in school, befriending the awkward, less popular ones and protecting the weak. One June on the last day of school, she won the Outstanding Citizen Award. Puzzled by what it meant, she characteristically gave it to another girl who was visibly upset by not being recognized with an award that day.

In high school Mary Brown was an honor student and active member of Student Government. She organized food drives and fundraising events such as car washes and dances with ease, banding her classmates together in generous work and providing less fortunate people with the things they needed for a better life. Her giving spirit was obvious to everyone who knew her. One year her dad got hurt at work and required surgery. When he returned home, she asked for permission to do her assignments at home for a few weeks so she could help her mother care for him. Her senior year the school counselor called her in to discuss her plans after graduation. Without hesitation she announced that she was going to nursing school in the fall. She wanted to help others.

Mary's instinct of putting others first was probably what drew her to Roy Caldwell. They met when at a church picnic. He had recently found work at one of the manufacturing plants near Low Field after being honorably discharged from the Marines. He was a quiet man, withdrawn and shy in public settings. She had to work hard to pull any conversation from him, but as they spent more time together, he shared his intellect and his heart more openly with Mary and they discovered a common love for one another. Shortly after they were married, most of the plant closed and he was forced to find new work. The unemployment benefits included retraining so he learned to drive trucks and got his CDL. Low Field was near the several interstate highways and the Ohio Turnpike and trucking companies were always hiring new drivers. He always had work.

The early years of their marriage were joyful and active, but both of Mary's pregnancies and childbirth experiences were difficult and took a toll on her health. Roy was driving cross-country trips most of the time and would be gone five or six days in a row depending on the weather and the details of the delivery route. Slowly they both got worn down and settled into lives of sullen mediocrity. Instead of being rejuvenated by seeing each other again after a long week, they sunk into complacency and boredom with each other and the repetitive pattern of their lives. Eventually they quit asking each other about the absent parts of their week. They both sought out the numbing solace of a drink to help them through their wearisome routines. Roy spent many lonely hours working outside as Mary toiled in the kitchen. Neither of them was ever genuinely happy again.

The late October wind pushed away the billowy clouds of the morning and the sun greeted a few friends that made their way into the church for Mary's calling hours. The five family members stood in a row just beyond her casket. They greeted and wept with the friends and acquaintances that passed by her thin, rigid body. They thanked everyone for attending her calling hours. Some of the people took seats in the empty pews to wait for the funeral service and others left to return to work or other tasks. Only two of Colton's friends paid their respects—Travis and Kelsey.

It was the first time Colton and Kelsey had seen each other since the day of the shooting. Colton's heart soared when he saw her; he smiled for the first time in weeks. During the years they dated, Kelsey had gotten to know Mrs. Caldwell well enough to call her momma M. Mary enjoyed having another female in the house, someone who she could talk to about decorating, recipes and women's clothes. Kelsey brought out a goodness and kindness in Mary that had been buried deep in her personality from the years of callous drudgery that dominated her marriage. They laughed about things that Colton didn't think were funny and enjoyed each other's company. Her spirits were lifted by the possibility of Colton having a life with Kelsey, and when they broke up, Mary told her son to do whatever it took to get her back.

Kelsey knelt and prayed beside the casket and then walked toward the family greeting her former boyfriend first, "I'm so sorry Colton. I just can't believe she's gone."

"Thanks Kelsey," he said with tears in his eyes, "it's great to see you. My mom would be happy you're here."

"I had to come and pay my respects," Kelsey said. "She was like my second mom."

"She loved you Kelsey, and so do I," Colton said with jarring frankness.

"No Colt, not now. I can't talk about us," Kelsey said shaking her head as she wiped tears from her eyes.

"Can I call you sometime? Just to talk," he pleaded.

"Not now Colton. I'm so sorry for your loss," she said moving-on to greet the other family members.

Kelsey left the church in haste. She had tried to do the right thing by attending the calling hours—be a good friend and show her support for Colton and his family during these terrible days, but she had no intention of making a complicated situation even worse by sending

Colton an unintended message about their relationship. It was just like him to use such a horrible situation in such an inappropriate way to try to play on her sympathies. Then again, she understood that he was probably in shock by the recent events that had sent his life spiraling so steeply out of control. He was probably just reaching out to her in an attempt to deal with the turmoil and unexpected chaos that had become his new reality, desperate to talk through his confused emotions with an entrusted friend. Regardless, she was determined to not allow her emotions and sadness for Mrs. Caldwell to compromise her feelings about Colton. Their relationship was in the past, and as far as she was concerned, it was finished. Today was a time to show respect to his mother.

The two hours went by and the remaining visitors and family members slid into the rows of wooden pews for the funeral. Colton and Clayton sat next to each other in somber silence. A feeling of emptiness filled their bodies; neither had to say a word because their shared loss extended far beyond conversation. Pastor Mike ceremoniously took his spot in the front of the church altar, next to Mary's casket.

"Friends and Family, we are gathered here today in the presence of God to say goodbye to our friend, our daughter, our wife and our mother, Mary Caldwell. Let us pray—Lord, bless and cherish this soul that was your faithful servant on earth. Keep her in your company and protect her until we can be reunited with her in your glory. Amen."

The pastor continued the service expressing kind and sensitive memories of Mary's life. He shared a few personal stories about her that he had learned from talking to her friends and family members. His remarks were powerful and thoughtful. Everyone laughed a little and cried a little during the service. At the conclusion, he asked everyone in attendance to stand and recite the Lord's Prayer together. Then he gave them logistical instructions for getting to the cemetery for the burial rights and the brief luncheon celebration to follow.

There was a final prayer before Colton, Clayton, Roy and Clyde accompanied the casket down the long aisle to the back of the church where they carried her body down the steps from the church and placed the body of their mother, wife and daughter into the hearse.

"Lord, we give you our friend and loved one for your eternal care. Mary's work on earth is done. We ask that you give us the strength to carry on in her absence; our hearts will be filled with grief and emptiness until you, in your infinite wisdom, call us to join her at your side. In Jesus's name we pray, amen."

Not a person in the church could comprehend the finality of those words with a dry eye.

49

THREE POLICE CRUISERS were parked strategically in highly-visible positions of the school parking lot forcing the Town Hall Meeting attendees to recognize, at least subliminally, the presence of law enforcement officers as they entered the school. The meeting was scheduled to begin at 7:00 PM, but an hour before, several television crews were already setting up cameras on tripods and taping their microphones to the podium. School officials made the decision to move the meeting to the gymnasium in order to best accommodate the capacity crowd. Concerned and curious citizens started to arrive shortly after 6:00 for the best seats and the flow of community members into the facility didn't stop for well over an hour. Seeing that no more seats were available, many guests ended up standing two or three people deep near the walls underneath the basketball goals. The latest arrivals were forced to mill around in the hallway and crowd into doorways hoping to hear the various statements and remarks with stretched necks well after the meeting had started.

Following the reciting of the Pledge of Allegiance, a Low Field student sang the national anthem.

The board president greeted the crowd, "Good evening ladies and gentlemen—I'm John Fitzpatrick, President of the Low Field Local Schools Board of Education. We would like to welcome you all to this very important community meeting. Tonight's program will begin with a series of speakers on the topic of Low Field's response to school violence and later, an equal portion of time will be devoted to comments and questions from you, the audience. As you know, we were all shocked and saddened by the unthinkable shootings that occurred at *our* high school a few weeks ago. Thankfully, no one was killed but the fact that two of our students were wounded by bullets in the parking lot during school dismissal is totally unacceptable. The wounded students were hospitalized, and I am happy to report tonight that both are now recuperating at home and we hope and pray that both of them make full recoveries. We realize now that we were lucky, but we cannot assume that our schools will never be the target of violence again. Rather, we must use this incident as a wake-up call of sorts to evaluate our comprehensive approach to preventing future school and community violence. We are committed to doing everything in our power to prevent a similar act from ever happening again in our schools. This evening is a starting point for that initiative. I ask you to please listen carefully and respectfully to all the opinions and points of view that are presented tonight and feel free to express your own opinions later in the meeting. Only by working together can we create a safe haven for our students, staff and parents. On behalf of the other board of education members, I thank you for being here tonight. Now, it is my pleasure to introduce the Superintendent of the Low Field Local Schools, Mr. Jim Collins."

There was a light applause.

"Thank you Mr. Fitzpatrick," said the superintendent. "For the past two decades, schools across America have become easy targets for mentally-ill people seeking attention and fame or angry people looking to retaliate for something that happened to them by inflicting mayhem on innocent members of society. All of this is a relatively new phenomenon in our culture. For those of us who grew up not that long ago and never gave a thought to being in danger while attending school, it is hard to accept that school security is an absolute necessity today. In the past six years, we have installed exterior and interior security cameras at both of our schools and locked all of the schools' exit doors so people can't enter the building without an electronic pass key or by entering through a monitored door after identifying themselves and stating the purpose of their business. Also, we started a Student Resource Officer Program in conjunction with the Low Field County Sheriff's Department that provides a deputy devoted specifically to safeguard the people in our schools during the hours of operation. We've made progress and our schools are much safer than they were a short time ago, but in the flash of a few seconds, things can go terribly wrong and our students and staff can be in perilous danger. The shooting that occurred at our high school a few weeks ago is a sobering example of why we should not believe that our work is done. We are hopeful that through meetings like this one tonight, we are able to get new, reasonable ideas that can be implemented in a cost-effective manner to make the Low Field Local Schools a safer place. Thank you and it's my pleasure to introduce the Low Field Chief of Police, Harlan Hadley.

"Thank you, sir. Listen people; we all want our schools and our kids to be protected from people who might want to harm them," stated the chief directly. "I'm going to get right to the point. Tonight I have a simple proposal from a police perspective to address the safety issue. I believe the best course of action is for my department to hire two additional officers that can be assigned full-time to the schools, one at each location, five days a week during school hours. That would put an officer in the building when school is in session that has the proper training and capacity to stop any kind of perpetrator with bad intentions. The students and the teachers would feel safer, and we'd have a cruiser parked in front of both buildings all day long as a signal to anyone who was thinking about trying something that we had an armed officer inside at all times. And this wouldn't cost that much, maybe $40,000 total for the year, and our community would have done the right thing to protect our kids. Law enforcement personnel are trained to prevent these kinds of problems or situations from ever occurring, but, when bad things happen, we know what to do. Also, we can work with the teachers and the principals to prevent gun violence in the schools. That's my idea in a nutshell. The next speaker is Deputy Perry from the County Sherriff's Department."

"Thanks Chief," said the SRO. "It's a pleasure to be here tonight and it's my honor to serve the students, staff, and community members of Low Field on a regular basis. This is my fifth year as the Student Resource Officer assigned to Low Field. The Low Field County Sheriff, Paul Alexander, and Superintendent Collins brought me on to start the program and, in my opinion, we've been very successful at making the schools a safer place. As the SRO in the district, I coordinate many national safety programs in the schools such as the Seat Belt Safety Program and the Safe School Zone Program. In the past few years at the high school we have instituted many important safety initiatives such as the Prom Promise, the Don't Drink and Drive and the Don't Text and Drive Programs, just to mention a few. I also work with Chief Hadley and the officers in his department by assisting them with domestic issues that involve our students, and my presence in the schools along with the police cruiser that I drive in the district serves as a deterrent to criminals entering school grounds.

"I've helped the district implement new safety procedures by doing crisis training with the staff and coordinating the writing of the safety plans in both schools. Also, I get to know the students personally, and, because of that relationship and trust, they sometimes share confidential information with me that oftentimes helps the principals prevent problems from ever occurring at school. Obviously, I can only be in one place at a time, so I try to spend a portion of my time in both buildings every day and I deliberately vary my schedule so it is not predictable to someone who might be looking for a pattern. I just wanted to take a few minutes to inform you about the SRO program. It's a good program and the program works. There are hundreds of them around the country, and I attend state meetings a few times a year to bring new ideas back to Low Field and continue to improve the program. Thank you. I would now like to introduce a parent, Mrs. Debbie Carter."

"Hi, I'm Debbie Carter and my daughter Julie attends the elementary school. Her first few years at the school were wonderful. She was a happy child who was learning and making new friends. We were so happy we had moved here so our daughter could attend the Low Field Schools. For third grade, our daughter's teacher was Mrs. Nelson. Julie loved her and was having another good year in school. Then the shootings at Sandy Hook Elementary School in Connecticut took place. When that happened, my husband and I tried to make sure our daughter didn't hear about it. We'd turn off the television, and we never discussed that terrible tragedy in front of her. But she found out about it anyway. All of a sudden, she became afraid and didn't want to go to school. She had many questions, and my husband and I did our best to answer them, however, for a long time, probably two months, she was different and she felt different about school. Her grades got worse and her personality changed. Somehow, we got through the school year. In the summer we tried to have fun every day. We went to the park and had picnics, she had friends over to play and we took what we called weekend vacations with her to the zoo and a waterpark. Gradually, her spirits and personality improved.

"Julie started fifth grade this fall and her grades were better and she looked forward to going to school. Then there was the shooting at *our* high school. Her world flipped over again. Now, she doesn't want to get up in the morning and we're reliving the same problems we had as a family a few years ago.

"Ladies and gentlemen, the shootings and violence in our schools affects our children even if the wounded students aren't their classmates. They understand at a very young age that these victims were innocent students just like them who came to school to have fun, see their teacher and friends and learn new things. Then the system failed them and one of these unthinkable, despicable acts happened at their school. No child should have to live with those thoughts. No child should have to live with that fear—especially when they come to school. From a parent's perspective, I hope we use this evening to make our schools a safer place where the children of Low Field feel protected when they walk through those doors each day, ready and happy to learn and grow. Thank you. I'd like to introduce Mr. Keith Byler who is the president of the teachers' union."

The teacher received the loudest applause from the crowd.

"Hello. Most of you know me—I grew up in this community and graduated from Low Field High School. I care about this school district and community more than anyone in this room," Keith stated. "The day after the shooting at the high school, all of the teachers got together and we had a meeting to discuss what we could do to make our schools safer. There were a lot of different ideas expressed, but there was total agreement in one thing—we had to do something right away that would raise the level of protection for both our students and the staff. So, over half the teachers, twenty-four in total, decided to take a dramatic step in the right direction; we agreed to become certified by the state law for a concealed carry permit. We've already taken the class where we learned a lot about the law, gun safety and how to use a gun to protect ourselves and others."

"During the past few weeks, we have practiced extensively firing our weapons and we've gotten proficient at hitting our target consistently. Our idea is simple—have twenty teachers trained and armed to counter anyone who comes into our schools with a gun. We know this might be a controversial idea to some, and we realize the board of education would have to pass a policy that supports the idea, but we hope that all of you and the majority of community residents will be in favor of us providing this layer immediate, direct protection for the students by our school staff. That's twenty times the protection we have now, and with all due respect, ten times more protection than the Chief's plan. *Show-of-force* is an effective tactic used by our military and law enforcement personnel whenever they encounter a hostile situation. We believe this idea would make our schools the safest in the country and it wouldn't cost our taxpayers a cent. The teachers have paid for the training themselves and we will continue to fulfill the required gun range practice shooting at our own expense. We owe this to our students and we need to act now!"

Mr. Byler returned to his seat on the stage. There was mild applause and a conversational buzz in the room. The board president returned to the podium and informed the crowd that there would be a ten-minute break and when the meeting resumed the floor would be opened to the public for questions and/or comments.

Following the break the crowd slowly returned to their seats and the second half of the meeting began with mostly comments, a few disguised as questions. Each person made their way to a single microphone stand in a center aisle of the room. They took turns making comments. The panelists took notes with the intention of responding to any questions at a later time.

"It seems to me that we have the same ineffective security plan as most schools; it slows down law abiding visitors through surveillance cameras and door buzzers but a determined person could easily shoot their way into the schools and have their way once inside. The system is basically worthless against a serious attacker."

"I'm a parent of a kid in the elementary school and I think we need a cop in each building and we need bullet-proof glass and doors at all of the entrances of the schools. And bullet-proof glass in the windows of the lower floors and classroom doors with locks that could stop someone inside the school from getting to the students."

"I just have a question; do the schools inform the local police about students with violent behaviors and mental health issues so they can force them to seek treatment? I mean a lot of the school shootings around the country are done by disgruntled students who carry weapons into school in backpacks or instrument cases."

"Yeah, I agree with the last speaker, and to take it one step further, what about adults in the community who make threats against the government or make comments that suggest they are capable of committing an act such as a mass shooting; can we do anything to force these kinds of nut-jobs to be evaluated for their mental stability?"

"Lawmakers need to ban assault style weapons and large capacity magazines if we are ever going to have a chance of preventing these kinds of public mass murders."

"Let's face it people, the only way to protect kids at school is to string walls of barbed wire around the buildings and turn our schools into prison fortresses."

"Why don't we create a community hot-line where people could call in anonymous tips and report dangerous people to the authorities? You know, like a crazy neighbor or someone who threatens to harm innocent people. We all know who the violent people are out here. We need a way to report suspicious people to the authorities and hopefully stop them before they kill someone."

"I'm all for increasing the level of security in our schools, but I think we have to be realistic about the cost of implementing some of the ideas that are being proposed. There are a lot of older people who live out here on a fixed income. My kids are grown now so it really doesn't affect me. I like the teachers' plan—it's cost-effective and provides a broad blanket of security."

"Mr. Byler, in the teachers' plan, which teachers will carry a gun and where do you intend to keep the guns? I'm wondering if you are planning for these teachers to wear holsters with guns and live ammunition."

Keith looked at the board president who nodded so the union president stepped up to the podium and answered, "Well, we would have to work out the details of a new policy with the administration, and, as I said earlier, the board would have to approve the plan, but we have a few ideas so far. Our thinking at this point is to let the public know that twenty teachers in the Low Field Local Schools have a concealed carry permit from the state of Ohio and the board has given them the authority to have those guns with them at school to serve as security against a violent attack. Probably the guns would be locked in safe keeping but readily available if needed. We don't think the students or the public should know which twenty teachers are approved for the policy or where the guns are kept, but the superintendent could have the list so he would know the details of the force. We could also establish a cell phone alert system amongst the teachers as a way to quickly communicate with each other to mobilize in the event of an attack, and we would have practice drills after school and on weekends to be prepared for different types of problems."

"Mr. Byler, it's my understanding that the teachers' contract expired last year and I've heard you and your people are currently working without a new contract? I just want to thank you and the teachers. I mean this is a great thing you're doing and it's a good step in the right direction by the union to work with the community to save money because most of us can't afford to pay more of our money in taxes."

Keith quickly returned to the podium and responded, "Yes; we have dedicated teachers who will do whatever it takes to make our schools great and to protect our students."

Mr. Fitzpatrick stepped up to the podium and redirected the line of questions, "Ladies and gentlemen, just a reminder to please keep your comments and questions focused on the issue of school violence. Thank you."

"Is there any truth to the rumor that the school district has already been sued by family of one of the kids who got shot? I heard they're suing you for millions."

"Mr. Fitzpatrick, I know you want us to only talk about school safety, but what if the levy doesn't pass this time? I think you owe the people here an explanation of how you think you're going to protect the children and increase your security without any more money from the taxpayers to spend. Let's face it, that levy has failed five times now. I think the people are going to tell you again, we're tapped out and can't afford to pay for another levy. You people have to be more creative and not take the simple approach of always asking for more money."

Against his better judgment, the board president again stepped to the podium and responded, "Yes it's true that we already have a very serious financial problem and if the levy doesn't pass we will be in a crisis situation. Again, the levy is a renewal which means it does not increase taxes, but it is not the topic for tonight's meeting."

"Yeah but this meeting's a waste of time if you're not going to have the money to change anything related to security unless the levy passes because I don't think it has a chance in hell of passing," someone yelled anonymously from the crowd.

"We hope the levy passes, sir."

The man stood after the turned heads for all intents and purposes had already identified him, "People around here can't afford more taxes. You keep asking us for more money but we don't have it. The schools need to do what we do in our homes; if there isn't any money, you do without. And if there's less money, you cut back; you don't keep spending and hoping for more money. I've got news for you; it doesn't grow on trees."

The man's comments were followed by a mummer of laughter and some applause as he proudly sat down and tipped his cap to the restless crowd.

"I understand your opinion, but as I said, that topic is for another meeting," stated the frustrated board president. "If there are no further comments regarding school violence, then we'll close tonight's meeting. Thank you for coming."

"Hey, what about the responses to the comments?" someone yelled from the stands. "We need answers."

The panel members stood and the board president switched off the microphone signaling the conclusion of the meeting. Fitzpatrick's final words were drown-out by booing and murmurings from the unhappy crowd. The disgruntled people knew he had denied them the spectacle they had hoped to witness by attending the meeting.

The mob mentality could easily be stirred by only a few impassioned voices, especially as the tenacity of their protests increased and the cords of their civil unrest bound them angrily together against the perceived injustice of the district. Members of the media worked feverishly to reposition their equipment in the hope of getting live interviews with the most vocal members of the community. Jim Collins leaned over to the board president and commented privately to him as a different reporter and camera lights closed in on the stage.

"Good job, John," said the superintendent. "You put out the sparks before they turned into a wildfire."

"These people," said a shaken John, "I'll never understand them. They don't care about the issue or really want to make things better—they just show up to complain and cause trouble."

Jim nodded and stoically replied, "Unfortunately, it's no different than medieval mobs five hundred years ago—they just come to see a good show."

50

WILL AND LUKE exchanged text messages and emails several times in the week following the state golf tournament. Neither of them had a steady girlfriend at the time, but they shared their opinions and insights regarding potential dates from each other's school and used social media outlets as ways to explore the backgrounds of the possible candidates. They wrote informal critiques of their respective teachers and schools and continued their discussions of colleges and their goals for golf and adulthood.

They also discovered a shared passion for video games. They both played the most popular games created for young males—some were sports-related but their current favorites were those that realistically immersed gamers into the world of warfare. Luke invited Will to sleep over the next weekend. If he was well enough, they could play golf, work-out and play video games and take the videos of Will's swing that he needed to send to the assistant coach at Mid Valley.

On Thursday, Will had a doctor's appointment after school. The gunshot wound was healing as expected, but the doctor didn't want Will to accelerate his recovery plan by exceeding the rigid recommendations of the physical therapists he saw twice a week at a rehab facility near the hospital. They had given him a single-page list of light exercises to help him regain balance and strength below the waist and yoga poses designed mostly to stretch the muscles during the healing process. Weightlifting was forbidden, even specific upper-body routines. The PT cautioned that most people were not disciplined enough to limit the routine exclusively to the area and that a set-back of any kind could result in permanent damage. Walking, however, was encouraged, so Will was given the okay to play golf as long as he continued to use a pull cart to tote his golf bag. Nine hole rounds were his limit for the rest of the fall, but Will was fine with that restriction. So long as he was allowed to be on the course and hit shots, he was happy and his life was regaining normalcy.

He found it strange how a person like Luke, who he'd viewed narrowly in the past few years as a golfing rival, was quickly becoming a good friend. It was a peculiar consequence of the shooting for which he was grateful.

Saturday morning was cold, in the low thirties, when they arrived at the golf course. A frost delay had everyone gathered in the Turning Rock clubhouse for nearly ninety minutes until the sun reached a high enough arc in the sky to melt the icy coating from the hidden areas behind the numerous pine and spruce trees that shaded many portions of the short grass throughout the course. Luke borrowed the golf professional's video equipment and the two boys drove a cart to the far end of the driving range to a teeing area that was typically reserved for private lessons. Luke set-up the equipment while Will slowly warmed-up; it had been several weeks since he'd last played, but eventually he found a good rhythm and tempo in his swing. They filmed videos of him hitting shots with most of his clubs with the intention of deleting everything but the best dozen swings. The video card was filled to capacity after forty minutes, so they returned the equipment to the pro shop and went out to play the back nine before the first eighteen hole rounds started to make the turn.

They were competitive with each other but both enjoyed the other's company. Neither of them played very well, but they had fun, having already accomplished the most important goal of the day. Later, they sat in a corner of the pro shop and selected the best swings from the range session and emailed them to Will's school account.

He would forward them along with his playing resume to the coach sometime later when they were back at Luke's house.

One section of Luke's basement was dedicated to fitness—a weight rack and bench were positioned on an area rug lined with plates of various weights and an assortment of dumbbells. A heavy bag and speed bag hung from the ceiling joists and a treadmill faced a small television in one corner. Will spotted the weight bar for Luke while he worked out. He was wiry, strong and worked out with greater amounts of weight than Will had expected from such a slim, tall person. Finally it made sense to Will why his tee shots were always twenty yards behind Luke's and why Luke hit his irons two clubs longer than Will—the guy was lanky, flexible and sinewy. Afterwards, they shared a pizza and played video games. The competition was fierce yet balanced by their newly evolving friendship. Hours went by unnoticed until finally Luke's mother brought two sleeping bags and pillows downstairs for them and said goodnight. The game finally ended at 3:00 AM and they lay down and talked for a few minutes before falling asleep.

"Thanks for today," Will said, "that was fun."

"Yeah, I had fun too, but you know what? We forgot to send the videos," Luke said.

"Oh crap. I'm too tired now," complained Will. "Let's do them in the morning."

"Sounds good."

51

Each Thursday from 4:00-6:00 PM the Low Field teachers had the exclusive use of the Fish and Game Club after school. Their cars filled the small gravel parking lot and the cracking sounds of their guns filled the air like a Fourth of July fireworks display. All together they fired hundreds of rounds from their newly purchased handguns. Colts and Smith and Wesson were the most popular choices of the *buy USA* teachers while those who had a taste for European sports cars preferred Glocks and Berettas. Their cases resembled smallish lunch boxes with locks and the investments they made in their weapons demonstrated a unified commitment to the security plan.

Bill Henry, the retired police officer and their concealed carry class instructor, had been contracted by the union to work with them each week on the firing range. His expertise was invaluable. As the frequency of their sessions increased, so did the teachers' safe handling of the weapons, as well as a marked improvement and comfort in their target shooting. By the third week he introduced some advanced training techniques and added mobility to their training exercises. He had the teachers run a few yards up to the firing line and drop to one knee before firing at the target. They quickly realized the importance of a steady hand, a quiet motion and a sharp focus when firing their handguns.

The ten teachers from the elementary school, consisting of eight women and two men, and ten teachers from the middle/high school with almost an exact opposite mix, nine men and one woman, made up the twenty teachers who followed through on the concealed carry permit and classwork. Bill pushed them during the sessions. He explained the nuances of the guns—how they needed to be handled and carried and each gun's firing patterns and features. He stressed the need to move confidently and smoothly with the weapon. He taught them proper aiming and firing techniques and made them practice the positions repeatedly each week in order to ingrain the movements into instinctive habits that they could rely upon in the event of a crisis situation. The teachers needed to be ready for anything. What they were doing was serious stuff; it could be a matter of life and death.

A few days before Halloween the air was cold and sunset occurred close to dinner time. A heavy grey sky hastened the fall loss of daylight and forced the session to conclude a half hour earlier than just a few weeks prior. Daylight savings was to switch the clocks the upcoming weekend and their practice rounds would need to be restructured to accommodate the group in the small, five-person indoor range. At the end of each firing practice, they would have a brief meeting in the main building. Guns were checked and everyone reviewed common safety procedures. Bill would discuss the lessons of the day, and they would finish with a question and answer session.

"Remember, until you receive your concealed carry permit, your weapons need to stay at home," Bill cautioned them. "You must go home after school and pick up your guns and ammunition before you come to the range. Do not, under any circumstances, leave your weapon in your car and do not take your weapon onto school grounds."

"Bill," one teacher asked with a wry smile, "why does shooting make you so hungry?"

"And thirsty!" added another.

"I make a motion that we move this meeting to The Airport," said another teacher.

"Here, here!" came the cheer from the group.

52

T HE TEACHERS HAD already carved out a Thursday night spot as regulars at The Airport. The waitresses who took care of the floor patrons reserved two long tables for the teachers at the far end of the restaurant. They were loud bunch. Routinely they drank more than a dozen pitchers of beer, ate sandwiches and baskets of fries and onion rings. She didn't mind serving the atypical gathering for the establishment because they left a generous tip. They were friendly people by and large and had a cheerful group spirit which was just what everyone expected from a collection of teachers. It was easy to tell they were both colleagues and friends. In an odd way the teachers had grown closer to each other through the bonding of their decision to take up arms and protect the schools.

One of them held up a frosted mug after the first pitchers of beer had been distributed around the table and said, "A toast—to the most dedicated militia of educators in the history of the world!"

"Aye! Yeah!"

"You can tell he's a history teacher," another replied laughing.

"Yes, but we are still lacking one element," the history teacher said.

"What's that, professor?" asked another.

"A name; we need a name—a designation for our group," he stated. "All the great assemblies that changed the world have a name; a moniker, as it were, for the history books."

"Like what? Have you thought about this already?" others asked.

"No I haven't, but we're getting surprisingly competent with our weapons and I think we need for something that bonds us together for our mission.   Let's brainstorm ideas.   Does anyone have paper and a pencil?" he asked.

"I do," said an elementary teacher, "fire away.   No pun intended."

"The Untouchables."

"The Low Field Militia."

"The Ready and Willing."

"The Defenders of Peace."

"The Secret Brave; no, The Brave 20."

"The Mysterious Ones."

"The Low Field 20."

"The Secret List."

"Any more?" the history teacher asked sensing the group was tiring of the activity.   "Alright, give me the list."

The teacher tore two empty shell casing boxes into small scraps of papers.   They wrote the name of each suggestion on a piece and stuck them on the dart board wedged into the wire circles that divided the areas of the target.

"Everyone gets three throws, and when we've all had a turn, we'll count the number of holes in each piece of paper.   The one with the most holes is the name for our t-shirts and jackets; the official licensed products for the group.   We can even ask the PTA to sell them as a fund-raiser for our ammunition.   Bullets make great stocking stuffers at Christmas and what says *I Love You* more at Valentines' Day than a 9mm shell casing?" he laughed.

They agreed to an embedded warm-up throw a piece so each teacher took a turn and threw four darts at the board and torn pieces of the bullet boxes.   Conversations resumed in clusters but everyone kept an interested eye on the action.

One of them turned to their instructor and asked, "Bill, how do you think we're really doing so far?   Be honest."

"Actually, everyone is doing great, especially for so early into your shooting careers," he replied. "As your teacher, I'd give the group a solid A minus."

They laughed and Keith said, "I agree. In fact, I can't believe how quickly everyone has learned to shoot and handle their weapons. I guess it all comes down to good instruction."

"I just hope it helps pass the levy," another teacher added.

"Well, we received a lot of positive comments from the community at the Town Hall Meeting."

"Yeah, I think our idea will make the difference in the election. We've been so close the last two times," Keith said, "but I think the voters will realize our solution to Low Field's response to violence is the most comprehensive and cost-effective proposal."

"We only need to flip a small percentage of the senior citizens to win the election. The more they think about it, they've got to love this idea," added another teacher.

One of them continued, "My dad said he overheard a bunch of them talking about it at The Diner last weekend—very positive comments from what he could make out."

"That's good because they always vote against school levies, whether they're renewals or not. They're cheap or broke or just don't care, but usually if they see anything on the ballot for us, they vote no. It's going to take something special like our teacher militia to drive a strong turnout at the polls," Keith added.

A call came from the leader of the dart-throwing activity.

"Anyone else?" the history teacher asked loudly. "Has everyone thrown their naming darts?"

Two of them gathered the papers from the dart board and tossed them on the table.

"I've got two holes in The Ready and Willing," said one tabulator.

"None in the Untouchables. Whose idea for a name was that anyway!?" she said laughing.

"One for the Low Field Militia."

"I think I have the winner here; can anyone beat six holes?" asked the first person handling the scraps of paper. "No? Then it's official— we are from this point on to be known as The Low Field 20!"

The group cheered and whooped in joyous camaraderie.

"More beer!" one yelled.

53

DARON DID SCHOOL work every day. As soon as he heard his mom's car door shut and her vehicle rumble away down their section of the crater-filled gravel road that circled and crisscrossed the trailer park, he would get out of bed, usually around 7:15, motivated to make the most of his time alone. He had a pattern, a ritualistic beginning to his mornings that started with a cup of coffee while watching The Morning Sports Show on television. A half hour would pass quickly, but that was all he would allow himself before dressing and logging on to the Academy's website. In the inaugurating weeks of the program, he tried to do his schoolwork dressed in pajama bottoms and t-shirt, but after a few weeks of losing interest and returning to bed, he realized he was getting nowhere and needed to change his pattern. When he explained the predicament to his mom, she suggested that he might be more productive if he got dressed for the day as if he was going to school.

The change in attitude and purpose was dramatic. Methodically he would work through each class. The goal each day was to work seriously for the entire morning and make progress in all three subjects, reading a chapter, answering review questions, taking quizzes and tests and completing writing assignments and projects. The classroom chat rooms were actually fun. He was surprised how friendly the teachers were to him and the other students. It was a good way to take a break and communicate with another person. They expressed genuine concern for him and the other students that he had never experienced before from teachers. He figured they must be mostly younger adults and possibly shared the awkward sense of alienation from society with their students. Daron would make at least one written submission in every subject before he would allow himself to logout. Lately, he would work quickly so he had the entire afternoon to himself. His resentment toward the Low Field and Colton actually began to wane as he became more comfortable and appreciative of his new-found freedom.

The early winter chill was making it difficult to start his truck. He feared the battery needed replaced so one afternoon on his way to Akron, he stopped at an auto parts store and got a price. The salesperson was friendly but the price was unexpectedly high, even if Daron performed the labor.

He had been thinking about a part-time job but when he discussed the idea with his mom she didn't like the idea.

Brenda said, "You've got the rest of your life to work; enjoy your school years while you can."

She was undoubtedly right but he needed some spending money for gas, food and things that came up, like the battery replacement. His grandparents had given him savings bonds every year for his birthday, and, even though he promised he would never cash them for anything but to pay for college, he didn't ask permission or even mention his plan to his mom. He figured they were his to use and he wouldn't make a habit of doing it so he stopped at a bank and cashed one in. Keeping his truck in good working order did not constitute a frivolous purchase in his mind, it was basically a necessity. A few days later he took care of the battery himself.

He planned to replace the battery in the parking lot of the auto parts store. Having little experience working on cars, he lifted the hood but grew reluctant to make the repair, concerned with the possibility of getting electrocuted from a jolt from the new battery. Fortunately another customer noticed his hesitation and volunteered to help him make the switch. The truck engine fired immediately and driving away he felt a new level of confidence and self-reliance. Maybe he should join the service as soon as he finished his classes at the academy and received his diploma. His Uncle Ray retired from the Army after twenty years and he already had a pension and had found a new job. College was another option—so was applying for jobs and starting to work. He could move to Florida; the south was the new north according to an assignment he had just completed, so jobs in that part of the country were supposedly plentiful. There was really nothing to keep him in Ohio but his mom.

As he drove the rural roads, his mind swirled with ideas. Some required more boldness than others; some were simply dreams shared by all youth—fame, fortune and fun. But there was a feeling of excitement regarding his upcoming decision. Coincidentally in one of his classes there was a discussion of how people arrive at important crossroads in life and how the decisions they make at those moments affect the rest of their lives. He sensed he was approaching one of his first significant crossroads as a young adult. He was grateful to have the afternoons to contemplate his life journey and the independence of becoming a man.

His mom got home early from work one afternoon—he, too, had just arrived a few minutes before. Quickly, he turned on the computer and assumed the look of an overworked student.

"Hi," she said entering their home.

"Hey, you're home early," Daron said.

"Yeah, I took a few hours vacation to run a few errands."

"What's in the bags?"

"Oh, just a little surprise," she answered with a smile.

"A surprise; well let's see what've you got there," he said reaching for the bags as he walked from his desk and toward the tiny kitchen.

"Wait," she said, "I said it was a surprise." Brenda turned her back towards him, pulled something from the bag and then spun around holding up the garment with her arms extended toward him. It was a dark brown hoody with the words CLEVELAND BROWNS across the front.

"Do you like it?"

"Sure, but I don't get it," he said quizzically, "you don't even like football."

"You're right, I don't like football, but I didn't think we could go the game on Monday night dressed like hicks from Low Field. Surprise! She flashed tickets from her purse. Guess who won Brown's tickets?" she said happily.

"Cool mom. How did you do that?" Daron asked.

"I answered a few very difficult trivia questions on a radio show yesterday," she said proudly. Then she admitted, "Actually, I was the third caller and a six year old would have known the answer to the question. But anyway we're going to the big city to see a professional football game."

Daron hugged his smiling mom. He hadn't seen her so happy in so long.

"Thanks, this will be fun," he said.

"Yes," she agreed, "and we deserve to have some fun for a change."

She was right. For Daron this fall, the season of his senior year, had been the worst of his life. So many adult issues had been coming at him and the rush to make difficult decisions and find his place in the world had wrenched his nerves and clogged his mind. His mom knew the weight of his racial burden was now fully actualized within him. The decision she made years ago to enter into a relationship with his father forever impacted both her life and her son's life. Her moral strength of character allowed her to interact with the world directly, knowing in her heart that love trumped the color of a person's skin. Playing her small part to weaken societal prejudice had become a focal point in her life, but now the issue had been unintentionally thrust upon her son. For Daron, being half black and half white had not been much of an issue when he was growing up in Akron, but as he approached his eighteenth birthday, he rarely thought about anything else.

Since the shooting, Daron felt self-conscious about how he looked to the people of Low Field. Suddenly, others' eyes were fixed on him, and he could feel their searing gazes locked on his face even after he had passed them by. The realization that his personal journey into early adulthood was complicated by others' beliefs and biases left him confused and angry. His inner conflict was inescapable. Being resentful would not change his situation, but he struggled to accept his situation with a sense of peacefulness and grace.

His mom had sacrificed everything for him including her own self-gratification in life. At times he was angry at his parents for selfishly having a baby without giving full consideration to the difficulties it created for him. At other times, however, his appreciation of his mother's compassion, protection and guidance grew to unequalled heights. Daron realized she was his best friend, certainly now and probably forever, and this made him a very lucky person. His thoughts and feelings continued to swirl within him but he knew his rock lived in the same dingy trailer as he and that she was always there for him, especially during this troubling stage of his coming of age.

All he could say was thanks.

54

ELECTION DAY WAS only 48 hours away, and the school district was in the crosshairs of peril. A sixth consecutive failure of the levy would necessitate immediate and drastic action. A reduction in services and programs in a small school district like Low Field meant people would lose jobs. Many of the employees were both born and raised in Low Field or are people who now called the community home. There was good and bad in this fact. If the teacher or bus driver was respected and their extended families wielded influence in the community, the employee might be a valued representative for the support of the schools. However, in many cases, the generational history, rivalry and competitiveness between families and individuals and the echoing effect of a negative decision or a personal slight of a student had caused a pervasive disharmony among the residents that was as deep and wide as an ocean. The collective negativity towards the district was similar to the layers of an onion, and the attitudes of many people brought tears to the eyes of those attempting to improve the situation and overcome the stagnation.

Innocent occurrences such as which student was selected to sing a solo part in the third grade Christmas Concert; which student was blamed for leaving a lunch table with debris and was punished by staying in from recess; which student was honored by being selected into the National Honor Society; which student didn't get to play as many minutes as another athlete in a game; and so on and so on, over years and years of daily interactions formed an accumulation of varied opinions, often negative, that had a rippling effects on families. These rigid beliefs were silently expressed several times a year at the polling locations.

The weekend prior to the election, in a last-ditch attempt to garner support for the renewal levy, the teachers presented more specifics of their plan for arming a representative group of teachers with handguns to the public through a handout that was distributed at the local grocery stores, pharmacies and gas stations. Saturday evening they hosted an informational meeting and fundraiser dance for adults at the Low Field VFW Hall. The event was festive but only lightly attended by the usual friends and family members of the teachers. Several board members who delicately walked the line between being the ultimate authorities over school matters, as well as being neighbors, friends and in some cases family members, also came to the hall to support the efforts of the teachers. Student safety was the new rallying theme behind the push to get the levy passed. The flyer's message was concise.

Support Your
Low Field Schools
On Election Day
The Safest Place for Students
In the USA
Thanks to the
The Low Field 20
Please Vote Yes!

The people of Low Field gravitated toward any controversy, especially when it involved the schools, and school levies always sparked a fire storm of debate in the local restaurants about the merits of the proposal, as well as dredging up stories of past wrongs and the shortcomings of the school district. In the weeks before an election, yard signs would begin to appear for various governmental positions and issues. Neighbors got to know each other on a deeper level based upon which signs were staked near the street on their properties. On the other hand, the absence of specific signs also revealed much about a household's opinion, especially regarding the schools. Words were never exchanged because it wasn't necessary.

The appeal for increased security in the schools was a gamble the teachers were willing to make. However, many people viewed the idea of arming twenty teachers throughout the schools as a desperate ploy for support of the levy and, in some cases, ludicrous and danger-ous. It became a joke in the community that the teachers were play-ing a game of *election* Russian roulette. Regardless, the controversial nature of the issue had heightened tension throughout the commu-nity to a fever pitch and the turnout for election voting was expected to be a record number.

For the past twenty years, the Low Field economy had spiraled continually in a downward trend. Many residents were now retired and growing older and their children had left the area for better em-ployment opportunities or a more vibrant lifestyle. Finances had become a legitimate concern for these people when they were faced with voting for or against monetary issues. The combination of the communities' shrinking collective wealth and the number of dis-gruntled constituents who held a grudge against the schools seemed to consistently polarize the people in a way like no other—on one side, positive citizens who understood the value of good schools in their community and shared in the conscious responsibility to sup-port educational opportunities for all children, or on the other side, negative residents who for a vast array of personal reasons had long since chosen to never endorse a school issue again—new funding ini-tiatives and renewals of existing taxes both received equal but brief consideration by the later group; no.

The gathering's attendees at the VFW rally were dressed casu-ally, many in jeans. They were like-minded, for the most part, al-though the attendance of a few people was puzzling to some based on loyalties of the past. Keith Byler constantly surveyed the crowd and on more than one occasion sent his wife or another teacher specifically to speak to certain individuals in order to probe their motivation and agenda for being present at the function.

"Hey Walter, thanks for being here tonight," said the union vice-president to a particular attendee. "I figured you were on the other side this time around."

"Who says I'm not?" replied Walter. "I haven't talked to you since my grandkids graduated from Low Field."

"I was just curious, Walter," said the teacher, "I mean Low Field isn't Las Vegas, and you probably could have found something more exciting to do tonight than attend a school levy fundraiser."

"I don't know; I mean the idea of twenty gun-toting teachers isn't what I'd call boring," Walter responded. "If you don't mind me asking, where in the world did you come up with this idea?"

"Actually we're not the first school district to think of it—we've spoken to a few educators out west who work in small districts with very few staff members that carry weapons. They're mostly principals who have military or law enforcement backgrounds but their school districts have authorized them to carry weapons as a deterrent to violence," explained the teacher.

"Is that so?" Walter said. "That's a strange notion to me to allow loaded firearms in schools."

"Yes, but when you think about it, we've had a student resource officer in the schools for a few years now and he always carries a loaded weapon in the school. All we're talking about is increasing the saturation of the adults with access to a gun in case some deranged person comes into our schools with the intent to harm our kids. Really, what's wrong with that? I mean what could go wrong? We're just making things even safer for our students, and it's not costing the taxpayers a dime," the teacher said with increasing enthusiasm.

"Well, I'll tell you something," Walter said, "I agree with you, and that's the real reason I'm here tonight—to show my support for you folks. Over the years, we've had our differences of opinions on some things that happened but I think you're doing the right thing this time. I just wish more people in the community knew or cared about this. I mean Tuesday is not looking good from what I hear just from talking to folks out and about. It's too bad you don't have a way to get the word out a little better."

"Um, actually we are planning a big surprise before the election that should help us get the message out in the community," leaked the teacher.

"Oh what's that?" asked Walter.

"I can't say just now, Walter, but you might want to keep your television on for the next few days. We've got several things planned that just might wind up on the local news. Hey, anyway, nice talking to you," the teacher said shaking Walter's hand. "I better get around and see some more people, but thanks for coming tonight, and if you have some time, make a few phone calls before Tuesday and ask your friends to give us a chance this time. There should be plenty to talk about."

55

Novemeber mornings in Low Field were typically crisp and cool; this Monday was no exception. The approaching dawn illuminated the sky with a slow-motion back light; the sun peaked above the horizon partially shrouded by a narrow band of clouds, their radiant edges tinted with hues of glowing pink tangerine.

The man watched all of this through the window of his room in the Honey Creek Motel. By a count of vehicles parked outside of the rooms, he had been one of only two occupants in the motel the past four nights. The desk attendant and property owner tried to engage him in small talk but he was careful to keep his responses both brief and vague. The only clue the man gave for his stay was that he was in the area to visit his niece and nephew who lived near Watson City. He paid in cash for four nights cleverly feigning the rates were so low that he might as well pay in cash rather than add the expense to his credit card. He told her he would not need room service during his stay, doing his green part to help save the world.

Each morning he would drive his aging mini-van out of the lot before 7:00 AM and would return in the early afternoon. He kept to himself and tried not to arouse suspicion. Each evening he would move small bags of groceries, beer and other items in from his vehicle. When he was in the room the drapes remained open across most of the front window, and he sat in a hard chair near the corner watching the peaceful view of the lake and soaring sky through the bare, scraggy branches of the oak trees that stood tall between the road and the shore. He contemplated the action he was about to take—the effects it would have on his life and the lives of the children.

The bus stop was to the north, up the side road of the motel about three-eighths of a mile. He shaved, showered, dressed and carefully checked his personal belongings and weapons. Nothing was left in the room. He gathered the dirty sheets and towels and piled them on the stand near the television. His coat was a parka style Marine issue that he had purchased from the Army-Navy surplus store near home and this morning he pulled on a black stocking cap and a pair of insulated work gloves. The two handguns were holstered around his waist and concealed by the length of the coat. He placed the shopping bag with his dirty clothes and wallet in the van and walked on the berm of the road, his back to passing traffic.

Several years after the steel plant closed his wife died. His only daughter had long since moved out west. She had a busy life and they rarely spoke to one another. So the combination of his loneliness and the need to work led him to the job of driving a school bus. He loved the students and they loved him. Most of them called him Uncle Dave. He greeted them twice a day with a genuine smile and heartfelt greeting. On their birthdays, he would bring them a cupcake and lead the other children on the bus in a singing of Happy Birthday. At Christmas, the families made the effort to bring him small, personal gifts. He drove for fifteen years and getting to see them grow up year after year filled his personal family void.

Dave frequently lectured other drivers about safety and preached about a driver's responsibility to protect students at all costs, even if it meant arriving a few minutes late on either end of a run. His grizzled face would tense and the deep wrinkles would shift as he discussed his driving philosophy with the other employees. He refused to use the size of the yellow bus as a means to drive aggressively with such precious cargo on board. The building principals and the bus supervisor would debate the point of timeliness with him, but Dave's prudent and cautious argument would usually allow him to have the last word. Everyone was bewildered by the ferocity and passion in which he stated his point-of-view.

When the first grader fell asleep on his bus and he left him alone in the parked bus for hours until his frantic parents, school officials and the police found the child, no one could believe it was one of Dave's students. When he parked the bus for the evening, he would follow the protocol of walking the bus aisle and checking the seats and surrounding areas for forgotten or lost items, so the mistake was unimaginable both to him and his supervisors. He found a book bag near the back of the bus and in his haste to place it in his van so that he could drop it off to the student's house before the little boy's mother scolded him, Dave forgot the finish his final inspection of the bus. Unfortunately, the precedent had been set when a similar situation had occurred in another district and his punishment, in spite of his ardent apologies and union mediation, was the immediate termination of his duties.

One of his fears during his years as a driver was the difficulty of protecting his students in an emergency. He contemplated terrible and convoluted scenarios often because he wanted to be ready for anything. An accident, a flat tire, a sick student, a sickness to himself, a heart attack, a terrorist attack—they were all possibilities. Other drivers thought he worried too much about such unlikely events, but his motto became, "you can't prepare for an emergency when you're in one."

The Low Field teachers' plan made perfect sense to him. The fire-power of twenty armed and trained teachers would serve as a bold deterrent against a crazed gunman entering their schools and would certainly provide a suitable defense against such an aggressor. In fact, in his view, bus drivers should also be permitted to carry concealed weapons, because the unique parameters of their jobs made them the lone adults charged with the care and custody of their students for several hours a day with absolutely no back-up. The parents entrusted their children to him not only for a safe ride to school but for their protection against a hostile and uncaring world. He was in the position to show the community of Low Field how anything can happen at any time. The teachers' plan was a good one and he would show them why it should be expanded.

He watched the bus approach the stop near the bottom of a ridge. A middle school aged student stood alone as he had the previous two school days. Dave had watched the stop several times in the past few days. The plan had been rehearsed in his mind over and over. The student stepped onto the bus, and Dave approached the driver as she reached for the door extension handle.

"Pardon me ma'am; I know you're busy but can you please tell me if you drive for the Low Field Schools?" Dave asked rhetorically.

"Why yes I do," she replied.

At that point Dave aggressively got on the bus and closed the door. The three students and the driver were initially startled and dumbfounded.

"Go!" Dave growled. "I said drive!"

One of the students screamed while the other two looked wide-eyed and shocked at Dave.

He turned to the students, smiled and said, "Don't worry kids; nothing is going to happen to you. Uncle Dave just needs a ride."

He reached across the steering wheel and switched off the driver's transmitter.

He leaned down close to her and quietly said, "I drove bus for fifteen years so don't put on the flashers or do anything to call attention to this vehicle. Now, turn left twice, get back onto the road along the lake and follow it for a while to the north; and drive slowly."

"But we'll leave the district," she said questioning his instructions.

"I know; that's okay," Dave said calmly. "Just drive slowly until I tell you to do otherwise and nothing will happen to you or the children."

From a crouched position beside the driver he scanned the road in search of a stretch with no houses and views blocked by woods. Finally, he pointed at a gas well access road.

"There; back into that access road and park the bus," he said.

The woman's face and neck were flushed scarlet with nervous emotion. She looked up and said to him, "What are you planning, mister? These are children and you're scaring them."

"Don't think about being a hero. Just do as I say and no one will get hurt," Dave assured her.

She nervously backed the bus onto the gravel service road; the reverse signal rhythmically echoed through the rising mist of the morning air.

"Turn the engine off," Dave said. "Now we wait a while until someone misses you."

Several minutes of silence seemed like an hour. The three students were quiet and still. Dave walked back and forth through the bus nervously trying to think of something to say to the students that would calm them. The youngest, a small boy, was looking down and shaking. Dave could see he was trying to hide his crying face. He sat in the seat near the youngster and waved his hand near the boy.

"What's your name, young fellow?" asked Dave.

The boy wouldn't look at him; his arms were wrapped around his book bag. Dave didn't like that a child so young had to be involved in his mission. He touched the boy's arm.

"Come on with me," Dave said. "You can sit up front by your bus driver. What's her name?"

"Miss Maxine," the boy answered softly.

"Okay. Well bring your bag and sit here behind Miss Maxine," Dave said.

He gently placed his hand on the child's back and walked him forward a few seats closer to the driver.

"There, you can sit here and be the assistant bus driver this morning," Dave said.

"It's okay, Brandon. Yes, you can help me today," Maxine said comforting the boy.

Dave walked back and forth again in the aisle peering left and right out of the windows. A car passed slowly by, the driver holding up his hand to Maxine.

"Just wave to him," Dave said, "and smile Maxine. Give him the thumbs up sign."

She smiled, gestured *okay* and waved as the driver continued down the road. Five long additional minutes passed. The silence in the bus was jolted alive with the startling ring of her cell phone. All of them were wide-eyed and alert.

"Sorry," she said, "I set the ringer as loud as it will go so I can hear it when I have a full load on board."

Dave quickly said, "Don't answer it."

"But, they're going to wonder why I didn't pick up," Maxine responded.

"I said don't answer it this time," Dave repeated.

Dave scanned the road then looked back at the other students. A girl quickly returned something to her coat pocket. Dave quickly walked down the aisle to her.

"Hey, what are you doing? What do you have there?" Dave said.

He reached into the girl's coat pocket and grabbed her phone. He read the message.

"Dammit. Why'd you do that? Everything was going fine. Don't you understand? I'm doing this for you," he said with frustration.

"Doing what, holding us hostage on our bus?" said the girl directly looking up at Dave.

Maxine's phone rang loudly again. The younger boy started to scream. Dave's instincts took over and he ripped a gun from under his coat. He fired a shot through the roof.

"Quiet," he screamed.

His eyes spotted a police cruiser approaching slowly from the left. Dave crouched down to the level of the high student seats closing toward the driver's position.

He said softly but sternly, "Maxine, get the kids and go to the back of the bus." He turned toward the students and continued, "Come on everyone; just like your emergency evacuation plan that I know you've practiced. Everybody up and go quickly to the back of the bus. Just wait with them back there Miss Maxine. Give me your phone."

Dave answered the call and listened to the voice on the phone.

"Everyone is fine and safe. Yes sir, Maxine is with them. I'll tell you what I want—I want the officer to stop where he is and I'll drive the bus to the school," Dave said.

Dave sat down in the seat while he attempted to hold the phone with his shoulder to his ear. He put the gun on the floor.

"Where are the keys? Maxine!" he said angrily.

"Sorry," she replied holding them up, "force of habit."

"Throw them here," Dave said loudly.

She threw them from her crouched position as she moved half-way through the bus. The keys bounced off the windshield and fell in the two-step well area near the door. Maxine seized her opportunity as Dave fumbled to hold onto the phone and extricate himself from the driver's seat that she kept tight to the steering wheel.

"Come on kids," she said quickly to the students.

She cracked open the emergency door and jumped to the ground as the alarm sounded the seal had been broken.

"What are you doing? Get back in here," Dave screamed.

All four of the hostages were gone in an instant, running scared with adrenalin into the wooded area behind the bus.

"Shit," Dave said to himself.

He started the bus and hammered the accelerator spewing gravel and mud from the drive as he steered the rocking bus onto the road slamming into the side of the cruiser with the front corner of the bus. The police car was knocked into the ditch and the officer, who had been on foot walking toward the bus with his gun drawn, bolted to safety away from the lurching bus. He fired several shots into the side of the yellow tank, the emergency door flapping open and shut as the vehicle roared away. He ran down the service road calling to the driver and the children.

Dave was hit by a bullet. His left arm was bleeding and he couldn't lift it. He could hear the approaching sounds of sirens toward him. Fight or flight he said to himself. The whole point of today's exercise was to point out to voters the need to approve the teachers' plan and extend it to the bus drivers. He had to think quickly.

The emergency door of the bus continued to swing open and closed, banging and echoing through the empty hull of the bus as Dave maneuvered the large vehicle around corners at an unsafe speed heading toward the lake. He saw a boat launch access road and swung the bus around a close corner between a series of pylons that signaled the ramp and launch area. He skidded the bus to a halt with the engine nose slightly submerged into the water, as if the yellow tube was getting a drink. He left the engine running as he gathered his weapons, Maxine's phone and calmly walked to the rear of the bus. Police cruisers converged into the abandoned area with a show of force that provided him with the answer to his question—fight.

Three police cars raced into the small parking area. The drivers swung their vehicles sideways for protection in case the capture got violent. Instinctively they fanned the cars in an arc about one hundred feet from the rear of the bus. It reminded Dave of a television drama. He stood on the edge of the emergency escape, his eyes scanning back and forth as the officers drew their weapons and crouched on the opposite sides of the three cruisers.

Maxine's phone rang. Dave held the phone in his right hand and a handgun limply in the other. A surge of blood covered his left hand and drops fell rhythmically to the ground from the gun barrel—the arm hung listless and straight. The pulsing of his heart was profound and his mind was struggling for clarity as he attempted to calculate his best option. His breathing was heavy and labored as he spoke to the officer.

"Yes. My name is not important; my reason for being here this morning is important," Dave said.

The office followed Dave's lead and said, "Tell me about that sir; tell me what's important about this morning."

"Kids are just as unsafe on a bus as they are in school. Bus drivers need to carry guns too in case a crazy person tries to hurt them on their way to school or on the way home. That's what is important about this morning; that's what I needed to show everyone. A crazy person can take over a bus easier than they can get into a school and start shooting people. Parents and teachers need to know that; voters need to know that; school officials need to know that. I showed them, I showed them that this morning," Dave said weakly.

Dave's vision blurred and he slowly swayed to one side against the door jam. He expected a firestorm of gunfire that would rip painful holes throughout his body—his final testament to a cause. He stood proud before them, but before it could happen, the gun slid from his crimson grip and he fell face first onto the gravel below in a sickening thump. His mission was accomplished.

56

M R. COLLINS SPENT the first hour the voting polls were open greeting people on the corner of the sidewalk that led into the back door of the elementary school where the precinct volunteers and booths were located for the day.

His generic greeting and message was, "Good morning. Thanks for coming out to vote. Please consider supporting your schools today. We need your help passing this levy. The money will be spent wisely on students."

And so on, were the comments he used in an alternating fashion as voters approached from the parking lot. Most people would either pass him without any recognition of his comments or would utter only a brief and grunted response. A few supporters would shake his hand and echo sentiments of encouragement.

When the buses began arriving with the students, he abandoned his post and walked along the sidewalk that edged the perimeter of the building to the school's front doors where the central office was located. He had been through the turmoil of elections so many times over the years that by 8:00 AM he had a pretty good idea based on the attitude and volume of voters in the first hour whether they had much of a chance to win the community's support. It was informal and unscientific exit polling to say the least, but, by the time he reached his office, opened the door and said good morning to his secretary, his gut told him the levy would fail again. Her facial expression and the nod of her head seemed to ask the question that he answered with his hand—thumbs down.

"Long day coming L J," he said.

She handed him several messages from missed phone calls; two board members and a local television reporter.

"Yuck, did I ever tell you that I have grown to hate Election Day?" he asked. "I better call John before the day begins to take on a life of its own."

"It seems like I've heard you say that before, boss," she said with a sad smile.

He closed the door to the office, hung up his sport coat, turned on his laptop and called the board president.

"Hi John," the superintendent said. "How are you today?"

"Hey Jim," he replied, "just fine thanks. How's the turnout over at the elementary school?"

"Pretty busy. I'd give it an eight out of ten on a volume scale," said Jim.

"The fire station was packed this morning when I voted. Probably not a good sign," lamented John.

"No, probably not."

"Hey, all we can do now is wait and see," said John. "On a different note, I went to the teachers' affair on Saturday night and heard something interesting."

"What's that?" Jim asked.

"One of the teachers was talking to Walter Franklin," John started to say.

"Really? Walter was there?" Jim said with disbelief.

"Yeah that's interesting in itself but my wife was nearby and overheard Ryan saying that there was going to be a big surprise before the election that would get everyone's attention and would be on the news," John said.

"Wow; you think they had something to do with yesterday's bus incident?" Jim asked.

"I can't say for sure, but Kim was certain he said that something was going to happen before the election," John said.

"My God, they're bigger fools than I thought if they set up that disaster of a stunt. A few of the guys I spoke with this morning were furious about that debacle; one said he couldn't believe we let that happen on a bus and wouldn't give the district a cent," the superintendent said.

"I hope there's no connection but who knows?" John said. "I guess we shouldn't say anything until the police finish their investigation. Let's hope it was a coincidence. Have you spoken to Chief Hadley yet?"

"Yeah he called last night," Jim said. "The fella was unconscious or sleeping most of the evening when he got out of the recovery room and the nurses asked them to come back this morning to question him and get his statement."

"Did you make any precautions this morning with the drivers?" John asked.

"Yes. All of the drivers had a volunteer assistant ride with them this morning—mostly family members, friends and a few parents. It was probably unnecessary but I thought it was a good idea for the students to see another adult and I haven't heard of any problems," Jim said.

"Well, I'll let you go. Please let me know if you find out anything and I can help call the other board members with an update. I'm in the car this morning calling on a few customers but I'll be around all afternoon if I can help," the board president offered.

"Will do," said Jim, "thanks John."

Jim sat back in his chair stretching his arms above his head and arching his upper back. The constant, silent stress of never-ending problems was taking a toll on his mind and body. An emptiness accompanied most days as the merry-go-round of his daily grind went round and round. His job was less about leadership and more about parenthood. Increasingly he felt like the father of an expansive, dysfunctional family. Happiness was less and less frequent and potential tragedy and heartache loomed over even the most routine of days. Statistically, his tenure in the district had doubled the typical lifespan of a superintendent and he now knew why most people in his position seek new jobs every few years—the people of Low Field knew everything about him and he knew everything about them and the perceptions were mutually dark and objectionable.

57

WILL THOUGHT SUNDAY afternoon might be a good time to finally
visit Abby. First, he called her home in case he was mistaken.
Her mom said his visit would be welcome. She gave him directions
because their home was located at the end of a seldom-used road and
was difficult to find.

"About three miles out of town watch for the abandoned, weathered barn that has a collapsed roof," she said, "and turn left at the next
road. It's at the bottom of a swale so reduce your speed."

The house was a large, log cabin A-frame whose deep walnut
color matched the bark of the red oak, sweetgum and locust trees in
the surrounding woods. It was built in a small clearing cut into an
elevated ridge several hundred yards back from the road. The house
was the last one on a dead-end road that bordered the Pine Hills
Preservation Park in the far southwest corner of the school district.
The area was scarcely populated and very rural, but too hilly for ag-
ricultural activity. This was a place for nature lovers—people who
enjoyed hiking, hunting and watching wildlife. The setting could
have been from a movie. A wide creek cut a seam through the forest
from the higher ground on his left to the falling terrain on the right
side of the road. The tires made a different sound as they rumbled
over the wooden bridge. He had never driven on the road before, and
the further he traveled, the passage became increasingly narrow. The
woods thickened, becoming denser and darker with trees hugging

both sides of the road so closely that he felt like he was journeying in a different century deep in an Ohio wilderness.

The peacefulness and privacy of the property matched Abby's personality—or at least what he knew of it. They had been classmates for twelve years of public school, but he, like most of their other classmates, never really got to know Abby beyond the surface level of hellos and goodbyes. She was quiet and reclusive, but her art revealed a lively thinker who preferred to interact with the world through a medium of serious visual expression rather than trite verbal exchanges.

"Come in, Will. How are you?" asked Abby's mother with a genuine smile.

"Fine, thanks, Mrs. Olson," replied Will, "how are you doing?"

"I'm well," she said. "Please, let me take your coat. Here, follow me; Abby's in the back of the house in her studio."

"Thank you, ma'am. Wow this place is really cool," said Will looking up at the heavy beams and large window panels.

"Thank you. We've lived here for quite a while. In fact, the house was built just before Abby was born. We fell in love with the property and knew this was the place for us. The trick was making the house fit in with the woods, so we ended up with lots of wood and glass," she explained.

"It's really awesome," Will said. "You and your husband are visionaries."

"Why, thank you."

They weaved through an open cabin-look space with large windows with shapes he thought reminiscent of geometry class. Several large build-in bookshelves flanked either side of a wide opening to a sunny, spacious room. As he approached, he saw Abby seated in a wheelchair hunched over a table working on a drawing. Pencils and Artgum erasers were scattered about—tools of the artist this day.

"Abby, honey," her mom said, "Will is here."

"Oh hi, Will," Abby replied.

"Hey Abby, how are you feeling?" Will asked.

"I'm okay," Abby said with a positive look. "How's your leg?"

"It's getting better every day," he said. "Thanks."

"Pull up a chair," Abby said pointing at a small side chair near one of the walls.

"Okay. So, tell me, what are you working on?" Will asked.

"Oh, I'm just doing some technique drawing of the woods—trying to achieve aspect and depth and dimension in such a busy landscape. I mean our eyes easily differentiate spacial variations but it's not as easy to replicate in art," she explained.

"Yeah, tell me about it; I never progressed past stick figures," he said looking closely at the drawing. "Wow, that's really good. Those trees look amazing; it's like a black-and-white photograph."

"Thanks. Do you want it?" she asked simply.

"Are you kidding?" he said with surprise. "Sure, I'd love to have it. I'll get it framed and hang it in my room."

"Well then let me sign it for you," she said carefully adding her signature near the bottom right corner. "Please take it away before I draw myself hanging by a noose in one of those pin oaks."

"What? Come on, Abby," Will said smiling, "things will get better."

"Yeah sure," said the artist. "You know I could draw a hole in my stomach and title it *My Day From Hell*."

"I'm sorry Abby for what happened," said Will.

"I keep wondering if there was some reason why we got shot. Don't you?" she asked earnestly. "I mean you, too, must have wondered why Colt's bullet hit you and not one of other two hundred people in the parking lot that day; haven't you?"

"Sure. I've thought about it," he confessed. "The only way I can explain it is I just figure lots of things happen to people totally by chance. I don't believe it was God's plan like we were being punished for something. This time I think it was a fluke that we got hit—more like a random coincidence, rather than for some grand purpose. I see it as bad luck, I suppose."

"I guess I'm more fatalistic than you, at least on the shooting. The way I remember it, there were a couple of hundred people walking through that lot at the moment Colt starting shooting and we were the unfortunate ones to get hit. Lindsay was right next to me, a foot away, and she's fine. Ever since that day, I've been thinking about the thin line there is in life between opposite things—success and failure; happiness and sadness; life and death. Just because we were walking in an arbitrary path that the bullets were flying, you and I have to deal with this shit for the rest of our lives," Abby said.

"You're right. It's certainly not fair and we do have to deal with this forever. Some guy called me into the office at school the other day. He's like a psychologist or something. Anyway, he got me talking about the shooting and my feelings and what I thought about Colton and a bunch of other stuff. But, in the end, after about an hour of talking, I asked him why he called me into the office. And do you know what he said?" asked Will.

"No, what?" she asked.

"He said just so I could talk to someone about the trauma of what we experienced. Not that it was going to change what happened or make sense of it, but just talk about it," Will explained.

"Was it helpful for you?" she asked.

"Hey, I know your situation is totally different than mine and I'm probably being a tool for suggesting that just talking about what happened is going to make it any better, but it felt to me like a situation where you're mad at someone and you argue and get it out and then later on it's just over. I guess the anger is gone," he said. "Anyway, after I talked to this guy, Dr. something-or-other, I did feel better, and the whole mess just seemed further away from me, more in the past. The other thing I realized was that as bad as it is to have been shot, the situation could have turned out much worse.

"Yeah, I can see that; actually it's probably a good idea," she admitted. "I am angry that I got hit by that bullet that could have paralyzed me for life and I'm angry with Colt for that, but I'm still searching for an explanation for why it was me, and you, who got shot."

"Sure. I understand your frustration," he said. "I'm mad at Colt, too."

Abby continued, "I mean, he was so reckless and stupid. Why in the world would someone be so self-absorbed to think he could start shooting a gun in a crowd of people and assume no one would get hurt or that he had any right to do that? It's just ludicrous. I still can't believe he just opened fire without any conscious thought of the possible consequences to others. What did he think was going to happen?"

"I know, it makes no sense whatsoever, but that's almost the point," said Will thinking out loud. "He must not have been thinking, right? He's had a bunch of concussions and it's like the rational part of his brain is turned off or damaged. I don't know how to explain it; it's just a mess. He created a big mess for all of us."

"Yep," she agreed. "Hey, I'm sorry for going off on you. None of it was your fault either."

"No problem; I think it's all part of us just working through our frustration. God, I sound like the school psychologist—that's so lame. I'm sorry," Will said laughing.

"Don't be," Abby said. "It's so nice of you to come by to see me and for us to have a chance to talk. I guess we'll always share a part of Low Field history together."

"Oh yeah, we're famous, in a weird way," said Will.

"Hey not everyone can brag that they were the first two shooting victims in the school's history and lived to talk about it," Abby said smiling.

"They should put us on the cover of the yearbook. Don't you think?" Will asked.

"Yeah, that's the least they can do," she said with a smirk. "What a legacy; the cover could have an overlay of raised, bloody bullets for accent and texture. I'd be glad to design it for them."

"Wow, you really do know your art," said Will

"A little," Abby said. "There's so much to study and learn. It's paradoxical—the more I learn about art, the more I realize how much more there is to learn. And I guess one thing the shooting has taught me is to not wait. I have a bone fragment from my surgery and every time I look at it I'm reminded how fragile our lives are; let's face it, we could be gone in an instant."

"You're right. Maybe that's the answer to the question you brought up a while ago," Will said. "Neither one of us will probably ever take our health or our lives for granted again."

"Yes," she agreed. "And I now realize that we should pursue our passions with conviction and single-mindedness."

"And that we shouldn't wait to chase our dreams," Will added. "I'm glad I came over to see you. You are such an inspiration to me Abby."

"What? Get serious," she laughed.

"I know that probably sounds corny but I mean it," he said. "This is crazy but Jack's mom is the President of the PTA at the Elementary School and the other day she asked me to come speak to the PTA about the shooting, I think to reassure them about sending their kids to school. I'm supposed to talk about what might be done to improve school security and that kind of stuff. Would you want to come with me and maybe share your opinions?"

"I don't know. I'm not much for public speaking," said Abby.

"Well I know you didn't expect that, but the offer is there if you'd like to join me, and I'd welcome the company because I'm not big on giving speeches either," admitted Will. "Oh, have you heard the latest? The teachers want to get guns and keep them in their classrooms?"

"What?" she said surprised at his statement.

"Yeah," he said, "crazy, right?"

"That's absurd. Why? So more kids can get shot? Have they lost their minds?" Abby asked.

"I know," Will agreed laughing, "maybe we can tell the PTA that arming the teachers we know at Low Field is far more dangerous than any lunatic or terrorist.

Abby laughed and said, "Let me think about it, Will. I might go with you; having more guns in the schools would just add to the problem and would not improve safety. What are they thinking?"

"They're nuts," Will agreed, "and maybe we're the right people to tell them that."

58

Until the growth spurt Clayton experienced during his sophomore year, he had stood almost a foot shorter than his older brother most of his early teenage years. The additional inches he grew now gave him the same lanky, six-foot body type and appearance of Colton. Despite the efforts of Low Field coaches to recruit the younger brother to play traditional sports in high school, Clayton spent his free time doing outdoor activities such as hunting and fishing when he wasn't working on the farm or in the sandwich shop. He was an excellent marksman with any type of weapon, bow or firearm. Roy encouraged his son's interest in hunting by setting up targets for the boy to shoot with his first BB gun rifle and a child's bow when he was barely six years old. Clayton would practice for hours, and once his father had the prerequisite safety guidelines firmly entrenched into the boy's routine, he would leave him alone in the back yard and continue his work in the barn, occasionally checking on him through the window.

When he turned eight, his father bought him a starter .22 rifle for his birthday. In short time, he became proficient enough with the gun that his father took him into the woods and taught him the basic principles of hunting. The thrill of killing squirrels and crows hooked Clayton on the sport. By age ten, Roy invited Clayton to join a neighbor and him for the fall hunting seasons and his responsible approach quickly made him a regular. He was always a calm, quiet boy, preferring to listen and learn from the older men. He had thoughts and opinions but, like his grandpa Leon, kept them to himself, even as a child. During the past few years, he was permitted to use adult guns and his love of shooting sports became the single most important passion in his life. Becoming an Army sniper was his goal after high school graduation.

The day after the school shooting Clayton went to work early at the sandwich shop. The owner, Jerry Wilson, promptly pulled him into his office.

"Hey Clayton, I meant to call you but we've been busy all day," Jerry said.

"Why, what's up?" Clayton asked.

"Well, I was going to tell you to take a week or so off; you know, stay home with your family for a while," he said. "Then I'll give you a call when I need you to come back."

"I'd rather be here," Clayton said, "and keep busy."

"Look Clayton, you're a good worker and you know I like you," Jerry said, "but I don't need the controversy affecting my business."

"What do you mean?" Clayton said getting agitated. He could feel his skin getting warm.

"I'll be straight with you. I know you didn't shoot those kids at the school, but your brother did and everyone in this town knows you and Colt," Jerry said. "I'm going to have to let you go Clay."

"That doesn't make any sense," Clayton angrily said. "I didn't have anything to do with what Colton did at the school; why would you take that out on me?"

The man held up his hand and said, "It probably doesn't make sense to you right now, but trust me it's nothing personal. It's just business."

"Well Jerry, that's the lamest bullshit I've ever heard," Clayton said. The boy tossed his work cap on the man's desk and turned to leave. When he got to the door, he abruptly stopped and pulled off his shirt exposing his bare torso. He balled the shirt and threw it with all his might at the surprised man who instinctively ducked to avoid being struck in the head with the employee garment.

"Clayton, never leave a job in a bad way," Jerry cautioned.
"Too late, Jerry," Clayton stated, "I already did."
"Don't come back," Jerry shouted.
"Oh, you haven't seen the last of me," Clayton promised.

59

Kelsey and Erin were in the basement rec-room watching television late into the night—mostly music videos and reality shows looking for laughs and cute guys. They made a frozen pizza and popcorn and after Kelsey's mom and stepdad had been in bed for hours, Kelsey climbed onto the kitchen counter and got down a bottle of rum which they added in lavish amounts to several glasses of diet soda. They were having fun texting other friends and each other and sending screwy pictures of themselves back and forth long past midnight.

Suddenly they heard footsteps on the stairs and Wyatt's voice quickly followed, "Hey you girls got to keep it down; your mother and brother and I are trying to sleep. In fact, I want you to go to bed."

"Sorry," Kelsey said, "we'll turn down the TV and go to bed as soon as this show is over."

"No ifs, ands or buts about it. As soon as this one is over, go to bed," Wyatt said.

"Okay," promised Kelsey.

Wyatt shuffled back up the stairs mumbling something as he walked away. Kelsey tiptoed to the basement door and quietly closed it.

"He's such a jerk," Kelsey said, "I hate him."

"He kind of gives me the creeps," Erin said with a grimace.

"I don't think I'll ever get married. I think my mom wanted a guy around for my brother and me, but I wish she had never married Wyatt," Kelsey said.

"I don't like the way he looks at me staring with his googly eyes. It's always like he's looking at a piece of meat or something. It just creeps me out being around him," Erin said.

"Yeah, I can't imagine my poor mom, you know, having to have sex with him," Kelsey said making a face and suppressing a laugh. "Yuck."

Erin laughed hard then stifled the sound covering her mouth with her hand.

"Oh my god," Erin said, "he's probably one of those guys with a little dick."

Kelsey burst out laughing too before she buried her face in a throw pillow.

"Not like Colt," Kelsey said making a face at Erin.

"What? You and Colt had sex?" Erin asked.

"No; but I saw him naked," Kelsey said. "One day I was over at his house and he didn't know I was waiting for him in their living room, and he walked through the room after taking a shower. It was so funny. He's walking along butt naked drying his hair with a towel and he sees me and just stops. And I'm staring at his thing, probably with my mouth open. It looked like a horse's thing it was so big. I cracked up and he ran out of the room. He does have a nice butt, too, by the way."

They both laughed and then Erin said, "Oh god, that's so funny."

"I told him afterwards I was never having sex with him, ever," Kelsey said.

Erin grabbed a tube sock from her boot and stuck one end in the front of her pajama bottom so the sock hung down long between her legs. She swung the sock back and forth laughing.

"Did it look like this?" Erin asked with a smile.

"Maybe, that's closer to a pony" Kelsey said giggling.

"Well come here, Kelsey," Erin said quietly, "let me show you some real pleasure."

Erin stood over Kelsey with the sock dangling down at her face. Kelsey reached up and pulled both the sock and Erin toward her.

"Come on then, big boy," Kelsey said playfully.

Erin gently pushed Kelsey to her back and got on top of her. She jokingly started to hump Kelsey while she fondled one of her breasts.

"How do like that, Miss Kelsey?" Erin said biting Kelsey's ear lobe and gently pulling it with her teeth.

"Oh you're too big," Kelsey whispered, "but don't stop."

Kelsey lifted her head and kissed Erin's cheek and neck. Suddenly they were both serious. Kelsey pulled her friend down onto the sleeping bag and hugged her close. Erin kissed Kelsey on the lips and they held their embrace, exchanging tongues and kissing slowly with feeling. They explored each other's bodies for a while, both with their passion fueled by the spontaneity of the moment. Quietly they undressed each other, their hands carefully moving to places that neither had ever allowed another person to feel. It was the most exciting experience of both of their lives. When they finished, they lay together holding one another, caressing, their bodies wet with sweat.

Kelsey got up and pulled on her warm-up pants and t-shirt.

"You okay?" Erin asked.

"Yeah, I'm fine," Kelsey said with a smile. "How about you?"

"I'm great."

Kelsey laid down next to Erin and said, "I don't know what just happened, but I certainly didn't expect that."

"Yeah, me neither," Erin said.

"Well, I had fun—I enjoyed it even though you're no Colt," Kelsey said.

They laughed softly together.

Then Kelsey added, "In fact, I think I enjoyed that more than if you were Colt."

"Me too," said Erin holding Kelsey's hand as they lay on the bed looking up at the ceiling and wondering to themselves what it all meant.

60

OOTBALL FANS WALKING into Cleveland Stadium couldn't remember the last time the team had hosted a Monday night game. The wind coming off of Lake Erie made the temperature feel at least fifteen degrees colder than the thermometer reading of forty-five that pulsed on and off between advertisements on an neon bank sign across a street and a small green space to the south of the parking lot. The fans' level of excitement, however, had a counter-balance effect on the frigid air.

Daron and his mom both wore three layers of clothing under their Browns hoodies and each had a hat and gloves stuffed into the pouch of their sweatshirt. They were early by almost two hours for the start of the game thinking the kickoff was an hour earlier than the scheduled 9:00 PM. The tickets Brenda received from the radio station were only commemorative passes for the event, so they needed to pick up the official tickets at the Will Call window at least thirty minutes prior to game time. They bought hot chocolate and waited in the vicinity for what Brenda described to Daron as his second surprise.

"Hey, look at you two! You look great, like real Brown's fans," said the large man smiling as he walked toward them with a tall slender woman holding his arm. The couple both wore black leather coats and dress hats.

Daron smiled and said, "Uncle Ray, I didn't know you were coming to the game."

Daron and his uncle shook hands and bumped chests.

"Well your mom really knows how to keep a secret," said his uncle. "This is my girlfriend, Olivia. This is my nephew, Daron, and my sister-in-law, Brenda. She's the brilliant trivia expert who won the tickets."

The attractive woman smiled and said, "Nice to meet you both. Ray has told me so much about you."

"So, how are you doing young man?" asked Ray. "You look bigger; you must be working out."

"Yeah a little," Daron admitted. "You know, I've got some more time on my hands."

"That's cool. I'm glad you're putting the time to good use," the man said. "Let's find a gate and go check out the Browns."

They had end-zone seats in the northeast corner lower field section about fifty rows up from the field. It wasn't a great perspective on the game but there were definitely worse seats in the stadium. The enormous banks of lights gave the interior of the oval facility the appearance of daytime but the concrete structure held the arctic chill like a walk-in freezer.

"Man, it's so cold in this place," Rafer said shaking his shoulders.

"Yeah, my mom kept making me put more layers of clothing on before she would leave and I guess she knew what she was talking about," Daron said.

"So, the last time I saw you I think was when I had just gotten home from Iraq," Ray said.

"Yeah, it was right after you got awarded the Purple Heart; in fact, your second Purple Heart," Daron said.

"Yeah, that's right. Earning that one was rough; real rough," said his uncle. "Let's switch seats; this one is my good ear so I can hear you better."

"You're a war hero, Uncle Ray," Daron said, "and nobody can ever take that away from you."

"Not that many people care about that, but, yes, you're right and that's nice of you to say it like that. So, what's up with you? Your mom said you hit a bump in the road," he said.

"Yeah, my senior year got disrupted a little, but it's cool. I'm actually enrolled in one of those electronic charter schools where you do all of your work on a computer and I like it. I don't have to sit in boring classes any more and the only classes I have are the ones I need for graduation; that's it. And as soon as I'm done with them, I'm finished with school and I get my diploma. So technically I can move on with my life right away without having to wait until the summer to make decisions about my next move," Daron said.

"So what are you thinking?" asked Ray.

"I'm not sure right now, but I've narrowed the choices down to three options: moving to Florida and working, going to college at Akron or joining the Army," said Daron.

"Okay, I like it," Rafer said, "those all sound good. Which one are you leaning toward now?

"I haven't told my mom but actually I'm pretty sure I'm going to join the Army," Daron said. "That's one reason why it's so cool that you're here tonight. What do you think I should do? I mean, is the Army a good option or a bad one?"

"The Army is a good option for the right people. Most of the guys I served with fell into one of two categories—the ones who had shitty home lives and no future other than winding up on the streets and either ending up dead or dealing drugs or the ones who were basically pissed-off young males who grew up playing too many video games and needed to have someone structure their time and tell them what to do. Both groups of guys were just trying to find their bearings in life," Rafer said. "You know, as I think about it, there was a third group. There were a lot of guys who really had a passion to serve their country and came from families that had a legacy of service in the armed forces. Those guys were real patriots. They took the whole 'red, white and blue' thing to a real, serious level. And that's the group I'd put you in."

"So how about you, Uncle Ray?" asked Daron. "Which of those groups were you in?"

"Honestly, I think I was one of the pissed-off video game guys trying to find myself, and the Army provided me with a great place to think about life and death and my future. It was good for me to spend those years growing up and learning how to be a man."

"Yeah but it sucks that you had to do that in a war," Daron said.

"That was okay; in fact, it was a great place to think about the big issues of life because you didn't know what was around every corner. Those first few months in Iraq I was terrified every minute about IUDs, snipers, suicide bombers, car bombs and all the people. It was a total mess. You had no idea who to trust and you never felt safe. But living with death staring you in the face like that every minute of every day really helped me focus on what I believed in and what I wanted to do with my life if I lived to get out of that desert mess," he admitted.

"God, that had to be awful being in a place like that," Daron said.

"It was rough, really rough. I saw a lot of death. I saw friends get killed and maimed right in front of me. And the car bomb that got me wounded the second time was fifteen yards from me, but it wasn't my time, I guess. I just happened to be on the right side of the hummer when it went off—the shrapnel just got me in the legs and blew my one eardrum out but I'm still alive," Rafer said.

"Man, Uncle Ray," Daron said, "what went through your mind when that happened?"

"It's scary. I was scared, no lie, because you know some really bad shit just happened and you were in the middle of it, but it literally takes you a minute or two just to figure out if you got hit or honestly if you're even alive," Ray said. "I mean, when that blast went off I got knocked down like a rag doll. I remember looking at the vehicle flipped on its side and I was holding my ear and touching myself to see if I could feel my fingers. It happened in an instant, a millisecond."

"Wow," Daron said," I don't know if I could handle that."

"You would; you would. Army training is the best in the world and once you get deployed you kind of get numb to your fear and you just do your job. It's a weird feeling, but it's the only way to survive. You just get lost in the mission, and it actually sharpens your focus as a soldier," the boy's uncle said sitting tall.

"That is some serious shit, man," Daron said shaking his head.

"Oh yeah, it's some real serious shit, but it forced me to become a grown man and it gave me a chance to figure out what I wanted to do with my life. And you know Daron, ultimately, the Army gave me a future, too. I'm going to school now because of my service. I mean, don't get me wrong, everyone who serves pays a price," he said. "And now, I have good days and bad days, but in a few years I'm going to be the first college graduate from my family and hopefully become a teacher and coach and help kids realize their dreams."

"Cool, man," Daron said shaking his uncle's hand. "You'll be a good one, too."

"Thanks, Daron," Ray said as a loud cheer rose from the crowd. "Look, here come our sorry Browns."

"Yeah, do you believe how the Cleveland curse lives on?" Daron asked.

"It's crazy man," Rafer said. "I've been watching this sorry-ass team since I was a little kid and then they left the city...and man, they've just sucked every year since they've been back. I don't know if they'll ever get it together."

Daron just shook his head in agreement as there was nothing else to say. To one side of their seats and behind them were a dozen or so fans from the Bills who had made the trip from Buffalo to Cleveland. They appeared to have started their party many hours before entering the stadium. Several of the men seated behind Daron's mother and Olivia were making personal comments about the four of them. His mom stood, pulled at Olivia's arm and glared at the men.

"Come on Olivia," Brenda said angrily, "let's go to the restroom."

"Where're you going, sweet cakes? Come on, don't run off," said one of the drunken men, "we're just trying to make some new friends with some Brown's fans."

Brenda pointed a finger at the man and said with stern serious-ness, "Just shut up, okay? Just shut up and keep your stupid remarks to yourself."

"It's okay, baby," said another man. "You're obviously a cool babe; I mean you've got the bi-racial kid and don't mind if your man is do-ing you and a black woman too. Just relax and be cool with us."

Ray and Daron stood and let Brenda and Olivia pass them. The men then turned in unison facing the rows of rowdy men in Bills jerseys.

Daron pushed up the sleeves of his hoody and yelled, "Man, you got a problem with my mom?"

Three or four of Buffalo fans stood as well, towering over the others because of the elevated seating.

One of them said, "No, we kinda like your mom."

"What? You assholes need to shut your mouths," Daron said.

"What if we don't want to?" said a man pointing at Daron. "You better sit down little Oreo."

"Who you calling an Oreo, you fat slug. Why don't you get up and we can settle this here and now," Daron said.

"What, all of us against just you and your daddy?" the man said laughing. "Or is he just your mom's chocolate treat for the week?" He lifted the large plastic cup of beer in his right hand and pretended to trip spilling most of the beer on Daron.

The row of four men stood looking down, laughing and baiting a full-blown confrontation. Ray had been quiet but now sprung into a trained combat rage. He pulled two of the men forward over the seats sending beer into the air like yellow rain. Before one of the other men could even pull his hand back in preparation of throwing a punch, Ray sent an upper-cut into the man's groin and slapped him hard on the side of the head. The fourth Bill's fan flung his full beer glass at Daron. He threw the hardest punch of his life and connected with the man's face. Blood rushed from the man's broken nose as he sat back in his seat screaming obscenities.

"Come on, Daron," said Ray, "let's get out of here."

Ray pulled Daron and the ladies past him toward the aisle, all the while glaring fiercely and daring the others in the visiting group to make a move. He was ready to take on all comers no matter how many started his way. He stood and stared at the group.

"I didn't think so," Rafer said.

Flustered and shaken, the four of them made their way to a concourse area where Daron's mom got him napkins from a condiment stand. She helped him dry his sweatshirt while Rafer and Olivia talked to one another nearby.

"Are you okay, honey?" she asked.

"Yeah, I'm fine, mom," Daron said. "Are you and Olivia okay?"

"Yes. I'm so sorry," his mom said. "They were just saying the most ridiculous and offensive things to Olivia and I—I just couldn't take any more of it."

"Mom, its fine," said Daron. "They got what they had coming to them."

Several security workers and police officers approached them to talk. Their heart rates were still accelerated and their breathing was rapid.

One of them said, "Folks, please we need you to come with us."

"Officer you don't know what those drunk men were saying to us and one of them poured a beer on my son," Brenda said.

Rafer spoke up and said, "It's okay Brenda, let's just go with them."

Within an instant, they were led into a room on the inner portion of the stadium. One of the men in security clothing grabbed a towel from a cupboard and tossed it to Daron.

"Are you okay, young man?"

"Yes sir, I'm fine," Daron said.

"Good. Okay folks we're going to ask each one of you to tell us what happened. It's going to take a few minutes, so please sit down and relax for now. Can we get you anything to drink or eat?" the security guard asked.

"Officer, we didn't do anything wrong here," Brenda insisted. "Those men started this whole problem. We were just talking and waiting for the game to start and they were saying awful, terrible things to us. My god, what a mess."

"Yes, ma'am we heard that from other fans who witnessed the incident. Please just relax. We just need to hear from you what happened so we can write it correctly in our report."

The four of them gathered their emotions and made statements. They used the restroom. The muffled noise from the stadium signaled the beginning of the game. The giant structure actually moved with the exuberance of the crowd. Several other stadium workers in brown blazers and orange shirts entered the room and talked quietly to the police and security workers. One of them approached Daron, Ray and the slightly traumatized women. He was carrying a new Brown's team jacket still wrapped in plastic.

He extended it toward Daron and said, "I guessed a large; is that correct?"

Daron and the others smiled and the boy said, "Perfect. A large is perfect. Thank you."

The other man in a brown blazer put his hands up and said to all of them, "Folks, we are very sorry about what happened and we don't want you to leave with that as your memory of tonight's game. So, on behalf of the Cleveland Browns, we'd like to offer you an opportunity to watch tonight's game from the comfort of one of the owner's private skybox suites. Of course all of your food and beverage needs will be taken care of, as well. Does that sound like something that you'd like to do?"

The four of them looked back and forth at each other and Daron shook his head emphatically yes. He snapped the front of his new jacket shut and shook out his arms. Smiles appeared on all of their faces as they walked in pairs out of the room, their arms linked.

"Man, talk about turning lemons into lemonade!" Ray said as a police officer and the Brown's attendant escorted them to the luxury of the private viewing room near the fifty yard line.

61

THE EARLY WINTER sun hugged the southern horizon as it passed over Low Field. A century-old, defunct and now abandoned church sat on a lonely unkempt lot across the street and down a ways from the Caldwell residence. From his bedroom, Colton would lie in bed and watch the mystical sight of the intersection of the sun's rays and the weathered cross atop the church spire. On cloudless days this time of year they created a morning shadow of a cross on his window. It slid gently from left to right moving across the threadbare linen drapes—a strange, distorted and wavelike sign from god.

Before his mom's death, Colton always thought of the cross as a good omen; it was God's way of letting him know he was being looked after. It was comforting and gave him the strength to follow his passion, playing football better than anyone else who had ever put on a uniform to represent Low Field High School. Even in the most difficult times when Colton had been injured and the migraines wouldn't stop, he believed a divine spirit was in his corner protecting him from the worst. His mom would remind him of God's presence in his daily life—the guardian angel sitting on his shoulder, providing safety and strength from life's travails as well as giving him the spiritual guidance to do good deeds and to make proper choices, whenever temptation entered his mind.

Since her passing, however, he was confused by God's will and even began to have doubts about a merciful deity in his life. She was such a good woman; she had never done anything remotely bad that he knew of, especially when it came to her interactions with other people. In fact, she always worried about how friends and neighbors were getting along and wondered if they were in need. She would send the boys to take a few of their chickens' eggs to the elderly people on their street as a way of simply checking on them.

"Tell them your mom sent some eggs and ask them if they need you to do anything. I want you to be neighborly, boys, and don't accept any pay for it. If someone wants to give you money, just ask them to leave some extra in the Sunday collection basket. We all have an obligation to help each other—that's God's will," was her lesson and message.

So why did God take her? He and Clayton needed her now more than ever. Colton was never as confused and conflicted about his life since his discharge. Some days he slept hours longer than usual; other days he could barely sleep at all. Fits of depression were coupled with ecstatic mood swings of optimism and despair. His future was perilously in the balance. Today's hearing would challenge his faith. As he dressed, he thought of the lessons she had taught him, the values she had preached and the belief that she had given them in a benevolent God who loved his children the way he knew his mother loved him.

In the back of one of his dresser drawers he kept a note his mother had written to him years ago after a classmate had drowned. She had written it to give her young son comfort and solace during his first encounter with death. It was a short note that read:

Dearest Colton, I am so sorry you have lost your friend Jimmy. Some things that happen don't make sense, but remember God has a special plan for each of us. Death on earth is not the end of life, but simply a new beginning. Love, Mom

Colton sat on the corner of his bed and read the note several times holding it gently in his fingers. He examined his mother's handwriting.

As he read the message his eyes pooled with excess tears. The memories of his friend had faded like the ink on the paper, but his mother's words of guidance were as powerful now as a decade ago. The simple note was his most prized possession from his mother; he felt her presence in the room when he held it. A tear fell from his cheek creating a wet dot on his beige slacks. After a few minutes he stood up and carefully refolded the note and put it in the envelope, tucked away for safekeeping.

Colton slipped on his only sport coat, an all-purpose navy blue blazer that his grandfather had told him would go with just about any shirt and tie and would get him through just about any function. He checked his hair and the knot of his tie in the small mirror of his dresser. He pulled back the drapes from the front window allowing brilliant sunshine to fill the room. His mother loved sunny days. She would say to him and Clayton in the bright kitchen while they ate breakfast, *God is smiling on us today boys.* He wished more than ever that she could be with him today. Colton would make the best of the situation, settling for her spirit and wisdom to accompany him through the inspiration of the sun.

62

Attorney Morris asked Colton's grandparents to drive him to the courthouse and sit in the first row of the audience. They were proud, honest people who wore the toll of the past month's events on their faces with concern and graven soberness. Their lives, too, had unraveled in a harsh tailspin. Both in their eighties, the stress of their family troubles had shrunk them even further than the gradual fading that comes through time. Their pale faces barely stood above the half-wall and railing that separated the officers of the court from the public.

"All rise."

Judge Stevenson sat at the bench and opened the folder to the first case. He said loudly, "Please be seated. Mr. Reardon, what are the charges?"

"Your honor the state charges Colton Edward Caldwell with the possession of a loaded firearm in a designated school zone, three counts of reckless endangerment, two counts of attempted murder and inducing panic in a public location," the prosecutor said.

"Mr. Morris," said the judge looking over the top of his reading glasses.

Morris stood and touched Colton's arm giving him the direction to also stand. The attorney buttoned his suit coat and whispered the words into Colton's ear, "Stand tall."

"Your honor the defense requests that all charges be dismissed because of my client suffers from the recognized medical condition, TBI, or Traumatic Brain Injury which he sustained during the past three to five years at no fault of his own representing both Low Field High School as a decorated football player as well as proudly serving in the United States Army. My client is a victim of the system, your honor. Furthermore, your honor, I would ask the record to reflect that earlier this week I filed a written claim against the Low Field Local Schools notifying the superintendent and board of education that we plan to file a lawsuit on behalf of my client for the pronounced damages he has suffered because of their gross negligence and their failure to treat his medical issues as well as their inability to protect him during his seasons as a high school football player while in their care and custody.

The judge looked at Colton and said, "Young man, state your name."

"Colton Edward Caldwell, sir," Colton said.

"How do you plead?" asked the judge.

"Not guilty, your honor," Colton replied.

"The defendant's request to have all charges dismissed is denied. This case will go to trial in this courtroom within ninety days. Is that sufficient time for both of you gentlemen?" the judge asked.

Mr. Reardon glanced at Mr. Morris and then answered the judge, "Ninety days is fine for the prosecution, your honor."

"Your honor," said Colton's attorney, "I respectfully ask that a one-hundred twenty day extension be provided to my client and his family. The defendant's mother was recently murdered, and while the police investigation is underway, my client and his family are under considerable stress and they are attempting to reorganize their daily responsibilities. Moreover, my client is currently undergoing extensive medical tests and treatments to determine the extent of his condition and to return to trial within the court's timeline would cause an undue hardship on him."

Judge Stevenson paused for a moment considering the request and then stated, "The court understands the complexity of the issues surrounding the family. A thirty day extension is granted, but I am also ordering the defendant to remain on house arrest in the interim. Mr. Morris I want a full medical report for the defendant sent to the Prosecutor's Office and the court within sixty days. Next case."

He pounded the gavel. Colton's attorney took his arm and led him to where his grandparents were standing. He bent over and talked quietly to them. His tall figure looked like a giant giving commands to children.

"Mr. and Mrs. Brown, we need as much time as possible to elapse before the trial so the hoopla surrounding the shooting can die down. I'll file for another extension in a month. In the meantime, I'd like to proceed with the lawsuit against the schools as a means to an end. The more sympathy we can garner for Colton in the weeks ahead, the better the chances we can get these charges reduced or dropped by the prosecution. Or, we might be able to use our lawsuit as a bargaining chip to get them to throw out the case. So far the prosecutor's been unwilling to budge on the case going to trial but sometimes things change. So it's going to cost you a little more money as this drags on, but the more we're on the offensive, the less we have to play defense, to use a lousy football analogy, and we've got a better chance to get an acquittal for Colton," Morris explained.

"Well, Mr. Morris, we'll do whatever you think is best to help Colton, but can we pay you over time?" asked the old woman. "We're both retired and his father has been out of work for the past month and we've had the expenses of a funeral and such, so we don't have a lot of cash sitting around to pay you right away."

"That's fine, ma'am," agreed Morris. "As long as you're in agreement with my ideas on how we should proceed, I will just roll the court cost filing fees and my hours onto a credit statement for the family and we'll work out a payment plan or you all can just pay me whenever you have the resources to do so."

"That's kind of you, sir," she said. "We're good for the money. Even if we have to sell our farm, we will pay you what we owe you. Thank you."

"Yes ma'am; you're welcome," Attorney Morris replied. "I'll be in touch Colton. For the time being, you do exactly what the judge ordered."

63

On Election Days, Mr. Collins asked the principals and staff to exhibit a 'business as usual' approach so community members entering the buildings to vote were impressed with the quality of education taking place without undue fanfare or gimmicks. In the past, student leaders would greet individuals as they entered the buildings, holding doors open, offering refreshments and giving directions to the polling areas. But these well-intended attempts to connect students to voters often backfired. Voters would be heard making comments such as,

"Why aren't these kids in class learning?" or

"So they think they can sweet talk a 'yes' vote from me with a cute kid."

And so on. So now a simple home-made sign and an American flag designated the entrances for voters to use and only parents and other volunteers stood in the parking lot to inform visitors as to the importance of a vote in favor of the school issue.

Maxine was scheduled for 9:00. They were to discuss the events of the previous day. She was to bring in a written statement of what happened and attend the meeting with a union representative and the bus coordinator so it could all be documented and made official. Jim Collins was on the phone with a member of an Akron television station explaining the financial necessity of the levy and the possible consequences of another election loss when a rapid knock on his door was followed by the elementary principal peaking quickly around the edge with a grey look on his face.

"Sorry to bother you," he said, "but we just received a bomb threat."

Jim's secretary quickly stepped past the principal and shot a time-out signal to the superintendent.

"Steve's on the other line," quickly added L J. "There's a bomb threat at the high school, too. He's already called the police and evacuated the building."

"Oh shit," said Jim to the reporter. "I'm sorry, Jerry, but I've got a situation here and I'm going to have to get back to you."

Jim stood and waved the two people in the doorway to come into his office and close the door.

"Who took your call and what did the person say?" he asked the elementary school principal.

"Jackie," he said nervously, "she told me the person just said a bomb was in the building and it would go off in ten minutes."

"Damn it. Did she recognize the voice or the age of the caller or anything distinctive about the call?" the superintendent asked. "I guess what I'm asking is did she think the caller was legit?"

"Yeah, she's very experienced, as you know, and she seemed pretty upset," the principal said. "I think it's real."

"Alright, what do you want to do?" asked the superintendent quickly.

"I think we should at least clear the building," said the principal.

Jim pondered his options momentarily and then said, "Okay, I agree."

"On my way," said the principal leaving the office.

Jim shot up from his desk and shouted to the principal, "Wait, Bruce. Announce to everyone that we're going to have a fire drill before you pull the alarm. Tell Jackie to keep quiet about the call, and once everyone is outside get your custodian and you two do a walk-through looking for anything unusual, especially in the library and around the polling stations; you know where the public has been coming in and going. I'll meet you after I talk to Steve. And keep everyone outside until we talk or I give you the okay sign."

"Got it," said the principal.

Jim used his cell phone to call Steve.

"Hey," answered the high school principal.

"I got your message," said the superintendent with haste. "What's going on now?"

"Well, we just about have the place empty," Steve reported. "The last of the teachers who comb the restrooms and stairways for kids in hiding are coming out now."

"What about the voters and election workers?" asked Jim.

"They didn't want to leave the polling site unattended because one of them thought none of the votes would count and everything would be voided if they left the polling area," said Steve, "but we finally got them out when we told them we would lock the doors and secure the area."

There was a protracted silence from Steve's end of the call. Finally he said to Jim,

"The Police are here now, and one of the volunteer fire fighters just pulled in, too. Hold on a minute."

Jim could hear the cruiser's siren pulsing frantically louder as it approached the principal. He could hear Steve explaining what had happened to them. The principal stepped away from them and returned his attention to the superintendent.

"Ah, Jim," Steve said, "we have another problem."

"Another problem? What are you talking about?" asked the superintendent.

"These guys refuse to check the building for the bomb," said Steve.

Jim answered, "What? Why?"

"They said it's our building and we have to check it," reported the principal.

"You have got to be kidding!" Jim said incredulously.

"No, I'm not."

"Well, get your custodian and you guys walk through the building looking for anything unusual," Jim said.

There was another pause and then Steve said, "Jim, I'm not comfortable with doing that."

The superintendent replied, "What do you mean?"

"I mean I've got a wife and kids and the $25,000.00 life insurance policy from the district won't go very far—it's just not worth it to me to get blown up checking for a bomb. Besides, I've never received any training related to bomb detection, so I'm not going in there and I'm not asking my custodian to go in there either to look for a bomb," Steve said. "It's probably just a hoax called in by one of those losers who transferred to the charter school, but I'm not about to find out otherwise and make my wife a widow at forty."

Jim held his head with his free hand and held the phone down at his side. He thought to himself, 'I couldn't make this up; it's so ridiculous.' But this was no time to get into a power play with the high school principal over insubordination. His instincts and experience told him to proceed cautiously because all employees do have rights protected by law. He, too, had rights, management authority, but in the spur of the moment he wasn't sure if sending a person into a building to check for a bomb would pass the test of him making a reasonable request of a person he supervised in a legal proceeding. And what if there really is a bomb in the school?

"Well then keep everyone outside until I get there," Jim said with dour resignation.

As his car approached the center of Low Field, Jim passed several cars full of jovial students, music thumping loudly as the vehicles crossed paths. Other students were walking toward the corner intersection of town presumably going to the sandwich shop and frozen dairy treats store for food and fun. He should take a few minutes to chase them back to the school grounds but there was a higher priority for his attention. He parked his car in the neighboring church lot and approached the crowd looking for the principal from the back of the building.

"Here he is," Steve said to one of the police officers in the parking lot. He turned to Jim and said, "Chief Hadley wants you to call him."

"Not now," Jim said angrily, "you go get the students who are walking to town and get them back here. They are your responsibility."

"I told them they could go get lunch," Steve replied. "What I am supposed to do? It's their lunch period and this isn't going to be over soon."

"So you just gave a bunch of students permission to leave school grounds to get lunch in town even though we have a closed lunch policy," Jim said clarifying Steve's actions with him.

"Well, I figured these were extenuating circumstances," Steve said. "They said they'd behave."

"Wow, you and I are going to have a meeting when this mess is over," promised Jim.

"Why? These kids have to eat. I only told some of the good kids it was okay—I wouldn't send the derelicts to town unattended," Steve reasoned. "Besides, in another hour they go there anyway after school and hang out. I mean, they do live here, Jim."

Jim shook his head and walked away toward the building fumbling to find his master key for the high school.

He turned his head and shouted back over his shoulder to Steve, "Go get your students back here now."

He walked slowly down the lower level hallway, his eyes scanning back and forth. The stillness and coffin-like silence gave this walk the same eerie feeling he had when he was the last person to leave the elementary school building after board meetings. Turning the lights out and feeling his way to the exit always quickened his pace and he habitually scanned the corners and edges of the building exterior as he walked to his lonely car through the midnight darkness. This time the lights were on but it was impossible for one man to thoroughly sweep a 100,000 square foot building for a bomb in a timely manner. He needed a specially trained dog and a handler to help him; he wondered how long it would take to get one to the premises. Maybe he would get lucky and the bomb would explode in a different part of the building. He was amazed as he started through common areas as to the numbers of book bags, sweatshirts and odd boxes that littered the space, perfect hiding places for trouble.

After fifteen minutes or so he heard his name being called. It was the custodian.

"Wesley, what are you doing in here?" Jim asked.

"I've been looking for the bomb, too. When I saw you go back into the building, I figured somebody's got to help. Actually sir, I didn't look in the classrooms; but I know every square inch of this place like the back of my hand, and I've looked at all the obvious places someone would be likely to place a bomb and I think it's all clear," the custodian said.

"But what about the boxes in the library and those poll workers' tote bags and coats? I mean there are a million places to put a bomb," Jim said.

"Yeah, you're right but I figure those old ladies aren't suicide bombers so they probably don't have a bomb nearby where they're sitting while people vote. Plus, I recognize every one of those boxes from years of cleaning around them. I ask that librarian every week to put that stuff up but he's a hoarder of sorts and the stuff just sits month after month until he has to do something with it before I threaten him in the spring with the summer cleaning crew," the older gentleman laughed.

"Okay, I'm good with your assessment," Jim said. "I think I'll tell Steve to get everyone back in here."

He walked to a series of doors and waved to the principal to bring the staff and students back into the building.

Jim turned and said, "Hey Wesley, thank you."

"You betcha, Mr. Collins," Wesley said with a wave. "Now let's just hope no bomb goes off."

The custodian walked away coughing and laughing hysterically at his attempted joke.

64

KELSEY AND DARON had been communicating with each other on-line. Both were enjoying the electronic school experience and progressing at quick and methodical paces through their classes. A component of the software allowed students to socialize with each other via chat rooms that were linked to their individual accounts and were set in-sync with class rosters. They were both enrolled in the same senior social studies class titled, Contemporary Issues of American Democracy. The class hit on a multitude of current social issues, some that were very personal for both of them such as gay rights, racism and second amendment gun rights.

As the weeks passed since the shooting they had drifted apart both going in different directions, pursuing interests that further separated them from one another. In an odd way, they realized their relationship had ended without any drama or even a conversation. But for Daron, Kelsey had been the first girl in Low Field who had the backbone and unbiased vision to simply view him as a man, and not a biracial man. He respected and appreciated that in her and he knew she would hold a special place in his memory as one of his first serious girlfriends, and they had fun together in the few summer months their friendship had progressed into a dating relationship. He couldn't help but transpose their experiences onto those of his parents, albeit twenty years removed from each other. It helped him gain an appreciative perspective on what his mother and father had endured at a similar age.

For Kelsey being with Daron during the months they were dating was part of a personal journey, trying to discover who she really was as a person and what she wanted in a relationship. She always felt that she was different from other girls and dating Daron allowed her to experience a non-traditional friendship with a male. Initially she thought her rejection of the norm had something to do with her mother and stepfather's relationship, but she had recently come to realize her feelings really had nothing to do with them. The years she and Colton had been girlfriend and boyfriend, she now realized was a typical early adolescent experimentation with the opposite sex. As she contemplated their involvement on a deeper level, she recognized Colton and she had very little in common other than shared roots, both being born and raised in Low Field. More importantly, they were very different from one another in terms of their separate views of the world, long-term ambitions and life goals.

Daron was the first to suggest the idea. He and Kelsey exchanged text messages.

We should go visit Abby would your mom let you go with me
   Yeah that's really a good idea I'd like to talk to her about what
happened the day of the shooting and c how she's doing
   How about early this week I can pick you up
   Ok I'm going to give her a call and c if Tuesday will work
   Cool

Daron sent Kelsey a text to let her know he was on his way to pick her up. She was ready, and even though she hadn't cleared the idea with her mom, both of her parents were both at work so there would not be a problem. It was the first time they had talked face to face since the open house at school. They got caught up on what had been going on in each other's life, and, as they both expected, there was no spark between them. The shooting had finished their relationship for good. Kelsey mapped Abby's home address on her phone and helped Daron with the necessary turns and directions. His pickup traversed the gravel driveway up to the house. Both he and Kelsey were amazed looking up at the house.

"How cool is this place?" he said.

"Really," Kelsey said, "I'd love to live here."

"I had no idea a place like this was anywhere near to Low Field," Daron said shaking his head. It's unbelievable. Are you sure this is the place?"

"That's the right address—1599 Park Line Road," she said pointing to the numbers on the mailbox.

"Alright," Daron said. "Are you ready for this?"

Mrs. Olson led them into the dining room and motioned for them to be seated.

"Abby's finishing up with Miss Hyde. She brings her assignments from the teachers at school and makes sure Abby understands what she's supposed to complete for the week. She's called a home instruction teacher. She comes once a week and makes sure Abby is keeping up with her classes while she's at home. Why don't you two wait here at the table and I'll get you something to drink," Mrs. Olson suggested.

"Thank you, ma'am," Daron replied.

"Yeah, thanks Mrs. Olson," Kelsey said.

"She's nice."

"Yeah," said Kelsey, "just like Abby."

"Do you know Abby very well?" Daron asked.

"Not really. I mean we've been in school together for twelve years, but I don't think anybody knows Abby very well. She's probably the smartest person in our class," Kelsey added, "but she's a very quiet, private person."

"Oh," said Daron. "We were in the same homeroom the first year I was at Low Field, but they're only a few minutes long so I never got much of a chance to talk to her."

They had waited only a brief time before Miss Hyde walked past them with her bookbag and coat.

"Hey you two," said the young, pleasant teacher, "how are things going?"

"Fine thanks," Kelsey offered.

"Yeah, fine," said Daron.

"Great; well, you take care."

"You too, Miss Hyde," Kelsey said.

Abby voice echoed from the next room, "Come on in you guys."

They walked into the greenhouse type drawing room. Abby sat in a wheelchair wearing a long sleeve t-shirt and sweat pants.

"Hey, you look great," Kelsey said nervously. "It's so nice to see you."

"Thanks, and thanks for coming over," Abby replied. "Hi, Daron."

"Hey Abby," he said, "are you feeling as good as you look?"

"Yeah, yeah I'm just great," Abby said sarcastically.

"I'm sorry; I didn't mean to be condescending," he said.

"No, that's not it," Abby said shaking her head. "I'm sorry; I didn't mean it that way. Will stopped over the other day and he had the proper perspective on the situation. He made me realize things could be worse, much worse, so all things considered, I'm doing fine; thank you for asking. Please, you two grab a chair and make yourselves comfortable."

"Abby, I don't know how to say this any other way but directly— we just feel terrible about what happened that day and we wanted to just come by and tell you how sorry we are and say that if there's anything we can do for you now or any time in the future, please don't hesitate to ask," Kelsey said quickly becoming emotional.

"Thanks Kelsey. It's nice of you both to come by and I appreciate the offer," Abby said. "I want you both to know, I don't hold any kind of resentment or grudge against either of you. Colton is the only person I'd like to kick in the balls."

They all laughed.

"I think there's a long line of people who want to kick Colton in the balls," Daron said laughing. "In fact, can I be right behind you in the line?"

"Sure," Abby said with a smile. "He was just so stupid that day to start firing a gun in a crowded parking lot. It was the most narcissistic, unaware and nonsensical thing I've ever witnessed. Hey, if you don't mind me asking, what actually happened between you guys?"

"Believe it or not, very little," Daron started to explain. "He came up to me in my truck while I was waiting for Kelsey to come out. Out of nowhere he got real testy and stupid with me and when she got out there he started giving us both some crap about how he didn't want us to be dating. And then he flashed the gun he had tucked into the waist of his jeans, so I just hit him hard with the truck door and we took off. We didn't even know for sure if he had even fired the shots at us until the police picked us up later that afternoon. I mean we heard the bangs, but my truck kind of sucks and there was so much commotion and noise that we really didn't know what had happened until later."

Kelsey said, "What Colton did was just ignorant. I heard they filed a bunch of charges against him and I hope he gets in big trouble for doing this to you."

"I don't know," Abby said, "some days like today I'm really mad at him and other days I get in a mood whereby I'm more accepting of it; kind of like just being in the wrong place at the wrong time. I mean every day in our life unexpected things can happen. Most days they don't, thank goodness, but I'm pretty certain in my mind that Colton didn't mean to hurt me or anyone else that day. He's just a pampered jock and he probably thinks he can do anything he wants to do, even if it makes no sense and is unbelievably dangerous."

"You know, we hear about forgiveness all the time at church but you're a better person than me, Abby," Daron said shaking his head. "You are definitely right though—bad stuff can happen to any of us at any time of any day. What you said really puts things in a proper perspective."

"Someone in the hospital was saying to me that everything happens for a reason; we just have to figure out the reason," Abby said. "I think the incident was a crossroads moment for all five of us who were involved. Our lives were forever altered by those few seconds and the choice Colton made to fire those shots at you two. The irony is that four out of the five of us had no free will in the matter."

"Wow, you're right, but it's going to take me a minute to get my little brain around that thought," Daron said.

"I'm sorry, I didn't mean to get philosophical about this whole thing, but lately I've been thinking so much about what happened," Abby apologized. "And I figure Colton was always the kind of person who does most of his thinking with his balls so that day was really no different than most for him. That's why I would like to kick him in the balls; it's sort of a slap across the face for most people."

"Abby you're such a funny and smart person," Kelsey said. "You have the ability to think so deeply about things it makes my head spin, but I'm really just so glad you're okay."

"Thanks Kelsey. All in all, I'm very lucky according to the doctors who treated me. They said if the bullet had entered one inch further to the left and hit my spinal cord directly, I'd be dead or in a wheelchair for the rest of my life. But now they've been telling me that they think by graduation, I might be able to walk across the old stage at the high school, so that's a good thing," Abby said.

"A very good thing," Kelsey echoed.

"So how is old Low Field High School these days?" Abby asked.

Daron and Kelsey looked at each other. He extended his hand deferring to her to comment.

"Well, we don't really know. They pretty much kicked us out after the shooting," Kelsey replied.

"What? Why would they do that? It's not like you had guns or pulled the trigger on Colton's gun," Abby said. "That doesn't make sense, but I guess I'm not surprised that they made another bad decision."

"Yeah we didn't think it made sense either, but Daniels didn't give us much of a choice. So we both enrolled in an electronic charter school called Classrooms Without Boundaries and its fine," Daron said. "We're both doing okay and we'll graduate this year so in the grand scheme of things it's probably no big deal."

"That is total crap," Abby said bluntly, "but so typical of that place. Well, I have an idea. Would you two do me a favor?"

"Sure, anything," Kelsey said.

"Yep, anything," Daron added.

"It's kind of a big favor and it might take a lot of time," Abby said wincing.

"Abby, no problem," Daron said. "You name it."

"I'm going to do a sculpture commemorating the day of infamy and I'd like the two of you to be my models. What do you think?" Abby asked.

Daron laughed and said, "I'm no underwear model, but count me in."

"Sure," Kelsey said, "it sounds like fun."

"Actually it's a little boring, but it would be great to have you both in the piece. I've got a few ideas swimming around in my mind, but I don't have it all worked out yet, so maybe we'll start in a month or so—probably between Thanksgiving and Christmas," Abby said.

"Do we have to be nude?" Kelsey asked. "I mean I've seen sculptures on television and they're mostly nude or just have a leaf covering their private parts."

Daron added, "And they always seem to be missing an arm."

"You don't have to be nude unless you want to," Abby said laughing.

"No," Kelsey said relieved. "I just wondered."

"Man, that's great because I don't know where I'd find a big enough leaf," Daron laughed.

"Don't worry, you two will be fine," Abby said. "Even Colton's balls could be a model, and we all know those stones are dumb as rocks, as the saying goes."

"Well in that case we should be fine," Daron said nodding in agreement.

65

FOLLOWING A VERY long day of work, Jim finished Election Day with the Low Field tradition. A *Victory Party* complete with cake, punch and speeches was being held in the high school cafeteria for the volunteers who gave so much of their time running the campaign and for the friends and supporters of the schools who hoped to continue the proud traditions of the school district. The area began to fill after the dinner hours. Families, retirees and employees all joined together to talk and laugh and hope together that the current campaign had been effective enough to sway the volatile two percent of the voters that always seemed to control the outcome of an election.

Historically, the community was divided evenly on school levies. For decades the results typically ended with the issue either winning or losing by a percentage count of fifty-one to forty nine one way or the other. Recently, the district had lost the support of the significant two percent evident by a consistent losing streak of five straight election defeats, even though the ballot issue was simply a renewal of existing funds. In the past that group would serve as a conservative voice of reason lending their support to the district faithful for renewals but joining with the angry voters to reject initiatives that called for expanding funding or making capital improvements to the buildings or grounds by raising taxes.

Long before Jim Collin's tenure as superintendent of schools began, the changing demographics of the community's voters had made passing any levy a challenge. Residents were growing older and many

were retired living on fixed incomes. Student enrollment had gradually, yet steadily declined as younger families were not moving into
the district and those who did had fewer children. The economic
conundrums of the nation, both macro and micro, had a constricting
squeeze on taxpayers who had the ability to voice their dissatisfaction with politics and government most directly at the local level.
Voting no on a school or fire levy was an outlet for pent-up frustration against the system at large, both in general and specific terms.
And no amount of persuasion or reason could trump the sometimes
illogical satisfaction that came with casting a vote *against* something,
usually at the local level.

Jim was exhausted but the students and people in attendance
were excited and perpetually optimistic. One of the district's retired
teachers who enjoyed the political process would spend the hours following the official closing of the polls stationed at the County Board
of Elections Office where they would post the final results of each
election on a large series of rolling bulletin boards in the spacious,
front hallway. As soon as the last voter tallies from the precincts
were released, he would call a designated person, usually the school
board president, with the election result. Everyone would gasp in
silence when the signal was given that the phone call was received.
The whole election process reminded Jim of Ground Hog Day in
February for two reasons: first, they followed the same notification
procedure over and over again with unerring sameness, and second,
the regularity of ballot issues prompted by renewal cycles from decades prior caused the district to have an issue in front of the people
at almost every election which was way too frequent and, in his opinion, doomed the outcome.

The evening was drawing on rather late because of the number
of issues and candidates on the ballot during a general election in
November. Finally, as the time approached ten o'clock, John held up
his hand and walked through the aisle toward the microphone set up
on the stage at the north end of the room.

"Hi Don," said the board president talking both into the phone and the microphone. "Yes, I can hear you. We have a hundred or so people still at the *Victory Party* and we've been waiting to hear from you. Do you know the results?"

The expression on John's face went from optimistic to dejected in an instant and made his subsequent comments irrelevant.

"I see. Thank you so much for calling," he said.

He touched the face of the phone and returned it to his blazer's side pocket.

"Ladies and Gentlemen, that was Don Perkins, our retired high school social studies teacher calling us from the Board of Elections with the results from today's election," John said. "But before I tell you what he reported I want to take just a moment to thank everyone on the levy committee for their fantastic efforts—I think you'll agree the information regarding the importance of this renewal levy was communicated in a clear and concise manner to our community. I want to thank the other school board members and the administrators for their unending efforts for the welfare of the students of The Low Field Schools and I would personally like to thank all of you—community members, teachers, bus drivers, cafeteria workers, parents, and students—for being here tonight and for working so diligently to gain the financial support of our community so that we can continue to offer the best educational experiences for our young people and prepare them for the challenges of the workplace and their place in our society."

After a lengthy pause, he stated.

"I regret to inform you that the levy failed by a slim margin of just five votes. But this means, as we know from previous elections with similar results, that there will be an automatic recount of the precinct tallies and the absentee ballots and military votes in the coming weeks, so don't count us out yet; we could still win this election!" he said with a forced positive expression.

A reserved response of sporadic clapping a few cheers followed his pronouncement. He left the microphone and joined the other board members, shaking hands and consoling each other with pats on the back and shoulders and nods of consolation expressed toward one another.

Jim's prognostication from the morning hour greeting voters was unfortunately correct. This sixth failure of the issue meant the likely necessity to return to the ballot through a costly special election in February, just after Ground Hog's Day. Compounding that frustrating expense of time, energy and spirit, he had the realization that his work in the coming weeks would include the preparation of cost-cutting proposals related to staffing levels, educational programs and services for the next school year. State law and the employees' collective bargaining agreements had early deadlines in these matters and called for the timing of decisions and notices to begin months prior to the start of the upcoming year. The demoralizing recommendations needed to be approved by the board and delivered in writing to the employees in the next few months, during the most difficult period of the current school year, the winter months.

The overwhelming negativity of today's results both personally and for the district at large were pulsing like the strobe light beacons of a heat stroke in Jim's eyes as he expressed simultaneous gratitude and condolences to the people leaving the party. His mind was numb with fatigue and he mouthed clichés and lukewarm inspirational statements in rote fashion.

He said things like, "Don't give up; we'll get 'em next time; thanks for your hard work; and you are our MVP's."

And so on. Near the end of the line, Keith Byler approached him and shook his hand rather stridently. He leaned into the superintendent and in a soft but determined tone he delivered the union's assertion knowing full well what the defeat of the election would mean to his members.

"Jim, we'll be on strike in January and you and the board better take action on our cost-saving proposals that don't impact staff or program. A great place to start would be the elimination of the SRO program and the insertion of the concealed carry policy for the Low Field 20," Keith said directly. "We're going to get these people's attention, whether they like it or not. Think about it."

66

JUDGE STEVENSON WAS swift and punishing when he ruled on Mr. Caldwell's case. The charges added up quickly against Roy—*theft* of a lawn statue that they relocated near Daron's truck; *criminal trespassing* and committing a *hate crime* when he and Clayton decorated the trees in front Kelsey's home with toilet paper; *U. S. Postal mailbox tampering* when they placed the white dunce cap on the post and painted KKK on the mailbox; *aggravated menacing* when the duo sent the threatening emails to Daron and Kelsey; and *contributing to the delinquency of a minor* for involving his younger son in the series of escapades. He allowed the man to make a statement before reading his decision. In a shaky voice Roy Caldwell read from a card given to him by his attorney.

"Your honor, I am very sorry for the problems I created with my actions. At the time, I was very upset because of my son Colton's troubles at the school, and I know I demonstrated very poor judgment in the decisions I made at that time. Including my son Clayton in these deeds was another mistake that I deeply regret. And I am very sorry to the families I upset by my actions. In the last month my family has been in chaos. Your honor, I ask for your understanding and forgiveness in this embarrassing, unfortunate situation," he said softly.

The judge shuffled some papers in a folder and placed a new one on top of the stack. He spoke in a deliberate and stern tone, his eyes fixed on Mr. Caldwell's as he glanced down occasionally to choose his words.

"Mr. Caldwell in reviewing this case, the court finds your actions on the day in question to be especially troubling, on one hand because of the nature of your transgressions and on the other hand because you are the sole provider and primary adult role model for your sons. The poor judgment you demonstrated that resulted in the list of charges shows a particularly shocking lack of ability on your part to make good decisions and provide proper guidance to your children, most notably your younger son. I am very tempted to turn his custody over to the County Children's Services Board and order them to find a foster family to assume his care, given that the health concerns and ages of the boy's grandparents doesn't qualify them to be a proper choice at this time," the judge said. "Your actions were both illegal, but also, and of equal importance to me, immoral and racist, which I find repugnant for a parent in the twenty-first century. I find you guilty on all counts and I order you to pay a fine of $5,000.00 and serve two years of probation, the first sixty days to be spent incarcerated in the county jail on the weekends from 6:00 PM Friday evening until 6:00 Sunday evening until those sixty days have been served. At those times, your younger son will be required to stay with his grandparents, Mr. and Mrs. Brown, at their residence. Let me add, if you have any citations or incidents with the law during this probationary period, you son's custody will be assigned directly to the Children's Services Board without appeal. Do you understand my decision?"

"Yes sir," Roy replied.

The judge pounded his gavel and said loudly, "Case dismissed."

Attorney Morris turned and faced Mr. Caldwell looking down into the haggard man's eyes.

"Good; that turned out well for you and your son," said the attorney.

"Bullshit," Roy fired back, "if that little prick wasn't surrounded by a bunch of police officers I'd go right up to him and kick his scrawny, drunk ass. He's not taking Clayton from me, and he's not my daddy lecturing me like I'm some kind of child."

Because the man's agitation was becoming more obvious to those in the courtroom, including the judge, the attorney quickly took Mr. Caldwell by the arm and led him from the room. In the hallway he resumed his comments.

"Look Roy, you screwed up and that judge could have made your life a living hell. He's allowing you to work and to keep your son in his home, so you need to get control of yourself and be grateful he didn't hand out a harsher punishment," Morris reasoned.

"I just don't like him," Roy said. "Everyone in this town knows he's got kids with three different women and spends every afternoon in the hotel bar before he goes home. He's got a lot of nerve passing judgment on me."

"Not many people like the judge who hears the case against them and, yes, he's human with human flaws like all of us, but believe me, he took it easy on you, so don't screw this up," cautioned the attorney.

"Okay. So now what?" Roy asked.

"The Clerk of Courts will have you sign a few papers down here at the window and then you are free to go home and get back to work," answered Mr. Morris.

"Okay. Thank you," Roy said shaking his attorney's hand. "When do I have to pay that $5,000.00 fine?"

"We'll ask the clerk to establish a payment plan that extends over the probationary period," the attorney said. "It's usually not a problem as long as you keep up on your payments."

"So, I have two years, right?"

"Yes," the attorney responded, "can you handle that?"

"Sure, as long as I can get back to work," Roy said.

"You're free to do that during the weekdays starting tomorrow," Morris said.

"That little drunk is lucky I can't touch him," said Roy quickly turning temperamental again. "I'd rip that shiny robe off his skinny ass and tie him up in it like a straightjacket."

"Okay, let's go see the clerk and get you out of here," the attorney said shaking his head in disbelief.

"Yeah," Roy agreed, "I better get out of here before I do something stupid."

67

THE PUBLIC PORTION of the Special Board Meeting was very brief. There was the call to order, the pledge of allegiance, and a roll call followed immediately by a motion to adjourn to executive session to review and discuss personnel matters. The large crowd, recruited by the teachers whenever they desired to pressure and sway the board towards the union's position on a particular issue, glared with somber scowls at the board members, the treasurer and superintendent as they excused themselves for the sanctuary of the board office.

"Wow, even though you know it's coming," said one board member, "it's still always uncomfortable when the room is packed with their friends and families."

"Yeah, I hate facing the angry mob," another said. "Oh well, what do have for us Jim?"

"We've got a few things for informational purposes and then two important decisions that we'll need to take action on when we go back up and resume the meeting. First of all, I want to fill you in on the bus incident with the stranger who took Maxine and a few of the kids hostage. He is out of the hospital and in the county jail," Jim reported. "The police have interviewed him and it's their opinion that he truly planned and carried out the entire fiasco by himself because he agrees with the teachers and believes bus drivers also should be granted the authority to carry guns in order to fend-off possible kidnappers or terrorists or parents who try to use the bus as a place to snatch a child or cause a problem. As some of you know, we were

— 305 —

initially concerned that he had been set-up by the teachers as a pub-licity stunt to gain support for the concealed carry idea before the election, but again, Chief Hadley is certain the man acted alone and has no connection with the teachers. I guess he just wanted to show the voters that arming the adults who are in charge of the students is a correct manner of protection. Maxine and the students are all fine. I met with her and her union representative and she has asked for a medical leave to receive some counseling."

"Why does she need counseling?" one asked.

"She claims she was traumatized by the incident and is now hav-ing trouble eating and sleeping," Jim replied.

"Oh, bull," said another board member.

"How about the kids?" asked one, "I'm concerned about how they're doing."

"The guidance counselor has talked to all of them and their par-ents and we are planning to have a psychologist, Dr. Cramer, from the county educational service center also evaluate them and discuss the incident with them to see if he she thinks any of them required additional counseling," Jim added.

"I guess we'll just have to wait and see."

"I agree," the superintendent said. "The second thing we need to discuss is the failure of the levy. As you know, we will now have to prepare a reduction-in-force plan for next year and at our next regu-lar meeting I will share that plan and make a recommendation for your vote. It's going to be rather involved and the cuts will have to be deep to counteract the loss of revenue from the expired levy. Zack, would you please review the funding cycle and share the numbers with the board?"

"Sure, Jim," said the treasurer. "The levy that was defeated again this week expires on June 30th. It generates $2,800,000.00 per year. So we are down to our final chance to renew it, but that will re-quire the board to pass a resolution tonight to place in on the ballot in a special election in February. Your action is required tonight in order to meet the deadline for filing that request with the Board of Elections."

"So obviously we're going to pass that resolution tonight, right?" one of the board members asked.

"Yes, that's what I'd recommend," Jim said. "Zack, what does it cost the district to place the levy on the ballot in a special election?"

"Well, that depends on the number of other issues on the ballot. The overall cost of the running the election is split equally by the number of entities who ask for the election," the treasurer explained.

"Well what if we're the only entity?" asked one of the board members.

Zack explained, "In the past when we've asked the board of elections officials that question the answer has been approximately $75,000.00."

"Wow, the hole just keeps getting deeper," said a board member shaking his head.

"The way I see it, we don't have any choice," John Fitzpatrick said. "We've got to pass that when we go back up there; everyone agree?"

The nodding of heads confirmed consensus.

John continued to lead the discussion and asked the superintendent, "So Jim, how many teachers and other employees do you think will have to be cut in your plan? Have you even had a chance to work on that yet?"

"Yes, I have a draft that calls for the elimination of non-essential services that are not required by law, namely bus transportation of the older students and all sports and extra-curricular activities. That will save almost $500,000.00. Then we can enlarge class sizes to the maximum numbers allowed by law and the teachers' contract, and as far as I can ascertain at this time, we could reduce about four teachers by doing that. I will have to review the reduction of courses not required by the state, elective courses we offer and non-mandated services throughout the district. Enrichment courses such as Home Economics, Shop, Art, and Foreign Languages will need to be reviewed, as will services like the elementary guidance counselor and the school nurse. Eliminating those kinds of positions will help us come up with another sizeable amount of savings. Lastly, we can consider cutting the custodians, the secretaries, and the food service workers back to a bare bones, minimal level in order to come up with the rest of the money," the superintendent said.

"How about administrators?" another asked. "You know the unions will want to see cuts there too."

"Yeah, the teachers have already spread that around the community that they want to see those positions cut first," said another board member.

Jim said, "Yes, and even though I don't want to see us lose any supervisory personnel, I will look at everything including the principals and the transportation and custodial supervisors to see if we can reduce a position or two in those ranks. The Student Resource Officer and the Technology Coordinator are two other places we'll have to consider eliminating."

"There's not going to be much left," one member said with a frown.

"And why would anyone send their kids here after those kinds of reductions?" asked another.

"Yeah that's pretty ugly," said another. "I'm glad my daughter graduates this year."

"Truthfully, if we have to do this, I'm going to look at open enrollment in Watson City for my kids," said one of the board members.

"I can't blame you or any of the other parents who explore alternatives and options," another agreed.

John pulled the group back to the agenda and asked, "All right, what else? I'm sure they're getting restless up there."

"Just two other quick items," Jim stated. "I received this today; here's a copy for each of you. It's an Intent to Strike Notice from the teachers. They plan to go on strike starting the day we're supposed to return from winter break, January 3rd."

"Oh for God's sake," one lamented. "That is just great."

"Well, they've been working without a contract this school year hoping that would help convince the community to pass the levy," Jim reminded everyone. "For all intents and purposes that means a wage freeze but some people think they're just waiting until the levy is approved so they can negotiate raises with the money."

"It doesn't work that way," Zack said. "Without additional funding, there's no money for raises unless we cut staff to create a new revenue source."

"Would we do that?" asked a member.

"For the past few years we've tried to make soft cuts by reducing staff through attrition but the problem is that no one wants to retire," Jim said candidly. "The economy is terrible and people are worried about their retirement incomes. Their pension increases if they work additional years and everyone is spooked by the cost of healthcare because the state retirement system keeps threatening to eliminate that benefit for retirees."

"Oh, god, what a mess," said a board member. "So the teachers are going to strike, what else do we have to discuss before we go back up there?"

"The fourth and final item is the concealed carry policy on school grounds. Even though I'm not a proponent of this idea, I'm going to make a recommendation, and here's a copy of the language for you to review," he said passing out another paper for each board member. "It's a draft and I haven't heard back from our attorney yet but the recommendation is to suspend the SRO Program effective next Monday and to approve a motion that will allow twenty teachers to have handguns in lockboxes in their classrooms for the sole purpose of defending themselves and our students in the unlikely event of a terrorist attack on our schools. Every teacher and every classroom will be equipped with a lockbox but only twenty will have weapons in them."

"How will we know who has a gun?" John asked.

"There will be a secret list that the principals and I will have," Jim explained. "The Low Field 20 will be the teachers who have guns in their lockboxes."

"Oh, I don't like this," said one board member.

Another quickly responded, "I don't either."

"Believe me," Jim said, "if I thought there was a better option, I would recommend it to you."

"I think we should study the proposal and vote on it next time," another suggested. "Maybe we should get a committee of stakeholders to explore this option as well as other ideas."

"Oh, why namby pamby around?" asked another board member. "Let's just do it. The likelihood of a terrorist attack at Low Field is like getting hit by lightning, twice."

"I agree the levy defeat necessitates we take aggressive action and this might actually be the first in a series of cuts and changes that will wake people up about our situation," another said as the lively discussion continued.

"John, you've been taking it all in; what do you think?" Jim asked the board president.

"Personally, I think it's ludicrous and irresponsible, but I understand the arguments both ways. I don't think delaying the vote and involving more people in a committee study will help us though. I guess I don't know how I'll vote until we get up there," he admitted. "I'm sorry folks."

"Fair enough; two in favor, two opposed and John will cast the deciding vote. That's a good thing at least to show the board was split on this issue; that's reasonable," Jim added.

"Okay, let's go back up," John said.

They all gathered their papers and folders and reconvened in the library in front of the standing room only crowd. The treasurer performed roll call and wrote the time on his copy of the agenda—8:07 PM. The board president thanked the people for attending the special meeting and informed them that there would not be an opportunity for public comment and that the board would be adding a vote on two additional resolutions from the superintendent.

The initial resolution to put the levy in front of the voters again in a February special election passed unanimously. There were several people who called out from the crowd at the conclusion of the vote.

"What don't you people understand about NO?"

"Yeah, that levy has been voted down six times."

"Quit wasting our money on special elections."

"Order," John said pounding his gavel for the first time anyone could remember. "Ladies and gentlemen you will be removed if you can't refrain from commenting and interrupting the board's business."

The second resolution simultaneously called for the immediate suspension of the SRO Program and the approval of twenty teachers, who under a new school policy, named Policy 20 for easy recognition and reference, to be permitted to possess secured handguns in their classrooms for the sole use of defending the students and staff of The Low Field Local Schools in the event of a terrorist attack or life threatening invasion of the school. The treasurer called out the board member's names one by one and recorded each vote.

"Mr. Reynolds?"

"Yes."

"Mrs. Thompson?"

"No."

"Mr. Hicks?"

"No."

"Mr. Cassidy?"

"Yes."

"Mr. Fitzpatrick?"

Following a protracted pause of ten seconds that felt like ten minutes, the board president replied softly.

"Yes."

"Pardon me?" shouted a person from the back of the library. "Sorry, we couldn't hear him."

John raised his head and said loudly, "I voted yes."

Zack quickly responded, "Thank you. Motion approved three votes to two."

"Motion for adjournment," called the board president.

"So moved," the treasurer noted.

"Second," called another board member.

Zack called for the vote, "All in favor."

"Aye."

"Meeting adjourned," said John.

A rush of people swelled toward the board members, treasurer and superintendent who were all trying to disperse and return to the board office. Sporadic clapping and cheers occurred as people stood and wrestled with coats. The mob attempted to engage each of the officials in a debate regarding the problems of the district. Jim made his way out of the library into the hallway and was greeted by Keith Byler.

The superintendent said to the union president, "Well, you got what you wanted. Let's try to make it work."

"It will work," Keith proclaimed with his typical sense of self-assuredness. "We now have the safest school district in the state; in fact, probably the country. We're going to be famous for this. You can just sit back and take all the credit, like usual."

"I don't want anything to do with this one," Jim said, "the credit or blame will be all yours."

A television reporter and her camera person approached Jim Collins asking for an interview. He declined not wanting to open the floodgate of possible questions this late in the day after so many hours of stress and when his mind was full of frustration and apprehension.

He wasn't sure what he would say and a reflex from past experiences made him very wary of the media.

"Why don't you get a comment from our union president," Jim said pointing to Keith, "this gun thing was his idea."

68

THE TEACHERS' LOUNGES in both schools were abuzz then next morning as staff members arrived for work. Some of the teachers were pleased with the board's decision, others not so sure they could embrace the new safety paradigm. The more veteran teachers were the ones most shaken by the idea of their colleagues having the authority to brandish handguns with live ammunition just feet from them and their students. Their dissention was soft-spoken but obvious to everyone by their lack of engagement in the conversations. A meeting was called for after school to discuss the idea and share specifics of the new program. Undoubtedly, the Low Field 20 would be the hot topic throughout the day.

What Keith Byler and the teachers didn't expect was the reaction from the outside. A student office worker knocked on his classroom door just ten minutes into first period with a stack of phone messages.

"Mr. Byler," the girls said, "the secretary said to bring these to you."

"Okay, thank you," he replied taking the handful of notes.

Keith glanced through them curious of the identity and affiliation of the callers. He was surprised to find requests for phone interviews and comments from local, state and even national networks regarding the new plan. Moreover there were messages from three significant political and social organizations—The American Civil Liberties Union, Mothers Against Drunk Driving and The National Rifle Association. He had expected the idea to spark a reaction but this response far exceeded his expectation. During his second period planning period he decided to return a few of the calls just to get an idea as to the line of questioning and to give him a chance to prepare more polished responses as he advanced through the messages to the more high-stakes callers.

"Yes, we believe the plan serves as a comprehensive deterrent to anyone who would contemplate violence against the staff or students in the Low Field Schools," he told a member of a local television channel.

"The community totally supports the plan from the research we've conducted throughout the community," he responded to another media person.

"We know of several districts in the southern and western parts of the country who have similar plans in place but we know of none that are as extensive and far-reaching as our strategy," Keith said to a national news network correspondent.

"We believe this plan will make our district one of the safest school systems in the country and serve as a model of effectiveness and efficiency for others," was another of his responses.

The journalists rarely interjected their opinions, interested more in Keith's comments and perspective as they developed their stories. As he expected, the national organizations had already taken firm stances either for or against the idea, offering to support the plan or to protest it in the coming weeks. The mushroom effect was far more reaching than Keith had expected but he had to face it. His idea was extraordinary, controversial and at one far end of the spectrum, revolutionary.

The day was an exhausting end to the week, but as Keith entered the library to face his colleagues and fellow teachers, he took a deep breath and exhaled it in dramatic fashion before he spoke, exhilarated by their notoriety.

"Well, this has been quite a day," he said. "Whose idea was this anyway?"

The uniform laughter relieved some of the tension from the people.

"Keith, we have a present for you," said a young female teacher. She approached the union president and handed pinned a plastic, child's police badge to his shirt pocket. The way we see it, you're the new sheriff in town; this isn't Mayberry but you're sort of the Andy character and the rest of us are the Fifes—I'm Sherri Fife, that's Jordon Fife and over there is Luke Fife. So what do we do now, boss?"

Keith admired his badge and smiling said, "Well, for starters, you're going to have more than one bullet, so for now, we need to schedule a shooting session for this weekend. Seriously, one thing that is paramount for this program to work is for all of us to exude supreme confidence and competence to everyone we discuss this with in the coming days."

"Keith, we all know who in this room took the concealed carry classes and have been attending the classes at the Fish and Game Club. Do you have any ideas how we're going to keep this information private and somewhat a secret from our students and outsiders?" one of the teachers asked.

"Seriously, that's the million-dollar question," Keith said. "I have to admit, one of the cornerstone elements of this plan was for an intruder to not know which of the gun boxes actually contain a firearm. So it is imperative that everyone in this room adopt and portray the mindset that each and every one of us has a gun in his or her lock box, and when students ask you if you're one of the Low Field 20, you have to look them in the eye, smile and tell them you hope they never have to find that out. It is extremely important for us to have total anonymity when it comes to where the guns are actually located throughout the buildings if this plan is going to be successful."

"Okay, so we all have to go home and all weekend practice saying what you just said in front of a mirror. I already had students ask me if I was one of the *packing teachers*," one man said. "So we all need to sound very convincing when we tell our students we hope there is never a problem in Low Field that requires us to open our lock boxes."

"You're exactly correct, Bob," Keith said. "Everyone has to be convincing, because you will get asked. Let's face it, kids love puzzles, people love puzzles, and figuring out which of you are the Low Field 20 just became the most interesting puzzle in this town."

"So how is this going to work?" an older teacher asked. "I mean so we all say the same thing when asked about the boxes."

"We purchased sixty-five 'state of the art' lock boxes that can only be opened with the thumb print of the teacher," Keith explained. "The boxes will be mounted on the side of the teachers' desks in every room this weekend. Obviously the Low Field 20 will have their prints coding into their boxes early next week in private and we will test them several times to insure they're working properly."

"So, that's it?" asked another. "The rest of us who are not part of the plan or maybe disagree with this plan have no say? I mean, there will be a gun box mounted to my desk on Monday morning, whether I'm opposed to this idea or not."

"We understand that some of you disagree with this idea," Keith admitted. "Frankly, we're asking everyone, and that means each and every one of you, to get on board and support this initiative. The community is strongly in favor of this plan and we know it is going to set our district apart from others and make Low Field the safest place for students and staff in the state. In fact, that sounds like a new marketing plan, doesn't it? Listen, we all hope this is a preventive measure that we never have to use, just like we hoped the SRO would never have to use his gun, but he still carried one on his belt every day just to be prepared in the event of an emergency. We're doing the same thing only we're doing it twenty times better. In fact, I hope you all feel safer because of this program. In time, I believe those of you who disagree with this idea, will come to find we are all safer because of the Low Field 20.

A young male teacher stood up, looked around the room at his peers and said, "Keith, on behalf of all of us, I want to thank you for thinking outside the box and doing the superintendent's job for him by coming up with this plan. It's sad that we have to teach and run the schools."

"Thanks Terry, but if this is what it takes to get the community to support us, it will be worth it. I want to thank the nineteen other teachers who were courageous enough to support and become a part this idea. Now before we get out of here for the weekend there's one more important announcement. I wanted all of you know that the LTA Executive Committee voted unanimously today to file An Intent to Strike Notice with the board, so start saving your money for the beginning of January. It's very likely that we will be on strike."

"Oh my God," said one of the veteran teachers thinking out loud, "don't you and the others think this is bad timing? I mean right after Christmas break."

"We discussed timing at great length, and it was the consensus of the committee that from now on we need to be more assertive in all of our dealings with the voters and the administration. We've been more than generous by taking a softer approach this year and working without a contract, and they still rejected the levy. The next thing that will be coming from the administration will be job cuts and program cuts. We can't kid ourselves any longer," Keith warned. "The financial outlook of this district is bleak. Amy talked to the treasurer and he told her the state would probably assign a Fiscal Oversight Commission to the district since the levy has failed so many times and the budget projection for next year is even more in the red than this year's budget. The state only allows a district to operate so long in with an imbalance of expenditures that exceeds revenue and then it steps in to do what the local board hasn't done. So we're going to become a district in financial emergency and that will mean the loss of many of our jobs."

Keith pointed to a senior teacher who was holding his hand up, "Stu, you want to say something?"

"Yeah, thanks Keith. Look, we all have to get on the same page right now. This situation is like war and we are in a warzone. If we don't stick together and do what's necessary, we could all perish. Everyone in this room needs to get on board about both the Low Field 20 and the impending strike—I mean this," he said forcefully, "no fence-sitters. I've been in this district my whole career, and the only way to get through this is to stick together whether you have a difference of opinion or not. We have to be unified on these issues or we'll get fractured, and this place will crumble like some sand hut in a third-world country. I mean it!"

"Okay," Keith said, trying to reduce the tension amongst the group, "the war analogies seem a little over the top for me but I do agree with Stuart, and I think all of us realize his assessment of our situation is correct. We're headed into some difficult times, and we have to have each other's backs. So please, people, think long and hard about what was said here today, and if you have any questions or concerns, please give me a call this weekend. It's been a long week and I'm sure all of you want out of here as much as I do. Any other questions or comments?"

A young teacher said loudly, "Just one, Keith. Who's buying the first round of drinks at *Pete's* to toast the Low Field 20?"

69

THE CALDWELL FARMHOUSE kitchen was square and small. The round table at which the family ate their meals took-up most of the floor space originally designed for the cook. The years of family tradition started when the boys were very young and Mrs. Caldwell could feed the boys in their high-chairs while she prepared the various meals for the day. Over the years, these early customs became habits worthy of preservation in her view, despite the fact that the boys had developed into young men and the family had outgrown the space. The kitchen felt comfortable to everyone. It was the place the boys did homework and school projects, recounted their daily experiences, solved problems, discussed dreams for the future and learned life-lessons from their parents. It was also the place where meetings were held, especially when there was a serious topic that needed discussed by the family.

Roy looked up from his bowl of soup and said to Colton and Clayton, "You boys listen up. That judge is holding our feet to the fire; no screw ups from now on. Do you understand me?"

"Yeah, Pa," Clayton said.

"Yep," was Colton's response.

"So, every weekend for the next year or so, I'll be locked up and you two will be on your own. Now Clay is supposed to be at your grandparent's house so I think he should at least spend part of the day there. Clayton, I want you to park your jeep there. Colt, you drop him off at school in the morning, and then Clay, you walk to work after school. If you're not scheduled, get a ride home or Colton will have to pick you up and drop you off. Just do some work for your grandparents until it gets dark, and then Colton can pick you up to sleep here," the father said. "You boys understand?"

"Yeah," Clayton said, "that sounds fine but why do we even have to bother going back and forth puttin' on a show? I mean, why can't Clay just drive his Jeep back and forth and then I can pick him up after dark?"

"Then you'd have to drive him back over there every morning. It doesn't make sense," his father said getting agitated.

"What's the difference?" Clayton asked.

His father responded pointing a finger at his younger son, "Because if they check to see if we're following the judge's orders, and they might check on Clay any time of the week because those damn social workers are always on duty. I talked to your grandparents and they agree with me. Okay?"

"Sure."

"Yep."

"Alright, good," said Roy. "I'm going into Canton tonight to pick up a load and I'll be gone for the early part of this week. I've got to go to Kansas City and then pick up a return load in Chicago. I should be home Thursday evening. There's food in the frig and I left $40.00 on the counter for you to get more groceries if you run out of food. I hate to leave you boys tonight but I've got a chance to make this run and start to make up for some of the lost wages from the past few weeks. You boys gonna to be alright?"

"Yeah pa, we'll be fine," Colton said. "You take care out there."

"Yep, I'm always careful. Now I want you boys to listen carefully," Roy added. "We don't have much in this world. Your mom and I did everything we could over the years, but life's not easy. The one thing we gave you both is a good name and it's up to each of you to preserve that. We'll get through this rough patch and come out the other side stronger for it."

Roy got up from the table and put his dishes in the sink.

"One of you clean up the kitchen later," he said. "Be good, and I'll see you Thursday."

Mr. Caldwell took his coat and cap from the hooks that lined the walls going down the steps to the back door. He put them on and banged the door shut. Colton and Clayton hung out inside for a while playing video games on the TV in the living room.

"I need some air," Clayton said. "Do you want to go out back and shoot squirrels?"

"Sure."

Most of the leaves had fallen in the woods behind their house. The hard red oaks and pin oaks were still full of the brown wedges that held stubbornly to the limbs like vessels synched tightly to a dock during a storm. The air was crisp enough for the boys to see their breath as they walked. Hunting had become something they took for granted, years after their father and grandfather had exposed them to the simple joy of spending time in nature. When they were very young, they walked quietly behind the men observing the techniques of the hunt. Typically the men walked with shotguns through the fields of neighbors and friends who were kind enough to allow them to hunt their land. Being experienced and neighborly, the two older men cared for and were respectful of the property. Both welcomed the opportunity to keep the wildlife population under control and maintain a proper balance of animals in the area. When Colton was just old enough to read, he noticed the repeating signs and asked his father about them.

"No Tres-pass-ing. What does that mean, pa?" the boy asked.

"It means no one's allowed to be on Mr. and Mrs. Baker's property," his father explained.

"How come we're allowed to be here?" Colton asked.

"They gave us their permission to hunt today. Your grandpa has known them for many years and he asked them if it would be okay for us to walk out here and hunt a little," answered his father.

"Oh."

"Those signs are on the trees so hunters know they have to have permission to be in these woods," Roy said. "They can't just come out here and hunt without talking to the people who own the land."

"Okay, I understand," Colton said. "Well, I'm glad grandpa knows Mr. and Mrs. Baker 'cause this is fun."

"Yep, hunting is a great sport, son," his father said, "as long as you're very careful and very quiet."

"Can I shoot the gun today?" Colton asked.

"Maybe a little later," his father answered. "For now, you just watch and learn."

"Okay pa," Colton replied.

Clayton and Colton had been through this small patch of wood a thousand times. Every year as they grew older, the woods seemed to shrink in size. They each carried a .22 caliber rifle using the training they had learned from years of tagging along as kids. Clayton stopped and slowly lifted his hand to the left pointing at a spot twenty yards ahead. Colton touched his index finger to his lips and motioned for Clayton to take the shot on the black squirrel once it left the tree. He slowly knelt in position and waited for the right opportunity. As soon as the rapidly moving animal hit the ground he fired a perfect shot hitting the squirrel and sending it into an airborne double flip. The animal fell to the ground thrashing momentarily in the brush, alighted softly on a blanket of leaves before the stillness of death eradicated the animal's pulsing.

"Nice shot, little brother," Colton said with a smile.

"Why thank you, big brother," Clayton said with a nod.

They spent the next two hours in the peacefulness of the woods. As the sun's late afternoon blush washed the horizon with a magnificent citrus hue, they turned and started back to the house dragging a short rope with three dead squirrels tied neatly at one end like cans from the back bumper of a car announcing a newly-wed couple on their way to celebrate the beginning of a new life. The time spent had been both fun and therapeutic. Like most siblings they shared a bond that eclipsed description—their memories, their experiences and their blood connected them forever.

The boys talked about their parents, especially their mom and what she had meant to each of them. Their current situation was a disaster but Colton tried to encourage Clayton to stay strong and follow Jesus's teaching the way their mom would have wanted, hopeful that everything would work out for the best. Colton found himself quoting his mother.

He said to his brother with a smile, "Remember mom would tell us that God is always there for you, in the good times and the bad times, and he doesn't keep score."

70

L ATE SUNDAY EVENING Mr. Caldwell was getting sleepy about two hours east of Kansas City. He stopped at a twenty-four hour service center to rest and purchase gas. He filled the truck and decided to stretch and walk around so he parked his rig and walked a ways down the road to a diner to have a light meal. He sat on a stool and put his cap on the counter.

"Evening," the waitress greeted him. "Coffee?"

"Sounds good; and a hamburger with everything but hold the onions," he replied.

When the woman returned with his coffee Roy asked, "Ma'am, would you have anything that might help me stay awake for a few hours?"

"Well, we have the High Octane Red energy drink on the counter," she said pointing to a small display near the cash register.

Roy leaned in closer to the woman and said, "I was hoping you might have something a little stronger in the form of a tablet."

"Oh, well let me see," she said searching with her hand in the front pocket of her apron. "I might."

She turned her back to the counter.

"I do happen to have something that will work for you but it's $10.00," she said.

"That's a little rich," Roy said. "Let me see how much cash I have. Okay."

She pulled a small piece of tin foil from the pocket of her apron and slid it under the saucer of his coffee. After finishing his sandwich and a second cup of coffee, Mr. Caldwell set a 20 dollar bill on the check and told her to keep the change.

His knees and back were stiff as he walked from the diner to the truck. He walked around the trailer checking it and stretching his body a little more before he climbed up into the cab. He rubbed his eyes and yawned after completing his log and clasping shut his seat belt. Maybe a shot or two from his flask would give him the jolt he needed to finish the drive. He could park in the overflow lot at his destination until the morning hours brought in the workers to open the dock and help him unload the trailer. He could sleep a few hours once he was on site and hopefully be refreshed enough to start on the next leg of the trip. He used two long swigs of Wild Turkey to wash down the pill so he was sure to get to town without falling asleep.

Traffic was light as he exited the interstate, merging onto local roads for the final ten miles to his first destination, a distribution center on the outskirts of the city. The dense Missouri woods were cut tight to the edges of the road, and a formidable layer of fog added resistance to dawn's lifting of the dark cloak of night. Mr. Caldwell was alert for deer; his experience told him the first hour of daylight was the most dangerous time for animals to wander onto the roads while grazing for food. He passed a familiar lumber yard located on a long, sweeping bend in the road that opened early. It was a stretch where traffic sometimes bottlenecked during traditional work hours. Trucks would go in carrying large, pine tree trunks ready to be cut into finished lumber and there would be trucks leaving the site with pallets of fresh two-by-four studs stacked efficiently on the trailer on their way for delivery at construction sites. He slowed because the entrance provided little time to react to large vehicles making gradual turns to and from the roadway. It was a dangerous spot but today he only encountered a pickup truck full of firewood chunks of pine, probably tree scraps unsuitable for lumber-grade sawing but good enough for a secondary use.

Finally, a pale light illuminated the sky behind him. They were rolling along in tandem and picking up speed when the pickup gradually drifted left of center heading directly at an oncoming pair of headlights. Suddenly, the driver of the pickup reacted to the brash horn of the semi-truck approaching in the opposite lane and pulled his vehicle swiftly back to the right barely avoiding a head-on collision. He swerved off the road and onto the berm barely missing a tree. Instinctively, he jerked the truck hard back toward the road bouncing through a depression before his tires regained traction from the pavement. The load of two-foot pieces of tree, however, became unsettled and many spilled from the open truck bed bouncing off the asphalt like popcorn in oil. Three pieces tumbled and spun straight into the grill and windshield of Mr. Caldwell's cab. The weight of the tree chunks and the force created by the speed of his truck made the objects sound like a succession of shotgun blasts when they slammed into his vehicle. He slammed on his brakes and his engine made a loud growl as he downshifted through the gears. Shattered glass exploded in front of him and showered his startled face with a myriad of crystal-like pellets. A deadly piece of cut pine struck him directly in the face killing him instantly.

His semi tractor-trailer rolled into the deep drainage ditch that edged the road sending the loosely attached vehicle careening violently into the trees in a surreal tumble that shook the quiet surroundings with a thunderous boom, crushing trees and sending debris into the air for a hundred yards. The driver of the pickup watched the calamity in his rear view mirror. He pulled off to the side of the road, called 911 and nervously reported the accident. Within twenty minutes a state trooper, volunteer fire department engine and several ambulances were on the scene. A dozen road-side flares were lit and placed in succession, dotting the road and creating a single lane for traffic to navigate around the accident. The officials quickly reviewed the crash site and performed a safety assessment of the catastrophe. They determined a subsequent explosion or a dangerous spill was not likely and started the mundane task of recreating and documenting the details of the accident. Others began the clean-up of the site in a methodical, perfunctory manner. All involved knew the worse part of the day would be for those charged with the grim task of identifying the victim and making the proper notifications to the trucking company and the local authorities near the victim's home. The Low Field Police Department was delegated with the horrendous chore of notifying the next of kin with the staggering news.

71

THE TWO LOCAL real estate brokers were both inundated with requests to list properties *For Sale* following the board's decision to arm twenty teachers in the two school buildings. The sixth failure of the renewal levy added to the frenzy and many families with school-aged children viewed the events of the past few weeks as the tipping point from which they could no longer support the schools and remain residents in the district.

A sub-committee of the PTA quickly reassembled themselves as the Concerned Mothers for Action or CMA to thwart the problem. A ribbon campaign was initiated. As a sign of support for the schools, property owners were asked to tie oversized ribbons to trees and mailboxes in front of their homes. At first, the simple sign of solidarity was accepted by many, but the initiative quickly died out when numerous mailboxes were spray painted and clubbed with baseball bats in the early morning hours one day by individuals determined to suppress the plan. The police had no leads on the identities of the vandals, although many people had a hunch who was responsible for the wrongdoing. People removed the ribbons fearing an escalation of property damage, and the cost of subsequent repairs outweighed the symbolism of sponsorship.

Another group, Parents for Change, was established to study the current state of the schools and voice opinions from parents directly to school officials. A website was developed that served as an open forum for people to make comments and offer advice with the promise of zero censorship. Visitors to the site were asked to express their opinions openly and honestly without fear of reprisal and without judgment. The website functioned for only two days before the vicious statements and personal attacks from bloggers left the group no other option than to shut it down.

The day it launched, logical thinkers made reasonable appeals to the community at large related to the long history and proud traditions of the schools in hopes of unifying the two groups of constituents that either strongly supported the institution or those who vehemently opposed it. In the creation of the forum, an attempt was made to establish common ground, such as the relationship between good schools and property value, as the starting point for constructive discussion and commentary meant to address the financial problems facing the district. Unfortunately, within a few short days, the in-fighting and wild allegations about school employees, unsavory comments about families and children and hateful insults toward both the administrators and board members only served to widen the chasm in the community rather than bring people together.

For months Daron's mom also had been considering moving out of the district. The fact that he was a senior and would probably leave home following graduation had her thinking about moving to a location closer to work. Making her decision even easier was the courtesy the landlord had offered—a month-to-month rental agreement. For two years she never missed or was even late with a rental payment so now she had the option to move at any time as long as she provided the owner with a month's notice. And he promised to refund her initial deposit if there was no damage done to the trailer after they moved out.

The incident at the football game had left her shaken, recalling the bigotry and small mindedness she had experienced as a white female teenager dating a black man. Race relations had improved only slightly since the civil rights movement and prejudice continued to exist in the hearts and minds of many people in the United States who were slow to let go of old notions, even if they had no bearing on them whatsoever. She still remembered the private conversation she had with Sister Catherine one day in high school.

"God doesn't see skin color, Brenda," said the nun, "only the goodness and belief in a person's heart."

"Sister, then why did God even create people of different skin color?" the girl asked.

The nun asked her, "Do you see Douglas as a man or a black person?"

"Both."

"When you see him as only a man," the nun said, "you will know you have lost your own prejudice."

"I think notions of race are too deep to lose," Brenda said.

"Cultural and sociological biases are real and powerful, I agree," admitted Sister Catherine, "but I like to think that man and woman were created in God's image, and as people have multiplied and spread around the world over thousands of years, natural adaptations have occurred out of necessity that make people have different appearances. But we are all still God's children."

"So I should disregard the relatively recent history of our country and the effects that slavery and black culture probably had on my own beliefs and look far deeper into history as a way to erase what I've been taught, consciously or subconsciously?" Brenda asked.

"I think that would be a good place for you to start. I would also ask for God's help for discovering what's truly in your heart. Brenda, you are a lovely, smart young woman," the nun said. "Trust yourself—you know what's right. Follow your own path; it's your decision."

The conversation was liberating and profound at the time because she knew she was pregnant. The conflict in her mind between her religious beliefs, societal and political norms and her own family's strong expectations of success had her pitted in the most significant emotional struggle of her life. Dating Douglas was one thing, but being the mother of an interracial baby weighed on her during the early months of her pregnancy with unimaginable pressure. She read an anthropologist's explanation of creation that expounded the notion that suggested from what was known about the origins of mankind that all the people in the world could ultimately be traced back to a set of parents or a small number of parents from a region in north Africa that over hundreds and hundreds of years migrated throughout the world, and over centuries, differences in appearance and language developed that explain modern questions of evolution. To her it seemed strikingly similar to Sister Catherine's creation theory and that eased her feelings of doubt. Intellectually, she began to view Douglas solely as a man with no differences from other men. By her sixth month when her pregnancy was obvious to everyone close to her, there was no uncertainty in her heart, only joy.

The problems she faced over the years from others were *their* issues in her mind, not hers. Now, however, she viewed the move from Low Field as an opportunity to experience a more open culture than the one she had lived in with Daron for the past eighteen years. Perhaps it was time for a new job and a new life on one of the coasts. In the evenings when Daron was out, she spent time searching for employment and real estate options in California. The more time she studied the options she only regretted she had not looked into them years earlier; life for both her and her son might have been easier.

She resolved to have a serious conversation with her son regarding race. In some ways their situations were very different—she being a female Caucasian and he being a male of mixed race—but they both stood together when it came to their experiences dealing with prejudice. Perhaps if she cooked his favorite sit-down dinner, it would provide them with the opportunity to talk about race and their futures. The water was boiling when she heard his truck park and the door close.

"Hi babe," Brenda said. "Where have you been?"

"Mom," Daron said directly, "did you hear the news? You're not going believe it—Colton's dad got killed this morning. His truck went off the road."

"Oh my God," she said covering her mouth with a hand and shaking her head in stunned amazement, "that poor child."

72

As the tragic news spread among the residents of Low Field about the accident, people reacted in total disbelief. The news more than anything in recent years served as a crisis that pulled the community together in support of the two boys and their grandparents. The news spread in every conceivable fashion—texts, social media forums, phone calls, and word of mouth by concerned friends and neighbors as well as gossipers. Regardless of how they felt about Mr. Caldwell or his sons, everyone was universally stunned by the relentless tragedies that continued to strike the family. Throughout Low Field the comments were consistently tinged with sadness and disbelief.

"Their mother was just buried less than two weeks ago."

"All those poor people have done is go to the hospital, the courthouse and the funeral home."

"Those poor boys; what in the world are they going to do?"

"If they didn't have bad luck, they wouldn't have any luck at all."

Churches started collecting money for the family as did virtually every business in the town. Plastic coffee cans with slots cut in the lid were circled with homemade paper signs expressing heart-felt, simple messages, such as *Help the Caldwell Family* and *The Caldwell Boys Need Your Help*. Pledges were made by people at a bank that set up an impromptu fund for Colton and Clayton. Food was donated by area restaurants and grocery stores. The boy's grandparents were staying at the house with them and politely opened the door and received the goods graciously from the people making deliveries, but everyone who saw them said they looked like ghosts in shock. No one had seen either Colton or Clayton for days. Word around town was the boys were upstairs in the house and refused to take visitors or phone calls. Funeral arrangements were being handled by Mr. and Mrs. Brown who supposedly told the funeral director that Colton and Clayton were so shaken by their father's death that they might not be well enough to attend the calling hours or his memorial service.

One afternoon, Colton climbed out his bedroom window onto a section of roof and jumped down into the side yard without his grandparents noticing the escape. He drove off in his pickup truck and it wasn't until they called him for dinner that they discovered his disappearance. That night he didn't come home. They called his cell phone repeatedly only to discover that he had turned it off and left it in the bottom drawer of his dresser. The next morning, Mr. Brown reluctantly called Chief Hadley. He asked them to stop by the station and officially file a missing person report with the police department. The truck information was emailed to law enforcement entities throughout the area, state and region. A full day went by and there was no sighting of the boy or his vehicle. News of Colton's disappearance shot through the community; young and old alike were talking about the former high school football star as if he might be suicidal. Search parties were organized as people desperately sought to find him before the tragic cycle of sadness was expanded further.

Will and Luke had driven to a driving range in the eastern suburb of Watson that had covered, heated hitting stalls. They each hit a large bucket of balls and took some video of each other's swing with Luke's tablet. The sophisticated golf software allowed them to analyze their swings in slow motion and from different angles. They were both eager to improve and to send almost flawless video to prospective college golf coaches. The national signing day was sometime in January, and despite getting letters of interest from many colleges, both of the boys were still hopeful that they would receive firm offers from programs with more famous reputations in the coming four to six weeks.

On the return trip to Low Field, Luke took a series of back roads rather than the state highways. The roads rolled steeply up and down, and when they achieved the right speed, the dips gave them both the odd feeling like the bottom of the car was falling out from under them. Their stomachs felt sick at first but after a few more of the humps they adjusted and were fine except for their uncontrollable laughter. They passed a small park called The Ledges that was famous for the mystical series of caves and narrow walkways that had been chiseled between and under an unusual collection of huge rocks, undoubtedly dispersed and arranged by glaciers centuries ago.

"Oh wow, The Ledges," Luke said. "Do you want to stop?"

"Yeah, but the place is never open," Will said. "Someone always seems to drown in the quarry or get killed falling off a cliff and then they close it for the rest of the year."

"Man, I remember going there as a kid," Luke said. "That place is wild."

"It is really creepy and scary," Will agreed. "Did you ever go there after dark?"

Luke looked at Will and said, "No, that would be crazy. Hey that gate looks open."

Luke slowed down and sure enough the entrance gate just past a huge boulder was open. The swinging pipe structure was unchained from a rusty post that it was locked to with a heavy chain.

"Is this an employee drive?" asked Luke.

"I don't see any sign," Will answered. "Let's drive up a ways."

They weaved slowly on the single lane road climbing deeper into the tree and rock-lined forest. The rocks were unlike any they had ever seen in this area of the country—deep charcoal in color and jagged with sharp edges.

"Do you want to park and hike a little?" Luke asked.

"Sure. This place is so primitive," Will said looking around at the scenery. "It feels prehistoric."

Luke pulled off in a small lot. They grabbed their fleece tops from their golf bags, locked the doors and started down a path between two mammoth boulders that was so narrow they had to turn sideways to get through the twenty feet and back out into the open.

"I hope you're not claustrophobic," Will laughed. "This place is so cool; I had forgotten how weird it is."

"I know," Luke agreed, "you feel like you're going to run into Indiana Jones or some ancient people with blow darts."

"Hey, look over there," Will said pointing at an object in the woods. "What is that?"

"I don't know. It Iooks like a car or a refrigerator," Luke said. "Let's go check it out."

They pushed through the heavy brush trying to avoid scratching their faces and eyes in the hopes of getting a better view of the object.

"It's a pickup truck," Luke said.

"Oh my God, that's Colton's truck," Will said in disbelief.

"Who's that?"

"The guy who shot me in the leg," Will said.

"You're kidding; well, he's not in the cab," Luke said looking through the side window. "Are you sure this is his truck?"

"Yeah, the *Jesus Lives* wood sign in the back window is unmistakable," Will stated. "And he's been missing for the past two days."

"We better look for him," Luke said.

They frantically tried to track Colton's movement from the truck through footprints and a path through the bushes. They started calling his name as they walked, their eyes scanning wildly left and right.

"Colton; Colton Caldwell," Will called loudly.

They followed a scruffy path and came upon a dark, black-hole of a cave. Slowly the boys entered the opening touching the walls with their hands and sliding their feet to avoid tripping.

Will called into the deep recess of the cave, "Colton. Colton. It's Will Harper."

"Man I wish we had a flashlight," said Luke. "I don't feel like going any farther. Some wild animal or worse could be hiding in there."

"I agree, we better stop," Will said. "I'm going to just let my eyes adjust for a minute and see if I can make out anything. Colton. Colton, it's Will Harper. Are you in there?"

Suddenly a rock flew past them and crashed into the wall.

"Holy shit," Luke said stumbling toward the light of the cave opening. "Somebody's in there."

"Colton is that you?" Will said warily.

They heard a moan. Will's eyes were now able to make out the white of a pair of shoes. He walked in and got closer to the person.

"Sir, are you okay?" Will asked. "Holy crap it's him, Luke. Colton, are you okay?"

"Who are you?" Colton asked in a soft, confused voice.

"Will, it's me, Will Harper. Are you okay, man? Will asked. "Come on, let's get you out of here."

"Who are you?" Colton asked again.

Luke rejoined the two in the cave and said, "Man, he's messed up. Is he hurt?"

"I don't know," Will answered. "Colton did you get hurt? Are you injured?"

The boys pulled Colton to his feet and he mumbled, "I don't know; where are we?"

"Oh wow, we've got to get him out of here," Will said. "Help me Luke. Let's get on either side of him and take him back to your car."

They couldn't get a cell phone signal until they had driven out of the park and a few miles down the road toward Low Field. Will called his dad who had just gotten home from work.

"Where are you?" his father asked. "Slow down; Will, you're breaking up and not making much sense."

"Dad, Luke and I found Colton. He was in a cave at The Ledges. I don't know if he got hurt or what but he doesn't know me and didn't know where he was when we found him. It's a long story; I'll fill you in later. I just want to know where to take him." Will said.

"It sounds like he's disoriented or delirious," Mr. Harper said. "I wonder if he hit his head. Take him to the emergency clinic on Hawks Ridge Road. I'll meet you there."

73

KELSEY HAD BEEN working late doing homework assignments, the pattern she developed after the first few weeks of computerized classes in her new school. She thought her brother, mom and step-father had long since been asleep when she heard a faint knock on her bedroom door and her mom peaked in.

"Hi honey," her mom said peeking through the cracked door, "got a minute?"

"Sure mom," Kelsey said.

Kelsey turned her attention away from the computer and spun her desk chair toward her mother who sat down on the end of the bed.

Her mom looked deeply at her and said, "I need to tell you something."

"Okay, mom, what's wrong?" Kelsey asked sensing her mother's burden.

"Wyatt and I are getting divorced," Stephanie said directly.

Kelsey paused for a moment considering her response and finally said, "Good."

"Really," her mother said with surprise. "I was afraid you'd be upset."

"You're kidding, right?" Kelsey said with a quizzical look. "Mom, I think that's great."

"This is a little surprising to me," she said, "but I'm glad you're okay with it."

"It's been pretty obvious that he's not happy and doesn't want to be here anymore," Kelsey said.

"How did you see that so clearly when I couldn't?" her mother asked.

"I think he hides his true feelings around you more than he does to Brian and me. And he seems to always find reasons not to be around much anymore. Let's face it, the other thing that's obvious is that he's been drinking more and more," Kelsey said candidly.

"Yeah I guess it's pretty classic behavior that's something's wrong," Stephanie admitted, "but I guess I hoped you two hadn't noticed."

"We'll be okay, mom," Kelsey said.

Kelsey sat next to her mom on the bed and hugged her from the side. They sat quietly together for a while.

"Thanks, honey. You're right," Stephanie said, "we're going to be okay. It's going to be a rough couple of months but we'll get through it."

"Is he still going to be here?" Kelsey asked.

"No, he agreed to move out this weekend and we're going to see a lawyer on Friday to start the legal proceedings. Eventually we're going to have to sell the house, so we'll be moving, too, after it sells," her mom explained.

"Did you tell Brian yet?"

"No," her mom answered. "I figured I'd wait until after this weekend. Do you think he'll be upset?"

"I don't know for sure, but I doubt it. Wyatt doesn't seem to do that much with him anymore," Kelsey said, "except yell at him about chores and cleaning up after himself."

"I hope you're right. I'm so glad you're not upset with me," her mother said.

"Mom, we'll always be best friends, no matter what," Kelsey said. "In fact, since we're sharing important news, I've got some for you as well."

Her mom's face brightened and she sat up with a renewed sense of happiness and expectation.

She said to her daughter, "What's your news Kelsey?"

The girl looked directly at her mom's face and said, "Mom, I'm gay."

"What?" her mom questioned leaning back from her daughter. "I mean how can that be? How do you know?"

"Erin and I are together," Kelsey said.

Her mother sat stunned, her hand holding her mouth, looking at the floor and shaking her head back and forth in a negative manner.

"Honey, are you sure this just isn't a reaction to your recent experiences with the boys you've dated?" her mother asked. "I have to be honest, you don't seem gay to me."

"I wasn't sure at first but now I know," Kelsey said.

"How do you know?" Stephanie asked her daughter.

"The first time Erin and I were together intimately, I was pretty confused, but the more I've thought about it," Kelsey said, "I realized I've known deep down for some time, but I wasn't sure how to deal with it."

"What does that mean?" her mom asked sincerely.

"Even when I was little I felt like I was different from other kids, like when they'd separate the boys from the girls for certain classes in school. Now I realize that I've just always been more comfortable with girls than with boys. And I am so happy when I'm with Erin," Kelsey said. "It's so easy to be with her, and we have fun, real fun together. I never felt this way when I was dating Colton or Daron. With Erin, everything seems to come natural to me and there's no pressure, no stress. I feel at peace, and I can be myself for once in my life."

"Honey I respect what you're saying," her mother said, "but this might just be a phase, so I wouldn't make too big a deal about it."

"Mom, it's not just a phase," Kelsey insisted. "This is real. I'm gay and I'm sure of it."

"Alright, that's fine Kelsey," her mother said sensing her daughter's agitation over her response.

They sat together again in quiet, this time holding hands.

"Well, have you two told anyone else?" Stephanie asked.

"Nope," Kelsey said, "you're the first to know. But Erin is planning on telling her parents sometime soon as well."

"Well, thank you for telling me first," she said.

Stephanie Boyd stood and wiped a tear from her eye with the sleeve of her robe. She touched her daughter lovingly on the shoulder.

"Let's wait to tell your brother for a few weeks if that's okay with you," her mother said. "He's still young and I don't want to overwhelm him with all of our important news too quickly."

"Sound good," Kelsey agreed.

"Good night, sweetie," her mom said standing and retying her robe belt.

"G'night, mom," her daughter said. "Remember, we're going to be okay."

74

WILL'S FATHER ALERTED the medical facility and the Low Field Police about the discovery of Colton Caldwell and his need for emergency treatment. They frantically converged on the urgent care center and arrived within minutes of Luke, Will and Colton. A nurse and attendant were waiting for them as they pulled under the overhang that protected patients from bad weather who were transitioning from a vehicle through the emergency doors of the facility.

"Let's have him lie down on a stretcher and take him to 105," the nurse directed.

The attendant got on one side of Colton supporting his body and Will assumed the same position on the other side of Colton's limp body, both serving as human crutches to the staggering young man.

The attendant said, "Here you go buddy, let's just sit down on the edge and then we'll help you lie down."

He clicked shut a strap around Colton's chest and another around his upper legs. The nurse returned with a blanket and covered Colton. They rolled him down the hallway toward the back of the facility. A pair of automatic doors anticipated their approach and swung open revealing a network of computers and technical equipment. They maneuvered the gurney and patient around a tight corner and into a vacant room.

The nurse pulled closed the large cloth curtain and said to Will and the others, "Wait out here please."

The attendant stuck the top of his head around the edge of the curtain door and said, "Thanks for your help."

A male nurse entered the room and started to gather the pertinent statistical information for Colton, taking quick temperature and blood pressure readings. He tried to communicate with the young man who remained drowsy and incoherent. Then a doctor came into the curtained area and began washing his hands while talking to the patient.

"Hi," the doctor said, "I'm Dr. Quinn. What's your name?"

Colton opened and closed his eyes in a slow, rhythmic pattern and said, "I don't remember."

"What do you remember?" the doctor asked.

Colton lay with a blank look on his face.

"Do you know how you got here?"

"No," Colton replied.

"Well, two of your friends found you and brought you here. I think one of them is named Will. Do you know Will?" the doctor asked.

"No."

"They told me your name is Colton," the doctor said. "Does that sound right?"

"I guess," he said. "They have been calling me that."

"Good, so you remember people calling you Colton?" the doctor confirmed.

"Yeah," Colton said.

A police officer stepped unobtrusively into the room.

"They found you at a park," the doctor continued. "Do you remember that?"

"Not really," said Colton.

"Can you tell me anything about what you did today? Or yesterday?" the doctor asked.

"No, sorry," Colton answered.

"Okay, Colton, that's okay," the doctor said. "Joe is going to bring you a pill and a snack and then I want you to just rest here for a while. Okay?"

"Okay."

Dr. Quinn and the police officer talked in the hallway for a moment and then joined the others in the waiting room lobby. Following introductions the doctor offered an initial prognosis.

"From my quick evaluation of the patient, I'd guess he is suffering from amnesia, but we won't know for sure what the problem is until he rests for a while and we do a few tests. The officer informed me about his parents; are his grandparents here yet?" Dr. Quinn asked.

Will's dad answered, "No, but we called them and they're on their way."

"I'll have to wait to talk to them about treatment, but thank you fellows for getting him here so quickly," the doctor said to Will and Luke. "You probably saved his life."

He shook Will and Luke's hands.

Upon their arrival, Colton's grandparents were taken in to see him. He didn't recognize them either. His grandmother leaned over his weary body, hugged and kissed him.

"I'm so glad you're okay, Colton. I love you," Clare Brown said.

Colton suddenly lifted his head and looked quizzically at the old woman. He turned his head looking at different angles at her face. She could tell he was trying to match the image his eyes were sending to his brain with the appropriate memory of her personage.

Finally his head fell back to the pillow and he said, "Thank you."

A short time later, the elderly couple sat in a small conference room with several large glass walls with the doctor.

"My guess is that he has amnesia caused by trauma to the head. Unfortunately he can't help us yet, but he has some swelling on the back of his head so maybe he tripped and hit his head on a rock or accidentally bumped one with his head which is a distinct possibility based on where he was found, but we won't know for sure until we get him stabilized and he gets some rest," the doctor explained. He paused for a moment, thinking and added, "Another cause for his condition might be is what's termed retrograde amnesia. This type of amnesia is often caused by a traumatic psychological event, like the loss of a loved one. So, from what I've been told, this is also a possibility based on what your grandson has recently been through."

"What's next, Dr. Quinn?" his grandmother asked.

"I suggest we have Colton transported to Akron General where they have the equipment to perform a CT scan so we can determine if there is any injury to his brain," said the doctor. "Who's his or your family doctor?"

"Ours is Dr. Curtis," she answered. "He's been talking to Colton's new doctor at the VA Hospital in Cleveland, but I don't know his name. I believe some of those tests are already scheduled for next week."

"Great, then I'll give Dr. Curtis a call and we'll find out where our records should be sent. Then it sounds like the doctor at the VA facility will become Colton's primary physician for the treatment of this problem. So, do you have any questions?" Dr. Quinn asked.

"Just one," Colton's grandmother asked. "Will our grandson recover from this condition and regain his memory?"

"That's difficult to say," the doctor answered honestly. "Many patients do but there is no standard treatment for amnesia that has been found to work for the majority of people who suffer from this disorder, and your grandson's amnesia may have multiple causes which could compound his recovery time and possibly limit the extent of the memories that do return to him. It's very hard to say in these cases and they are all very unique. But keep your spirits up and good luck. He is young which helps; I hope he does fine."

75

THE FIRST DAY of the Low Field 20's rule of the schools came and went without incident. The entire staff was on alert fearing that there would be some kind of challenge to their authority. Once the students had been dismissed and were on their way home via the busses or car-pools, the LF20 met in a remote classroom at the far end of the elementary building. Keith Byler was still alert and animated fueled by the anxiety of the day.

"Okay, so let's review a few important issues," he said feeling the way a field commander must when addressing inexperienced troops. "First of all, did everyone check their lockbox at some time today in order to verify the hand passcodes were working?"

Keith paused and carefully scanned each and every one of the teachers for an affirmative response.

"Good," he said, "I assume no one had a problem?"

Again he made a slow scan of the room, carefully checking with each staff member visually for a confirmation.

"Okay, that's great. Now listen carefully, people," Keith said slowly, "Now, I know, as we discussed last week, that none of your guns were loaded today, but tomorrow morning, I'd like each of you to arrive at school ten minutes earlier than usual and move your live ammunition from your pockets or purse or wherever you had your rounds today and into your guns. Then, obviously, lock the boxes. Any questions?" Again, he scanned the room and then said, "Good."

As the union president looked over his notes and was ready to move onto the next item one of the teachers asked, "Sorry Keith, but I do have one question," he asked. "Did Steve see you today? He stopped me in the office and asked if we had our guns because he had his in his office. I was surprised because I didn't think the principals were part of our plan."

"What?" Keith said with dismay. "Why did that fool have a gun in his office? Listen, as all of you know, the board approved the twenty teachers on the secret list to have weapons and there was no provision for administrators in that motion. So, to answer your question, no, I didn't see Steve today, but I will call him tonight and question him about it. As far as I'm concerned, there's no way he should have a gun in his office because he is not part of the Low Field 20. If any of you hear that he does have a gun at school tomorrow or any time after that, please notify me immediately. I think we'll have to notify the police if he does that again. Thanks for letting me know about that; unbelievable. Anything else? Anyone?"

"Is the emergency response training still scheduled for this coming weekend?" another teacher asked.

"No. Thank you for asking; I received a call today from an agent with the FBI who said he couldn't be here until three weeks from this Saturday. So, please mark your calendars for the second Saturday in December, 9:00 AM here at the elementary school; we'll have donuts and coffee starting at 8:30 in the cafeteria and you can dress casual. Those of you from the middle and high school, please bring your guns with you, so remember to take them with you on the Friday before that day when you leave school. So that's Saturday, December 12th, here at the elementary school; plan on arriving between 8:30 and 9:00 AM with your weapons and I'll send out an email that week to remind everyone."

Another teacher sheepishly raised his hand and said, "Keith, I was told today by a student that the word going around the student body is that this whole idea is just a scam, some sort of scheme by us to make people feel safe so we could get rid of the SRO. The student who mentioned that also challenged me over and over to show him my gun, and I was just wondering if anyone else was approached by other students with that same apprehension and story."

"I was too," said another, "so I showed him. It was Jimmy Phillips, the board member's kid so I thought I better show him so he could tell his dad that this is real and we were ready for an emergency."

There was an immediate undercurrent of conversation amongst the teachers in the room.

"Whoa, okay people listen up," Keith said. "First of all, Nick, and this goes for everyone, please don't let anyone, not students, not parents, I mean no one bait any of you into first of all revealing if you are one of the Low Field 20 because you immediately become a target in the event of a crisis and you spoil the anonymity of the program. Secondly, no one is to ever remove their weapon from the box unless we are in a code orange emergency situation. It is of paramount importance that we never remove the guns from the box for any reason other than a code orange emergency—does everyone understand that? These are two cardinal rules of this program that everyone must abide by if we are to be successful."

The group nodded in approval and the teacher who had succumbed to the temptation to show the student his gun apologized to the group.

"Listen everyone," Keith continued, "this is public relations 101. None of us can let down our guard for even one minute—that means to your husbands or wives, boyfriends or girlfriends—and especially not in casual conversation. You have to practice and rehearse your responses to a variety of inquiries and not allow yourself to reveal the secret identity of the 20. I'm sorry to get emotional, but all of our reputations are dependent on the ability of everyone is this room to deal with this issue with the highest degree of confidentiality and professionalism, or trust me, this whole idea will collapse like a house of cards."

"Keith, we all appreciate the level of confidence you bargained for with the board on our behalf, and I think I speak for everyone when I say that all of us will do our best to serve the union and the district with the utmost seriousness when it comes to protecting the students and the other staff members in the event of an emergency," a teacher said. "We all probably underestimated the severity of the commitment, but I'm sure we'll all do what it takes to preserve both the anonymity of the identities of the teachers as well as the secrecy of the location of the weapons in the schools. It's just a very new paradigm for all of us and it will take some getting used to."

"Thanks Jeff; I'm sure you are absolutely right. This is a monumental new undertaking for all of us, and we will have to make the adjustments necessary to insure its success. Well, does anyone have any other comments or questions before we get out of here?" Keith asked. "Yes, Kelly."

"Keith, I'm so sorry but I have to tell you all, I told all of my classes today that I'm one of the Low Field 20," Kelly admitted. "And I'm terribly sorry to say this but they didn't believe me so I showed them my gun. I'm so sorry."

A loud groan swelled from the people in the room.

"Oh my god," one of them groaned loudly expressing dismay for everyone in the room.

76

J IM COLLINS FELT like his world was spinning out of control. It wasn't unusual for his job to entail maintaining a delicate, orderly balance between managing the everyday routines of the school district necessary for children and adults to make methodical progress throughout the year, and the unexpected and unpredictable chaos that frequently befalls every human organization. He had experienced a similar wobbly feeling before but never had the equilibrium of the district's parts been so far out of harmony with each other. Now the scales were tipped far to the left of center, and he had a serious concern that if the community sensed the turmoil, it would give those people who were so inclined an opportunity to exacerbate the problems and use the situation to further their case that the district was in a state of dysfunction beyond repair, and frankly, not worth saving.

To make matters worse, he received an email and phone call informing him that the failure of the levy had indeed caused the district to descend into the lowest category on the state's reporting system—a designation of *Financial Crisis*. By law this prompted the immediate assignment of a Fiscal Oversight Commission from the State Department of Education to oversee the district's highest management functions. They would assume the administrative and fiscal supervision of the central office. In fact, the consultants were also given the authority to determine all personnel and policy matters, superseding the power of the board of education. Moreover, the committee had the final say on any and all decisions regarding the economic matters of the schools. In essence, this meant they were in charge of everything.

They would take control of the district, supplanting the typical hierarchy of power established more than a century ago in state law and thus relegating the superintendent of schools, the treasurer and the local board of education merely to serve in figurehead positions, puppets kept in place to carry out the wishes of the oversight committee and approve their recommendations through official board action so the committee's plans for the district met the formal, legal requirements of state statute. The lead consultant was driving to Low Field and Jim was expected to clear his calendar and meet with her later today.

As control of the district was slipping through his fingers, Jim thought about his frustration with Steve for refusing to help him check the high school following the bomb threat. One of his primary goals since being hired by the board more than seven years ago had been to establish a sense of teamwork and collegiality amongst the administrators. Jim wanted each of the principals to feel like they had the autonomy to run their own school but also work in a spirit of shared responsibility when it came to resolving difficult problems.

The more he thought about the situation, he believed Steve's refusal was rooted more in the decline of their personal relationship and an erosion of mutual trust rather than truly being an issue of safety. He wished there was a way to fire Steve, but the political impact of such a decision through the typical employee evaluation process was a landmine that was sure to explode on both of them. Maybe the refusal to follow a reasonable request from his superior would at least give Jim merit for an insubordination charge on his evaluation during the next review cycle prior to Steve's contract renewal. After hearing the details of the incident, the school's attorney advised Jim to not pursue any negative or retaliatory actions against the principal regarding the event. His opinion was that if Steve truly thought there might be a bomb in the building, then Jim's request for him to check for it was not a reasonable request.

"But we had six hundred people standing in the parking lot, and students inciting panic by calling their parents saying a bomb was in the building. People were waiting to vote," Jim argued. "The news media was called, for God's sake. They showed up and were filming and reporting live on camera. It was a mess and everyone knew it was a hoax. And the person in charge added fuel to the fire by impulsively getting on the intercom system and announcing there was a bomb threat rather than just evacuating the building through the typical protocol of a fire drill alarm."

The attorney calmly stated, "Jim, he didn't do anything wrong."

"Maybe," the superintendent said, "but he made things worse and then refused to help fix the problem."

Again the attorney said evenly trying to reason with Jim, "If he thought there might be a bomb in the building, the case could easily be made that he showed prudence by getting the people out of the building and not letting anyone go back in."

"Oh god," Jim said, "this is so frustrating. What if I refused to go into the building, Henry?"

"I guess you would have been forced to dismiss school because of the emergency and send everyone home," the attorney said.

"But it was Election Day," Jim continued to argue. "You would have me create that kind of problem by disrupting an official election in my district because of a bomb threat?"

"Jim, listen to me," the attorney said, "you're losing your perspective. Look at it from the other side of the coin. Let's say a bomb had gone off. Steve would be hailed a hero and a person who used good judgment by not putting any of the people at risk, whereas you would be viewed as a person who put yourself and the custodian who helped you search the building in grave danger by not taking the threat serious. It might sound funny, but maybe you should have sent everyone home, including the election workers, and simply called the FBI and waited for them to assemble the proper equipment and personnel to check for the bomb safely."

"Henry, you don't understand, school districts receive bomb threats all the time," Jim said. "If we sent everyone home and called the FBI every time we got a phone call or some kid scribbles a note on a piece of toilet paper, we'd never have school and we be the laughing stocks of the state. I'm sure every government entity and most businesses assess and ignore threats like this all the time. If we didn't, a few crackpots could shut down the whole country."

"Jim, again, pull back and think like a superintendent. 9/11 changed everything in our world. I think we all realize anything can happen anytime and anywhere. I mean look at your bus hostage situation. Did you ever once in your life think you'd be dealing with something like that? Look at this situation with your teachers and their guns. This is crazy," the attorney stated, "but the world is a different place."

"I'm sorry Henry," Jim said, "but I refuse to believe this is the new normal."

"I know it's hard to accept," Henry said, "but unfortunately, it's *your* new normal."

"Thanks," the superintendent responded sarcastically.

"Sorry, but I think you've got bigger issues that need your energy more than Steve's refusal to help you check the building for a bomb. I would suggest that you just let that one go," the attorney advised.

"I know you're right Henry," Jim said. "In fact, you have no idea how right you are because I'm looking out the window and here comes the chairperson of the Fiscal Oversight Commission that's going to take over the management of the district. I'll talk to you soon."

"Who did you get assigned to work with?" Henry asked.

"Honestly I don't remember her name, maybe Dr. Reed," Jim guessed trying to recall her name from the email.

"Is she an attractive Black woman?" the attorney asked.

"Yeah," Jim said. "Do you know her?"

"Yep," Henry said with a sardonic laugh. "You definitely have bigger issues to deal with, my friend. I'll talk to you soon."

77

THE PTA MEETING was being held the Monday before Thanksgiving. The group decided to turn the usual November business meeting agenda, which typically was light and hosted no more than ten to fifteen moms due to the impending holiday, into a public debate on the merits of the new district policy that permitted up to ten armed teachers in each of the school buildings as a deterrent to school violence in Low Field. The policy had been in force for a little over a week without incident, however, not without significant controversy in the community.

Will and Abby were the guest speakers for the evening. Their comments were to be followed by public comments and questions that would be recorded, transcribed and submitted to the Board of Education and Superintendent. The two victims of the only shooting in Low Field history planned to meet at a rear entrance of the elementary school library. They had compared notes for several nights through emails, texts and phone conversations and felt prepared with what they considered to be a useful commentary on both their experiences and their beliefs of what would make the students of Low Field both safer and better prepared in the future if a school shooter would make one of the schools the target of an attack.

The main parking lot was full and cars resorted to parking along the edges of the driveways into and out of the lot as well as in makeshift rows on the front lawn of the school property. An over-flow, standing-room-only crowd was jammed into the small, elementary school library. As the starting time approached, the officers quickly decided to move the meeting into the gymnasium which held more people. The night custodian stretched out the bleachers and rolled two racks of folding chairs near the doorway of the gym so people who preferred not to climb the bleachers could help themselves to a chair and place it on the gym floor. A podium with a built-in sound system was rolled into the center of the floor and small row of chairs was evenly dispersed on either side of the lectern with a long folding table in front to hold papers. An American flag in a heavy circular brass stand was hastily brought in and placed at one end of the table and chairs. People gathered belongings and grudgingly made their way into the gymnasium after one of the PTA officers announced the change in rooms.

Abby used a combination of walking with crutches and a portable wheelchair to navigate through the building. Her mother, father and Will were with her for support. Many people greeted her with smiles and kind words as she made her way to the presenter's area with Will. They recognized most of the PTA officers as parents of school-aged children of different ages but who regularly attended events in the district or spent hours and hours volunteering in the schools. A tall gentleman in khaki slacks, a light blue dress shirt and a black leather jacket was seated at the far end of the table; he nodded to Will when their eyes met just prior to the start of the meeting.

"Good evening everyone; I'm Barbara Prescott, President of the Low Field PTA. It's my pleasure to welcome you to this evening's program and I thank you all for attending. At the head table tonight are Faith Dolan, our vice-president, and our featured speakers for tonight's debate, Will Harper and Abby Olson, two seniors from the high school, and Mr. Alan Leggett, a regional officer with the National Rifle Association. Thank you all for being here. I've asked our two students to start tonight's meeting by sharing with us their memories of that dreadful shooting just weeks ago at our own high school. Will, would you or Abby like to begin?" she asked looking down from the podium at the two students.

Will nodded and replaced Mrs. Prescott behind the microphone. He tilted the flexible arm slightly higher and cleared his throat.

"Hello everyone, my name is Will Harper. Looking around I don't think this gym has seen so many people since last year's Christmas show, so please excuse me if I have to look at my notes but I'm a real amateur when it comes to public speaking, especially when it's in front of so many dignitaries. I'm sorry, I don't know what I meant by that," he laughed nervously shaking his head.

Will spent the first few minutes of his time summarizing his activities and experiences in Low Field prior to the day he was shot. He stressed how important his passion, golf, was to him and explained how he had put himself in a position to qualify for the state tournament which had been his main goal for the past few years. Gradually as he continued speaking he gained confidence and felt more comfortable in front of the large crowd as he shared his recollection of the shooting.

"Leaving school that day was like every other day. A majority of the students were making their way onto buses or out to the student parking lot when we saw the argument between a few students near the pickup truck. I never actually saw the gun. Their argument only lasted a few minutes. Then the truck engine made a loud noise and sped away from the person on the ground and we heard gun fire. We were all shocked by what happened. It happened so quickly and no one expected that one of the people in the argument, who was someone we all knew, would start firing a gun with so many people around. The next thing I remember, I was on the ground and my leg was bleeding and it hurt like I would imagine a hot poker would feel burning your skin. I had never experienced that kind of pain before in my life. I knew I had been hit but I had no idea how bad my injury was or even if I could walk at that point. I remember Mr. Daniels talking to me and riding in an ambulance. And then I just closed my eyes and thought my golf career was over. But I was the lucky one that day. I'd like to now introduce a classmate and friend of mine who wasn't as fortunate as me, Abby Olson."

There was loud applause and many people stood while they clapped to honor Abby. She gained her balance with the crutches and made her way to the podium.

"Thank you, Will," Abby started, "thank you very much everyone. Will asked me to share his time which I'm honored to do and I thank him for the invitation. As Will said, that day seemed like any other day at dismissal time. The upper-class students were all having fun and laughing on the way to our cars, happy that the day was over. Then there was a moment in time when our reality flipped upside down and we realized we were in the middle of a serious confrontation. I remember seeing the altercation before the truck accelerated toward the people, and then, Colton sat up slightly from the pavement and I'll never forget noticing the flash of his gun against the sunlight just before the shots were fired. Everything kind of slowed down for me in a surreal way and when the bullet hit me I doubled over and dropped my books. I was instantly knocked on my back. I literally thought I was going to die within a few minutes. The pain was unlike anything I had ever felt before and it hurt so bad I couldn't scream or cry. I just thought I was this close to death."

She held up her hand with the thumb and index finger a small distance apart.

"I haven't had a chance to thank publically the people who saved my life—from Mrs. Andrews, the EMTs on the way to the hospital, and of course, all of the doctors and nurses who have been so wonderful to me since that day," Abby said. "I can't thank them enough for their treatment and for giving me my life back. Will said he was the lucky one that day, but I, too, feel pretty lucky. Thank you."

Abby made it back to her wheelchair with Will's help. Mrs. Prescott introduced the man from the NRA.

"Good evening everyone. I'm Alan Leggett, and I'm happy to be here tonight. Those two young people are wonderful representatives of this fine community and give all of us hope in the future of our great country. The NRA is thrilled they are healthy and weren't hurt worse or even killed during that startling act of violence they were caught in as innocent bystanders. They are exactly the reason why the NRA fights to preserve our rights as citizens to protect ourselves as our forefathers intended in the Constitution of the United States when they wrote the Second Amendment," he stated. "Did you know that a senseless and often tragic act of violence occurs every fifteen seconds in our country? School shootings have increased 500 percent in the past thirty years and no community, rich or poor, urban or rural, is immune from a potential catastrophic situation. Thankfully, we do not live in a police state, and as Americans we value our civil liberties more than any other people on the face of the earth. The best way for us to preserve our God-given rights and freedoms is for us to retain the ability to protect ourselves and our families against individuals who would do us harm. I'm sorry, I get very passionate when I talk about our great country, and when I see two strong, young students like Abby and Will, they make me proud to be an American.

Kelsey, Erin and their friend Megan had slipped in late, having had to park on the soccer field behind the building. They missed Will's opening remarks but heard the other two speakers after pushing past some of the people in the hallway and finding a place to stand on the far side of the gymnasium.

"I don't like him," Erin whispered to the other two. "Too much flag waving and apple pie."

"Yeah," Megan agreed, "he seems sincere but get off the *Proud to be an American* shtick."

"Really, and what is he even doing here?" Kelsey asked. "I mean why did the PTA invite someone from the NRA to speak."

"My guess is they set it up for him to debate Abby and Will," Erin suggested.

"Okay," Megan said, "but what could he possibly say against them? I mean, they got shot."

"Oh, just watch the spin he puts on things; he's smooth," Kelsey warned.

Mrs. Prescott returned to the podium and posed a question for each of the speakers. The green and white scarf around her neck matched her eyes and complimented her ebony colored hair.

"The first question is this: Does the plan for twenty of our teachers to be armed with handguns in their classrooms provide an effective deterrent against a school shooting and make our schools a safer place? Will, would you please respond first?" the PTA President asked.

"Thank you. Absolutely not," Will answered defiantly. "The Low Field 20 plan, as it's being called, in fact puts our students in greater risk for two reasons. First of all, by approving this plan, our schools have now become a special target for anyone trying to make a name for himself or seeking fame by committing a school atrocity simply because of the extra challenge Low Field 20 represents. A shooting at Low Field would now be viewed as a great accomplishment. These kinds of people value the publicity and fame associated with this kind of senseless violence and we just made ourselves one of the most prized targets in the state, or nation for that matter. Second, having more guns in the hands of more people just increases the likelihood that someone will get hurt; it doesn't lessen the possibility, in my opinion."

Mrs. Prescott removed the microphone from the stand and said, "Thank you, Will. Abby, would you like to respond, please?" She handed the microphone to Abby so she could speak from her wheelchair.

"I agree wholeheartedly with Will. In our situation, one gun in one person's hands caused each of us to be seriously injured and affected our lives forever. I hate to think how much worse the situation could have been if there was even just one more gun in someone's hands that afternoon. And think about this; if Colton had not been carrying his gun that day, we wouldn't be here tonight debating this topic. I believe the correct response is to pass laws in this country that strictly limit who owns guns and who, if anyone, has the authority to carry and use them. If it were up to me, the only people allowed to own and carry guns would be soldiers in the military and law enforcement personnel. Thank you," Abby said handing the microphone back to Mrs. Prescott.

"Mr. Leggett," she said.

He stood at the podium and carefully chose his words. "Thank you, Mrs. Prescott. Let's face it people, these two young people have lived through an enormous trauma in their lives that none of us want for any of our students. I have great respect for both of them and it is very important that we listen attentively to their opinions tonight. This is a very complex issue—one with valid arguments on both sides. I believe there are fundamental rights that all Americans have regarding self-preservation and protection of their loved ones. Over two centuries ago, laws were established that are just as relevant today as they were then related to the right to bear arms. We're blessed with talented and dedicated law enforcement officers in this country. They would give their lives, unselfishly, to protect our students, no matter what the name or location of the school, but they can't be everywhere. They are human beings with limitations and burdensome job responsibilities, and they work in a system that is reactionary. They react to situations and respond most of the time after the damage has been done or the crime has been committed," Leggett said. "Don't get me wrong, that's not their fault. It's the system's fault, and we suffer because of it. If you are in your home one night with your children and someone breaks in, are you going to ask the intruder to stop what they're doing for ten minutes so you can call the police and wait for them to arrive? No, you have a few precious seconds to respond and protect your loved ones. My point is this, bad guys in our society already have guns and they will always find ways to get guns, so for politicians to ban them would only affect law-abiding citizens, and, in fact, put law-abiding citizens in greater danger. We need to train every American citizen to safely own personal weapons and also teach every adult how to defend himself or herself against criminals and others who would do them or their loved ones harm, and that is the NRA's mission. We are a stronger nation if every American family can protect themselves against the forces of evil."

He sat down to a scattered, but vociferous smattering of approval.

"Will, this next question is for you. The question is, are you convinced that the Low Field 20 could protect our students and staff against an invasion in our schools by an intruder who wants to commit murder against innocent people?"

"This probably is not going to surprise anyone but my answer to that question is no," Will said. "In fact, that's my biggest problem with the program. I think having ten or so teachers with guns in each school during a hostage situation could prove to be disastrous. I mean, I know they are well-intended, but ultimately, I don't know how well they are prepared to confront someone who intends to harm people and who has no regard for life, including his own. I think we would be better equipped to deal with such a person if we fortified our schools and classrooms with protective measures that would obstruct and frustrate the intruder until the proper authorities, who are trained to deal with this type of situation, like specialized swat teams, arrive and confront the individual."

He handed the microphone to Abby who added, "I agree. I can't imagine a worse-case scenario than having twenty of our teachers armed during school. Will and I know most of them pretty well. They're very nice people who really care about the students, but if they start running around brandishing guns and trying to nullify someone with hundreds of rounds and assault weapons, I think they will be dead before they even see the intruder or get a shot off. I mean, they're teachers, not police officers or soldiers and I don't think any of them have adequate training in combat or life and death situations. So simply arming them and asking them to be heroes who protect the entire student body against a school assassin is flawed reasoning; it's basically ludicrous. We should have bullet-proof glass and steel doors and secure locks that can be secured instantaneously with one push of a button if we really want to protect people. I think we should prevent the gunman's access to students before he can harm anyone. That would be safer than putting twenty more loaded guns in our schools."

"Mr. Leggett."

"Thank you," he said. "Well this might surprise you but I agree with Will and Abby. The Low Field 20 will only be successful if they are trained responders in an emergency. This has been one of the NRA's long-standing missions for the past fifty years. We provide professional training to law enforcement personnel and we host an annual skills contest not fifty miles from here for those individuals. It's the largest single sporting event in our country and it's serves as a high-level training exhibition for police officers in Ohio and all around the country who have signed on to serve and protect us. The same training that law enforcement personnel go through is what I would recommend the Low Field 20 experience as soon as possible so they are better equipped both individually and as a group to confront an intruder in the schools. I know the teachers have received gun safety training and have been approved for concealed carry permits, but I agree, more training is necessary to enable this group of dedicated teachers to respond swiftly and decisively against someone wanting to harm students in your schools. The NRA is ready and willing to assist in the training of your teachers, and I am here tonight to announce that we are prepared to offer free tuition, room and board, to all of the Low Field 20 in firearm proficiency and tactical response at our Erie location during the teachers' spring break. This will save the school district almost ten thousand dollars and will not cost the taxpayers one dime."

The meeting continued at an intense pace for another hour before the PTA officers sensed an appropriate amount of comments had been made on both sides. They distributed index cards throughout the audience and invited everyone in attendance to submit a question or express an opinion before adjourning the meeting. Questions were to be written to any of the three panelists, and as a summary to the evening, Will, Abby and Mr. Leggett would respond to one final question.

Erin, Kelsey and Megan scribbled questions on cards and passed them impulsively to a PTA mom who had gathered a handful.

"What did you ask, Meg?" Kelsey asked.

"I asked Will when he became such a stud and if he wanted to go out this weekend," she smiled. "No, I'm serious, I really did."

They all laughed and nervously bumped into each other.

"You're crazy," Kelsey said. "What did you ask Erin?"

"I asked the NRA guy if he would shoot a mentally-ill family member who was pointing a gun at him and was threatening to shoot him," she said with a shrug of her shoulders. "How about you Kelsey, what question did you ask?"

"Well, I asked Abby if her middle name was Grace," Kelsey said, "because she is so cool and poised for someone who almost died two months ago—she's inspiring."

Will and Abby were talking quietly to themselves. Abby looked pale and tired from the excitement of the event; perhaps she was not strong enough for such a taxing few hours. Will stepped over to Mrs. Prescott and spoke close to her ear. She shook her head in affirmation and returned to the microphone.

"Ladies and gentleman; first of all thank you for participating in this very important forum. I'm sure we all gained insight into the difficult situation our schools find themselves in and we hope all of you will continue to be engaged in the discussion. I want to announce a slight change in the final activity tonight. Ms. Olson is not feeling well and needs to leave, but Will has requested that he have a few minutes to make a statement for both of them. Will," she said inviting him to the podium a final time.

"Thank you, Mrs. Prescott. Since the shooting, Abby and I have talked a lot about the changes we believe would make Low Field a safer place for all of our students and residents," he said. "So, hopefully with the help of the Low Field Police Department, the Low

Field PTA and all of the students in Low Field, tonight I am proud to announce the formation of the Abby Olson Foundation. One of the primary purposes of this non-profit foundation will be to institute a gun collection and gun buy-back program in our community. Our goal is to significantly reduce the number of guns in Low Field. We know that our community has a proud hunting tradition so this drive will be complimented with an effort to register the guns of those individuals who own them for the purpose of hunting sports. This register will be a source of information regarding the types of fire arms and locations of them in our community. This data will help mental health workers and the police in coordinating their efforts to insure guns don't end up in the hands of the wrong people. We also believe assault weapons and large capacity magazines have no place in society. These are military and law-enforcement weapons and we plan to gather signature petitions that support legislation banning the sale of these products to citizens. We hope true sport hunters will agree with that goal. The third effort of the foundation will be to raise funds that will be used to make the Low Field Schools the safest buildings in the state and hopefully a model for the entire country. Equipping our school buildings with bullet-proof glass, steel-plated doors and the best security systems and cameras available will be our goals, along with providing safety training to all school employees and making sure the necessary resources are available to protect the students of Low Field from the moment they step on school property until the time they leave to go home. We've got a lot of work to do but we hope all of you will join us in our journey. Thank you all for being here, and if you don't mind, I need to get Abby out of here ahead of all of you so her parents can take her home to get some needed rest."

He confidently walked over to Abby, released the brakes on her wheelchair and pushed her down the center aisle that split the two halves of the bleachers. Everyone stood and honored the two students with a thunderous applause as they left the gym. Abby's face was drawn and serious but as they left the room she held up the Low Field "*L*" with her right hand in acknowledgement to the crowd and a small smile graced her face. Will leaned over and gently tapped her fingers with his palm.

"High five," he said smiling.

"Nice job, Will," Abby said, "you've got a future in politics."

"Thanks, but no thanks," he laughed. "I'm just a golfer and now my days are going to get pretty busy working for the Abby Olson Foundation."

78

At the high school, Steve and Keith crossed paths in the hallway between two early morning classes.

"Hey," Steve said.

Keith replied, "Good morning."

"Can you stop in to see me later?" Steve asked. "I have an idea to run by you."

"Sure," Keith said, "I needed to see you too."

The two men were similar in more ways than either recognized or was willing to admit. They were stubborn, self-righteous, and competitive people who enjoyed the power that was inherent in their leadership positions. Secretly, the union president coveted the principal's position. He was certain he could do the job better than Steve. Over the years, Steve made decisions or handled situations in a manner that made the teachers gasp and shake their heads in disbelief. His intuition and initial judgment were typically so contrary to those of the staff or parents that many people had lost confidence in his ability to manage and lead the school during an era when public scrutiny and testing assessments were at such an extraordinary pitch.

Rumors had swirled since Steve first was hired in the district that he was awarded the position more through political influence rather than the time-honored tradition, at least in educational settings, of working one's way up the hierarchy of positions earning promotions through years of experience and good work. The support and trust the staff and most parents had in the principal were at an all-time low since the shooting and controversial events that followed. Keith made up his mind to confront Steve directly from now on when he disagreed with him. In the past, he had adopted a more congenial relationship based on a notion of inherent respect for both positions, the one he held and the one he wanted to hold.

By the end of the day when the two men were finally able to get together, both were exhausted by the usual ups and downs of working with young people as well as the additional demands they shouldered from managing so many adults.

"Hey, thanks for stopping in. Would you close the door, please?" Steve asked. "I've got an idea that will get more support for the Low Field 20."

"We've got the board's support," Keith said, "and I think that's enough."

"Listen, let's just say, hypothetically of course, that a guy comes into the high school cafeteria loaded with guns and ammo and threatens to start killing students. Maybe he gets all the people to line up against the wall or has them kneel the way they practice for a tornado, and it looks like he's going to kill them execution style with an assault rifle. Then you and I, and maybe another teacher or two, burst into the cafeteria and surprise him with a quick show of force, all of us with our guns trained on him so that he has no option but to surrender. We've got hundreds of witnesses that the plan is working perfectly, locked and loaded. What do you think?" the principal asked.

"If you're suggesting we stage a school invasion and subject a bunch of students to a fabricated near execution, I don't like it," Keith said.

"Well, we'd have to work out the details for sure," Steve said surprised that Keith didn't agree with his plan, "but why don't you like it?"

"I don't want anything to do with a contrived scheme like that," Keith said. "Someone could get hurt; something could go wrong and

I won't be a part of it. Frankly Steve, I think that's a stupid idea and I can't believe you think it's a good idea."

"Well, you people don't like any of my ideas," the principal said.

"That's pretty much true."

"You know, maybe you could explain why you and your son were in the school last Sunday morning at 4:00 AM taking scrap metal from the shop and loading it in your truck," Steve said. "I don't think that was a good idea."

"What are you talking about?" Keith said, his skin starting to flush with emotion.

"You know perfectly well what I'm talking about. Your building access wand was used to enter the building on Sunday morning and you're caught on camera with your son committing theft." Steve said.

"Listen, we were just picking up that junk that's been setting there for months creating a safety hazard before some student got hurt on it and sued you and the district," Keith explained. "We were just doing your job."

"My job doesn't involve stealing school property in the middle of the night and neither does yours," the principal said.

"We were getting that junk out of here so it could be recycled and the money donated to athletic department. We were going to surprise you and the board by taking care of it on our own time when school was not in session," Keith said.

"That sounds good, but a very strong case could be made that you were stealing school property," Steve said. "I don't see a check; where's the money?"

"My son's going to take the stuff to the scrap yard in Boylan one day this week, and then we were going to take the check to the treasurer and make the announcement. Anyway, you've got a lot of nerve accusing me of theft. I grew up here. I graduated from this school. I've given everything to this district," Keith said angrily.

"Yeah, what I see is that you've taken a lot more from the district than you'll ever give back," Steve said standing up.

Keith Byler also jumped to his feet and said, "Why, you prick."

The two large men came together in a mighty clash of overweight ex-athletes similar to Sumo wrestlers attempting to establish physical control over one another from a standing hold position. One jerked the other from the side and they tumbled with a loud, hard fall into the drywall sending the light studding of the wall off its mark. The secretary and several teachers collecting their mail at the end of the day were started and ran to the office door. One of them tried to enter but the nob was locked so he knocked rapidly and raised his voice.

"Everything okay in there?"

The men were holding each other on the floor behind the principal's desk in a tight upper body grasp, struggling back and forth for control. After a few seconds, one of them released his grip.

"Stop. If they see this, we could both get fired," Steve said. He turned his face toward the office door and said loudly, "Yeah, everything is fine. I just tipped over in this old chair."

The other let go and the two awkwardly stood and straightened their disheveled clothing. Both were breathing hard and were flushed with adrenaline and a residue of anger.

"You've got two days to have that check on my desk or I'm going straight to the board with the video," Steve said pointing at Keith.

"You'll have it," Keith fired back, "but let me tell you something; if you bring your gun into this school again, I'm going to have you arrested, and you can kiss your career goodbye."

"What are you talking about?" Steve asked sheepishly.

"Don't bullshit me, Steve," Keith said pointing at the principal. "I know you've had a gun here since the board approved the Low Field 20, which, for your information, is against the law. You're not on the list and you don't have permission to have a weapon in a school zone. It's called a felony, dumbass, and I'll be happy to take you down."

"Just have the check here by Thursday or we can both go down in flames," Steve threatened.

79

A CROWD OF HUNDREDS of people formed a long, snaking line that weaved back and forth inside the funeral home and continued outside stretched from the doors and wrapped around two sides of the building. They were all waiting to pay their respects to the surviving members of the Caldwell family. It seemed as though everyone in Low Field wanted to show their support to the two boys who had unimaginably lost both of their parents within a six week period. People felt the need to see Clayton and Colton personally, to shake their hands, hug them, cry with them and express their sympathies. The mood was solemn and serious. People chatted quietly with others in front and behind them in line. As the line curled back and forth across the large main room in the building, people got a glimpse of the family members, walls of flowers and the closed casket through a large open doorway on one end of the viewing room.

The family receiving line started with the boys' surviving grandparents, Mr. and Mrs. Brown, seated at the head of the casket and followed in order by Clayton and then Colton. As the hours wore on and depending on the closeness of the visitor, they would occasionally stand or sit. Clayton, dizzy from trying to recall so many people's names in succession and without time to think, got in the habit of asking each person who shook his hand or hugged him to also introduce himself or herself to Colton whose mind was in even worse shape to remember the visitors' names.

"This is my brother Colton," he said, "would you mind introducing yourself to him?"

No more explanation was needed because the word had spread throughout the community about his amnesia. The hospital tests revealed that Colton had indeed sustained an injury to his skull while walking through narrow stone-lined paths at the Ledges. His doctor, however, concluded his current condition was compounded by the undue levels of stress and emotional trauma he had experienced in recent weeks. The physical bruising of his brain coupled with the psychological effects of his life events produced a tandem of problems that would take months if not years to overcome.

"I want to leave," Colton announced to his grandmother.

"Well, there are people who've come to pay their respects, Colton," she said. "It would be rude for us to leave right now."

"I don't care," he said, "I can't stay any longer."

"Clayton, why don't you take Colton outside to get some fresh air," she suggested.

"Sure," Clayton agreed, "let's go out the back Colton."

The two brothers looked uncomfortable in their ill-fitting, inexpensive black suits. Neither knew how to tie a necktie properly so their grandfather did the best that he could with his arthritic hands and slipped the ties over the boys' heads before they left home. The old man had always worn clip-on ties to church and Mr. Caldwell avoided wearing ties altogether, so very little traditional knowledge of masculine dress attire had ever been passed down to the boys. Their only pairs of dress shoes, black ones worn only to church, were scuffed around the toes and neither had the slightest inclination to shine them with shoe polish. They leaned against the side of their grandfather's truck. Clayton put a pinch of chew inside his lower lip and offered some to Colton.

"No thanks," Colton said.

"What's wrong?" Clayton asked. "Does your head hurt?"

"Yeah, a little," Colton said. "I'm just frustrated. All of these people seem to know me but I don't remember any of their names."

"Did any of them look familiar to you?" Clayton asked.

"Yeah, I know I've seen a bunch of them before but I can't remember anything about them. I don't want to stay here. Do you want to leave?" he asked his younger brother.

"Yeah, let's get out of here," Clayton agreed. "I'll tell grandma and grandpa that we need to go home."

"The people can just go past the casket and pray on their own," Colton proposed.

"I suppose," Clayton said. "Let's go back in and I'll tell Grandma Clare."

They returned to the room where their father lay. Their grandparents looked exhausted but continued to politely shake hands and hug the visitors one by one as they passed by, each one uttering a few gentle words of consolation. Clayton made his case to their grandmother. She whispered to her husband and then motioned for the funeral director to come over. He listened to her nodding his head in approval. Within a few minutes the family was being escorted out of room through a door on the far end from the casket.

One of the men in black suits working for the funeral home approached the family and said, "Excuse me, Colton, this young lady has been waiting to talk to you."

"Kelsey," Colton beamed, "hi, how are you?"

"I'm fine Colton," she said hugging her former boyfriend tightly. "I just wanted to tell you how sorry I am about your dad. He was a good man."

Clayton and his grandmother both caught the fact that Colton recognized Kelsey and called her by name.

"Colton, do you remember Kelsey?" his grandmother asked.

"Yes," he said, "she's a good friend of mine."

"That's right," his grandmother said, "she was your girlfriend."

"I remember," he said. "Kelsey, we're going to leave. Do you want to come over to the house?"

"No Colton, I'm sorry I can't, but thank you for asking," Kelsey replied. "Erin's waiting for me in the car."

"He can come too," Colton suggested.

Kelsey gave the others a puzzled look.

"Erin's a girl, Colton," Clayton said with exasperation. "Don't you remember Kelsey's friend Erin?"

"No," he said, "I'm sorry, but I don't."

"That's okay, Colt," Kelsey said, "I'm glad I got to see you before you left, and again, I'm so sorry about your dad."

"Thank you and thanks for coming to see me," he said.

Kelsey stood and wrapped a scarf around her neck and picked-up her purse from a small table in the hallway. They all moved together past the man holding the door open for them. The family climbed into the large seating area of a waiting limousine. Colton stood facing Kelsey, his hand holding onto the wrist of her coat.

"Kelsey," he said, "for some reason I can't remember much of anything right now but I do remember that I love you. I remember that I love you."

She patted him on his chest with her free hand, pursed her lips, not allowing herself to say another word, and simply nodded to him, turned and walked away.

"Kelsey. Kelsey," he said.

"I'm sorry for your loss, Colton, very sorry," she said as she walked away without turning around.

80

A VAST WASH OF afternoon sun lit the sitting room on the south side of the Olson house that had been converted exclusively into Abby's living space since she came home from the hospital. A dresser and her bed were moved into the room and walkways were carefully designed so she could traverse the area without difficulty and easily get to the necessary parts of the house, including her adjoining studio. A large drawing table dominated her art room, leaving little space for models to pose as subjects for her art. Nevertheless, Kelsey and Daron created space at one end of the room by relocating a few straight chairs and a floor lamp elsewhere, under Abby's direction. Erin, who had recently joined the nearly fifty other students who had enrolled into the Classrooms Without Boundaries charter school, had completed her school assignments for the day and came along with her friends to experience the preliminary work of the artist. She too helped with the furniture arrangement.

"Okay I'm sure you know how this works," Abby said with a straight face. "Daron and Kelsey, take your clothes off."

After a few seconds of everyone looking quizzically back and forth, Abby prodded them along.

"Come-on, don't keep the temperamental artist waiting," she said.

"Is she serious?" Daron asked Kelsey quietly.

"I don't know," she said.

"Oh never mind," Abby said, "you're both taking too long. I was just kidding anyway. But why don't you both stand back to back over there—Daron pretend to be holding a handgun in your right hand pointing it at that window in front of you and Kelsey, with your left hand hold this cup in the palm of your hand. There, that's good; I like that. Erin, would you take a few photos of them so they don't have to stand there for the next three weeks."

She handed a small camera to Erin and instructed her on its use. Erin circled them snapping photos with a digital camera and flash. She held the camera up high and then low getting stills from a variety of angles and from 360 degrees. After previewing the photos on a small screen at the back of the camera, Abby asked them to pose standing next to each other, first holding hands and secondly, with an arm around their backs. While they were finishing the additional photos, Will arrived. A new idea came to Abby, and she had all four of them stand back to back forming a square pillar. Finally, she asked the foursome to stand in a line facing her and place their arms around behind each other. One of the two on the ends held up a peace sign with a free hand and the other held up the Low Field "L." She took photos of the four friends posing as she had requested and then in silly positions.

"Great," Abby said, "I think I have plenty to work with now. Thank you all. Now, if you would take all of your clothes off. Okay, just kidding. I guess I'm a horny artist who needs to see skin, but seriously, you all have such great bone structures. You should consider modeling for the Art Departments where you go to college. It's easy money compared to manual labor or donating your blood for beer money."

"Thanks Abby. Is that it?" Daron asked.

"Actually, if you don't mind, I'd like you to come back a few times after I work up the final draft for the sculpture. At first I was considering iron or scrap aluminum, but last night I was thinking of trying my hand at stone. I've never done anything of this scale before and I've only worked with limestone once, so this promises to be at least a six month adventure," she said.

"How are you going to do this, your school assignments plus work on the foundation?" Will asked.

"Well, I'm basically done with school," she said. "I've got enough credits to graduate already. I'm just taking my two last required classes through home instructions and then I'm finished, and being at home all the time gives me the flexibility to work on things whenever I'm motivated, which is really cool. Don't you guys like the flexible schooling so much better than being stuck in high school classes for one more boring year?"

"Oh yeah, it's awesome," Erin volunteered. "I had no idea I would like it as much as I do."

She caught herself and toned down her enthusiasm.

"Sorry Will. I forgot you're stuck in the hallowed halls of Low Field," she said.

"It's okay," he said, "I've got the early senior release so I only have three classes in the morning and then I'm out of there anyway, which is really cool. By the way since you're all here, I passed out these new flyers we created for Abby's foundation and here's a copy for each of you. Our first event is coming up next weekend. We got approval to host an anti-gun rally in the stadium and everyone I talked to is interested and said they would attend."

"Great," Abby said. "What did they think about the masks and toy guns?"

"Well, that's what has everyone so jacked-up about the rally," he said. "They think it's going to be so cool that everyone is going to be incognito. It's kind of like Halloween all over again. We should have a lot of fun and I gave petitions to a bunch of seniors who are supposed to start to gather signatures against Policy 2, so everything seems to be moving in the right direction."

"That sounds cool, but I'm out of touch and I don't know what that means," Daron admitted.

"Oh you'll have to come," Abby said. "Next Saturday at noon we're planning a rally against the new policy the board of education approved that permits a bunch of armed teachers at the schools instead of the SRO. Our brainstorm was to have everyone wear a mask or camo-paint and be armed with a toy gun, you know the way a terrorist or a kook hides his face because subconsciously he knows he's doing something wrong. Well, then, during the rally we're going to have everyone lay their guns on a huge paper canvas that has the Low Field 20 painted on it with the international symbol for *NO* painted over it in red. Then we'll take photos of everyone with their masks on and some with them off. Hopefully, it will demonstrate how we have to get the whole gun thing under control or else everyone could be a menace to society. At least it might get people to think about the need to participate in the real gun collection and gun buy-back program we're going to start with the PTA and the police department."

"And start the gun registration program," Will added.

"That sounds like a great idea for the rally," Kelsey said.

"Yeah, and we're having Jimmy and Rob's band play, and we invited the television stations. It will be the Low Field version of Woodstock. There will be a few speakers but we're going to limit their time so it doesn't get boring. It should be fun," Will said enthusiastically.

"Oh Abby, I bought us a couple of those black bank-robber stocking caps that go down over your face with just the cut-out holes for your eyes and mouth," he said. "I almost bought you a pink one but I decided black was more versatile and menacing."

He pulled the winter knit hats from a plastic bag and tossed one to Abby.

"Oh I forgot," Will added, "you have this option as well."

He lifted a hard white plastic hockey face mask from the bag; a horror movie favorite.

"There's also this option," he said laughing. "I'm guessing people might figure out who you are anyway because of the wheelchair, but what the heck."

"Yeah, I like that one," Abby said with a smile. "My mom found us a few old water pistols in the basement. One even looks like a real gun—the other one is a Pink aquamarine rifle."

"Erin, we could wear panty hose," Kelsey said.

"That would be good," Erin responded, "or burqas."

"No, I think Daron should wear a burqa," laughed Kelsey.

He smiled and replied, "I just might do that, or maybe a Lone Ranger mask or a paper bag with eye holes like the Browns' fans I saw a few weeks ago."

"All of those should really get the old people's attention," Erin said.

"They're invited too," Abby said. "Maybe we can create something that will unify this crazy community instead of always having half the people for one thing and the other half against."

"I don't know Abby," Daron said, "there are a whole lot of people in Low Field who just enjoy hating on anything."

"Yeah, there called old codgers," Kelsey said.

"Someone called them crusty," Will said, "crusty codgers."

Abby had the last word, "I don't know about you and your parents Will, but I think my parents are going to sue those crusty codgers for a bunch of money."

81

ONE OF THE teachers brought Keith a copy of the student flyer for *Rally Against Guns* demonstration, the kickoff event for the Abby Olson Foundation. Another teacher left one on a table in the teachers' lounge so everyone could see it as they passed through the room during their preparation time or at lunch.

"Dammit. Don't these kids see we're doing this for them?" said a teacher who saw the flyer for the first time during his lunch break. "Why does everything we do for this district have to be such a struggle?"

"No one cares about their rally," another said. "They'll be lucky to have twenty people show up for something like that on a Saturday in December."

"I think it's supposed to snow on Saturday," another teacher laughed.

"Well, remember, getting the levy passed is the most important thing we face as a union. The board and the administrators can't get it done, so unfortunately, we have to do it for them. Maybe we should have a rally of our own," another suggested.

"That's a good idea," another agreed. "We can get our people out and get the news media here too."

"But, I'm thinking more than a pep-rally," continued the teacher who proposed the idea. "What if we show them an example of our preparedness by making a video of how we are organized to respond in case of an emergency? For instance, we could film a teacher quickly getting his or her gun from the lock box and getting in a ready position to take out the target once he comes through the classroom door. I'll bet that would get thousands of hits on the internet."

"Yeah, I like that idea," agreed another. "We could video some of us converging on the target using our communication system with our guns drawn and moving through the halls toward the shooter's location."

"I don't know," cautioned another, "it's sounds like a propaganda documentary like terrorists groups put out. We'd have to be careful."

"Yeah, and we'd have to shoot the video without revealing any one's identity," said another teacher. "I guess we could video the action with a pair of those camera glasses or have the tech coordinator follow us and film the teachers from behind."

"I like that idea," Keith said finally joining in the conversation. "Tom, will you get a few of the 20 together and come up with a tentative idea or script so we can get everyone together in a few nights and make this happen? Maybe someone could post the video on YouTube and if it's done properly, it could really help our cause."

"Yeah, sure, I'll get back to you by Friday," Tom said. "Maybe we can shoot the video over the weekend."

"Good, thanks," Keith said.

Conversations regarding Abby's Foundation and their mission to make Low Field safer by significantly reducing the overall number of guns in the community and revealing the names of gun owners through a registration data base stored by the police department soared like an opera through the places people gathered for food and banter in town. People either loved or hated the plan.

Those on one side of the issue believed it was an unrealistic yet valiant start to establish restrictions and limitations for gun ownership that seemed necessary for a civilized society. They believed gun rights had stretched too far towards one end of the spectrum. Normal people had no reasonable need to own assault rifles of extralong magazines. Moreover, even sportsmen who were ardent hunters didn't own more than a few guns and those only for specific game. With the preponderance of violence shown in television shows, movies and video games young people had their consciences warped to concede acts of aggression and bloodshed were routine, daily events. It was totally unnecessary to promote the blurring of entertainment fiction with reality through easy access to powerful, destructive guns. Restrictions on many fronts needed to be implemented in order to challenge and change the current state of affairs.

On the other hand, many truly believed the issue was simply one of citizens' rights. Clearly the right to bear arms had been established as a constitutional amendment for a reason; a very good reason. Immediate, personal protection was the best way to counteract violent behavior. A gun allowed a person to neutralize a situation regardless of strength, age or gender. A gun was the ultimate counterbalance to a hostile attack and no one was immune regardless of wealth, color or location. Reasonable people acknowledged mentally-ill or individuals with histories of violence should have limited access to weapons or no access at all, but removing guns from all citizens or making a public record of gun owners was not a prudent or legal way of dealing with the issue. Moreover, politicians were as ineffective in dealing with gun rights as they were in dealing with most charged debates. Placing trust in politicians was like throwing darts blindfolded. If history had taught us anything, leave well enough alone; passing new laws or amending existing ones would only make things worse.

Once again, the community of Low Field found itself divided between two contradictory positions, this time opposite strategies to counteract violence in their schools—the teachers' plan of challenging hostile intruders with an unparalleled strength of force and the students' plan of correcting the flawed security of the schools by upgrading the system through several means—a comprehensive, costly renovation of the old buildings and a daunting reformation of the legal system that had as much political traction as bald tires on ice.

82

THE SECOND TIME Dr. Reed was in the district to meet with Jim
Collins the discussion became serious and tense. They sat across
the conference table in his office with stone faces and eyes often
locked each other's. Their cups of coffee cooled near the center of
the table, neither person relaxed enough to enjoy even sips of coffee
amidst the discussion. The pleasantries were over and Jim realized he
was now a pawn in her game of chess.

"You have a big problem, sir. Your community has repeatedly
told you they are not willing to support your school district the way
it currently operates and I'm here to tell you the state is not willing to
bail you out any more," she said.

Jim countered with a traditional argument used by many who
found themselves in similar positions, "I think the Ohio Revised
Code stipulates that public education is the responsibility of the state."

"The state funding formula approved by the legislature clearly
defines the shared financial responsibilities of both the local and state
portions of your district's revenue. As you know, the formula is complex but fair and is applied to all six hundred plus districts in the state.
Low Field has borrowed from the state emergency fund three times
and that is the limit by state law," Dr. Reed said.

"So what am I supposed to do?" Jim asked. "We've had a levy on
the ballot in every eligible election."

"And your constituency has answered that question every time,"
she said. "Now I'm here to force you and the board of education to

do what you should have been doing progressively as this situation worsened over the past three years—adjust the expenditure side of your annual budget so it balances with the revenue side of the budget," she answered.

"That's easy for you to say. For one thing, I've got negotiated contracts that the board has the legal obligation to honor that mandate certain teacher-student class size ratios as well as diverse curricular offerings required by the state department of education and the Board of Regents for college admission," Jim argued. "And secondly once we start cutting extra-curricular offerings, busing and academic programs, we'll simply accelerate the downward spiral of negativity and drive more families from the district, not to mention those types of cuts would violate the negotiated agreement with the classified staff."

"Well, that's the beauty of the oversight commission being assigned to Low Field—the financial problems in this district suspends your commitments to the state law," she said. "Now, money drives everything, including contractual obligations and compliance with educational mandates.

"I guess that will help control the arguments and fights once the unions understand that point," Jim conjectured.

"One of the only things I thought you had done right in the district was to get the teaching staff to agree to work without a contract," she said.

"They are, but our attorney advised me that in essence the old contract is still in effect," Jim said. "The union has a reasonable expectation that the issues covered by the previous contract are still in effect and guide our operations until a new agreement is negotiated."

"I'm not so sure about that opinion," Dr. Reed said, "but I've worked on enough of these commissions to know that the choices you have at this time are not pleasant; you must make very aggressive changes right now and we have the legal authority to carry them out."

"I feel like a political rope being used in a tug of war between the state and the community," Jim said.

"I'm sorry for that but I'm not just an enforcer sent here from Columbus. I'm also here to help you," she said. "Maybe you can use the Intent to Strike Notice that the teachers' union filed to help you win favor with the voters for the difficult decisions you must recommend to the board, with my approval, of course."

"That's a big maybe in this community," Jim said.

"Mr. Collins, you have a new primary concern in your management of this school district and the commission gives you the legal authority to fulfill that concern within state statute," she said.

"Which is what exactly?" Jim asked.

"Like any poor person or entity, pay your bills. By law, sir, that is your first obligation to this community," she said.

"I thought my first obligation was to provide a rich and meaningful education to the children of this community," Jim replied.

"Unfortunately, not now," she said. "Your first obligation is to provide whatever level of educational experiences you can that meet the state's minimum standards within your means," she clarified. "Offer what you can afford to offer."

"So, I've got to strip this system down to the state minimums?" Jim asked.

"Yes, and the state of Ohio and your teachers have given you the instruments by which to do that."

"Well, I'd like you to explain that to the board personally, if you don't mind," Jim said.

"Gladly, and you should schedule that meeting without delay. As they say, don't keep people waiting to hear bad news," Dr. Reed said with a wry smile.

Jim responded, "I agree, especially if I'm not the messenger."

"So, I'm going to take a restroom break and return a few phone calls and then when I come back, we can work on your plan," the woman said in a matter of fact manner.

She picked-up her cell phone and purse before leaving the room. Jim sat low in his chair, his chin in his chest and a hand rubbing his forehead. His secretary looked in through the doorway holding a home-style coffee pot in her hand.

"How about a refill, boss?" she asked.

"Sure. Thanks L J," he said.

"Not good news from the wicked-witch of the south?" she joked giving Jim an opportunity to release some of his obvious frustration.

"No, I'm afraid, not an ounce of good news. In fact, would you mind seeing if Zack is available to join us for the next round of fisti-cuffs?" Jim asked.

"Sure. I remember what my mom used to say to me and my brothers when things got tough—stand tall and keep your chin up," she said.

"Good advice; thanks L J," Jim said. "You know I always appreci-ate your support."

"Don't take it personal," she added. "Low Field has been this way forever."

"I know, but in the beginning, I thought we were getting it turned around," Jim reflected. "We got the focus back on the kids the way it should be, but then it all started to slide backwards."

"Like pushing water uphill; it keeps finding the low point. Why do you think they named this place Low Field two hundred years ago?" she laughed. "The people must have had a big smile on their faces when the village was established, or at least half of them did."

Jim smiled at his secretary.

"You have an uncanny knack of seeing through the crap around here," he said.

"I wear thick glasses and have thick skin," she replied. "What can I say? When you grow up in a place it becomes part of you like a family. And there's good and bad in every family—and it's not always a fifty-fifty balance."

"I'd take that right now," Jim said.

"Hey, right now we're seeing the dark side of people's personalities. Only time will swing the pendulum the other way," she stated.

"You're probably right but unfortunately we just ran out of time," Jim said continuing his negative reaction to the day. "By the way, who was the guy I saw coming up the walk a while ago?"

L J pursed her lips sideways and said, "More good news. It was a delivery from an attorney's office for you."

She grabbed a large manila envelope from her desk and handed it to the superintendent. She had already sliced open the top of the package open as was their usual procedure. He pulled the papers out and quickly read the cover letter.

"Oh, it just keeps getting better," Jim said. "We are now officially being sued by the Colton's family. How do you like those apples?"

83

A T THE VA Hospital in Cleveland, Dr. Rosenthal shined a pencil-sized silver flashlight into each of Colton's eyes, checking the dilation of each pupil and scanning deep inside for more clues that might shed insight into the boy's problems. Colton performed simple balance tests such as standing on one foot and touching his nose with his eyes closed. The doctor asked him a series of questions such as the name of the President of the United States, what year he had graduated from high school, the name of his best friend and then asked him to read a paragraph from a waiting room magazine. Moreover, he wondered if Colton still had headaches, if his appetite was normal and if he was sleeping through the night.

The standard treatments for retrograde amnesia included a few experimental medications, improvements in diet and nutrition, increased exercise, occupational therapy and something called image stimuli that might trigger an immediate recollection of a person or event from the past, enhancing the person's ability to formulate correct associations among memory fragments and clearing the psychological blockage from hindering or interfering with the intricate, normal functions of the brain. It was obvious to everyone that the series of stressful events Colton had experienced in the past few months must have contributed to his predicament. However, in Colton's case the history of football concussions and additional head trauma he had suffered in recent years complicated the diagnosis and rehabilitation cycle. The doctor had spent time at home the night before rereading concussion literature and refreshing his understanding of psychotherapy options. He had determined if Colton continued to be locked in an amnesiac stupor beyond a few days of this appointment, he would refer him to a neurologist in Cleveland for an additional assessment and diagnosis of his cranial nerves.

The news that he had recognized his former girlfriend at his father's wake and called her by her name elevated the prognosis for improvement. The overriding fear they were facing was that the more entrenched the malady, the more difficult, drawn-out and possibly unlikely was the hope for significant recovery. His grandparents had driven him to the appointment and were waiting patiently in the reception area.

"Colton, how do you feel today?" asked the doctor.

"Right now?" asked Colton. "Lousy."

"Do you have a headache?"

"Yeah, my head always hurts," Colton answered.

"Does the pain come and go, or do you have a constant headache?" the doctor asked.

"I don't know," Colton replied losing patience with the doctor's questions, "it pretty much hurts all the time."

"Have you ever had any seizures?"

"I don't know," Colton responded.

"If so, how many seizures have you had in the past three years?"

"I don't know," the young man said.

"How many hours did you sleep last night?"

"A lot; I don't know exactly how many," Colton answered. "I woke up a few times and watched TV."

"What did you have for dinner last night?"

"I don't remember. Dammit, what's with all the questions?" Colton said loudly expressing his irritation with the doctor. "I don't know what I had for dinner and what does it matter anyway?"

"Sorry Colton. It's important that I ask. What's my name?" the doctor continued.

He quickly covered his name badge.

"I don't know but you're my new doctor at the VA Hospital," Colton replied.

"Good; okay enough of that. I'm going to call your grandparents in now," he said.

They entered the room with only a nod, and at the direction of the doctor, sat in a pair of hard chairs near one end of the examining table.

"Mrs. and Mr. Brown, we received the results of the CT scan from earlier this week. Colton, you suffered a Mild Traumatic Brain Injury when you were at the park hiking; it's what we usually call a concussion. The good news is there is no bleeding in either lobe of his brain. The bad news is that the repeated cycle of concussions he's incurred over the past few years and the other stressful events of the last few months have resulted in this neurological amnesia, which simply means he's going to struggle to remember people and events from the past for a while. He might even have trouble remembering things you were just talking about as well. In simpler terms the brain's limbic system controls our emotions and our memories and Colton's has been injured. You might notice irritability, changes in his personality, disorientation and depression. These are some of the behavioral changes this kind of injury can cause in a person. So it might be tough for a while, and I just wanted you to be aware of these possibilities. Do you have any questions?" asked the doctor.

"What can we do to help Colton get better?" Clare Brown asked.

"Good question; I want him to start taking a few vitamin supplements each day and Colton, try to take it easy for a while," the doctor said. "If you feel tired, take a nap, because you need rest. I'd show him scrapbooks of photos and talk about things from high school and home that might help him start to remember more about his past. You can even talk about memories you all have together like trips you shared or holidays when you were together. If a few of his friends want to stop by, I'd encourage that as well. Any conversations he has with people can be therapeutic and might help him regain his memory."

"Thank you doctor," they said.

"You're welcome," he said. "I'd like to see him in a week. Jessica, the receptionist at the front desk, will help you with an appointment. Colton, get some rest; okay?"

"Yeah," Colton said and then added sarcastically, "thanks for wasting our time."

The doctor shook his head, closed the folder he had been recording notes on and left the room.

"Colton, that wasn't a very nice thing to say," chided his grandmother.

"Sorry grandma," Colton said, "but I could tell grandpa doesn't like him."

84

THE IMPROMPTU, SPECIAL meeting of the Low Field Board of Education was held on Tuesday evening. A public notice was issued the required twenty-four hours prior to the meeting's start time. The press release clearly stipulated that the board would adjourn to the private sanctuary of executive session specifically for the purpose of discussing personnel matters and the legal proceedings they were facing. Furthermore, the notice stated there would be no public portion of the meeting, in an attempt to dissuade people from attending the event. However, a handful of watchdog constituents arrived just prior to the 6:00 PM call to order and made it clear they would be also waiting patiently for the board later when they reconvened to adjourn the meeting. Their comportment dumbfounded the board members and administrators but over time the school officials learned to equate the attendance of the group with the community's distrust of the schools.

Their attorney was waiting for them when they returned to the board office. All five board members, the treasurer and superintendent took their usual seats. The attorney then filled into one of the two open chairs. Folders were piled onto the table and Jim asked everyone to grab a drink from the refrigerator or a cup of coffee from the fresh pot he had started before they went upstairs to the library to perform the perfunctory formal opening of the meeting in public. Snack foods and candy were scattered about the center portion of the table along with small plates and napkins. Everyone settled in for a long, serious conversation about the rapidly expanding list of district problems.

"I asked Henry to be here tonight so he could advise us on our options regarding the three lawsuits that have been filed against us," Jim said.

"Three?" one of the board members said. "I knew of one, but now we have three?"

"Unfortunately," Jim responded. "Most of you have heard about the first two from the Caldwell and Olson families and yesterday we were served with a summons and complaint from the Low Field PTA that claims the board took illegal action and violated state law last week when you approved Policy 20. That's why Henry is here. And I should mention that the chairperson from the Fiscal Oversight Commission will be here in about an hour for the second part of the meeting."

"Oh my God," another board member said, "we'll be here all night."

"Yeah," Jim agreed, "this could take a while."

Mindful of everyone's time, John Fitzpatrick assumed direction of the meeting and said, "Alright, I suggest we go in order and have Henry talk us through our options on the three lawsuits. From my stack of papers it looks like number one is the Caldwell suit. Henry."

"Thank you Mr. Fitzpatrick. So we're on the same page I'll summarize the charges against the board and then we can discuss the options. This one is a civil lawsuit that was filed two weeks ago in The Low Field County Court of Appeals. In simple terms the suit charges the district with negligence for allowing Colton Caldwell to play football his senior year with a known history of repeated concussions. They are claiming that not only did his playing with this condition cause him to lose college scholarship offers but also contributed to the medical problems that surfaced while he was in the Marines, ultimately leading to his discharge. Moreover, the suit claims that these injuries have caused a permanent medical issue that impaired his judgment and led him to fire the gun that injured the two students in October. The lawsuit is claiming enduring injuries to Colton and asking for monetary compensation."

"That's ridiculous," one member asserted. "So we caused him to bring a loaded gun onto school property and open fire in a crowd of students. I'm surprised it doesn't blame us on the deaths of his parents. I'm sorry for saying that, but this is just ridiculous."

"I know we're all very sorry for what's happened to Colton and his family, but we have to deal with the lawsuit now," the board president said. "Henry how valid is the lawsuit from a legal perspective."

"All three of these cases have one thing in common—they are legitimate filings that also contain elements of emotion appeal if they go to trial and were heard by a judge or a jury. In other words, we have to take all three very seriously," the attorney for the board said.

"What kind of monetary compensation are we looking at?" one person asked.

"It's hard to say," Henry answered. "First of all there would probably be a jury trial and if the district was found guilty of the charges then the judge would order the jury to establish the monetary settlement. Typically, personal injury lawsuits can be a very high number because they include medical expenses, pain and suffering, emotional distress and a calculation that tries to establish the potential financial impact on the person for the remainder of his or her life. Obviously, Colton is a young man and if you believe the injuries he sustained playing high school football caused his medical condition, he very possibly could incur astronomical medical expenses during the rest of his life and his life earnings could definitely be reduced over the next thirty to forty years. This is the problem with these kinds of lawsuits. It's impossible to predict how the emotions of the jury will affect the dollar amount of the settlement they might award to Colton if the district is found negligent."

"But this young man shot two of our students on school property and could have injured many more by his reckless actions," another board member said incredulously.

"Yes, I agree," Henry responded. "He broke the law and we will use that argument in our defense, but I suspect his attorney will attempt to separate the two actions in court. My guess is he will acknowledge his client's wrongdoing on the one hand and then on the other hand attempt to excuse Colton's behavior on his football injuries. In other words, I'm guessing he will make the claim that his client's judgment is permanently impaired because of the history of repeated concussions and it's anyone's guess if a judge or jury will agree or disagree with that assertion."

"But how do we know that he didn't hit his head as a child working on his grandparent's farm, or he got thrown from a horse and hit his head. I mean, isn't it a convenient claim to say his medical condition is exclusively a result of his football injuries?" another board member asked.

"Yes," Henry said, "we will subpoena his entire medical records from childhood to the present, but unless we are lucky, I'm afraid the majority of documented incidents of head trauma will be his football injuries."

"Jim," another asked, "don't we have athletic release forms the parents would have signed that acknowledge the risks of playing contact sports? I seem to remember signing a page like that in my son's athletic handbook a few years ago."

"Yes, but unfortunately, the athletic director discards those signature pages each summer in anticipation of the new ones for the upcoming school year," Jim answered. "So we don't have any for Colton."

"What? Why doesn't he store them for a few years?" another asked.

"I think we all know Mark is a little compulsive," Jim replied. "We already made an adjustment in that procedure and from now on athletic records will be stored for five years."

"Great," another responded sarcastically.

The level-minded board president said, "So, we can fume and vent all night but, Henry, what's the bottom line? What actions do we take?"

The attorney passed out copies of a document he had prepared to answer that very question.

"What I'd like to do, with your permission of course, is file this request with the courts to dismiss all charges and deny any wrongdoing on the part of the board, the superintendent and any school employees in this case," Henry stated. "Football is played by thousands and thousands of high school athletes in America. They all join their high school teams with a reasonable understanding of the inherent risk associated with playing the sport. Colton Caldwell is no different and the history of his injuries while playing football in Low Field include the district providing thorough medical care for him on each occasion as well as cautioning him and his parents about his continued participation. We have many coaches and administrators who can corroborate that position through depositions. So, what I'm saying is we have a defense and a counter to everything in the lawsuit, but going to trial is always risky and it is impossible to predict how this will play-out in a court of law."

"Are you suggesting we offer a settlement?" John asked.

"Probably not," Henry said, "but we might need to consider that option in the future depending on how this case moves forward in the system. If this lawsuit ends up in a trial, we will make a strong case for our side of the issue and push back each time his attorney makes a move. Depending on the situation we'll make the necessary responses in court and remain flexible with our options based on the sympathies of the judge and jury."

"Wow," a board member groaned, "what a mess."

The board president once again asserted his control of the conversation and asked, "Are we ready to discuss the Olson suit?"

"Sure," Henry replied.

"This complaint is virtually the same as the Caldwell lawsuit," Henry started, "however, this case looks much worse for the district for obvious reasons. Undeniably, Abby sustained very serious injuries on school property that have required expensive medical treatment that is on-going. This suit claims the district was negligent in providing a safe environment for students during dismissal from the high school that resulted in her sustaining those injuries."

"I know but how can we be at fault for Colton bringing a gun onto school property? I'm guessing our dismissal is no different than every school in the state. We live in a democracy, not a police state," a frustrated board member argued.

"And people are permitted to own guns. Someone can bring a gun to school, or to the movies, or a store any time," another added. "Isn't that just part of the risk we all assume living in a free society?"

"Yes, you both bring up legitimate points," Henry agreed, "and we will use both of those reasons as a basis for again asking that this suit be dismissed without cause."

Again he removed papers from a folder and passed them to the people seated at the table.

"There are several reasons why I started by saying this case might be more difficult for us to win. We have several problems trying to defend this lawsuit. First of all, several years ago, a new law required school districts to post highly visible signs in their parking lots, athletic fields and on all school doors stating that guns are prohibited from school property; unfortunately, that was not done. Second, the only adults outside at the time of dismissal were the bus drivers, who were in their buses, and the Student Resource Officer, who was standing in the middle of the road stopping traffic so the buses could leave the lot and enter the highway in uninterrupted succession. So basically, the entire student body of the high school and middle school were unsupervised and there are no written procedures in the student handbook that address a safe and orderly student departure from school property."

"So are we looking at monetary compensation again?"

"Yes, but this time with a twist," Henry answered. "This complaint claims negligence and failure to provide a safe environment and they are asking for punitive damages for all medical expenses, pain and suffering, emotional distress, and a settlement for her ongoing medical treatment and the physical problems associated with her injuries throughout the remainder of her life. They are also asking for a full and adequate correction of the security systems in both school buildings."

"I know the Olsons," one board member said. "My wife and I have socialized with them. They are reasonable people. Do you want me to talk to them?"

"Absolutely not," Henry cautioned. "Each one of you is named personally on the complaint as members of the Board of Education, so now that a formal lawsuit has been filed, none of you are to say anything to any of these people. Once the legal proceedings have commenced, only the attorneys communicate with one another. You are not to make any comments to anyone outside of this room on any of these matters—not even your family members. And, if members of the media ask you about any of these procedures, you are to tell them you are not permitted to comment on anything related to these legal matters."

"That's very important folks," John stressed. "Does everyone understand that? We can't even talk to our spouses about these lawsuits. The old rule about everything that is said in executive session stays in the room is especially true when the stakes are as high as they are in these lawsuits."

"That's correct," Henry reiterated. "Please do not let down your guard, not the slightest bit, when it comes to expressing your opinions or making comments about any of these cases. Simply tell people you are not permitted to comment on these matters."

"If we lose these, the amounts could be staggering numbers," one board member said soberly. "This could bankrupt the district. Isn't there anything in law that prohibits public entities from being sued?"

"Yeah and how about us?" another added. "I mean you said we are being sued too?"

"Technically yes," the attorney said, "but remember you purchase insurance as a board that protects all of you and the district in the event of such circumstances. In fact, I have already contacted them and their attorneys will help me handle portions of these litigations. Of course, the difficulty is that in times of crisis, just like with our own personal insurance, the same company that promises the world when they want us to purchase the policy, sometimes becomes difficult to deal with when there's a problem."

"Yeah, like now it's your fault and you caused the problem so they can refuse the claim," one said seemingly speaking from experience.

"Or they simply want to settle the claim and cut their losses," another said.

"That would be okay, wouldn't it, Henry?" John asked.

"Financially yes, but it would set a dangerous precedent for this school district because an out-of-court settlement is often viewed as an admission of guilt," Henry explained. "And that could make obtaining subsequent policies difficult or very costly."

"God, when is my term up?" another said sitting back in his squeaky chair.

"Yeah, you get on the board to make things better," another said, "and now we can't get a levy passed and the schools are back to being public enemy number one for most people in the community."

"Most days it doesn't seem worth it anymore, does it?" another said.

"It's rough," John said. "I mean I grew up here, graduated from Low Field and raised my kids in this community and now I'm frustrated. No wonder we can't get young families to move to Low Field."

"No offense Henry," another board member added, "but I hate it when you're at our meetings because it always means there's a problem, and it's usually a big problem."

"I know, but don't worry about it," Henry laughed. "I learned pretty early in my career that usually people don't call you with good news, so I've learned to not take it personally. On the other hand, I hope I can help you get out of this predicament."

"What about the third law suit?" Jim asked.

"Well, the good news is that, as far as I can determine in one day of research, you acted perfectly within your authority by passing the board policy that permitted the teachers to serve as a quasi-security force within the school buildings. Obviously, there is a state law prohibiting fire arms to be brought onto school property, but most schools permit authorized personnel, usually law enforcement officers such as your SRO to carry guns on school property with the purpose of creating a high degree of safety in the buildings. In this case, you have extended that permission to members of your faculty who have required levels of training and have earned concealed carry permits." Henry explained. "So, I'm always reluctant to say a situation is foolproof because anything can happen within the legal system, but it certainly appears to me that you did not violate state law by approving Policy 20 as the PTA claims in their lawsuit. I didn't have a chance to prepare the document for you but I would suggest that I file the response on your behalf that states our position and asks for the charges to be dismissed without prejudice."

"That sounds good to me," John said with a smile. "We're batting .333—one for three!"

"Too bad the other two could cost us millions when we don't have a dime to spend on education," another board member said.

"Speaking of being broke," Jim said, "Dr. Reed, from the State Department of Education Oversight Commission is probably waiting to be called in, if you want to continue. She is here to discuss our financial options, especially given the likelihood of the teachers' strike in January."

"Can we take a break?" one board member asked. "I think I'm going to be sick."

Everyone laughed, stood and stretched.

"Sure," Jim said, "let's take a quick restroom break and grab another drink if you want one. I'm going to ask Henry to stay if that's okay with everyone."

"Why not," quipped a board member, "it's only money."

85

Dr. Reed sat at the head of the table looking elegant in a navy pants suit and white blouse. She was, however, anxious to assert her authority with the group, having arrived with both a reputation and an attitude.

After everyone had returned from the short break and was seated, Jim started this portion of the meeting with an introduction, "We'd like to welcome Dr. Vanessa Reed. She is a representative of the State Department of Education who is the Governor's appointee assigned to chair the Fiscal Oversight Commission in our district for the remainder of the school year, because we are now officially designated by the state as a district in *Financial Crisis.*"

"Thank you, Mr. Collins, and it's a pleasure to meet all of you," she said. "Let me get right to the point, ladies and gentlemen. The state legislature has given The Low Field Local Schools two loans in the past two years and the district continues to languish in fiscal emergency. Your inability to connect sufficiently to your voting constituents and pass a levy to fund the educational activities in this community has created a very serious situation for both of us. My role as chairwoman of the oversight commission assigned to your district is rather straightforward. I am going to help you bring your expenditures in line with your revenue. There are simply no more loans coming from the state, so we must act swiftly and decisively to balance the school district's budget and that process begins tonight."

"Dr. Reed, when you say balance the school's budget, are we talking for next school year?" one of the board members asked. "I mean we can still try to pass the levy in February and May, if I'm not mistaken."

"Actually your final attempt to renew the levy will be in February. If the levy is not renewed on that attempt, that measure will be deemed expired and you will have to seek additional revenue in the form of a new levy to fund your operations," she said.

"Oh that's right," the board member said, "I'd forgotten this past election was the fifth time we had the levy on the ballot."

"That's correct," she said smiling, "a school district has six attempts to renew a levy. After the sixth failure, the levy is deemed expired by state law."

"This feels like a *feet to the fire* or *backs against the wall* kind of conversation," John said.

"Sure," Dr. Reed said shaking her head in affirmation, "and it should. You have no option at this point other than making the reductions you need to make in anticipation for the next school year. By doing so you are showing your community what kind of educational environment you will be forced to provide without the revenue from this levy. And you are correcting your financial insolvency in the state reporting system."

"So we're supposed to start hacking away at staff and programs right now in the middle of the school year? What about the students' welfare?" another board member asked.

"That's the appropriate question you need to take up with your residents," the chairperson stated.

"Jim's always told us the state has the obligation under law to provide for the education of its students," John said.

"That's partially true. Education is a shared responsibility of the state and the local board of education," she explained. "The funding is shared based on the wealth index and the regulations and policies are also shared. That is why you folks are elected as members of the board of education. Locally you have the authority to hire and fire employees, negotiate contracts and approve policies that govern the programs and services you deem important and necessary for your students."

"So why are you and this commission here in our district?" another asked.

"Because you are unable to meet your fiduciary portion of the agreement," she replied.

"What does that mean exactly?" a board member asked.

"You have not been able to pay your local share of the funding ratio for several years. So you've borrowed money twice from the state. There is no more money and your levy failed again. When a school district is in this situation, the state department of education declares the entity to be in *Financial Crisis* and sends a commission to manage the district's affairs," she explained.

"So we're out?" one of the board members asked.

"No, you still represent an important connection to the people of Low Field and your work is the best hope the district has to continue to exist," she said.

"Exist?" John asked. "What do you mean exactly?"

"If the residents of a community are no longer willing to support the funding of their school district, the state has the option to dissolve the district and provide educational services to the young people of the community in an alternative manner," she explained.

"So our district, that's been in existence longer than any of us in this room have been alive, could be extinguished, closed?" one asked.

"Sure," the oversight commission chairperson said candidly.

"I'm flabbergasted by this Dr. Reed," John said. "I don't mean any disrespect, but I can't believe you can just sit here and talk to us in such a matter of fact way telling us you're going to shut down this district."

"We're all adults sir," she said looking directly at John. "I realize this news is not easy to hear but I see no point in giving you misleading information. I like to present the facts. I'm sure The Low Field

Local Schools have a long and proud tradition, like most school districts in the state, but things change. I hope it doesn't come to this, but maybe your community is trying to tell you something like they no longer want the district."

"That's ridiculous," another board member said. "I can't believe this."

"Well, may I share some recent information with you?" Dr. Reed asked looking at some papers inside a folder.

"Of course," John said.

"The state reporting system is updated every week and contains a vast amount of data that your superintendent and treasurer can use to help make informed decisions," she said. "For instance, are you aware that in the past month your enrollment has declined by ninety-three students?"

"We've lost that many students in the last month?" John asked surprised by the statistic. "That seems impossible; our total enrollment is only slightly above 1,000. So you're saying we lost one tenth of our students in a month?"

"Actually, your current enrollment in grades K-12 is 817 students," she said looking up from the report she was holding.

John looked at the superintendent and said, "Jim, I thought we had 1,000 plus students this fall."

"You're right John," Jim said. "We thought we did, but as you all probably remember, every fall it takes a few months to find and count each of our students. They have many choices such as attending parochial schools, private schools, colleges, charter schools, home schooling, other districts through open enrollment or they just move out of our district. So the projected enrollment numbers we were using in August have changed for the worse and since the shooting and November election we have lost another hundred or so students to these various schooling options."

"This is where the legislature has really eroded public education," said one board member. "I mean when I was a student here, and that wasn't that many years ago, every kid in Low Field attended these schools except for a handful of Catholic students who always went to Saint Brendon's or the parochial high school in Culver. Now people have all of these choices and every one of them takes our local tax money out of this community."

"Yeah, why don't you go back to Columbus and tell them to quit killing public schools with all choice options?" another said angrily.

"It's all political," John said. "The legislators keep acquiescing to special interests groups in order to get reelected instead of doing the right thing and preserving the most important institution in our democracy—local school districts."

"Well, speaking locally, I've heard that this board's recent decision to pass Policy 20 is also having a negative impact on your enrollment," Dr. Reed said.

"Possibly," Jim said. "I was told about a dozen students withdrew in the two days following the board meeting."

"Yes, Jim's secretary confirmed that. Unfortunately, all of these changes in your enrollment figures negatively impact your funding as well, because a key element in the funding formula is the number of students you serve in the district," she said. "When the school year began several months ago it was projected that you would run out of funds in March of this school year, but, with the decline in enrollment that we just discussed, the new date for your funding to cross into negative numbers is mid-January. So that is why I am here—to help you make the adjustments to your staffing levels, services and programs that are necessary to extend your revenue through the end of the school year. If your levy would be renewed in February, then many of the reductions you will make in the next few weeks could possibly be restored, but in the meantime, they are required because you also owe the state back payments and interest on the two loans you've received during the past few years."

She shuffled her papers and locating the one she wanted said, "At this time the total you owe the state is slightly over four million dollars as I'm sure your treasurer can verify for you."

"Well, this news coupled with everything we discussed with Henry earlier this evening sounds like a disaster to me," one of the board members said with defeat in his voice. "Maybe we should just wave the white flag and call it a day, John."

"I'm not sure what news you heard earlier this evening," Dr. Reed said.

"Oh it's nothing, really," Jim said sarcastically. "We just had two personal injury law suits filed against us that will probably cost us millions of dollars and drive more families out of Low Field."

"Oh," she responded, "that paints an even darker picture."

"It feels like a black hole to me," said another board member.

Dr. Reed pursed her lips together, crossed her arms across her chest and looked at Jim Collins.

All Jim could say was, "Well, thanks for coming tonight, Dr. Reed."

86

CLAYTON TOLD HIS older brother that he had invited Travis over to their house to visit with him. The two friends had lost contact with one another since the second funeral, although Travis had attempted to reach out to Colton by calling and sending text messages to his friend's cell phone many times during the turbulent weeks. Colton's health was improving but Clayton had suggested to Travis that he should behave calmly and speak slowly around his brother, at least during the onset of the visit.

The two brothers were back at their house doing chores and hanging out together apart from their grandparents. In spite of the background noise from the television, the house seemed lifeless and eerily quiet. Growing up the boys had gotten used to their father not being around on weekdays but their mother's constant busyness more than made up for his absence from the home by providing them with the eternal presence of a steady hand in charge who effortlessly guided the family's daily activities.

Colton could easily hear the sound of Travis's truck through the thin walls of the house. It was built before anyone had thought of vertical insulation and the old clapboard siding hadn't been painted in more than a decade. The truck doors slammed twice and two sets of footsteps were audible ascending the wooden steps to the back door. Travis knocked and without waiting opened the door.

"Hey, anyone home?" he said.

"Hey Travis, come on in," Colton said getting up from his supine position on the couch.

"I brought food and a friend," he said stepping aside and revealing a tall, attractive young woman.

"Hi Colt," she said looking at his blank face, "it's me, Tammy."

She quickly walked over to Colton and hugged him, squeezing his torso tightly. The embrace sent primal impulses and instinctive memories through him. He wrapped his arms around her lissome frame and held onto her for a while.

"Hi."

"I hope you don't mind that I came too," she said holding his face between her cool hands.

"No," Colton replied, "of course not."

Travis stepped forward and shook his friend's hand. Both visitors removed their coats and hung them on the back of kitchen chairs. Travis pulled wrapped hamburgers and French fries from the bags and spread them in front of the chairs evenly spaced around the round table.

"Where's Clay?" Travis asked.

"Upstairs," Colton replied. "I'll call him. Hey Clay, Travis brought food for you."

Clayton responded loudly, "Okay, thanks, I'll be down."

"I got you the usual Colt," Travis said sliding a chocolate milkshake toward his friend's food.

"Great, thanks Travis," Colton said unwrapping the sandwich. "Wait, this is chicken."

Travis laughed and tossed a cheeseburger to his friend, "I'm sorry Colt, I couldn't help it," Travis said. "I just wanted to see if today was *a cold day in hell*."

"You dumb butt," Colton said with a smile. "No, it's not that cold, even though it does feel like hell around here sometimes."

They ate the food quickly while carrying on conversations about generic topics.

"That was good, Travis," Colton said sucking the last of his shake through the straw, "thanks."

"No problem bud, and now we have a treat for desert," Travis announced. He reached behind him and pulled two thin joints from a front pocket on his faded jean jacket.

"Tammy and I agreed that we should bring you a little marijuana, for medicinal purposes of course," he said with a smile.

"Okay, but let's wait a few minutes," Colton said.

They returned to the living room and Tammy sat next to Colton on the sofa. Travis took a seat opposite the television in the recliner that formerly was always reserved for Mr. Caldwell. As they continued to talk and watch music videos, Tammy placed her hand on Colton's thigh, occasionally squeezing and softly massaging a section of his firm quadriceps. Both visitors were privately encouraged by Colton's memory and ability to converse. Their friend's condition seemed better than they expected from the tales of woe going around town.

"Let's go outside and get some fresh air," Travis suggested.

"Good call, T. Bring your medicine and we can smoke in the barn," Colton said.

It was much colder in the barn than they expected. Colton lit some kindling in the wood stove and brought a few bales of straw for them to use as seats near the heat. They smoked a joint, sharing it peacefully.

"So where did you buy medicinal pot in Ohio?" Colton asked.

Tammy said, "A friend of mine brought it from Colorado. It's a chocolate blend."

"What?" Colton said laughing.

There was a sound from the loft. A small animal stumbled or slipped on the uneven floor board planks.

"What was that?" Tammy asked.

"Just a mouse or a rat," Colton laughed.

"Oooo," Tammy recoiled moving closer to Colton.

"Ah, we always have them because we keep the cattle feed in here," Colton explained. "I'll have Clay shoot them later; will you help me remember?"

"Yes," Tammy said quickly as they finished the second joint. "In fact, let's go back in the house."

Clayton was sitting at the kitchen table finishing his lunch.

"Thanks Travis," he said. "We haven't had any normal food in weeks. Our grandma is forever cooking stews and soups."

"And putting things in Jell-O," Colton added.

"Like what?" Travis laughed.

"Mostly fruit, but the third time you have one of her gelatinous creations the same day, you just want something hard to chew on, like some jerky, if you know what I mean," Colton laughed.

Clayton finished and brought the trash can to the table. He gathered all of the meal's waste papers, cups and napkins and stuffed them into the fast food bags.

"I might as well take the trash out and burn it," Clayton said.

"Hey, why don't you take your .22 and shoot some rats in the barn while you're out there, Clay," his older brother suggested. "It seems like they've been breeding again."

"Okay," Clayton said putting on his coat and removing his handgun and clips from a drawer. "That's all they ever do; eat and reproduce."

The friends continued to talk in the living room commenting on the music videos they watched on the country network. Occasionally they would hear the muffled sound of gunfire outside.

"So, Colt what are you going to do once you're feeling better?" Tammy asked.

"I don't know," he said, "probably just look for a job. Or I might go to school to be a truck driver."

"Dude, that would kind of suck for a guy with your abilities," Travis said.

"I know but I have no idea what to do since I washed out of the Marines," Colton said.

"I talked to a college recruiter at the KSU branch a few weeks ago," Travis admitted. "She told me there's money available for people like us."

"What do you mean?" Colton asked.

"Well, with our dads both dead, I guess we can get most of college paid for through a social security benefit," Travis said.

"What do you want to study Travis?" Tammy asked.

"I'm not sure, but I always liked science classes in school," he answered. "Maybe I could become a science teacher and terrorize the next generation of Low Field kids."

"You'd be a good teacher," Tammy agreed. "Once I save enough money, I'm thinking about going to school too."

"What do you want to do with your life," Colton asked her.

"I'd like to work in the fashion industry, and I don't mean being a cashier who sells clothes at Walmart," she said with a smile. "But my dad wants me to go to beautician school."

"That would suck," Travis said.

"Yeah, so I can stand on my feet and cut hair for thirty years," she said with a frown.

"And live in Low Field and have a bunch of kids," Travis added.

"Isn't that the truth," she said. "I can just see myself weighing 200 pounds and being miserable like every other woman I know. I plan on leaving this place and not coming back."

"I agree," Travis said. "I think it would be cool to be a geologist and work in the oil industry out west or in the south."

"It all starts with a dream and a plan," Tammy said.

"Amen sister Tammy, amen," Travis said sensing Colton's disinterest in their conversation. "So Colt, I'll take you to meet the lady at the branch if you want."

"Okay, maybe Travis," Colton said. I've got to get this bracelet off my ankle and get my head to quit hurting first though."

"I understand," Travis replied. "I'll be here when you're ready."

"Tammy, did you know I'm secretly in love with his sorry ass?" Colton said with a smile.

"I knew I didn't stand a chance with him here," she said.

Outside in the barn, Clayton threw the rodent carcasses down from the loft to the packed gravel and dirt surface below. Normally he would carry them out back on a coal shovel and burn them, too, but today he had a different idea about how to dispose of the dead rats. He scooped them into a cardboard box. On his father's makeshift workbench he poured gasoline into a small canning jar, gathered some rags and carefully placed the items on top of the rats along with his lighter. He left the box inside the sliding doors of the barn and returned to the house. He owed his former boss Jerry a response to his firing, but until now, had trouble conceiving of an easy and effective way to retaliate for his dismissal. Clayton returned his weapon to the drawer, hung his coat and stepped into the living room where the others were talking and watching television.

"I took care of the rats," Clayton said looking at his brother and Tammy who were sitting very close to each other again on the sofa, cuddling under a blanket and occasionally exchanging kisses.

"Great, thanks Clay," Colton said.

"Sure," he responded heading up the stairs. "You two should get a room."

"Ah you're just jealous," Colton said laughing with Tammy.

"Maybe we should," Tammy laughed quickly squeezing Colton between the legs. "Actually, Travis, we probably better take off. I have to be at work at 3:00."

"Oh, okay," Travis said getting up and stretching. "Colt, you take care of yourself and answer your phone when I call, alright? I mean both you and Clayton have been understandably quiet lately, but at least he responds to a text."

"I know, I'm sorry about that Travis," Colton said. "I haven't wanted to talk much lately, but I do feel better since you guys came over today."

"Chalk-up another victory to the powers of medicinal marijuana," Travis laughed. He shook his friend's hand and gave him a quick man hug. Colton, however, held onto his friend for an extra few seconds.

When Colton finally released him, Travis said, "God, I'm glad Clay didn't see that; he'd want all three of us to get a room."

87

Daron's uncle Rafer left a message on his cell phone inviting him to meet for lunch at the McDonalds in their old Akron neighborhood. It was a tired, worn looking building in desperate need of an update in décor, a thorough cleaning and a coat of fresh paint. He stood and waved when he saw his nephew enter the building.

"Hey Daron, how're you doing?" Rafer asked.

"Hi Uncle Ray," Daron said with a smile. "I'm good; how are you?"

"Good, good," his uncle replied, "glad you could make it. You hungry?"

"Always," Daron laughed.

"Go ahead and order first," the boy's uncle said. "Lunch is on me so get whatever you want."

"Really?" Daron asked. "Okay thanks."

They sat facing each other in a tight corner booth flanked on two sides by walls of windows. They ate their lunches without haste while reminiscing about the Brown's game. Finally, the real reason for the meeting surfaced—Rafer wanted to know more about the charter school Daron had been attending the past few months.

"So you're school is called Classrooms Without Boundaries?" he asked.

"That's right," Daron answered. "It's very cool. They provided the computer, printer and internet service and everything was real easy to set-up and use."

"And you picked your own classes?" his uncle asked.

"Well, one of the directors evaluated my transcript and basical-ly told me which four classes I needed to graduate, so that's what I signed up for," Daron said. "I mean, I could've taken more electives if I wanted to but why bother at this point."

"So, you're doing okay and will graduate this year?" Rafer asked.

"Oh yeah, actually I should be finished with the classes in a month or so," Daron told him.

"Really?"

"It's a self-paced program so I can go as quickly as I want to and I enjoy taking the classes online. And they have a special program for seniors that allows for early graduation, so right now I just feel like getting done and moving on with my life. Plus, that way I won't hold up my mom's plans," he answered.

"What's she planning?" Rafer asked.

"She's thinking about moving away from this area and getting a fresh start. There's a job opening in the bank she works for that's re-ally got her contemplating a new adventure," Daron explained. "Or maybe she's just having a mid-life crisis."

"Well, she deserves something better," Ray said. "I mean she's done right by you all these years since my brother died, but it would be nice to see her enjoy herself more."

"You're right; she's sacrificed a lot for me. That's why I'm trying to graduate early," Daron said, "so I can move on with my life and not hold her back from what she wants to do."

"I don't blame you one bit, young man," his uncle said. "If this wasn't home, I probably wouldn't have come back after I got out of the service. But I spent so many nights in Iraq dreaming about being home, that I told myself if I lived long enough to get on a plane back to the US, I was going to live in Akron for a while."

"So you're almost done with school too," Daron said. "What's next for you?"

"I don't know for sure. I'll finish my bachelor's degree next year and I might look to move after I do my student teaching and get my license. How about you?" his uncle asked. "Has anything changed since we last talked?"

"Not really although I'm leaning toward either moving to Florida near my grandparents or enlisting. In fact, what do you think about the Marines instead of the Army as an option?" Daron asked his uncle.

"You should talk to recruiters from both branches," his uncle suggested. "I'll go with you if you want. Either way, you'd be a great soldier. It teaches you discipline and skills and you can make it work for your future, too, if you sign-up for the college program when you enlist. Like they say, it's an adventure."

"Did you ever have any racial problems in the military?" Daron asked his uncle.

"Daron, I hate to tell you this but I've experienced racial problems almost every day of my life, no matter where I was in the world," his uncle said. "It's not something you ever get used to but you just learn to live with it."

"That's disappointing. I was hoping it might be different in the army," the young man said.

"It's different, but it's still there; whether it's black or white, yellow or brown it's still there and you just have to cope with it," said his uncle. "Speaking of race, are you still dating the white girl? I'm sorry I forget her name."

"No, Kelsey and I sort of split up after the shooting," Daron said.

"Was it your choice or hers?" Ray asked.

"Actually her parents' choice more than either of us, but it's cool," Daron explained. "I don't think it was going to work for either of us. In fact, she just came out."

"What? You turned a girl gay?" his uncle asked smiling. "I wouldn't tell anyone about that."

They both laughed and Daron waved off his uncle shaking his head.

"No, she just didn't know until this fall, I guess. I'm not sure how it all went down with her but I hear she's seeing another girl from school that she's been good friends with for years," he said.

"Hey, it happens and you're both probably better off if she's trying to figure out her *preferences*," his uncle said. "So tell me about your old school. I hear they passed some policy that allows the teachers to carry guns in class."

"What I heard was twenty teachers in both schools have permission to have a gun in their classroom but no one knows which of the teachers have the guns. They put a lockbox in every classroom and some have guns in them but others are empty," Daron explained.

"What kind of training do these people have?" Ray asked.

"I don't know for sure," Daron said. "I heard they got concealed carry permits."

"Well the whole thing sounds crazy to me," Rafer said. "A concealed carry permit is nothing; I mean you go to a class for five hours and take a third grade test."

"I know, it sounds nuts," Daron agreed. "I've heard a bunch of parents are really upset with the plan. Hey, one of the kids who got shot has us posing for a sculpture she's working on."

"Really? What's that like?" his uncle asked.

"It's cool; I mean we just go to her house and take off our clothes and pose for her," Daron said. "No I'm just kidding, we don't know much about her plan but she's a serious artist so I'm sure it will be good. She talks a lot against guns so I'm guessing that's part of the theme."

"Hey, guns kill," Ray said pointedly.

"We went to a meeting at the school last week and this guy from the NRA argued that people kill," Daron said.

"Bullshit. Most people wouldn't get killed in this country if we had stricter gun control. If you enlist in the Marines you'll see what I mean. Weapons are serious, complex instruments that take a long time to learn completely. They're not toys that someone can just pick up and then a month later think they can use effectively in a hostile attack. It all takes training and coordination. Those teachers are crazy," Rafer said growing animated by the conversation. "Do you know if any of them served in the military or have a law enforcement background?"

"Not for sure, but I don't think so," Daron answered. "As far as I know they're just a bunch of teachers with guns. Uncle Ray, you're going to be a teacher; you should meet with them and tell them what you think."

"Who's the union president?" he asked.

"He's a teacher in the high school named Mr. Byler. I think his first name is Keith," Daron said.

"What's he teach?" Ray asked.

"Not much," joked Daron, "although he's supposed to teach social studies I think. I'm not positive because I never had him for class."

"Maybe I'll send him an email and see if he'll meet with me," Rafer said.

"That's a great idea because you know so much about guns and how to fight bad guys," Daron replied.

"I definitely learned about all of that in the Army," Rafer said. "Do you want to come with me?"

"I'm not allowed on school property anymore," Daron said.

"What? Why's that?" his uncle asked.

"I don't know. They basically kicked me out because I'm black," Daron said honestly.

"What a bunch of shit," his uncle said. "Those people gave you a raw deal."

"That's what I said but it was just easier on my mom if I just went away and did the charter school to finish," Daron said.

"Well yeah," his uncle said, "it's always easier on the white people if the black guy just goes away, but that doesn't make it fair."

"I know, but, hey I was the outsider and it was easier for them to make me the fall guy," he said.

"The more I hear about this the more I don't like it, Daron," said Ray. "I don't like the way you were treated and I don't like the idea of having a bunch of guns in the hands of teachers who don't know how to use them. I think I'm going to visit the Low Field Schools and talk to some people."

"Don't worry about it, Uncle Ray," Daron urged. "It's really no big deal. I mean, it's over now, and I'm going to graduate pretty soon, so don't trouble yourself with them. Low Field is a bunch of rednecks who like things the way they've always been. It's not worth your time."

"With all due respect, I'll be the judge of that," his uncle said seriously. "Some things in life shouldn't be let go. It sounds like they disrespected you and your mom. They've got no right to make you pay the price for something that some white kid caused. I'm going to call that union president. You said his name is Byler, right?"

"Yep, that's his name," Daron said, "Byler."

88

THE DOCTORS AND therapists who treated Colton were guardedly optimistic regarding his condition. Within the first few weeks of his episode of disorientation at The Ledges, his brain had been scanned twice. The second exam showed no internal bleeding in the lining between the brain and the skull. Also, the swelling and contusion on the top of his head that they surmised was caused by a collision with a rock in the park had subsided significantly. Moreover, there were steady, encouraging signs that his memory was returning to near normal. He was able to remember more past experiences from years ago, and, even more encouraging, he recalled the people and events from the previous day or two, which demonstrated that his mind was effectively processing those activities from his short-term memory. Visiting with friends made him feel normal, even if only for a few hours. Spending time with them helped minimize the dim, misty veils that shrouded his memories.

At the suggestion of one of the doctors, his grandmother had moved all the family photo albums from both houses into his bedroom. Looking through the stack of faded and loose photos was a bittersweet experience for Colton. A photo of the family members taken years ago, that stripped away years of hardship and aging, would bring a smile to his face. Their youthful smiling faces subconsciously transferred the same happy expression to his face and in most cases he was able to recall the setting and approximate date of the photos. Sadly, however, was the recognition that his parents, the two people who shared the responsibility for his upbringing and cared the most for his well-being, were no longer present in his life; their absence became increasingly evident by looking at the photos.

Therapists and counselors alike were very concerned that both Colton and Clayton were verbally withdrawn and unable to articulate their feelings regarding the tragic losses of their parents. A common strategy used in these types of cases was to ask patients to draw pictures or write notes or letters. Colton was asked to write a letter to his parents. The content was of his choice; the charge was simply stated in this manner: If you could tell your parents something that you didn't have a chance to say before, what would it be?

Colton struggled for hours trying to organize his thoughts. His dad had taught him a great deal about engines and working with his hands. His mom was his rock; she was the person he could talk to about anything, the way best friends share their innermost fears and opinions. Like most people, his greatest regret was not thanking them enough for what they had both done for him. He decided that would be the central point of his letter to his parents.

Dear Mom and Dad,

I've been looking through some our old family photo albums recently. One of my favorite pictures was taken at grandma and grandpa's farm when Clayton and I were pretty young. We were both wearing new cowboy hats and mom you were leading their old horse Lucky around so we could take a ride on her. I think dad brought us the hats from a trip out west he had driven and were all very happy. Clayton and I also had our six-shooters strapped on in case we had to deal with some bad guys. The sun was shining brightly because both grandma and grandpa had sunglasses on while they were watching us ride. When we were little, we used to say Lucky was as big as an elephant; now I know why, because compared to us she was gigantic.

Dad, I didn't get a chance to tell you before you were gone that I loved the weekends we spent in the barn working on old cars or fixing the tractor. I learned so much about how engines work and how to use tools properly from spending so many hours assisting you and watching how you tear apart engines laying the parts carefully in an order so you knew exactly how to flawlessly retrace your steps and put the machine back together. At the time I thought you must have been a genius to keep it straight in your mind. Thank you for being patient teaching me about motors and how machines work and always taking the time to play catch with me. I'm guessing you would have rather rested or done something you wanted to do, but no matter what sport was in season, baseball or football, you were always willing to help a little kid get better at throwing and catching. Most of all, thanks for letting Clayton and me go hunting with you and grandpa and Uncle Boo and your friends. We learned so much from those days with you men that I hope we will use for years to come and maybe with our own kids someday.

Mom, I won't accept that you're not here for me to talk to about girls and school and various other problems I'm having in my life; that's why I still talk to you every night when I first lay down in bed. I know you're listening and sometimes I can hear your advice if I take the time to listen closely in the stillness of my dark room. I thought life was going to be so easy once I finished high school but you were right about that one too. You said life was often hard and really began after the fun of high school was finished. Wow, you were so right. Almost everything that's happened to me in the past six months has been bad. After Kelsey and I broke up my life's been nothing but a downward spiral. You always said a man needs a good woman to keep him grounded and I'm starting to understand what you meant. The leaves have fallen and most of the summer birds have headed south. I still put the feed out for the ones that stay in Ohio like you had us do so they had something to eat when their food supply becomes more difficult to find, and the cardinals and blue jays are out back every day the way you liked it. You will always be my best friend no matter what happens in the future. Thanks for always taking the time to sit and listen to my kid problems and help me through them. You are the best mom any kid could ever have.

I miss you both. Thanksgiving was the worst holiday ever. Grandma cooked but it just wasn't the same. The house is so quiet now, especially the kitchen. I never realized until now how much time we all used to spend in the kitchen doing chores, cooking, eating, doing homework or projects and just sitting around the table talking about our days. Now your chairs are always pushed-in close to the table and the placemats are never dirty or disturbed. It's so quiet— I never thought of you two as noisy people but our house used to seem alive when you were here and now it doesn't. I hope you both can reach down to Clayton in some way because he's in a bad way. I am too, but he's enough younger than me that he's really angry about you being gone and he's acting out in ways that aren't like him. He needs your help before he does something really bad.

Last night I went out to the barn with Serge and he was barking the way he used to when dad was out back working. I swear he knew you were there dad. I just watched him running around by the work bench and he stood barking at the tool shed door with his tail wagging. I tried to tell him you weren't there but after a while I realized he was trying to tell me you were there. It was so strange. We went up in the hay loft and opened the window boards. The sunset was full of pastel oranges and reds; your favorite type of sunset, and I knew you were with us, watching it over our shoulders. After the sun dropped below the tree line, we went in the house and watched the final light evaporate from the sky through the kitchen window, the way mom used to stand and gaze out at the solitary view of the sky while she dried the last of the dishes, humming or singing softly to herself. I fed Serge and waited for Clayton to come home, then I called grandma and told her we were both home and in for the night. My head hurts pretty much all the time these days, like it used to on Saturdays following football games. And I still can't remember everything from the past, but I wanted you to know that I love you both and miss you more than the words in this letter can express. I feel very lonely, but I know in my heart that you're with me helping me make good decisions and watching out for Clayton. Thanks for always being here for me. Love, Colton.

Although Colton knew the therapist wanted to see what he had written, there was no way she would ever read the letter. He looked the handwritten pages over and over correcting misspellings and changing words so each sentence said precisely what he wanted to say to his parents. A few tear drops fell from his cheeks and when he wiped them it smeared the text. But it didn't matter. He knew long before he crumpled the pages into a ball that his words were only meant for his mom and dad and he would never let them be seen by a stranger's eyes. What he felt about them was too personal for an outsider to ever know or read. Colton knew his parents would understand in a few days when he would have to tell her he didn't write a letter because he didn't know what to say.

89

THE FIRST FEW weeks of December in northeast Ohio are full of unpredictable weather for a golfer. One day the sun will shine and a single layer of outerwear is sufficient for outdoor activities while the next day begins with a frosty coating to the ground that gets covered with a sheet of snow that entirely conceals the grass and paints the rolling acreage of the course a bright white. For many golf courses the first snow of the season is the event that signals the closing of the facility for the year. Others, however, desperate for even sparse amounts of revenue, will allow enthusiastic golfers to walk the course whenever conditions are conducive to play throughout the winter months. Once the leaves have been blown into the woods from the short grasses and the workers who mow are progressively laid off for the season, the only winter chore for the remaining crew is performing maintenance on the equipment. From the warmth of the grounds building these year-round workers can also collect the greens fees and keep an eye on players during the early winter days.

Will and Luke were two of the golfers who knew which courses stayed open for play and would meet every afternoon after school to practice for as long as the shrinking daylight hours would permit. They played two-ball matches in order to increase the effectiveness of their work. Some days they would pick the better of the two shots and basically play a one person scramble from the best position of their two shots through each hole; this 'best ball' style promoted birdies and aggressive strategies. On other days they did the opposite, again hitting two shots from every spot but this time playing from the worse ball's position; this forced them to practice their recovery and escape shots and play more conservatively trying to maintain contact with par. Regardless, they had great fun because the courses would have only a handful of golfers competing for space. They would pull on stocking caps, rain pants, several thin layers of tops and fumble with gloves and cart mitts while they hustled around the golf course practicing the game they loved as the low sun quickly evaporated into the western horizon.

On snowy days the boys went to the weight room at Luke's high school in Harrison City. Off-season athletes such as football, baseball and soccer players would be milling around the facility more-or-less unsupervised, working through the stations doing upper or lower body sessions. They accepted Will into the fraternity and viewed the two golfers as unobtrusive because Luke and Will trained very differently from most of the others, not competing for turns with the heaviest weights. Through conversation, Luke became aware of Abby's foundation and wanted to meet her. After working out one afternoon Will gave her a call and the two boys traveled out to Abby's house. The garage door was open and they could hear soft music.

"Wow, this place looks like a ski lodge," Luke said as they walked up the gravel driveway to the house. Will smiled and shook his head in agreement.

"Hey Abby," said Will leading Luke into the garage, "my goodness, this is impressive."

"Thanks, it's coming along pretty well," she said with a smile. "Some art students from Akron U volunteered to help with the preliminary chisel work."

"Abby, this is a good friend of mine, Luke Redmond," said Will stepping aside. "He's wanted to meet you for weeks."

"Hi Abby, it's nice to finally meet you," Luke said surprised at her attractiveness.

A large smile lit Abby's face as her eyes met Luke's. She stood wobbly and a little hunched over but she looked proud and confident in front of her art. A navy and white handkerchief covered her long dark hair and her farmer's style overalls were blotted with a powdery film. Her neck and chest flushed scarlet with hives of excitement.

"Hi Luke," Abby said extending her dusty hand, "nice to meet you as well."

"So, Abby this is really starting to take shape," Will said. "How in the world did you get this huge stone in here?"

"If you look closely, you can see that it's actually six thin slices of sandstone with smooth sides so they can be abutted together and look like one massive piece. That makes moving it much easier and then later, once it's placed, the pieces can be affixed together with epoxy," she explained.

Will glanced at his friend and said, "I told you she's smart. What did you decide for your Low Field creation?"

"Well, I went through a bunch of ideas and drawings that ranged from what I'd describe as the angry victim of gun violence to criticizing the backward mentality of the gun-toting hillbilly, but I've finally worked through enough of the stages of forgiveness that allowed me to take the higher road," Abby laughed. "So over here is one of the final sketches that we're using to rough out the figures from the stone."

She escorted the boys to a large mural taped to a garage wall on the far side of the stones. It was a beautiful drawing of a line of children. From left to right, the sketched boys and girls showed the progression of childhood beginning with a toddler followed by four other school aged children of various ages, sizes, and shapes culminating with a high school student on the far right end of the mural. Each child was holding the hand or hands of the person next in line and all wore a simple, happy facial expression symbolizing the joyful innocence of youth.

"God, this is awesome," Luke said carefully scanning the detail of the drawing.

"Oh, thank you," she said. "I threw away a ream of angst-filled drafts while I was trying to figure-out a more timeless subject for the work."

"Would it be okay to take a few photos of the mural?" Will said trying to extract his cell phone from the pocket in his top. "Or maybe not yet?"

"Yeah, maybe not yet," she said. "It could change again, plus the unveiling of a work is more dramatic if there's an aura of anticipation, if that makes sense."

"Sure; I should have thought of that," Will said shaking his head, "sorry."

"Let me show you the stone. Feel along the top edge of a piece. Do you feel the metal eye screw?" Abby asked.

"Oh yeah," Luke replied touching the metal circle.

"That's how they can lift each piece for the final placement hopefully without damaging any," she explained.

"How did they get moved into here?" Luke asked.

"A skid-loader and heavy-weight dolly, believe it or not," she explained. "And four really big guys who delivered the pieces from the quarry."

"This is so cool. How did you learn how to do this?" Luke asked.

"Actually this is my first big sculpture. I did a small piece one summer at a workshop in Cleveland. And this one is a collaborative work," she said. "I'd be here for years if the art students from the university weren't helping with the rough shaping."

"Thanks for showing us your work, Abby," Luke said. "I feel like I'm in the presence of greatness, like a modern-day Michelangelo."

"Hardly, but I'm having fun again," Abby said with a smile, "and hopefully we can leave a positive tribute for the students of Low Field for many years to come."

"By the way," Will said, "I think everything is falling into place for Saturday's rally."

"I was checking out the webpage and social media postings earlier," she said. "Everything looks great. Do you honestly think many people will come?"

"I don't know," Will admitted. "A bunch of people at school have told me they're attending, but we won't know for sure until Saturday. We started this with a cause, an important cause, but as time goes on, I'm starting to realize it's probably just our cause. The students who weren't directly affected by the shooting forget and move on."

"You're right," Abby said. "Every day brings new challenges and issues for people and forces them to have short memories. Maybe we can capitalize on the current momentum the issue has this weekend, but as the holidays approach I get the feeling like the sense of urgency is slipping away. Let's just hope the weather cooperates."

"We definitely need some luck on that front, but my dad checked with the Legion hall and they said we could move it there at the last minute if we need to," Will said turning to his friend. "Hey you ready to get rolling, Luke? We better let Abby get back to work."

"Okay, sure," Luke said.

Will added, "Abby, I've also got the copies of the petition you emailed me, and Kelsey and Erin are putting up posters. Is there anything else we should be doing?"

"Are the arrangements made for the bands and the sound system in the stadium?" she asked.

"Yeah that's all set. Erin's taken the lead with Kelsey and everything sounds fine. They're using the parade floats to set everything on, so when it's each band's turn to play we'll just roll them to the center of the track and connect them to the power source. I talked to the head custodian the other day and he said it wouldn't be a problem," Will explained.

"Okay, great. That's all I can think of right now," Abby said. "Thanks for coming over, you guys."

"Sure, it was our pleasure," Will said.

"Great to meet you Abby," Luke said as he shook her hand again. "I'm really impressed by your sculpture. I can't wait to see the finished work."

"Thanks Luke, me too," Abby said with a coy smile. "It was nice to meet you."

She watched the boys walk down the driveway toward the truck. Will and Luke exchanged a high five as they laughed and walked.

"I told you she was cute," Will said.

"Man, I can't believe you've been holding out on me like that," Luke said softly punching Will in the chest. "She's more than cute— I'd say hot and smart. Wow, what a package. I've never met a girl like her before. You probably have your eye on her for yourself."

"No, she's just become a good friend," Will said. "I'd describe our relationship as kind of like a brother and sister since the shooting. We shared a very traumatic experience with each other that will always bond us together. I think she's doing a great job of working through a major ordeal and trying to get her life back together."

"Maybe she could use some support from someone who doesn't think of her as a sister," Luke said with a smile. "So what time are we going to the rally on Saturday?"

Will just laughed as Luke backed the truck into the turn-around and headed down the long gravel driveway away from Abby's house.

"I couldn't bring myself to tell Abby that a few of us have received threatening emails and notes warning us to cancel the rally," Will said. "The bums are probably just trying to intimidate us but they don't know I've looked Luke Redmond in the eye before making a four footer to win a match."

90

RAFER'S DRIVE FROM the city west to Low Field was snarled by an accident on state route 49 involving a box truck hauling produce. The brightly colored vegetables were flung from their open storage crates across both lanes giving the area the appearance of an asphalt garden. The weather conditions were icy. Earlier that afternoon he called the high school and left a message for Keith Byler explaining that he might be late, hoping the union president could still meet with him.

Parking lots and pavement encircled the old building. Ray drove the perimeter slowly taking a few minutes to see the entrances and exits from every angle. It was nearly 4:00 when he arrived. Student athletes were running wind sprints down one section of the first floor hallway while some others jumped rope in a different corridor, using every available space in the building, a necessity caused by the numerous demands for the gymnasium floor during the winter sports season. A sweaty, winded boy with acne pushed open the door for Rafer as he saw the man pull on several handles of locked doors.

"They're always locked," the boy said.

"Thanks," Ray said, "I'm here for a meeting with Mr. Byler."

"Oh he's probably in his room. It's on the second floor in the front of the building," the boy said pointing in the direction.

"Thanks again."

"Sure."

On his way there, Rafer passed the main office. He turned around and stepped inside. The secretary, Mrs. Cunningham by the name plate on her desk, repositioned the personal items on her desk and put on a long, satiny coat.

"Excuse me, Mrs. Cunningham?" Rafer asked.

"Yes sir," she replied.

"I'm Rafer Scott; I called earlier and spoke to you about a meeting I have with Mr. Byler," he explained.

"Why yes, how do you do?" she asked politely.

"Hi, I just wanted to thank you," he said. "You were very nice on the phone."

"Oh, thank you."

"I wondered if you have a map of the building," Rafer asked. "It's my first time here and I don't know how to get to Mr. Byler's room."

"Sure," she said handing him a folder from under the counter. She flipped it over revealing a floor plan drawing on the back, "his room is number 213." She drew a circle around that room and the main office so Rafer could navigate the simple pattern.

"Perfect, thanks again for your help and it was nice to meet you ma'am," Ray said as he left the office.

The ex-army lieutenant quickly walked to room 213 carefully cataloging in his mind a visual survey of the stairways and recessed doors he passed along the route. Something inside of Rafer wouldn't let go of the gnawing dissatisfaction he had when he thought about Daron's treatment by the school officials and people of Low Field—it felt like racism. Of the thirty to forty students he'd seen since entering the building, none was a person of color. Daron must have felt like he was living in a fishbowl every day for the past few years; that was something no white person in this school could understand. It put undue stress on his nephew and never allowed him to relax and just be himself. Growing up is hard enough to do without the added pressure of being the square peg trying to fit into a board of only circles.

He peered into the room and saw the large man in his early forties grading papers at his desk. The man was wearing a sweatshirt with Low Field written across the chest in script lettering. Keith looked up at Rafer and lifted his reading glasses.

"Hello, Mr. Byler? I'm Rafer Scott, thank you so much for waiting to meet with me," Ray said approaching the teacher with an extended hand.

"Mr. Scott, nice to meet you," Keith nodded and replied. "So you have to interview a union president for a class you are taking at the university?" He stepped around the teacher's desk and motioned for the visitor to join him sitting at a pair of student desks. Both men struggled slightly to fit their large bodies into the one-piece designs.

"Yes, thank you for giving me this opportunity," Rafer said.

"So, please tell me about yourself," Byler said. "I mean you're obviously not a typical undergrad."

"That's for sure. I'm attending college on the G I Bill," Ray explained. "I spent twenty years in the army after high school."

"Were you deployed into combat?" Keith asked.

"Yeah, four deployments, mostly in Iraq and Afghanistan, sandwiched with some medical rehab from some injuries," Ray said sharing more than usual with a stranger.

"How were you injured, if you don't mind me asking?" said Keith.

"One time I was wounded during a gun fire exchange and the second time I caught shrapnel from a roadside IED," Rafer said.

"Wow, that's rough," Keith said. "Are you okay now?"

"Mostly," Rafer admitted. "I have some dark spells like everyone who served and I'll never be totally free from the injuries, but at least I made it home walking. A lot of my friends came home in body bags."

"I'm sorry," Keith said. "So you have a Purple Heart?"

"Two," Rafer said. "They're in a drawer at home with some photos and important papers from that chapter of my life."

"Wow, that's impressive," said the union president. "Thanks for your service."

"You know when that courtesy of thanking people in uniform for their service started I was kind of sour because I didn't believe ordinary people in the airport or at the grocery store had any idea of the extent of the sacrifices people in the armed services truly make for their country," Rafer said. "The phrase seemed like a cliché. But after the weeks in hospitals and rehab facilities and the bouts of depression I went through, I started to realize that at least these people get the fact that I was serving our country and they understood and appreciated at least that; so thank you, and sorry for rambling on about it."

"No, no that's perfectly okay," Keith said. "I meant it sincerely."

"Thank you," Ray said, "and maybe some people in this community will start thanking you and the other teachers for providing security to your students."

"Oh you heard about that?" Keith asked.

"Yeah, sure," Rafer said. "Honestly, I was concerned at first, but I'm starting to come around on the idea."

"We've been practicing our shooting and I think we're ready for anything," Keith said confidently.

"Really?" Ray asked. "I wouldn't be so sure of that. A school is a soft target and very difficult to defend in an open society. For instance, are you prepared for a layer of tear gas? Or explosive charges? I mean there are a multitude of tactical maneuvers a person with any kind of military background or even just access to the internet could use to disrupt your response to them as a hostile intruder."

"Well, we're not at war," Keith said scoffing at Ray's statement. "Schools typically get attacked by a lone wolf type or a few disgruntled students who've played too many video games."

"That's a pretty naive assumption, Mr. Byler. I wouldn't want to be in your position if someone with a little more sophistication challenges you and your teachers," Ray said with a tilt of his head and pursed lips.

"I think we're fine," Keith said shortly. "That's enough about our plan, what do you need for your class?"

"Oh, I think I have enough," Ray said.

"Really, I thought you needed to know about union stuff and had educational questions," Keith said surprised at Ray's statement.

Both men wiggled and slid their way out of the student desks. Ray extended his hand to Keith and said, "The presence of guns is a very low level of preparedness, Mr. Byler. Way more is necessary for you and your militia to be truly prepared. In my experience, there's a huge difference between being smart and trained or just being lucky. Right now I think you're counting on a whole lot of luck if you think you can protect your students from an invasion."

"Well, you might be right, but I don't have time to do any more for this district than I'm already doing," Keith said, "so unless you want to share some of your expertise and help us, I'm afraid I'll have to take my chances for now."

"I'd be willing to help you," Ray said.

"Really? That would be great, in fact, we were thinking of making a promotional video of our team's response to a crisis either this weekend or next if you're available," Keith said.

"Okay, that might be a valuable training aid," Ray said. "Let's exchange phone numbers and you can let me know. I can show you how unprepared you really are for trouble."

"Alright," Keith said doubting the value of his offer to let Ray assist the LF 20. "I guess you can be the bad guy."

Rafer left the room and walked back toward the noise coming from the gymnasium. A middle school basketball game had started and a small crowd of people were milling around the hallway buying refreshments and talking. He went to a far corner of the hallway that surrounded the gym on three sides and stood in a doorway contemplating entrances and exits. He studied the floor plan on the folder and allowed his mind to photograph the numerous nuances of the building for his plan. Mr. Byler and the Low Field 20 were going to get quite the awakening in their response to the havoc and mayhem he planned to deliver to their plan.

91

THE COLD, HUMID conditions of mid-December nights often-times formed frost pockets in the low areas of soggy turf grass at Whispering Hollow Golf Club. Golfers were kept off the course until the sun was high enough on the horizon to heat the surfaces and turn the frost to water. This Saturday the ground frost was heavy and pervasive and a light hoar frost coated many of the bare trees in the dells and valleys of the course. Luke and Will sat patiently drinking coffees loaded with cream and sugar in the clubhouse with a handful of other hopeful golfers waiting for the okay from the greens superintendent that the course was finally safe and ready for play. Suddenly, Will's phone pinged and buzzed several times in rapid succession, signaling incoming text messages. They were from his parents.

> *Will, prob at the school*
> *Rally issue please call me*
> *Custodian called needs u at the school*

"Oh crap Luke," he said, "there's some kind of problem at the school. Do you mind if we scrap the golf this morning and head over there?"

"Sure, why not," Luke agreed, "I'm getting a headache from this coffee and it doesn't look like the frost is lifting anyway."

They arrived at the high school before 8:00 AM and saw the custodian removing a shovel from the bed of a pickup truck. The vehicle was backed up to a large pile of manure blocking the main driveway into the parking lot.   A steamy mist was rising from the top giving the illusion of ghosts awakening from a burial plot.

Luke looked at Will shaking his head and said, "What the heck."

"It's just the beginning," Will prophesized. "This could be a bad day."

Luke parked the truck in the front of the easement, parallel to the road. The stench was earthy and powerful.

"Good morning fellas," the custodian said. Then he pointed toward the stadium gates and said, "There's two more."

"Man that's not a good smell for a guy with an empty stomach," Luke said covering his nose and mouth with his hand.

"Ah you city boys," Will said with a smile.

Two identical mountain shaped loads had been dumped in front of the patron entrances into the fenced facility.

"That's a lot of bull shit to shovel," the older man said with a smile. "Please excuse the bad joke."

"Any other surprises Mr. Swanson?" Will asked.

"Just one more, at least for now," answered the custodian. "All of the tires on the floats are slashed. It seems as though someone doesn't want you kids to have this rally."

"I think you're right," Will agreed. "All the more reason to carry on with it."

Will took photos with his phone and sent them to Kelsey and Erin with messages asking for help. The girls posted the pictures to social media and started making phone calls. Within an hour a small army of twenty to thirty students arrived at the school. As the clean-up continued the band members started to arrive carting in their equipment and setting it on the mini-stages of the float decks. During the initial sound check they discovered the wires leading from the control center in the wooden press box to the speakers that hung on the tall light poles had also been cut. Harried students frantically called home and within a short time portable generators and basement speaker systems and amplifiers started to arrive from all corners of Low Field. The unified students supporting Abby and her notions about gun rights would not be deterred by the opposition.

The people on the other side of the debate were also organized and had their own plan. As the morning waned and they got closer to the midday start time for the rally, the scheme of the pro-gun rights coordinators started to become evident to the students. It reminded Will of the armies in colonial battles arranging their armaments in plain sight of one another prior to the beginning of a bloody skirmish. They were hosting a rally of their own in a neighboring practice field which sat directly beside the stadium. Will called the Low Field police department to complain about the situation. The only officer on-duty was a young, part-time deputy recently hired to work weekends.

"We could have a mess here," Will warned the officer. "Our rally is a school-approved activity but I doubt that their group has any permission from the principal or superintendent to hold their demonstration on the football practice field."

"I don't know," the officer said, "but let me do some checking and I'll get back to you."

Music accompanied the arrival of supporters to both rallies. Most of the students entered the football stadium wearing masks of one type or another over their faces. Hockey goalie masks, stocking caps, scarves and Halloween masks were the most popular choices and many brought an array of toy guns to donate to the symbolic surrendering of their weapons during the festivity. The majority of the people who gathered on the practice field were dressed in camouflage hunting or military attire. Some wore face paint to complete their outfits while many others simply wore sunglasses to conceal their identities. All were handed American flags which they displayed in a variety of creative ways. Members of the media scurried to comment and film both gatherings.

Abby was the primary speaker inside the stadium. Her remarks were sandwiched between the two musical acts.

"Social and political action is necessary for meaningful change," she began. "Gun control laws in this country are biased toward power rather than common sense. It is up to us to help alter the argument. Will Harper and I were just two of the 100,000 people who were shot this year in our country. More restrictions, better licensing and tougher laws are necessary if we are ever going to reduce the unnecessary injuries and killings caused by guns. Today we have five petitions that we are asking you to consider signing. The first calls for a ban on the sale of semi-automatic firearms to ordinary citizens. The second calls for a restriction on large capacity magazines for guns. The third calls for a comprehensive tightening of gun laws in this country including closing background check loopholes and a restriction of gun access to juveniles and people with mental illness. The fourth petition asks the Low Field Township Trustees to require that all firearms in this township be registered with our police department. And the final petition asks the Low Field Board of Education to reverse Policy 20, which allows almost half of our public school teachers to have access to firearms in our schools. Volunteers are passing around clipboards with the various petitions on them right now. Make your voices heard today!"

She waved to the students and was greeted with a thunderous, standing ovation. Her introduction of the next band could not be heard because of the extended, exuberant clapping and yelling from the students.

A few hundred yards away the ovation caused a reflexive glance by the several hundred people listening to speakers on the other side of the debate. The most polished and persuasive speaker was an employee of the National Rifle Association who had driven to the community from Virginia to help stir the emotions of the gun enthusiasts.

"These students," he said pointing toward the stadium, "are no different from the spineless politicians and super-rich liberals who are constantly attacking our freedoms. These incendiary factions must be stopped. Our forefathers pronounced that the right to keep and bear arms shall not be infringed when they wrote the second amendment of the United States Constitution over two hundred years ago. These people are still trying to take away our rights and our freedoms. We have to stand and fight together to defend our shooting and hunting traditions. We have to stand and fight together to keep the right to own guns to defend ourselves and our families. And we have to stand and fight together to eliminate gun control laws so everyday Americans like you and me are free from left-wing oppression. Now, get on your feet, wave your flags proudly and send a loud message across this field to that stadium that says you're not giving up your rights, ever."

The group jumped to their feet, cupped their hands around their mouths like human megaphones and sent an equally loud roar echoing back at the students. A few zealous members of the crowd, caught up in the emotional rhetoric of the speaker's plea, drew the handguns they regularly holstered as part of the concealed carry permit legislation and accompanied the group cheers with a repeated explosion of gunshots fired into the air.

In the stadium, several of the students misinterpreted the gunfire as shots being fired at them. A few of them started to scream, "They're shooting at us!"

A panic rippled suddenly through the group of students. Most of them, still wearing masks, had their vision compromised as they attempted to evacuate the crowded stands. Many tripped in their haste or pushed others in front of them causing a domino of falling students cascading out of control down the ascended metal seating of the stadium. Countless students were unintentionally trampled and crushed by other students once the alarm and terror overtook the capacity of the youthful crowd. From the ground the accident looked like a human avalanche snowballing down a steep hill. Will and Abby screamed in vain for everyone to stop. But their words could not be heard over the wails of the frightened students. In total thirty seven students suffered broken bones and well over a hundred sustained cuts, abrasions and contusions. Over a dozen were admitted to the hospital with serious but not life threatening injuries. Mercifully no one was killed.

The members of the news media crews abruptly received a dramatic ending to their story as the disaster was all caught on camera. The videos went viral once again bringing unwanted notoriety to the little community of Low Field, Ohio.

92

COLTON AND CLAYTON Caldwell were once again getting dressed into their Sunday clothes on a day other than Sunday. This day Clayton was scheduled to appear before the juvenile judge to determine the best solution for his legal guardianship and residency during the next few months until his eighteenth birthday. No more than a month prior, Clayton was ordered by the courts to stay with his grandparents at their residence a few miles out of town, but in reality, he had been living at home with Colton. Collectively, the family sat down and worked out an acceptable living arrangement for the boys as they gradually reassembled the pieces of their splintered lives in the weeks following their father's funeral. Clayton would call and check-in with his grandparents on the weekends and on weekdays would drive out to see them after school. He would do some homework and they ate supper together. The family had developed a safe routine whereby they spent adequate time supporting one another, yet had the freedom and privacy each of them needed while they made the personal adjustments to the new family paradigm.

That was until the case worker from the County Children's Services Board made an unannounced visit to see Clayton at Mr. and Mrs. Brown's farm early one Saturday morning. After exchanging pleasantries and acknowledging the suitability of the surroundings, the woman pressed Clayton's elderly grandmother regarding her grandson's whereabouts.

"So where is he this early on a Saturday morning?" she asked Mrs. Brown.

"He's out with his brother," the old woman answered. "They had some errands to run."

"When do you expect him home?" the case worker continued.

"I'm not exactly sure," the boy's grandmother answered. "You know how young people are these days. They don't always account for themselves."

"Does he have to work today?"

"No, he's not working at the sandwich shop, anymore," she replied.

"Oh, when did he quit his job?" the CSB worker asked while writing copious notes on a yellow legal pad.

"I guess it's been a few weeks since he had a falling out with the owner," Clayton's grandmother admitted.

"So he got fired," the worker clarified.

"Well, yes," she said slowly.

"Well, I'll be back a little later because I need to see Clayton and speak to him for my report," the woman added as she made her way to the front door. "Thank you Mrs. Brown."

"Oh you're welcome," she answered. "Miss, Clayton is a tormented soul; please give him time to open his heart so God can help him heal."

When the social worker left, Mrs. Brown sat down wearily in a soft chair near the television. She held her shaking head with her hand. She was doing her best to shore-up the family in this time of need but the lasting effects of her stroke made it difficult to fill the role of a parent in her grandson's life. Clare called out to her husband to call the boys and have Clayton come over to their house as soon as possible.

They had no idea where Clayton was or what he was doing and neither did his brother.

"I don't know where he is, grandpa," Colton said as he walked around the empty house for clues. "His jeep is gone and so is he."

So when the case worker returned two more times that day and even stopped at the Caldwell house, Clayton was nowhere to be found. He had packed the eleven odd cans of beer he found in the refrigerator into a brown paper bag and had taken a long, solitary drive out past the abandoned church on the hill with a remarkable, old cemetery. He and his friends would wander the grounds reading the headstones for glimpses into the history of the area. A half-mile further down the road was one of his favorite places to be alone and think, The Grand Reservoir. At a bait shop near the park side of the water, he stopped and bought some chips and cheese. For hours he sat in the car, sometimes starting the engine for some heat, but also walked along the rocky shore skipping rocks across the swirling texture of the grey water. In the late afternoon, a park ranger found him asleep in the vehicle surrounded by empty beer cans. Despite the calm approach of the officer, Clayton reacted with confusion and ill-tempered language, nearly causing the confrontation to end up in a physical altercation. Eventually the boy's mood quieted and he became sullen and depressed. The ranger had the jeep towed and drove the young man back to his grandparent's home, informing them all he would have to file a report of the incident the following Monday.

As Clayton finished dressing and attempted to finish tying a knot so the tie's length finished at his belt buckle, he looked at the small black-and-white photograph of his parents that sat graying on his dresser in the homemade oak picture frame his grandfather helped him make many years ago. How young and happy his parents both seemed with their hands on the boys' shoulders as they stood in front of their parents, both boys only half the height of their father. He knew time changed everything but he wished he could stop it for a while, or at least slow it down.

Judge Janet Drokin presided over the hearing. Attorney Morris informed the judge of the family's litany of difficulties and asked for an extension of Judge Stevenson's ruling that placed Clayton in the temporary custody of his maternal grandparents. Following testimony

from the CSB case worker, the judge interviewed each of the grandparents as well as Colton. The hearing had lasted well over an hour
when the judge announced a twenty minute recess. Everyone was
excused to the wide hallway outside of the court room. Clayton
looked around at the other people in the building. All of the people
looked poor and disillusioned, and most of them were black. Clayton
didn't realize any black people lived in Low Field County. A man
who worked for the judge called the attorney and the agency's social
worker into her office to discuss the case. A half hour later, everyone
was instructed to return to the small courtroom for the resumption
of the hearing.

Clayton sat next to Attorney Morris at a small metal table in front
of the elevated judge's stand. A bored, pudgy police officer stood
nearby with his back to the wall. Everyone waited in silence as the
judge patiently read through the papers in front of her, occasionally
jotting notes to herself on a pad. Finally she took off her reading
glasses and looked directly at Clayton.

"Clayton, let me start out by saying that I am extremely sorry to
have learned about your recent losses. The situation is unthinkable
to me. Every young person needs the unconditional love and support of his parents and it's not fair that you and your brother must go
through the remaining years of your lives without them. In my work
I see and hear of family situations that keep me awake and make it impossible for me to sleep. I know you will be on my mind tonight. My
heart hurts for the young people who come to this court and for those
family members who love them. It's important for you to know that
I carefully consider all of the information that's presented in court
from both sides before I make a decision regarding a young person's
life. I'm the kind of person who looks for a silver lining in every situation. I guess I'm an optimist. In your situation you are fortunate
to have grandparents who love you and are willing to care for you in
your parents' absence. You are also lucky to have an older brother.
Unfortunately, your grandparents have some health problems of their

own and they are at an age that makes it very difficult to be effective parents for a seventeen year old boy. Colton is also willing to assume the responsibility of looking out for you, but he, too, has a significant medical issue that he's trying to overcome and his situation is also compromised by the serious legal issues he's confronting. Before I tell you what I'm thinking, I was wondering if you would like to say anything, Clayton," she asked.

The boy looked at his attorney who nodded and motioned for Clayton to stand and tell the judge what he was thinking.

"Your honor, Mrs. Drokin, my brother and I have lived in the same house our whole lives. Sure, it's different there now without my mom and dad, but I have Colton and we have a lot of happy memories there. I'd like to stay there with him for the next few months. I promise you that I will go to school and I'll see my grandma and grandpa as often as you want me to. Thank you."

He sat down and the judge put her glasses back on and wrote more notes on the legal pad. After a few minutes, she put the pen and glasses on the folder in front of her and said, "Clayton, I know you will turn eighteen in a short time and then you will legally be an adult. At that time, you will be free to make your own decisions about your future, and I'm hope you allow your brother and your grandparents to play a significant role in helping you formulate a life plan that will provide you with happiness and prosperity. But in the meantime, I believe you need some help. You need the support of a family that can support you and help you get through your troubles for the next few months."

Before she stated her ruling it seemed to Clayton that she experienced a robotic personality transformation right before his eyes and became a different person than the one who just minutes before had been speaking to him like a caring human being.

The judge said, "The state awards temporary custody of Clayton Caldwell to the Low Field County Children's Services Board for placement with a foster family until his eighteenth birthday. The transfer of custody from the grandparents to the foster parents will occur as soon as an appropriate family is located by the case worker. Thank you all."

She stood up and walked directly into her office without saying another word. Clayton, Colton and their grandparents were stunned by the unforeseen decision. Clayton turned red with emotion. Suddenly he slammed the table with an open hand and yelled, "No, I won't go." The large attorney put his arm across the boy's chest pinning his arms from further actions. The police officer hastily approached the table ready to intervene.

"That's not going to help our situation, Clayton," the attorney said calmly.

"I don't care, I'm not going to live with strangers," Clayton said loudly. "That's never going to happen. I don't care what that judge says, I'm not going."

"Let's just take a walk outside," the attorney said motioning for Colton to help with Clayton.

"Come on Clay," Colton said grabbing one of his brother's arms. "Let's get out of here."

After he calmed down, the family drove back to Mr. and Mrs. Brown's house and had dinner. The conversation was sparse. They all knew Clayton was in no mood to hear words of consolation and nothing they could say would change how he felt about the judge's ruling. Their opinions were better left unsaid. He and Colton drove home after dessert. The unlit area darkened the night air to a deep black. Inside Colton's truck, Clayton turned on the radio with the volume uncomfortably loud to stifle Colton from talking. He slammed every door on the way from the vehicle and into his room. Colton turned on the television and gave his brother the privacy to deal with yet another blow.

At 3:00 AM the next morning, Clayton crept out of the house dressed entirely in black. He pulled the hoody over his head and walked to the barn. In the darkness he felt along the workbench and found a pair of work gloves. He picked up the box and walked through the neighbors' back yards and woods toward town.   There were no cars on the road. The crossroads were as quiet as a morgue. Without making a sound he slipped along garages and the backs of businesses until he arrived at the Jerry's Sandwich Shop. Along the front walk and the recessed entrance to the main door, he spread the dead rats he had collected from the barn the week before. They were frozen hard like small animal pelts with long, stringy tails. Once he was certain they would illicit the response he hoped for by passersby in the morning, he took the box to the side of the parking lot and knelt down beside the blood red Clothing Donations box that sat beside Jerry's storage garage. Clayton dipped each of the rags into the jar of gasoline one by one and then tossed them through the square opening into the four corners of the wooden box. He lit the last one with his lighter and tossed it along with the cardboard box and the lighter into the donation bin. As the fire expanded from one rag to another inside the box, there was a rapid succession of fiery explosions.   By the time Clayton had run a few hundred yards away and looked back, the entire box was engulfed by bright flames and sparks bursting through the roof. He was breathing hard from running back to his house through the uneven terrain of the woods, so he waited outside by the barn to catch his breath. He leaned against the small, rusting corn crib that had settled over the years against the back corner of the barn.   Within a few minutes his breathing returned to normal and he quietly reentered the house and sneaked up to his room. From the window he could see the glow from the fire that now included Jerry's storage building lighting the distant sky. When he got back in bed, he could hear the faint sound of the siren calling the volunteer fire department. He thought to himself, enough is enough; it's time for me to take control of my own destiny.

93

SINCE THE SPECIAL board meeting with Dr. Reed of the Fiscal Oversight Commission, a majority of Jim's Collins time had been consumed meeting with the district administrative team, union representatives and officials from the county Board of Education. Strategies were identified, developed and proposed to meet the mandate coming down from the commission to drastically reduce operating expenses for the remainder of the current school campaign as well as the upcoming school year. Ideas such as the elimination of non-essential programs and services, consolidation of programs with neighboring districts, delivering educational opportunities to students through cooperative county programs and less expensive electronic instruction were all suggested to the superintendent. Although some made sense and would save money over time, few could be implemented immediately and collectively would only offset a fraction of the district's soaring debt.

The Low Field Local Schools had received two loan advances from the state that were used to fund the daily operation of the district during the last eighteen months while the emergency levy was being repeatedly defeated by the voters. Currently, the mounting legal fees and possible judgments against the district, coupled with a precipitous decline in student enrollment further reducing state funding, subjected the treasurer to finance the district's ventures on a week-by-week basis, oftentimes through creative manipulation of line items in the budget. Because the school's primary mission was to provide services to students through staff members, the majority of a school district's expenses were directly tied to personnel costs. The only way to significantly close the gap between revenues and expenses was to reduce the number of employees who were being paid by the district. The hard decisions needed to be made and the choice to aggressively cut staff was being overseen and extolled by Dr. Reed from her auxiliary office inside the board room.

Jim developed a two-phase plan to address the deficit. Part one was scheduled to be implemented in January immediately following the holiday break. All student transportation, athletic programs and extra-curricular activities would be suspended, food services would be reduced to satisfy only the minimum requirements of federally funded programs and maintenance and custodial services would be outsourced to private firms. Furthermore, the kindergarten classes would be converted to half-day programs at the beginning of the second semester and several other classes and course offerings would also be eliminated at that time requiring an immediate reduction-in-force. Part two of the plan dealt with the necessary decreases in programs, curricular offerings and staff for the next school year. The two layers combined had a devastating effect on the educational opportunities the district could offer its students. No parent would be satisfied with the recommendation or the long-term results.

As Jim and L J were developing the draft of the board agenda, he sensed that next week's special board meeting would likely rank near the top of the list for the worst public fiascos he would be required to direct during his tenure as superintendent of schools. Once finalized, these advanced copies of the agenda were sent to all of the board members as well as the union presidents of both employee groups the weekend before the special board meeting. Although both unions were aware of the Oversight Commission's requirements and tactics through reports of its dealings with other unfortunate districts across the state, they were blindsided by the magnitude of the recommendations contained in the agenda. They had anticipated some negative adjustments and lay-offs in the coming months, but neither expected the swift and pervasive actions being proposed by the superintendent for board action the following week. They assumed the next step would only involve tactics designed to gain leverage and sway the community to finally approve the renewal of the levy in the February special election, not the full-bodied assault on their memberships that was contained in this proposal. The reach and scope of the cuts made it impossible for them to accept the recommendations without launching a momentous and hostile challenge at the board meeting.

John called the superintendent Saturday morning on his cell phone after he opened and read the copy of the agenda he received in the mail.

"Good morning, John," Jim said answering the phone while watching the school's fifth grade basketball team compete in a local weekend tournament.

"Hey Jim," the board president responded. "I just read through the agenda. Do we really have to go this far right now to satisfy the commission? I mean, the consequences are terrible."

"Yeah, we didn't have a choice John," he responded. "Dr. Reed, Zack and I analyzed the options and she was unrelenting until we reached certain thresholds of savings."

"I don't think this will help us pass the levy," he said, "and, furthermore, if the levy fails and these changes become permanent, they will decimate the district for the future. I mean, if we lose again in February, who in their right mind will want to live here?"

"Only people who don't need or value the schools," Jim replied soberly.

"We've got to find a compromising position with her," John suggested.

"I tried John. She wouldn't budge," Jim explained. "Our backs are against the wall and we've got no option other than to do what she says. The commission basically wields omnipotent power and authority. Until we resolve this money issue, we are all just straw figureheads forced to carry out their demands."

"Well then, why doesn't she stand up in front of the unions and angry mob and tell them what she's making us do," he suggested rhetorically.

"I've discovered that's the beauty of her position; she tells me what I have to recommend and then tells the board what they have to approve, all from backstage and shielded from the angry horde," he said. "The only advantage to us is that we can blame all of our decisions on the Commission."

"It's not fair that we're still out there on the front line defending and taking the fallout for her decisions," he complained.

"John, after spending the better part of the past two weeks with her, all I can say is we have to get used to it." Jim said. "She's persistent and ruthless and she's not going away any time soon. We are going to experience more strife and heartache than any of us ever anticipated while we're in this situation. She's got a job to do, and unfortunately, she's going to do it."

"I've never felt so helpless in my life," John said.

"There's a new captain at the helm and all I see is troubled water ahead," Jim said.

94

THE NIGHT OF the meeting, all of the board members made it a point to arrive early, getting in ahead of the crowd. A few minutes before the scheduled starting time for the meeting, Zack left the board office and walked up to the library to see how many people were in attendance. He returned to the office shaking his head.

"Well, how bad is it?" someone asked him.

"Bad, real bad," Zack replied.

"Who's up there?" Jim asked Zack.

"For starters, every employee in the district and their crazy families," Zack said, "the union field reps and I'd guess about three hundred other people. It's already standing room only with people out in the hallway."

As the starting time approached, the seven people steadied themselves for the difficult mob they were about to confront.

"Stick together," one advised.

"Say as little as possible," suggested another.

"I agree. When you do have to say something, keep it brief. We don't want to load the bullets in the gun," Jim said, surprised at his poor choice of words, "to use a bad analogy."

"Speaking of which, how many people up there do you suppose are carrying weapons?" a board member asked.

"I hope none of them," John answered. "Did we post those signs yet, Jim?"

"Yes, but that's a good point Sharon makes," he said. "I don't know how a concealed carry permit applies to this setting."

"Well it's a meeting on school property and guns are forbidden, right?" one of them asked.

"You're probably right but I don't know for sure," Jim admitted. "That battle is probably best left for another night."

"I agree," the board president said.

"Let's just try to not piss them off so much that they start shooting at us," another said with a smile.

"Well, let's go get this over with," Jim said looking at his watch. "Everyone ready?"

"Yeah."

"Alright let's go."

The board members kept their faces pointed forward as they walked past the overflow crowd toward the long tables at the front of the room. They sat behind their corresponding name plates. John asked the crowd to stand for the Pledge of Allegiance and Zack performed roll call. Jim presented a concise synopsis of the Fiscal Oversight Commission's role and functions now that the district had been officially labeled by the State Department of Education in *Financial Crisis* and then asked Zack to update the board and community regarding the monetary status of the district in his Treasurer's Report. Again, Jim was called on by the board president, this time to present an overview of his fiscal savings plan that had been ordered by the commission. He detailed the strategy with the aid of a power point presentation; his remarks were brief and matter-of-fact. Each time he called up a new slide outlining the specific aspects of the cuts, an undercurrent of groans and side conversations ensued within the crowd. On several occasions people from the hallway or far corner of the room called out, "Speak up" or "We can't hear you." He concluded his remarks to an ovation of boo's. Before the board voted on the recommendations, John opened the meeting to comments from the public. The room was tense and full of raw emotion.

Keith Byler hurried to the microphone, eager to make the first comment and establish the adversarial perspective for the teachers. He said, "Mr. Fitzpatrick, with all respect to you and the other board members, I see nothing on the agenda about administrative cuts. If the commission is now in charge of the district, I propose you start the personnel reduction-in-force with the superintendent. He's responsible for the mess we're in, and since the state is now in charge, I don't see where we need him anymore. Our problems have just grown and grown and grown with this guy. That will save a hundred and fifty thousand dollars right off the top and allow you to maintain the jobs of some of the people in this room who provide direct services to our kids."

There was a thunderous applause as Keith stepped away from the microphone. The classified staff's union president, Shawna Hastings, was next in line to comment. "Almost all of the people in this room live and pay taxes in Low Field. The employees of this school district get up and come to work every day and do their best to help our children grow and develop into the next generation of adults in this community. These people deserve an explanation from you all," she said pointing at the board. "We want to know how the mismanagement of this district is allowed to persist without the superintendent getting fired and none of you being impeached. I know by law we have to have a superintendent but why don't you just make one of the principals the superintendent and keep these dedicated people working with our students?"

Again, her comments were followed by a rousing applause and cheers of approval. John instinctively allowed his inclination to debate her suggestion.

"Well the superintendent has a contract that we are obligated to honor, so even if we made that cut we'd have to pay him anyway," he countered.

"Wait a minute," Keith said loudly returning to the microphone, "that's not true. If the commission says you need to save money by cutting personnel, he's included in that mix as well as the rest of us."

"We have obligations to all of our employees, who all work under contracts with the board," John said.

Jim hastily scribbled a brief note on a paper and slid it toward the board president who was seated next to him. It said, *Don't argue.*

Keith sternly persisted, "Teachers provide direct services to students, one on one. That is the fundamental relationship in education—a student, a book and a teacher," he said loudly. "Cut the other stuff first."

John read it and said, "Next comment."

The crowd again sounded its vociferous displeasure with the board president before allowing the series of public comments to finally resume. For the next hour, speaker after speaker made repetitive comments regarding the negative effect the cuts would have on the children of Low Field as well as property values, community pride and the reputation of the school district. The stress of the situation was nearly unbearable for several of the board members who never imagined such turmoil when they agreed to help the schools by running for a seat on the board of education.

"Two more comments," John said.

Keith and Shawna stood and made their way back to the microphone. The remaining people in line to speak allowed the two union presidents to make the final remarks.

Shawna unfolded several pieces of paper and held them up before she said, "Mr. Fitzpatrick this is for you and the board. This is a letter signed by every member of the Low Field Schools Classified Employees Union stating our position in support of the teachers' union. We hope you reconsider cutting any staff members tonight except for the superintendent, the principals or the supervisors." She ceremoniously walked forward and handed the paper to John. She turned and raised her arms in the air with clenched fists.

"Solidarity," she screamed.

A thunderous response of cheers and clapping shook the room. When the ovation subsided, Keith stepped up to the microphone and repeated the same actions as his predecessor.

He held several folded pieces of paper in the air and said, "Mr. Fitzpatrick, the Low Field Educators Association hereby serves you with this Intent to Strike Notice that starts in five days." The applause was deafening as he stepped forward and snapped the papers to John Fitzpatrick's outstretched hand.

The board president tried to regain control of the meeting for the board vote on proposed agenda items. One of the board members raised his hand with a question before John could ask for a vote.

"Yes, Mr. Hicks," John said acknowledging the board member's request.

"Mr. Fitzpatrick, and my respected colleagues on the board, it is with regret that I would like to announce my resignation for the Low Field Board of Education, effective immediately," the man said passing a letter down the table to the president.

A loud murmur rippled across the library.

Then the board member seated next to Mr. Hicks stood and said, "Mr. Fitzpatrick, I, too, would like to tender my immediate resignation from the board at this time." He passed a previously prepared letter of resignation down the line of board members to the president.

John was stunned by the unprecedented and unexpected chain of events. The crowd was abuzz and many people cheered for the two board members interpreting their resignations as support for the employee groups. John leaned over to Jim and Zack and asked them what to do.

"I think it's just like abstaining from a vote; if the board accepts their resignations, you still have three voting members until the vacated seats are filled," Zack said.

Jim replied, "You need a motion to accept the resignations and then call for a vote on that before you can vote on the rest of the consent agenda."

"I need a motion to accept the resignation of Mr. Hicks and Mr. Cassidy from the board of education," John said.

"So moved," replied the board member seated next to John.

"Second," the other board member said.

"Mrs. Thompson," John said to Zack.

"All in favor," Zack said.

"Aye," was the response from the remaining members of the board of education.

Mr. Hicks and Mr. Cassidy got up from their seats, and as they passed by the front of the board tables, shook the hands of the three remaining members who gave them quizzical looks. Their actions were accompanied by a stout applause and cheers of support from the capacity crowd. Mr. Fitzpatrick then called for a vote on the main proposal and the primary purpose of the special meeting. As he did so, the roll call was drowned out by the deliberate, noisy departure of the crowd. John's appeal for everyone to remain seated until the meeting was officially adjourned was met with indifference and defiance. The crowd ignored the final action of the board with an effective strategy of insolence, knowing the board would approve the recommendations in spite of their efforts of the past few hours but refusing to respectfully acknowledge the board's vote.

When the three board members, Jim and Zack finally pushed their way through the exiting crowd and returned to the board office, John removed his sport coat and slammed in on the back of his usual chair at the table.

"I can't believe those guys," he said referring to the unexpected resignations of the two board members. "I never saw that coming; did any of you?"

"No," Mrs. Thompson said. "They never hinted at that for a moment that I can remember or said anything to suggest they weren't in this for the long haul, through thick and thin."

"Yeah, I'm as shocked as you are," Jim said. "Someone must have gotten to them."

"Well the problems just keep piling up," Zack said.

There was a quiet moment in the room as everyone sat down and attempted to process the ramifications of the meeting.

Finally, Jim sat up straight in his chair and said to the remaining three board members, "John, you know what I've always said. All you have to do is ask and you'll have my resignation the next day."

"No, I know they came down pretty hard on you up there," the board president said, "but we need you more than ever to get us through this mess."

"Thanks, but think about it," Jim continued. "Sometimes the top person has to go in order for the healing to begin."

"I appreciate the offer, Jim," John said, "but I'm afraid we're a long way from any healing."

"Wow, what a mess," Zack reiterated shaking his head. "What a freaking mess."

95

T HE FIRST DAY of the Low Field teachers' strike established new low points for both the history of the school district and Jim Collins' career. At 4:45 AM he drove into the back of the elementary school parking lot. No one was out in the still darkness of the early December morning but he and the maintenance supervisor, who arrived at nearly the same time.

"Hey Rock," Jim said to the man.

"Mornin' boss," Rocky said.

"Thanks for coming in so early. Please get this building up and running and then go up to the high school and do the same," Jim said. "After that, just plan on staying there because the teachers probably won't be very friendly if you try to cross the picket lines."

"Okay, wait here," the maintenance supervisor said unlocking the door. With his hand, Rocky felt his way along the dark corridor until he found the light switch high on a pillar near the cafeteria.

"My goodness, I never noticed that switch was hidden up there," Jim said.

"I guess it was designed to be out of reach for the students," Rocky explained. "I'll check everything and then stop by your office to see if you need anything else before I go up to the high school. Or, just give me a call if you need anything today."

"Thanks Rock," Jim said.

In his office Jim looked out the front window at the empty street in front of the school. Three plain white work vans pulled into the lot in quick succession.   A dozen private security workers from the firm Jim hired to keep the peace during the strike burst from the vehicles all dressed in dark military-style jump suits.   They set up tripods with video cameras and pointed them directly at the ends of the driveways where buses and cars would challenge the impediments set up by the strikers. The leader of the security force came down the sidewalk waving at Jim.

"Good morning. How are you doing sir," he asked the superintendent.

"As good as could be expected," Jim answered.

"Everything will be fine," the man said. "I've done this hundreds of times. We know what to expect and we're prepared for it."

"Okay, I'm counting on you to keep the kids safe," Jim said.

"Yep, they're our number one mission," the man said. "We've just got to get them in and out safely. As long as your bus drivers don't balk at crossing the lines, we'll be fine."

Outside the first school bus was entering the driveway.

"There are your teachers," said the security team leader pointing at the bus.

"Really? Why so early?" Jim asked.

"It's easier to get them in before the picket lines get developed, so we put it in their contract that the day starts at 5:30 AM," he said.

"Good because I've placed all of my trust in your assurance that we could open the schools without problems during the strike," Jim said.

"It will be fine," the man said without hesitation. "You better go greet the subs."

A few hours went quickly as the principals arrived at work as well as the few classified workers who chose not to report off because of illness. By 7:00 the driveway entrances and exits at the road were clogged by striking teachers and their supporters, many seated in lawn chairs in preparation for the long, tense day.   They held signs and yelled through megaphones at passing cars to sound their horns in support of their work stoppage.

When the first bus load of frightened students approached the driveway, the strikers refused to move out of the way. The security firm closed in with their video recorders as did several parents who chose to also capture the events on film for various reasons. The bus was showered with lobbed tomatoes and eggs and several teachers moved to either side of the bus and pushed, rocking it back and forth, and eliciting screams from the terrified children. Unfortunately, they were seeing a different side of their teachers. Slowly the scared, yet determined driver, eased the bus through the picket line and then drove to the rear of the school. Jim greeted the anxious students and assured them everything would be fine as he walked with the group to the cafeteria.

Many parents, who chose to drive their children to school that morning, simply turned their cars around when they were challenged by the teachers at the picket line, determining the possible ramifications of the encounter outweighed the benefits of attending classes. Others, however, converged on the teachers with stubborn aggression. One young father screamed at them to get out his way as he made the turn into the driveway without reducing the speed of his car. A tragedy was narrowly avoided when a teacher who pretended to be tying his shoe leaped out of the way a split second before being run over by the charging minivan. Jim walked around the cafeteria attempting to converse with the young students who had followed his directives and had come to school in spite of the strike.

"Our schools will be open tomorrow with substitute teachers," he recalled watching himself say on the late night news the evening before.

Now as he walked around the cafeteria and saw the pale, frightened looks on the young students' faces, he wondered if his determination to remain in session was the best decision. He sat next to a small girl whose bright, pink backpack was almost as large as she.

"Hi, I'm Mr. Collins," he said quietly. "What's your name?"

She stared straight ahead and didn't speak.

"Are you okay?" he asked gently.

Her eyes bounced up and down and briefly in his direction.

He leaned sideways toward her and said softly, "Thank you for coming to school today."

He got up and left her alone with her young thoughts. Throughout the day, the image of the frightened little girl haunted Jim. The children were unfairly caught in the middle of a fight between adults and organizations. Today the strike was about control, power, money and jobs, and not about the students or their education. They were unwitting pawns in the struggle for balance between labor and management, employees and employer. Ultimately, the strike would both save the district and improve future educational experiences for students or it would hasten the further tailspin of the district toward its abolishment.

That afternoon, the superintendent received a fax from the State Employment Relations Board announcing the filing of an Unfair Labor Practice by the teachers who claimed Jim had breached their contract by operating the schools with substitute workers in their positions. Jim's chest hurt. He walked down the hall to the men's restroom and splashed water on his face. In the mirror's reflection, he saw the deep wrinkles and worry lines in his aging face surrounded by the grey hair he'd earned during his years at Low Field. He leaned against the wall drying his hands with a coarse paper towel, closed his eyes and breathed deeply. He rubbed his chest and thought about his family. His deliberations drifted as he looked deep into his heart and soul for answers to questions he had yet to formulate. The sheer accumulation of internal and external conflicts he lived with every day were taking a toll on his health and he wondered if he still wanted his job. He had offered his resignation but he knew John was right when he responded that leaving now would not help the district.

Jim rubbed his eyes and face with his hands and again looked at his haggard image in the mirror. This time he saw the semblance of his father and his grandfather. The genetic similarities among the generations of men became more convergent and overlapping with each year. He thought of the struggles they endured in their lives and their hopes for him. A sudden calmness filled him with new-found inner strength. He lifted his chin and thought of his grandfather's simple faith and personal courage and his father's quiet perseverance to live a normal life and his dedication to fatherhood. Both followed their hearts. Their journeys were inspiring and it took this moment of reflection to recall the contributions they had made to his life. Jim spent the remainder of the day making sure the students were okay.

The second day of the strike was considerably calmer than the first because of the temporary restraining order a judge had placed on the teachers which mandated they move their picket lines at least fifty feet from any school egress. The school's attorney had asked for the injunction early the first day of the strike and the judge responded before leaving the courthouse that afternoon. This action swung the leverage of the confrontation away from the teachers. Now the security firm's videos showed cars and buses moving freely in and out of the school properties without the same teacher provocations of the first day. Attendance improved to fifty percent following a dismal 30 percent on the initial day. After lunch, Jim received a surprising call from Keith Byler.

"Jim, can I buy you a cup of coffee?" Keith asked with ungraceful cleverness.

"What? Keith, what do you want? I'm busy." Jim said directly.

"A meeting, as soon as you are willing to meet with me," the union president said. "I'd like to discuss ending the strike."

"Okay, sure, but just you and me alone," Jim mandated. "Do you want to meet at the pavilion in the township park in an hour?"

"That's good, see you then," Keith said.

The security firm transported Jim wherever he needed to go during the day so he could safely get past the striking teachers. The van was peppered with eggs as the driver slowly proceeded past the picketers. A second security worker, who sat in the front passenger seat inside the van, filmed the irate teachers who swore and shook their fists at the superintendent. Jim was astonished to see the expressions of deep hatred on their faces. On their way to the park, Jim reminded himself that Keith could not be trusted. Too many times he had promised one thing and done something different. Additionally, over the years of Jim's delicate and important interactions with the union, Keith had a history of miscalculations and oversights regarding the community or issues facing the district. Jim had been stung by the union president once too often.

"I thought you said alone," Keith said when Jim stepped out of the side of the van.

"I am, and no tape recorders Keith," Jim said as he walked from the van to the pavilion.

"I don't own one," Keith responded.

"Okay, what's your idea?" Jim asked.

"In a nutshell, we will come back to work tomorrow and end the strike if you agree to hold the lay-offs until after the February election," Keith proposed.

"I can't do that. The commission won't allow it and the board already took action on that resolution," Jim said. "I'm surprised you don't remember that. I remember you and your lynch mob demanding that I be fired."

"Let me talk to that commission chairwoman," Keith said.

"She won't talk to you; you're the opposition," Jim replied. "She and the state commission think you and your union are the problem in Low Field."

"Every district has unions," Keith said. "We just want our fair share."

"Maybe the community is telling us that it's too much for the district to survive," Jim said.

"We're not going anywhere," Keith said arrogantly.

"One of her plans is to cut the district into pie shaped pieces and send our kids to the surrounding districts," Jim explained.

"Well, they're stupider that I thought," Keith said pausing to think of an alternative suggestion. "Then I don't know what to say, but this strike isn't helping either one of us."

"I agree with that," Jim said sensing Keith's suggestions were prompted by a waning enthusiasm for the strike by the teachers. "Look Keith, it's taken me a few weeks to get used to this idea, but basically the whole situation is now out of our control. The state is running the district and we can't get them out of here until we get the community to pass a damn levy."

"So we just throw-up our hands and take their crap?" asked Keith.

"I don't know. Yesterday and today I think we hit rock bottom and the way I see it, there's nowhere to go but up. But it's going to take a while," Jim cautioned. "I think the people in this community have enjoyed seeing the pissing match that's been going on between us and until we stop fighting and start doing what we're supposed to be doing, it will never change."

Keith walked around in a small circle, looking at the sky.

"I'll tell you what, I want three things," Keith offered, desperate for a compromise. "First you make passing the levy your number one and sole priority for the next six weeks; I mean mailings, talking to folks at The Diner and churches, doing interviews with the media, organizing your people to work, everything you can think of to get us over the hump. Second you try to stall the staffing cuts until after the election and third you take a voluntary pay cut."

Jim looked firmly at Keith and countered, "I'll tell you what, drop the ULP, end the strike today and come back to work tomorrow and for the next six weeks I'll do everything in my power to get that levy passed. I'll also do whatever I can to hold off the reduction-in-force until after the election and I'll offer to take a pay freeze in my next contract, but no pay cut now."

Keith paused and then said, "Deal."

"Deal," Jim said as they shook hands in good faith. "Teachers report at 7:15 tomorrow."

"Yeah, we know what time school starts," Keith said.

"Well, yesterday I couldn't help but notice that you were late to your own strike," Jim retorted as he climbed back into the van.

"Jerk," Keith called.

96

DARON AND BRENDA sat at the small table in their kitchen eating scrambled eggs mixed with diced onion and green peppers. Sausage links, wheat toast with jelly and coffee rounded out the hearty breakfast meal.

"Do you want more?" she asked her son. "There're some eggs left."

"Sure, this is really good and I'm still hungry," he said.

"You've got the appetite of a man," she said laughing.

"So mom, what do you want to do for your birthday tomorrow?" Daron asked. "Go shopping or go the movies?"

"Oh, I don't know," she said, "I'm thinking something different this year but I don't know if you'll like my idea."

"It's your birthday; we're supposed to do something special for you, not me," he said. "I'm good with whatever you want to do."

"Really?" she asked.

"Sure, I mean there's not that much to do around here on a Sunday," he said, "so, yes, it's your choice."

"Okay. This might sound like a funny request, but since my birthday is on a Sunday this year, I'd really like to go to church," she said.

"Church! We haven't been to church since we moved to Low Field," he said surprised by her birthday wish.

"I know, but I want to go to church back at St. Christine's, where my family attended every Sunday while I was growing up and where your dad and I were married and where you were baptized," she said.

"That's fine with me," Daron said now committed to honoring her request. "I don't know if my suit still fits though. Why do you want to go to church all of a sudden?"

"Well, I've been thinking about it for quite a while. We are both facing some very important decisions about the future and I remember how I used to gain strength and clarity from being in church when I was a younger person," she said. "I feel like both of us might benefit from some divine intervention right now."

"You're right, as usual," Daron agreed. "As I get closer to being finished with school, I'm totally conflicted as to what to do next. I realize I'm coming up on a very important life decision, but the choices just seem to be spinning; and, the more I think about the options, I just get more confused. No one idea seems to jump out as the right pursuit."

"That's exactly the way I feel too," his mother said. "My heart is telling me that we should move away from Low Field, but in my mind I don't see a clear path away from here."

"I know, honestly mom, I feel lost and trapped inside my own skin," Daron admitted. "Everything that's happened in the past few months has made me question everything about myself and my place in the world."

"Daron, you are a person of worth," she said. "At your age it's perfectly normal to worry about the future, and the decisions you make as a young adult will follow you for the rest of your life. When I look back, I realize there's a fine line in life between success and failure, happiness and sadness and the decisions you're facing will determine the direction of your life."

"Oh that makes me feel better," he said rolling his torso in exasperation. "How am I supposed to know what to do next?"

"That's why we're going to church tomorrow," she said with a smile.

"So is the priest going to reveal my future to me?" he asked.

"No. One of the biggest mysteries in life for all of us is what the future holds," she said, "and the only way to reveal your future is to live life fully; we all have to try new things and challenge ourselves to expand the richness of our lives."

"Oh God, how do you do that?" he asked.

"I think the events in our lives have ripples that carry meaning, and it's up to us to find that meaning," she said.

"What's that mean?" he asked.

"Well, for instance," she said thinking about his question, "remember when we lived in that furnished duplex with the piano and you used to take lessons?"

"Yeah."

"Well, I thought you had a real talent for music," his mother said. "But after the neighbor shot the other neighbor's dog and we had to move, you never asked about playing again."

"We didn't have a piano anymore," he said confused by her comment.

"My point is, your piano playing was natural and beautiful to me, but at the time, I thought that it wasn't as meaningful to you as it was to me, so I let it drop when you didn't ask about playing after we moved," she said. "Maybe I was wrong. But when I think about that now, I wonder if I had continued your lessons if it would have changed your life and opened a bright, new world for you."

"We'll never know now," he said.

"Why?" she asked. "I don't think it's ever too late to pursue a passion. I regret not doing certain things in my life but now I realize that was my fault for giving up on my dreams. Life constantly teaches us about ourselves but we have to be smart enough to learn the lessons. I believe things happen to us for a reason. If you still love music, we have to find a way for you to follow that path."

"I did really like playing the piano and I think I was pretty good at it," he said.

"You were very good," his mother said. "I had a teacher in high school—I can still remember her name, Sister Antonette—who told me that if you find a passion in life it's one of God's greatest gifts and you should do everything in your power to follow it."

"And in music, the color of my skin wouldn't matter," he said.

"Music is colorblind," said his mother with a smile. "It's one of those universal callings that come from the heart."

"I like that," he said.

"Honey, don't blame your future on your past. You have the free will to try anything and to become whoever you choose to become," she said. "There's a big world out there, and I hope you go out and see some of it."

"Mom, you're one of the smartest people I know," he said. "I'm so lucky to have you in my corner."

"I let life beat me down," she admitted. "I want something much better for you."

"So you think you made a mistake marrying dad?" he asked.

"No, that was not a mistake. I was true to my heart," she said. "Everyone makes mistakes, but we have to try things for ourselves in life as well as be smart enough to learn from others. No, marrying your father was not a mistake."

She got up from the table and cleared their dishes to the sink. On a return trip to the table she stopped behind her son, hugged his shoulders and kissed him on the side of his face.

"I love you and always will," she said.

He touched the side of her head with his hand and said, "me too."

The next morning they sat in the familiar pew Brenda's family had occupied for decades near the front of the church. She rubbed her hand along the oak bench and smiled, thinking back to the days when she sat between her parents, curious to understand the mystical teachings of the mass. She knew this morning somewhere in Ocala, Florida, her parents were seated in a similar pew listening to a similar homily from a similar priest. Consistency and tradition were a few of the hallmarks of the Catholic church and she smiled as Daron was able to instinctively follow the various parts of the service, reciting the prayers and responses without hesitation and knowing the correct times to stand, kneel and receive the blessings of communion.

This mass contained a requiem for the faithfully departed parishioners of the parish. Without hesitation, she grabbed her son's arm and led him to a side-alter to light an offering of a prayer candle in the memory of a loved one. Daron followed his mother's lead without saying a word.

When they returned to their pew and knelt for prayer, he leaned close to his praying mother and asked, "Who did we light a candle for?"

"Your father," she said. "Through his love, I now have you. I will always honor and cherish his memory."

She put a hand on his prayerful hands and squeezed them.

"I think it's time for us to leave Low Field," she said.

97

THE INTRUDER PREPAREDNESS Training Session, as Rafer referred to the exercise he was planning to conduct with the Low Field 20, was also scheduled for Sunday, a few tumultuous days after the teachers abruptly ended their two-day strike. Rafer's college semester concluded the week before so he had been planning for the educational activity every day, mapping the most dangerous locations including exits and entrance routes to discuss with the teachers, buying products he could use to simulate problematic changes to the environment and preparing his arsenal of ammunition and weapons to use in the drill. He had sent text messages to Keith, who had only responded to one because of the demands on his time caused by his union responsibilities. Keith informed Ray that the teachers planned on meeting him in the high school cafeteria at 2:00. The preliminary segment included receiving assault tactical training from Ray, followed by a live mock drill where Ray would simulate an invasion of the school and the teachers would rehearse a response to that threat. This was the portion of the afternoon that Keith wanted filmed for a possible promotional video about the LF 20.

In order for the video to appear realistic yet remain safe, Ray purchased three blank firing guns and a few boxes of matching 9mm blank firing ammunition for the teachers to use in the simulation exercise. He also purchased a pair of camera glasses he would wear to record his and the teachers' actions during the drill. That video could provide excellent insight for the teachers if they wanted to further advance their training at a subsequent event. Or they might splice the footage from the two videographers together for the final version of the promotional video. He bought a blank firing 9mm handgun and blank firing ammunition for himself as well. Lastly, Ray purchased a semi-automatic paint ball handgun that he intended to use for his primary assault weapon during the intruder simulation; the visual effects would be highly visible on the video. He sent Daron a text about the training session and invited his nephew to the school to witness the event. Unfortunately, he responded to his uncle, it was the same day of Brenda's birthday celebration and Daron knew his mom wanted to go out for Sunday dinner in her childhood neighborhood after church.

During the week, Ray made six home-made smoke bombs. He loaded them into his backpack with the other supplies he planned to use in the video. The old camouflage fatigues he wore in Iraq still fit him so he dressed from heel to toe like a soldier and headed to the school.

The teachers who made up the Low Field 20 were friendly to Rafer and he was impressed by how seriously they embraced their roles as first responders in the event of an attack on the school. For an hour he worked patiently with the teachers, nine women and eleven men, covering common defense strategies and techniques for combat situations. Most of the training was taken from his experience at basic training camp but he also touched on the most valuable combat skills he learned during his military deployments. He discussed situational awareness and teamwork. He enhanced what they had learned at the fish and game club regarding shooting from different positions as well as shooting at moving targets. All the people moved around the tables in the cafeteria taking cover and doing exercises designed to engage an active shooter. It was a consummate educational experience for the teachers who learned a great deal while being actively involved in the activities and having fun.

After a short break, they felt ready to film the video of the LF 20 team engaging and taking down a school intruder. The teachers were sent to a classroom.   Rafer pulled on a black ski mask, grabbed his back pack and moved to a secret location near a rear cargo entrance in the back of the cafeteria kitchen. He designed the exercise to start in a fashion similar to a game of hide and seek. The teachers were going about their normal routines in the classrooms when Ray entered a room near a stairway and quickly shot the teacher with a paint ball. The shot struck the unsuspecting male teacher in the chest spraying bright yellow paint on him and the chalkboard. The paint ball stung and caused a welt on the man. The teacher was surprised at the attack but was not injured. Rafer quickly put duct tape over the man's mouth and taped his hand together behind his back.

"You're dead," Ray said, "so you can't move or signal anyone with noises or a phone. Got it?"

The uncomfortable teacher nodded yes. From there Rafer quickly ran up the stairs and shot two teachers who were standing in the hallway talking. He accidentally hit the female teacher on the side of her head with a paint ball, and she screamed in pain as she sunk to the floor. Ray quickly taped them, but before he could move to a new location, another teacher bolted up the staircase with one of the blank guns. He was firing non-stop even though Ray had ducked around a far corner of the hallway. After the man emptied his clip, Ray calmly stepped into sight and shot the man in the mid-section with a paint ball, coloring his sweatshirt with a splatter of yellow paint that looked like the sun. Again, the stunned teacher was dumbfounded by the stinging of the paint ball shot and Ray quickly taped the man and ran down a different set of stairs. His next target was Keith Byler.

The union president had emerged from his room with a gun but Rafer easily shot the unsuspecting man in the back, causing him to groan loudly as he dropped his weapon and fell to his knees.

Ray taped him and whispered, "Sorry, you're dead, so just stay here and no phone calls."

Rafer climbed out a window onto the roof of a section of the first floor and climbed down using a downspout as a rope. He glanced through a window and saw six of the teachers having a heated discussion and pointing in different directions. They were planning their assault on the intruder. Ray grabbed three of his smoke bombs and crept to one of the outside doors, hidden by the half wall beneath the bank of windows lining the back wall of the cafeteria. He lit them, opened the door a small amount and tossed all three along the floor, tumbling inconsistently at the group. Dense smoke suddenly engulfed the cafeteria and he could hear the teachers coughing and yelling at each other. Three of them ran right at him through the rear doors of the cafeteria and he easily shot them all with the paint gun leaving them writhing in pain as he taped their mouths and hands.

He entered the cafeteria behind the shroud of smoke and moved quickly and quietly to one end of the large, open room. He took out two more smoke bombs and lit them. Accidentally, one burst open and sent a plume of fire rocketing into the air. The thin mesh window coverings exploding into flames and the fire quickly spread to the ceiling. The added smoke made the air in the room densely opaque and it was impossible to see more than a few inches. Ray now had a real emergency on his hands and started to panic and search for the other teachers who were likely to be overcome with smoke in the cafeteria. He had to find them and get them out of harm's way.

Eventually the sprinkler system activated showering the center of the room with a heavy dousing of water. The principal who had stopped by the school to complete some paperwork in his office was drawn by the noise and smoke to the chaotic scene. People were screaming the names of the other teachers while coughing and inadvertently knocking over chairs and tables trying to get out of the inferno. Ray could hear the loud sirens outside hailing the volunteer fire department to the school. The principal called the police station and reported the hostile encounter at the school. He grabbed his hidden Colt AR-15 from behind a bookcase and ran back to the cafeteria. Steve Daniels lined-up the weapon and braced himself against a corner section of the wall. He fired two shots at Rafer. The second shot struck the decorated Army Staff Sergeant in the leg knocking him off balance and crashing with a table to the floor. Smoke was billowing high in the room as the fire had now advanced across the ceiling and was burning every window covering around the open cafeteria.

Rafer didn't have a real weapon with him to defend himself from his unknown attacker. He ducked behind a table and fired four blanks in the direction of the principal who yelled in fear, "Take cover; he's got a gun!"

In his backpack, Ray found an elastic band and wrapped his wounded leg tightly with compression. He could hear the principal across the room talking to someone. The man's hands were shaking violently as he talked anxiously on the phone.

"I've got him pinned down, but I think he has a hostage," Steve said. "Okay, I'll wait."

The police sirens screamed loudly as they approached the building. They turned their cars as large shields and hid behind them with their guns drawn. There was a palpable silence while each person waited for the other to make a move. The fire had climbed up the side wall and was now burning the window coverings on the second floor. Steve ran out the front door of the school toward the police. He was holding his weapon with an outstretched arm high above his head.

He screamed, "Don't shoot; it's me, the principal."

Steve ran to one of the cars and knelt down behind a young, weekend officer.

"What the hell's going on in there?" the young patrolman asked.

"I'm not sure, I just stopped by the school and saw the fire and heard gun shots," he said, "but I recognize a bunch of our teachers' cars in the lot so this is real. I think I shot the guy."

"Is he alive?"

"I'm not sure," the principal said, "there was so much smoke I couldn't see very well, but after I took my shots, he took cover and fired back at me so I think he's alive, and he might have a hostage."

"Okay, well, I've been given my orders to wait until the Chief gets here," the officer said. "He's on his way."

Daron and Brenda were returning to Low Field when they heard the sirens. Several times Daron had to pull over to allow racing police cars and volunteer firefights to pass. As he approached the school and saw the wildly lit scene, he figured out the problem involved his uncle.

"Oh no, mom, this is really bad," Daron said.

"What are you talking about?" she asked with concern as she surveyed the fire and emergency vehicles across the front lawn of the school.

"I think its Uncle Ray," he said.

"What? Uncle Ray? I don't understand," she said looking at her son as if he was crazy.

"He sent me a text that he was training the Low Field 20 at the high school this afternoon and invited me to come and watch," Daron explained.

"Why didn't you say anything to me about this?" she asked.

"Because I told him we were going to Akron to celebrate your birthday," he said as he pulled his truck up aggressively near the crouching police officers.

"What are you doing?" one of the young deputies screamed at Daron.

"That's my uncle in there," Daron replied. "They were doing a training exercise and something must have gone wrong."

"Maybe or maybe not, but we're just waiting out here until the chief arrives," the man said.

"I think I shot him, Daron," the principal said.

"What? Why would you shoot him, you ass," Daron screamed.

"He had guns and torched the school," said Steve.

"I'm going in for him," Daron said. "He's a war hero. He wouldn't do anything that might get someone hurt."

"No you're not," said the officer. "Now you get back in your vehicle right now young man."

The man pushed Daron back toward his truck. He got in the driver's side and slammed the door.

"What's going on?" Brenda yelled at Daron.

He sat behind the steering wheel gritting his teeth together.

"Mom, get out of the truck," Daron said directly. "I've got to go in there and save Uncle Ray. The stupid principal thinks he shot him and he's going to die of smoke inhalation if we wait any longer."

She opened the door as her son started the engine. He backed the truck up and then pulled the gear shift down and sped toward the glass doors on the side of the cafeteria. His truck slammed into the steel and glass causing an explosion of diamond-like pieces of the breakaway safety-glass doors.

The boy jumped out of the truck and yelled, "Uncle Ray, Uncle Rafer where are you? It's Daron, Uncle Ray where are you?"

Daron stumbled through the smoke bumping into tables and knocking over chairs. He covered his nose and mouth with his hand as he looked for his uncle. Finally, he heard a man groaning and found his uncle nearly unconscious on the floor.

"Come on Uncle Ray," Daron said lifting up the man's arm and wrestling himself into position to help support his uncle's dead weight. "We've got to get you out of here."

The man had enough awareness and strength to cooperate with his nephew who helped him limp out of the building before they both collapsed in the grass. Two EMTs who had just arrived on the scene rushed to Rafer and Daron.

"I'm okay," Daron said to them. "Help him."

"Okay, we've got him now," one of the emergency workers said. "We've got him."

98

ONE WEEK BEFORE Christmas Day, the case worker from CSB called Clayton's grandparents to inform them that she had found a family in Plainview who were willing to serve as foster parents for their grandson. They were to meet one another on Thursday evening, and if everything went okay, Clayton would move into the host family's house on Saturday. Mr. and Mrs. Hoffman had two children of their own. The oldest, a daughter, was in her second year of college at The Ohio State University in Columbus and their son was a freshman at Plainview High School. They had heard about the Caldwell tragedies one Sunday in church. A friend suggested them as a possible host family to another member of the congregation who worked at the County Children's Services Board. When they were approached with the idea, they agreed without hesitation. Volunteering to help the Caldwell family in their time of need resonated with the Hoffmans' personal commitment to the church's mission. Helping others in need was simply the right thing to do.

On Thursday after Clayton got home from school, his grandmother told him to take a shower and put on the clean clothes she had laid out for him. He was sullen and withdrawn, as he had been since hearing the news, but complied with his grandmother's wishes and waited for the social worker, Mrs. Moreland, to pick him up. She, too, was invited for dinner at the Hoffmans' residence. Earlier in the week, a Low Field police officer had stopped at Clayton's grandparent's farm investigating leads regarding the fire and vandalism at

Jerry's Sandwich Shop.   Mrs. Brown confirmed both Clayton and Colton had stayed with them that night and neither boy could be involved in the destructive incident.   Sometimes life forces a person to tell a white lie, she thought, justifying her alibi.   Besides, Clayton's plate was already full of problems and there was no room for yet another one.   A time for reparations might come later, perhaps next summer.

The evening went fine from the perspective of the case worker.   The family tried very hard to welcome Clayton into their home and their hearts.   Mrs. Hoffman cooked a meal that was suited for a Thanksgiving feast and Mr. Hoffman proudly showed Clayton and Mrs. Moreland his new bedroom.   The family had cleared the peaked attic space in their small Cape Cod home and set up a bed, desk and television for Clayton.   The house was located on a residential neighborhood street in the small town and Clayton could easily walk to the high school, or street parking was permitted in front of the house if he was allowed to bring a vehicle to Plainview.   Clayton was polite but quiet for the two hour visit.   Each of the family members tried to engage him in conversation but he would only reply with short, one sentence answers.   He shook hands with the family, thanked them for their hospitality and he and Mrs. Moreland headed back to Low Field.

"Well, what did you think?" she asked.

"They are nice people," Clayton answered.

"I thought your bedroom was nice and private.   Did you like it?" the CSB worker asked.

"I like my bedroom at home," he answered.

"Clayton, you know the judge ordered you into a foster home for the next few months.   You have to accept his orders," she explained.   "Once you turn eighteen, you will no longer be in the juvenile system and you can move back home."

"I don't see why I have to move away from my brother and my family home for two or three months," he said.   "It doesn't make sense. This is my senior year and my friends are in Low Field. I'm getting decent grades and my grandparents are just a few miles away if I need something."

"I think the judge wants to change all of that for a reason," she said. "Sometimes a fresh start helps a person get back on the right track, and Mr. and Mrs. Hoffman would provide the kind of support that a young person can only get from his parents."

"My parents are dead," Clayton said, "and those people will never take their place."

She pulled her car into the driveway at Clayton's grandparent's house.

"Clayton, they're nice people who just want to help you," she said. "I'll bet your mom would want you to go live with them for a few months. And you can still visit your brother and grandparents once a week."

He didn't speak. After a full minute of trying to think of something to say to change her mind, he gave-up, realizing that debating the situation was pointless. He got out of the car and they went into the house. Mrs. Moreland summarized the evening for Clayton's grandparents and then left. She would pick him up at 10:00 Saturday morning and help him move his things into the foster home.

"I'm not going, Colt," Clayton said emphatically the next evening. "I called Aunt Peggy in Canada last night and she said I can move there until my birthday."

"You can't move to Canada for two months," Colton said shaking his head. "The judge won't let you go there."

"Why not? Aunt Peggy is a blood relative and she's a good person," Clayton said.

"Clay, just make the best of it for a few months and then you can move back home," Colton said. "It will be over before you know it. Plus, I was thinking, while your gone, I could paint the kitchen and living room in a color that you choose so we can start to make the house *our* house. I'll even paint your bedroom for you if you want me to."

"No, I'd rather you left everything the way it is," Clayton replied. "This is the way it's been our whole lives and I like it that way."

"Okay, I was just trying to help," Colton said.

"If you want to help, take me to Canada," Clayton said. "Or I'll just drive myself."

Clayton went upstairs to his bedroom and Colton could hear him opening and closing dresser drawers; he was packing the two suitcases the boys had found in their parent's closet. He came down the stairs wearing his winter coat and carrying the luggage.

"What are you doing?" Colton asked. His brother ignored him and went to the back door where he shoved his feet into a pair of boots. "Hey Clay, where do you think you're going?"

"To Canada," Clayton said slamming the door. Colton grabbed his leather jacket and jammed his feet into a pair of running shoes near the back door when he heard the Jeep engine start.

"Wait," Colton yelled waving and running down the driveway. Clayton barely slowed down enough to allow his brother to get into the passenger side of the vehicle and then he sped down the road heading west through the blinking traffic light in the center of Low Field. The older brother thought this was his only chance to save his younger brother from himself.

"Clay, you can't run away from this," Colton said.

"Sure I can," Clayton said. "Colt I'm not going to live with strangers so either help me or get out and I'll deal with this mess by myself."

Colton was silent as he thought through an array of possible responses, trying quickly to ascertain which one might get Clayton to listen to reason and act more sensibly. The one thing Colton knew was that he had to stay with his brother, especially while Clayton was stubbornly entrenched in his bout of self-destructive behavior.

Clayton drove in a northwest direction following signs to route 75 and Toledo. Obviously he had studied a map before bolting out the door on what appeared at the time to be an impetuous, reckless escapade. Now, Colton realized the trip to Windsor, Ontario had been a well thought out back-up plan for his brother. A few hours later, as Clayton continued his headstrong driving through the darkness, they passed a road sign for The Mossy Grove Bible College.

"Look, there's that school mom always tried to send us to for summer camp when we were little," Colton said trying to start a conversation.

"Yep, I actually wanted to go one year but you were going to football camp the same week and mom wouldn't let me go alone," Clayton said.

"Oh I don't remember that," Colton said.

"Well it happened; I'm not making it up," his brother said loudly.

"Clay, I didn't say you were," Colton said gently. "I better send Travis a text to see if he can stop by and feed the cows tomorrow."

"No," Clayton said. "Do you think I'm stupid? I know what you're trying to do, Colt."

"Hey, I'm not trying to do anything but get Travis to feed the cows," Colton said, "I'll show you the phone and the text before I send it."

"Yeah, I want to see it," Clayton said. "I don't want you calling the cops or sending out some dumb Amber alert."

"I'm not going to do that Clay," the older brother said. "Just relax and enjoy the ride. Check out all those stars." Colton pointed to the sky through the front windshield. "Remember when dad got that telescope for Christmas and we all used to go out on summer nights and try to see the North Star and the Milky Way?"

"Yeah," Clayton replied. "Hey Colt we better stop and get some gas at the next exit."

"Okay, sure," Colton said, "I've got to pee anyway and I could use some food. How about you?"

"Yeah, I'm hungry too," he said.

Colton typed the text message to Travis.

Hey could u please feed the cows tomorrow back door key for the house is hanging under the top step

He showed Clayton the phone before hitting send. "Is this okay?" Colton asked holding up the phone so his brother could read the message he had typed.

"Yeah," Clayton answered. "Would you buy me some beer and then drive for a while?"

"That's probably not a good idea," said Colton.

"Damn Colt, I just want some beer to help me calm down. You said you'd help me and now you won't even buy me a lousy six pack of beer and drive for a while," Clayton said loudly.

"Alright, take it easy, Clay," Colton said. "We'll see if there's any place open that's still selling beer tonight. It's pretty late and most places stop selling alcohol after midnight."

"Thanks."

Maybe the beer would make Clayton tired and maybe sleep so Colton had time to come up with a plan. They found an all-night gas station that sold snacks and beverages. He went into the restroom and sent Kelsey a text message

Hi Clay acting crazy we're driving to Canada dont know what to do???

He waited a few extra minutes in the small locked restroom to see if she would reply to his text or call him but there was no response. He bought beer, soda and snacks and returned to Clayton's jeep. His brother was in the back seat. He anxiously grabbed the beer from the bag and set it on the back floorboards. He opened one and took a long drink as Colton pulled away.

"God that's good," Clayton said. "Thanks Colt. This will bring me back from the edge of the cliff."

"What's that mean?" Colton asked.

"Every day I feel like I'm standing on the edge of cliff looking down a deep hole with no bottom," Clayton said, "and most of the time I just want to jump and join mom and dad."

"That's not cool, Clay," his brother said. "This has been a rough time for both of us but we have to be patient to understand God's plan for us; there's no other choice."

"Sure there is," his brother said. "I can jump."

"Don't talk crazy, Clay," Colton said.

"What's crazy about suicide?" Clayton said. "It's an option; some days it feels like a pretty good option. Honestly I don't care if I live anymore."

"I care if you live, Clay," Colton said, "Nothing can get mom and dad back, but I care if you live."

They rode in silence for a few minutes. Then Clayton said, "I just feel sad all the time Colt, and my life is empty. It's like there's no reason to get up in the morning."

"We both have some demons right now, but I believe mom would say we have to look hard to see light in the darkness. Giving up will only make things worse," Colton said, "if that's possible."

"Life pretty much sucks, Colt," his brother said quickly downing another beer.

"I had a dream a few nights ago. You and I were in Las Vegas playing in the worst game of Texas Hold'em poker in the history of mankind," Colton said. "We keep getting dealt one bad hand after another and the game wouldn't end. Every hand was a loser, time after time, and it just went on and on. Then after we kept playing non-stop for what seemed like two days, the dealer changed and we took a break. You and I went into the casino and there was this pretty girl handing out free drinks. We both got one and started talking to her. And we never went back to the game."

"And then what happened?" Clayton asked.

"Nothing; that was it," Colton said, "and I woke up."

"Well that's dumb," Clayton said.

"I thought so, too, at first," Colton said, "but you know how dreams are, sometimes they finish and make sense and other times you're just glad you wake up and you're happy it was a just a dream and the stuff didn't really happen. I'm thinking all of the bad stuff that's happened to us is kind of a dream and after a few months or maybe a few years we'll wake up from the dream and there will be something better, kind of like that pretty girl in the casino."

"Oh, I sort of get your point," Clayton said opening the tab on his fourth beer.

"We've had an unbelievable run of bad luck but better days are ahead. We just have to find the will power to get through it," Colton said. "We have to fight to persevere."

"Right now you have more will power than I do and you're a better fighter than me," Clayton said. "In fact you're better at everything."

"That's a bunch of crap. You can shoot a rabbit in the eye from fifty feet with a .22 and you know more about just about everything in life than I do," Colton said. "I still have never won a game of Trivial Pursuit from you in all these years."

"I didn't think you were trying," Clayton said.

"I was trying but there's not much to do when you don't know enough about most things to even make a guess," Colton said laughing. "By the way, I'm out of money. Do you have any?"

"No, but let me take a nap and I'll get us some in Detroit," Clayton said.

"Okay."

Colton wasn't sure what his brother meant with that statement but he decided to keep driving and let his weary, dispirited brother rest. During the drive, Colton collected his thoughts. He wondered what kind of identification Clayton was planning to use to cross the border. The last time the boys had visited their aunt in Canada was many years ago and a citizenship document was not required to enter the country. This time, with each of them carrying only Ohio driver licenses, he fully expected they would be turned away by the border patrol. They were only a few miles from the southernmost suburbs of Detroit when Clayton woke up. It was almost 5:00 AM but from the obscurity of the sky, it appeared more like midnight.

"I've got to use the bathroom," a groggy Clayton said from his cramped position on the back seat.

"Yeah, I could use a cup of coffee," Colton answered. "I'll watch for someplace to stop."

Colton exited route 75 at one of the exits in Southgate, Michigan. A Donut Shop was on a corner across from a strip plaza and a gas station. The area was developed with many small businesses but most were closed for at least a few more hours. A sign in front of the Donut Shop advertised twenty-four hour service, so Colton turned into the parking lot. Through the front window he could see several workers busily preparing for the upcoming morning rush.

"Hey, I think this place is open. What do you want?" he asked Clayton.

"I'll take a chocolate milk and a glazed donut," Clayton said handing a ten dollar bill over the seat to his brother.

"Okay, let's see if they're open," he said stopping at the speaker. A female voice greeted him.

"Thank you for stopping," she said. "What can I get for you?"

Colton gave her their order and pulled up to the drive-thru window. They exchanged money for goods and he pulled away. He handed the milk and the bag with the donut over his shoulder to his brother. As he was driving around the corner of the building to exit his brother stopped him.

"Colt, pull back around," Clayton said. "Would you try to exchange this donut for a chocolate cream-filled one?"

"Oh, okay," Colton said turning the jeep to the left for another lap around the building.

"Hey, let me out, I'm going to run in and use their restroom," he said. "After you switch the donut, drive over to that gas station and I'll meet you there."

Colton was too tired to argue and agreed to his brother's directives. He switched the donut and drove out of the lot. Clayton slipped in an employee entrance that was propped open, allowing the excess heat from the kitchen ovens to escape. He pulled the hood of his sweatshirt over his head and put his left hand in the front pocket of the hoody pretending it was a gun. The first girl who saw him smiled and then realizing what was happening screamed and covered her face. He walked directly to her and with his free hand on her shoulder, pushed her straight down onto her knees.

"Get down and stay down," he said with a fabricated deep voice. The other worker near the drive-thru window and cash register was trying to dial a wall telephone. Clayton grabbed the receiver from her and yanked the cord out of the mounted unit.

"Don't do that," he ordered. "Open the register and get down." She shook her frightened head no so he slapped her on the top of her head. The register looked like the one in Jerry's Sandwich Shop and he was quickly able to punch in a fake order into the point of sale and get the drawer to open. He quickly snatched all of the paper bills. There wasn't much but he guessed it was enough to get them into Canada.

"Now stay on the floor and count to one hundred slowly," he said. "And I might come back at twenty and if you're not counting, I will have to shoot you. Do you understand?"

Both young women shook their heads in affirmation and said, "Yes."

He ran from the building as fast as he could and jumped into the back seat of the jeep.

"Go Colt," he said breathing hard.

Colton looked at him and quickly surmised what his brother had done. "You jackass," the older brother said pulling away. At the entrance to get back onto route 75 he went through a red light to hasten their escape. For the next ten miles he exceeded the speed limit shaking his head and repeatedly checking the rear view mirror for police

— 492 —

cars. There were no sirens. As they continued into the downtown area he started to see signs for the border crossing into Windsor. He got off of the highway and dropped down onto a side street. There was a park with deserted, rusting playground equipment. The early peaks of dawn cast a hazy dimness over the area. No one was in sight. Colton parked the car and got out. He opened the back door and pulled Clayton out of the jeep.

"What the hell's wrong with you?" he screamed at Clayton.

"Nothing. I didn't hurt anyone," he said. "I just got us some money."

"Oh my God Clay, you are totally out of control," the older brother said holding the sides of his head. He pushed Clayton in the chest bouncing his back off of the side of the jeep. The younger boy lowered his shoulder and drove it into Colton's midsection sending them both to the ground in a furious wrestling match. They rolled over one another, each trying to gain the dominant top position. After a few minutes, Clayton was no match for his larger, stronger brother and released the tension from his body. He lay limp with his back on the ground and Colton sitting on top of him. The older brother raised a fist and held it in position to strike his younger brother. But he released his grip, and instead, wiped his face with both hands as he slid off of Clayton and sat beside the boy.

"Don't you see you're creating a bigger problem with all of the shit you keep pulling?" Colton asked.

"I don't care Colt," he said. "I'm sorry but I don't care."

They got on their feet and brushed themselves off. Clayton opened the back door of the jeep and grabbed his pistol. He pointed at Colton and said, "I'm driving." He tossed the gun into the back seat and started the jeep.

Colton closed his eyes and said, "Clay, all of this is my fault."

A few signs led them directly to the Detroit Windsor Tunnel which was the easiest place to cross the border between the two countries. A customs officer at the plaza stood in front of a gate and held his hand stopping them. The sunrise had quickly lit the early morning sky. He stepped to the driver's side window and tapped on the glass.

"Good morning," he said to them, "visas, passports or passport cards please."

Both boys looked at each other. They removed their wallets from the rear pockets of their jeans, withdrew their driver licenses and handed them to the guard.

"I'm sorry these are not sufficient to cross," he said. "You have to have the enhanced driver's license or one of the other approved documents."

"Oh we're just going into Windsor to visit our aunt for a few days," Colton said leaning forward to speak past Clayton. "She's sick."

"I'm sorry, but I can't let you through," the officer said looking into the jeep at Colton.

"She's real sick mister, isn't there any way you can get us through this time?" Clayton asked. "We don't have time to go home and get one of those documents. I mean, she might die."

The guard noticed the empty beer cans and noticed the grip of Clayton's pistol exposed slightly from beneath his cap on the back seat of the jeep.

"I'll tell you what, why don't you back up and park over there," the man said pointing to a paved area along a fence. "I have to go inside and check with my boss."

"Sure," Clayton said. "Thank you, sir."

The man stepped into the brick building at the same end of the row of lanes where he asked the boys to park. He was gone for at least five minutes and Clayton was getting anxious.

"What's he doing in there," he said impatiently.

"Just stay calm, Clay," Colton said. "We might pull this off; if not we just have to drive home and figure-out something else."

"No way," Clayton said reaching into the back seat. He put on his ball cap and reached back a second time. This time he deftly brought the gun into the front seat and inserted it into the front pocket of his sweatshirt.

"What the hell are you doing?" Colton asked suppressing his anger and concern.

The door of the building swung open and three armed officers ran toward the jeep pointing rifles at the boys. Clayton started the jeep and jerked it into reverse. The tires screamed and smoked. One of the officers fired a round hitting the front passenger tire. A loud pop and exhalation sounded and Clayton lost control of the vehicle. The jeep nearly tipped over but he managed to right its balance. He shifted into drive and accelerated the hobbled jeep toward the gate. One of the officers fired a shot through the front windshield grazing Clayton's neck. Glass showered both boys and the jeep crashed into one of the small guard huts between each lane and came to an abrupt, smoking stop. Colton instinctively ducked and many pieces of glass from the shattered windshield flew down the back of his shirt. Clayton drew his weapon and fired several shots through the empty front opening. He jumped out of the jeep and started to run away from the scene but he tripped and fumbled out of control falling hard onto the paved surface. He dropped the gun during the fall. He was dazed but tried to crawl back to recover the weapon. Colton dashed from the jeep toward his brother and kicked the gun far away from him. He got on top of Clayton like a human blanket and pinned him to the ground. The officers were confused but ran up on the two boys surrounding them with pointed rifles.

Colton looked up at them and said, "We're sorry. It was a mistake; we're sorry."

One of the officers turned his gun around and raised the butt of the weapon at an angle readying to strike Colton.

"Not my head," Colton screamed ducking and covering his head instinctively as the blow struck him in the shoulder, breaking his clavicle bone.

He raised the gun again in preparation for delivering another blow and one of the other officers yelled, "Enough; he's not resisting."

Colton rolled off of his brother wincing with pain. Clayton lay drained from emotion and weeping. With his good arm Colton grabbed the hood of Clayton's sweatshirt. He wadded the fleece and held it firmly against the wound in his brother's neck. Blood saturated the cloth and Colton's hand.

He looked up at the guards and said, "Please get my brother some help."

99

Just before Christmas the first heavy snowfall of the season blanketed Low Field. Abby had felt sick ever since the calamity of their well-intended rally. She wanted to do something that would make amends to the students who were injured at the foundation's event, but there were so many who were injured it was difficult to find a way to thank them for supporting the event and wish them well. She was going to send each person a card but it was almost impossible to determine everyone in attendance because of their masks. Through social media she sent out a generic message of appreciation but the gesture seemed hollow to her. Finally, her mother suggested that Abby host a winter party for her friends one evening between the holidays. On their property where he typically burned brush and leaves a few times a year Mr. Olson created a sizable circle with bales of straw and prepared a large bonfire for the students. It was a safe place on the edge of the dense woods where they could stay warm, toast campfire marsh mellow treats and enjoy the brisk winter weather.

Abby sent out another message through social media inviting her friends and asking them to share the time and date of the party with their friends. On the same message she announced that she was formally dissolving the foundation she had established with Will only a few months before. With a somewhat tongue-in-cheek comment, she said she lacked the intestinal fortitude required to be a social activist and would from this point forward be committed to expressing herself through a more private medium, her art. Any funds the foundation collected would be spent on a single initiative in Low Field, the gun buy-back program. Will sent Abby a text thanking her for the invitation.

Great idea A
Thx W
Can I help?
Sure
Why no more foundation?
Loss of innocence
Im sorry
Dont be lets have some fun instead
I'll be there a few hours early
Ok
Can I bring Luke?
Sure!
Great c u later

Over forty students attended the party, some underdressed for being outside, but Abby's parents sent extra blankets and coats out to the group and offered the extra boots and outside shoes from the garage to anyone who needed additional protection from the soft, full snowflakes. The fire burned brightly against the deep stillness of the woods. The crackling from the moisture inside some of the firewood accompanied the sounds of voices engaged in conversation and joy. A few students ran through the woods laughing and occasionally stumbling over tree roots. They made snow angels, had snowball fights and had the same kind of innocent fun in nature as they had when they were children. Most of them, however, stayed around the fire, enjoying its warmth and the stories of their friends.

Some told ghost stories but no one had an original tale. Kelsey brought up the folklore legend of the wooly bear caterpillar.

"I saw one a few weeks ago by the back door of our apartment and the stripe in the middle was huge, so that means we're going to have a really bad winter," she said.

"I think it's the opposite," Will said. "Isn't it if the brown stripe is narrow the winter will be harsh?"

"Oh, I don't know for sure," Kelsey admitted.

"Well, are you sure it had a stripe?" Erin asked. "Maybe it was a worm or a very small snake."

Everyone laughed and continued to pull melting treats off the ends of sticks. A few boys pulled shiny silver flasks filled with brandy from inside coat pockets and passed them around.

"Have you ever heard the one from the Farmer's Almanac that if the first winter snow falls on unfrozen ground the winter will be mild?" Kelsey asked.

"No," Daron said, "I don't think you should take up farming, Kelsey; in fact, you better move to Akron or Cleveland."

"What do they say about winter in the city?" Will asked Luke.

"Well, our urban legend is that it will be cold during winter and it will snow, especially in January and February," Luke said with a smile.

"That's brilliant," Kelsey said. "You've had such an advantage growing up in the big city."

"Oh yeah, Harrison is just below Turdville on The Forbe's list of best cities in America," Luke said.

Another boy lit a small joint and shared it with the people on either side.

"This is the best part about falling down ten rows of bleachers," he said. "Now I have an excuse to smoke dope."

"I think medical marijuana qualifies as some kind of folklore, doesn't it?" laughed Kelsey.

"Why, of course," the boy responded. "Your grandma and her grandma and her grandma all smoked pot; don't let them tell you otherwise."

"Well, I never have," said Abby.

The boy pulled out another joint from his shirt pocket and tossed it to Will who was seated a few places down from Abby.

"Now if anyone deserves some shwag it's you Abbs," the boy said.

Will lit the reefer and handed it to Abby. She sucked the smoke in and immediately coughed, laughing at her inexperience.

"Sorry, I'm a novice pot smoker," she said slowly bringing the joint back up to her lips.

"Pull a little smoke in slowly and hold it," Luke said leaning over towards her. "Here, I'll show you."

He took a drag and held his breath for at least ten seconds before exhaling the smoke.

"I don't know why you do that but that's the way they do it in movies and music videos," he laughed.

Abby did the same thing, this time to perfection. Everyone in the circle clapped.

"Welcome to Stonerville, Abbs," the boy said who brought the dope.

"Why thank you," Abby said, "I feel totally stupider now than I did thirty seconds ago."

"Stupider?" Will laughed. "Is that even a word? No more dope for you, Miss Abby. The world needs your brain too much to waste it on MJ."

"I think stupider is a word," she said laughing.

"Well, since I've been out here in the country," Daron said, "my neighbor grows sunflowers along one side of her trailer and every year they're a different height. This year they were taller than her roof and she said that means there's going to be a ton of snow."

"My granddad always said that, too," Erin said. "I guess it's true then."

"So, all it takes is two old people in Low Field to agree on something for it to be true?" Daron asked laughing.

"No," Will said, "you have to ask two more people who will obviously disagree with the first two."

"Oh what a world we live in," Abby said continuing to smoke. "Well I was reading this work by a spiritualist who explained how snow was a way God speaks to us from Heaven," she said with a smile. "The divine spirit in heaven is the teacher for us lowly students here on earth. The teacher sends a gentle snowfall to instruct the moronic pupils on earth a simple lesson of wisdom."

"What's that?" Will asked.

"Well you have to remember that every physical thing on earth has a spiritual complement. A teardrop is a physical element that represents emotion—you know, tears of pain or tears of joy," she said, "and snow is no different."

"Wait a minute, Abbs," said the boy, "I don't know if I'm the only one here who's getting lost, but I'll admit it. What lesson is the teacher sending us when it snows, Miss Grasshopper?"

He put his hands together in a prayerful way and bowed to Abby. She looked at him with a frown on her face.

"Technically, it should be Master Po but who cares," Abby said laughing, "please pass that joint back."

Her dad was outside working on something beside the garage.

He yelled up to the students, "Hey let me know if you can hear this."

Earlier in the day, he had mounted a wireless speaker to a tree near the campfire. He walked back into the garage and started a music tape of traditional Christmas songs. Suddenly Silent Night blasted through the woods startling every living creature within a mile.

"Too loud, dad," Abby yelled.

Others joined her and yelled, "Turn it down a little."

He adjusted the volume to a level where they could all hear it without covering their ears. Several of the girls started to sing along.

Will stood and raised his arms and stuck out his chest as a music conductor stands before a choir.

"Everybody, Silent night, holy night," he sang.

The others joined in and proceeded to sing carols for the next half hour. Most were surprised at how many of the lyrics they remembered from elementary choir performances, but others laughed at their inability to recall the words to songs they'd heard hundreds of times.

"I'm blaming it on the pot," Erin said. "I'll never smoke again."

"Oh sure, we all know your purse is full of wacky," someone joked.

Luke leaned over to Will and asked, "Do you think she likes me?"

"Sure, dopey," Will said. "God, it's like a romance novel or a Hallmark channel movie out here. Make your move."

"She's great when she's relaxed and not taking herself too seriously," Luke said.

"You have a good effect on her," Will said.

"I don't know, she's pretty smart and I'm just a golfer," Luke said as he closed his eyes and reached down and grabbed one of Abby's mittened hands. "You look cold."

"I am getting cold," she said sliding closer to Luke and resting her head on his shoulder.

He put his arm around her and pulled her in tight to his chest.

"Hey, Will, do me a favor and throw a few more logs on the fire," Luke said with a smile.

"Sure, anything for a friend."

100

TRAVIS LIVED FOUR miles from the Caldwell house. On his way down the winding roads he passed a disheveled man walking along the side of the road. It was Smokey. All of the students at Low Field knew the single, homeless man from his devoted attendance at sporting events. He was solitary and harmless. One legend had it that he was a former middleweight boxing champion and another that he was a prisoner of war during Vietnam. He got his nickname because his clothes always smelled like smoke, probably from cooking and getting warmth from open fires. Years ago the board of education had given him a lifetime pass to any school event as a way of helping the man, and he would stop by the school many evenings just to walk around the halls looking for dropped coins or interacting with the parents and students who had taken the place of his extended family. Travis pulled over and waited for the man to walk up to the truck. He leaned over and opened the passenger door a crack.

"Want a lift Smokey?" Travis asked.

"What a kind offer," Smokey said climbing slowly into the cab. "Thank you, young man."

"Sure, where are you off to this cold morning?" Travis asked.

"I'm going into town to see my friends," Smokey answered.

"What a coincidence, I'm on my way to a friend's house right now. Who are your friends, Smokey?" Travis asked.

"They're mostly at the church, but I have friends all over," he said. "Our lives are woven together for a reason."

"You're right. My friend and his brother are going through some tough times," Travis said, "so I've got to be there to help them."

"One of the best things to hold onto in this world is a true friend," Smokey said.

There was a pause in their conversation. The warmth from the sun was melting the light snow covering on the exposed side of the road. Travis was curious about Smokey's perspective on life. In fact, until a few minutes ago, he had never heard him speak other than to say hello.

"If you don't mind me asking, where do you live Smokey?" Travis asked as he continued the drive toward town.

"I have a few homes," Smokey said. "In the summer I live near the bike path shelter by the causeway and in the winter I stay in the stone barn at Lone Wolf Creek. I'm a lucky man."

Travis looked puzzled and rolled his eyes at the man's comment. "You have a great attitude toward life, Smokey."

"I believe the true meaning of life is to live simply and treat others with kindness," Smokey said.

"Smokey is your nickname, but what is your real name," Travis asked.

"Manny," the wanderer said. "You can call me that if you'd like."

"Okay, thanks Manny," Travis said. "I'm wondering if you have any advice for my friend. I mean, he's had some bad things happen to him recently and I'd like to help him out."

"Do you know the parable of the donkey and the farmer?" Manny asked.

"No."

"A donkey had fallen into a large pit and couldn't get out. He bayed and whined until the farmer finally came to his rescue. But the farmer could not see a way to get the animal out so he decided to fill in the hole. He shoveled dirt into the pit and the donkey bayed and whined. After a while the noise from the animal stopped and the farmer continued to fill the hole. In a few hours he was finished. He looked up and saw the donkey happily gallop away. The donkey discovered he could brush the dirt off his back and stand on it. The farmer filled the hole and the donkey escaped from his predicament," Manny said.

"Oh, I hate when I can't figure out the meaning of these stories," Travis said. "I was never good at riddles or parables."

"Well, let me help. The donkey shook-off the dirt life was shoveling on him and found a way to use it to step up," Manny said. "Your friend is facing one of life's challenges and he has a choice. He can whine and allow his misfortune to bury him or he can face the problem and discover a way to reverse his troubles."

"Ah, of course; that's a perfect analogy, or is it a simile? Oh whatever; thank you, Manny," Travis said. "I'll tell my friend what you taught me this morning."

"I'm just a messenger," the man said pointing at paved area where Travis could pull over. "You can let me off up there."

"Thanks again, Manny, it was nice talking to you," Travis said. "I hope you see your friends."

"No, I am the grateful one," he said getting out of the truck. "Tell your friend to search for peace in his heart, and, once he finds it, he will have everything."

Travis pulled away from the man. He noticed the smell of smoke lingering in the cab of the truck and smiled.

"Wow that was weird," he said softly to himself.

Travis turned into the Caldwell driveway and pulled past the house near the barn. He checked his phone again but still had not heard from Colton since the brief exchange of text messages the previous night. As he walked toward the barn, he saw the small gathering of cattle already under the lean-to on the west side of the building. They were waiting for their meal. He greeted the six cows with his usual countenance.

"Well, good morning, you pathetic excuse for a herd," he said loudly to them as they shuffled closer to the feed trough. "Daisy, Gertrude, Matilda, Oscar or whatever your names are."

He went into the barn and found the bags of all-purpose feed he'd watched Colton and his father provide to the livestock to augment the cows' primary diet of grazing and hay.

"You six are the laziest creatures on the face of the earth. All you do is eat, sleep and walk around in circles, or I guess rectangles," Travis said with a scowl. "Oh, and go to the bathroom, thank you," he added as one of the cows started to urinate. He shook his head and said, "What a life."

He finished spreading the meal in the tin trough and stepped back into the barn folding the empty bag and tucking it into the wood stove for the next fire. He glanced back at the content cattle lined up at the feed station, raised a hand to the animals and said in a small tribute to Manny, "May you all have peace in your hearts."

Travis closed the barn door and walked through the damp snow to back steps of the house. He found the hidden key and went in to check on the house. A folded American flag was sitting on the kitchen table; it was a funeral gift to the family from the Veteran's Administration in recognition of Mr. Caldwell's service to his country. On the table near the flag was a note and staple gun. Travis took the flag outside, unfolded it and attached it to the front of the barn so Colton and Clayton would see it when they returned home. He hoped they would agree with his placement of the flag. The patriotic display was a proper tribute to their father since he spent so much of his free time toiling unceremoniously in the barn.

Back in the kitchen, Travis washed the dishes and cleaned the table and counter tops. It reminded him of the way Mrs. Caldwell always left the kitchen. He wrote Colton and Clayton a brief note and left it on the table. Then he straightened up the living room by folding a blanket, fluffing some throw pillows and stacking a few magazines on the coffee table. In the corner sat Colton's acoustic guitar on a stand. Travis grabbed it and sat on the sofa softly playing the instrument. In middle school and the first few years of high school, he had taken lessons. Like so many other young people, he, too, dreamed of gaining fame and fortune through the entertainment business. He recalled how to play parts to a few of his favorite songs. He was surprised at how effortlessly his fingers returned to the correct strings and frets even though he hadn't practiced for a few years. He sang softly to himself and remembered why he had given up on a career in music; it took far more talent than he would ever possess and he just didn't have the kind of confidence and ego it took to stand up in front of people and sing. He didn't like the sound of his voice and could barely force himself to sing even in private.

It was important to be realistic about your limitations, he thought, while at the same time not selling yourself short by aiming too low. What a strangely important time in life he and Colton and Clayton were facing. They had numerous choices but the decisions they made in the coming months would impact their futures forever. Whether or not they would remain in Low Field or discover their destinies in some other part of the world, Travis knew he would always have fond memories and experiences of growing up so close to the Caldwell brothers. The times they shared bonded them inexorably together as lifelong friends.

Regardless of their whereabouts or circumstances today, the most important thing Colton and Clayton needed was, as Manny referred to it, a true friend. Travis decided he would be that friend, whether it was reciprocated or not. As he locked the door and walked down the back steps, he lowered his chin, and in his best baritone falsetto, sang the end of his *cousin's* song, "Forever and ever, forever and ever, forever and ever, Amen."

ABOUT THE AUTHOR

Warne Palmer is a writer, PGA golf professional, and educator who lives in northern Ohio. He holds a BS from The Ohio State University and an MA from Youngstown State University, and has worked as a high school English teacher, a principal, and a school superintendent. Author of Play Great Golf Now! and Left-Handed Golf Swing Fundamentals, Palmer's debut novel, A Road of Stones, is the first book in his upcoming trilogy, The Low Field 20.

www.ingramcontent.com/pod-product-compliance
Lightning Source LLC
Chambersburg PA
CBHW071628260626
47170CB00001B/15